TENDE

"Your towel, my lady. Prithee let it fall," he whispered languidly into her right ear. "I cannot oil your skin through a towel."

She turned away from him and, unfolding the towel at her cleavage, pushed it all the way down to her hips. His broad, warm palm seemed to span the width of her back, then his fingers slipped around to the side of one of her breasts.

Dana's breath caught in her throat, but she tried to tell herself she wasn't in the least affected by how good it felt to be touched this way by him.

His hand traveled up her shoulder and, in the space of an instant, he had her pinned, facing upward, on his brother's mattress. "Fortune has sent you onto my path and it is my duty to guard and to please you until it returns for you."

" 'Please?' "

"Ja, please."

She did not stop him as he resumed the work of lotioning her skin. She did not even protest, as his large, warm hand slipped down, beneath the linens . . .

* * *

"Masterfully crafted, captivating, unique, unforgettable . . . VIKING TEMPEST is an irresistible time travel. This is Ashland Price at her best!"
— Linda Abel, *The Medieval Chronicle*

"FIVE STARS! An incredible time-travel romance . . . one of the great novels."
— *Affaire de Coeur*

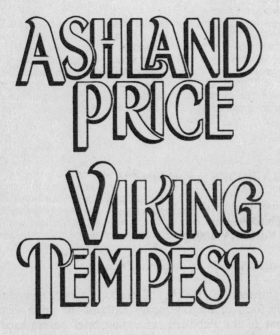

ASHLAND PRICE

VIKING TEMPEST

ZEBRA BOOKS
KENSINGTON PUBLISHING CORP.

ZEBRA BOOKS are published by

Kensington Publishing Corp.
850 Third Avenue
New York, NY 10022

Zebra and the Z logo Reg. U.S. Pat. & TM Off. The Love-
gram logo is a trademark of Kensington Publishing Corp.

First Printing: October, 1994

Printed in the United States of America

To Janice Parker Matsumoto—
for encouraging me to write
fiction long before anyone
else did. What a joy and a
blessing to have found you again
after all these years!

My thanks also to the Hennepin
County Library system of Minnesota
for their ongoing help with
research.

Chapter 1

Dublin, Ireland—July 1994

"Have another Irish Mist and try to forget about Steven, dear. *Time* heals all wounds."

Dana Swansen usually bristled at her mother's advice, but this particular counsel struck her as infinitely wise. She'd already managed to put lots of *space* between her and her most recent ex-lover. She'd left him five thousand miles behind in Minneapolis, in fact. But *time*. Now time would take a great deal more effort. More waiting and more desolation than she honestly believed she could endure.

She'd done it before, however, a voice within her reminded. She'd survived true heartbreak at least half a dozen times in her twenty-eight years, and she would somehow do so again, she told herself stoically, suddenly embarrassed by the tearful silence she was letting ensue on this pricey long-distance phone connection with her mother in Minnesota.

"Right," she managed to reply, doing her best not

to let the pain in her voice be heard. Her parents had looked so cheerful, so hopeful that she'd have a happy trip abroad as they'd seen her off at the airport, that she just couldn't let on how devastated she still was by her breakup with Steven. Now, even from across half a continent and an entire ocean, however, she was pretty sure her mom detected the defeated waver in her response.

"So what's on the agenda for your first day in Ireland?" Mrs. Swansen began again brightly.

Dana reached up to blot her eyes with the cuff of her satiny bathrobe. Then she felt around the hotel bed, upon which she was sitting, for the brochures that might refresh her memory as to the tour's itinerary. "Oh, you know. The usual bus-tour stuff."

"Such as?" her mother pursued, clearly not about to hang up until she felt her youngest daughter was on a better emotional footing.

Dana's fingers finally came upon the first day's schedule, and she halfheartedly read it aloud. "We're going to a stone circle and a coastal monastery tomorrow morning. Then lunch at a Wexford pub. And some place called 'Celt World' after that."

" 'Kelp' World?"

"Right, Mom," Dana quipped. " *'Kelp'* World, Jacques Cousteau's first Irish seaweed museum! No. *Celt* World. You know, like the Boston Celtics basketball team."

Mrs. Swansen gave forth a flustered laugh. She could be amazingly slow on the uptake at times— utterly hopeless at such things as programming her VCR or typing a single page on the home computer

Dana's father had recently insisted they buy. But she meant well, God love her; so Dana usually tried to refrain from making teasing remarks.

"Oh, oh, yes," the matriarch replied. "Sorry, darling. Well, that should be interesting, shouldn't it?"

Dana shrugged. "More interesting than kelp, I suppose. Look, Mom, we're running up a terrible long-distance bill, I'm sure. Judging by what I've already seen, the price of everything here seems to be twice what it is in the States, so I imagine the telephone service is no different. Why don't you let me get back to you in a few days? I'll probably be in much better spirits by then."

"All . . . all right. If you're sure you're O.K."

"I am," Dana declared, with as much conviction as she could seem to muster.

"But, before I hang up, tell me: have you met any of the Americans in your tour group yet?"

"Most of them. We were gathered at the hotel bar for a complimentary 'welcome-to-Ireland' drink, when our flights got in this afternoon. And, no, there don't appear to be any eligible males, if that's what you're asking." *Doubtless, it was.* "Just the typical collection of yuppie couples, senior citizens, and a handful of hopeless spinsters like me."

Her mother gasped. "What a thing to say about yourself! You're not even thirty yet. You break my heart when you talk that way, you know."

Dana emitted a whisper of a laugh. "I was just kidding, Mom. That's not really how I feel."

"It had better not be," she continued to scold. "You're so pretty and bright. And all those years in

college and graduate school. You know I'd have given
my right arm to have the opportunities young women
have these days."

"I know. I know." Dana sighed, hoping to stem any
further admonishment. She should have known better
than to even seem to be deriding herself. This was a
lesson she should have learned way back in her teenage
years, when she had, in passing, grumbled that her legs
were too fat, only to have her mom fiercely remind her
that she should be grateful she possessed legs at all.
Many people didn't, Mrs. Swansen had maintained—
parents, for the purpose of inducing guilt, being authorities on the less fortunate, including those starving
in third-world countries.

Dana rolled her eyes and fought the urge to groan.
God, what an awful cycle she'd fallen into! One failed
romance after another. Always followed by her parents' and *long-married* sisters' awkward efforts to assure her that "Mr. Right" was still out there for her
somewhere. Indeed, in her zeal to see her youngest
daughter finally married off, her mother had actually
broadened her limited wish that Dana "reel" in a doctor or lawyer to include any male without a prison
record.

"Now be sure you just relax these first five days of
your trip, dear, and let your tour guide see to everything. You've been working so hard lately that there's
no reason you can't take a little time off before getting
back to those tedious historical studies of yours.
There's more to life than moldy old Norse ruins, you
know."

If you spent half as much time thinking about you

life as you do the Vikings, you'd be a happily married woman with children by now, Dana mouthed, hearing her mother's usual conclusion to this particular sermon even before it was once again voiced.

But, to Dana's relief, it didn't come this time. Her mother had fallen mercifully silent for some reason, and Dana seized the opportunity to further assuage her. "O.K. I promise to leave the headaches to the tour company for at least a week. I'm not scheduled to meet with any museum curators until next Monday, in fact."

"That a girl," Mrs. Swansen praised. "I knew you'd listen to reason."

"Really, Mom. Let's not run up a bill when there's so little for me to report just yet. I promise I'll call you in a few days and let you know how things are going."

"All right then, darling. We'll be looking forward to it. Good-bye and take care."

" 'Bye, Mom. Love ya," Dana managed to conclude before the buzz of disconnection filled her right ear.

Her mother was gone. Her one true fan in all the world. Well, not including her father. Dana didn't honestly need her parents' continued assurances that she was lovable; yet the silence in her hotel room, as she set the receiver down, made her throat ache with an odd sort of despair.

Dear old mom is right, a voice within her declared. She was, in her own way, attractive and bright. Certainly worthy of a relationship more lasting than Steven, the attorney, or Michael, the C.P.A., or any of her other philandering mismatches had seemed capable of giving her through the years.

But it was more than that. More than a luckless love life at the root of her problems. While she knew tha her mother was terribly old-fashioned, terribly *wrong* to place so much importance on her finding a husband and procreating, there was something even more dis tressing about the woman's admonitions.

It was the part about Dana caring more about Vi king times than she did her own—the painful reminder that she had never really fit in somehow. Not even into the posh lifestyle her father, a successful dentist, had provided since her infancy. There had always been an unvoiced feeling among the members of her immediate family that Dana's steady focus upon her Scandina vian origins, rather than her American future, was not altogether normal or healthy.

To her relatives' credit, though, they'd managed not to criticize her choice of the obscure and fairly unmar ketable area of Scandinavian history in which to earn her master's degree. They'd even held their tongues as she'd taken one costly trip after another—to Norway Sweden, Denmark, and Iceland—in her zealous pur suit of knowledge about her seafaring ancestors. But now that she was pushing thirty, now that her *sixth* long-term relationship with a man had ended in an other heartbreak, they were truly beginning to worry about what might become of her. And, contrary to their impassive Norwegian-American natures, they were starting to come right out and say as much.

That was why Dana had chosen Ireland as her re search destination this time. Fair old "Erin" at least *seemed* a change of pace to the uninformed observer Such "laymen" simply didn't realize that the Irish

towns of Dublin, Waterford, and Wexford—or
Water*fiord* and Wex*fiord* as their Norse founders had
named them—were more Viking than Celtic and were
blessed with Nordic artifacts so rare, even the cities of
Scandinavia could not claim to possess their likes.

"If you wish to know a race's secrets, look to where
they raided, rather than where they lived," one of
Dana's history professors had once declared, and
she'd long suspected there was some truth in it. She
was, therefore, about to find out for herself.

She got up from the hard double bed and crossed
the room to look out the picture window. Dublin in
July was even more sweet and green than she had
imagined. The gorgeous pink of wild roses and the
purple of heather could be seen here and there; and the
narrow, winding streets of this ancient city were filled
with Irishmen and women whose fair features bore
witness to their blond Viking forefathers.

She sighed and leaned up against the window's deep
sill. She felt peaceful here for some reason. Though
she'd only been in Ireland for a few hours, she was
strangely at home in Dublin—her own flaxen-colored
hair and large blue eyes mirroring the coloring of so
many of the locals.

She'd made a lot of mistakes in her twenty-odd
years, but she felt certain that coming to Ireland was
not one of them. Even before her plane had touched
down, she'd gotten the distinct sense this wasn't the
first time she'd been here. Though she'd never visited
it in her present life until now, some buried part of her
definitely *remembered* this land. And fondly.

There had been many of the same sights back then.

The same fragrant flora, the same blue-green Irish Sea. And re-experiencing these made her feel as if she were paging through a favorite picture book she hadn't seen since childhood.

But something was different now. Something. *Something.* She felt certain the missing element would occur to her, if she searched her mind for it long enough.

Finally it did, after she set out her clothes for the next day's tour and sank into bed in the hope of catching up on some of the sleep she'd lost during the long flight from the States.

Trees. That was it! She remembered an Ireland with lots and lots of trees. Not the largely deforested country it had become in the past three hundred years.

How had a land, whose inhabitants had once so devoutly worshipped trees, managed to be stripped of so many of them? she wondered.

Whether simply out of need for rest or some desperate flight of fancy, she continued to recall Erin from a time when its only foe was the occasional shipload of Norsemen. And, though she already knew the dangers of it, it was more *recollection* than dreaming that at last drew her into the deep sleep she craved.

If time did indeed heal all wounds, as her mother had claimed, Dana was about to discover what slipping back through ten centuries or so might do . . .

Chapter 2

She already knew what the tribesman was going to do to her. She also knew that she would more feel than witness it.

The only sights and sounds she was aware of were those overhead: the brightness and warmth of the late-summer sun and, of course, the trees. Birch, she believed they were or poplars perhaps, with silvery leaves that flashed like coins in the breeze.

This was always the way it began. And, though she was lying spread-eagle, her wrists and ankles bound to the cold stone altar upon which she rested, she did not yet feel the fear she knew would follow. Nor did she know any particular shame at her nakedness, for this, she had been told since childhood, was a most sacred rite, one which no man would dare deprecate by leering at her young flesh or making lewd remarks.

Nevertheless, she realized it was because of her dis-robed state that she never seemed able to visualize more about the encounter than the soft blue of the sky and the seemingly approving twinkling of the trees that towered all about the open shrine.

She was simply too mortified to look anyone in the eye, and in keeping with this, she saw only the lower half of the man who finally came to claim her. She remembered seeing nothing above his waist as he shed his crimson robe and knelt down upon the altar, between her tensing legs. Then, without pause, he penetrated her, his forcefulness telling her he'd surely been worked into some sort of herb-induced frenzy by the men of their clan.

She cried out at having him drive himself into her in so heedless a manner. She had expected it to be painful. She simply hadn't anticipated its taking her breath away. No one had warned her that the first thrust would hurt so that she'd be too numbed to feel the ones that so rapidly followed.

In time, however, she knew the depths of her would stop fighting him. She knew the rope that bound her feet would begin to give a bit with his repeated pushes upward. She would herself adopt the primitive rhythm of it, as her ears became filled with the unified claps of her surrounding kinsmen, their striking palms seeming to set the ever-increasing pace of this holy coupling.

She would, without aid of the inflaming aphrodisiac they'd given her partner, become as swept up in the act as he . . . his firm, sweat-moistened flesh gliding over hers again and again and again until all her mind seemed capable of focusing upon was the feeling of him moving in and out of her.

The rapturous throbbing within her finally began to command all of her senses. The sights to which she'd

*been clinging—the trees, the sky, the sun—started to
fade as they were usurped by the marvelous sensations
he was causing.*

Then, all at once, she heard a sharp ringing, a sum-
moning just off to the right of her, and she felt herself
sit bolt upright.

She groaned at having the dream, this odd reverie
she'd experienced since girlhood, so abruptly interrupted.

"Hello," she managed to croak, as she clumsily
lifted the receiver of her bedside phone.

"Front desk ringing you up, Miss Swansen. You did
request a seven o'clock wake-up call, did you not?" a
dulcet Irish voice inquired.

Dana reached up with her free hand and rubbed
sleep-blurred eyes. "Um. Yes. Yes I did. Thank you."

"You're most welcome," the woman returned.

With that the intruder, the shatterer of her dream
was gone, and Dana hung up the phone to again face
the plans the travel agency had made for her.

Damn it! There was nothing more annoying than
having an erotic dream interrupted, she thought, flopping onto her side and curling up into the fetal position. Why couldn't the front desk have waited until the
terrifying part, the part where she was about to be
sacrificed to some pagan god or other and she genuinely needed someone to intervene?

Maybe, if she closed her eyes again and tried very
hard, she could slip back into the ravishment scene
from which she'd just been torn. Perhaps, *this time* she
would actually catch a glimpse of the face of the mysterious young man who had come to her in her sleep,

in this unspeakably carnal way, since her preteen years.

Though she hadn't fully understood the act back then, the images had been the same. He'd deflowered her, roughly claimed her, so that the first of her sacrificial blood was spilt even before her executioner arrived.

The dream never changed. And, seemingly because of this, she never managed to get a look at her appointed lover. She'd come to know the scent of him, the feel of his demanding tumescence, well enough; but—damn it all!—she never succeeded in making out his features. And, thanks to the front desk of Dublin's Darby Hotel, this time had certainly been no different.

Naturally, she'd tried to assign some meaning to the dream through the years. Not just because it was recurrent, but also because it seemed more lifelike, more vivid than any of the other dreams she'd ever had. The pain, the pleasure of it were so real, in fact, that she sometimes woke feeling as though she truly had been ravished. The depths of her pulsated and ached, and her wrists and ankles felt chafed as they would if she had, in actuality, been bound in such a way.

Ah, God, what was the use? she thought with a defeated sigh. Then she rolled onto her other side and pushed herself up to a sitting position. Over the course of sixteen years, she hadn't succeeded in making sense of this haunting bit of her subconscious, so it seemed unlikely she ever would.

She was probably just sex-starved, she decided. Too long away from the intimacy she'd known with Steven to expect much more of her psyche than such a bestial scene.

She rose and made her sleep-drunk way to the room's closet. She'd been warned that it could suddenly become chilly and overcast on Irish summer days, so she'd have to remember to bring a sweater along this morning.

Breakfast was every bit as awful as any she'd been served in Scandinavia. It included runny eggs, undercooked bacon, cold toast, and—horror of horrors— stewed tomatoes! No wonder it was the only complimentary meal of the day in this tour package. There was absolutely no danger of the hotels coming out on the losing end with such revolting offerings!

Making what small talk she could with a table full of the Americans she'd met the day before in the hotel bar, Dana managed to choke down a cup of very strong tea, while silently resolving to ask for later wake-up calls henceforward. Nothing missed, she reasoned, if she simply waited until lunchtime to eat.

"Miss Swansen, our Scandinavian history instructor from the University of Minnesota, isn't it?" Dana heard a male voice hail, as she was walking back down the hotel corridor that led to her room.

She turned about to see that it was her tour guide who'd addressed her.

"Or I should say Ms., shouldn't I now?" the middle-aged Irishman amended with a good-natured grin. "As you American ladies seem to prefer."

She reciprocated his smile, the disarming twinkle in his green eyes seeming contagious.

"We've neighboring rooms," he explained, withdrawing his key from his pocket, as Dana reached her door. "Well, in Dublin, anyway. But who's to say what the room assignments will be, once we move on to the east?"

"Dana's fine," she declared.

"What was that?"

She gave forth a soft laugh, realizing that his was the face of the classic Irish charmer, just open and smile-lined enough to allow him to get away with such straightforwardness. "I mean, you don't need to bother with 'Miss' or 'Ms.' You may just use my first name."

"Fair enough," he said with a nod. "You call me Ian, then. Just up to get your things, I presume, since the coach leaves in five minutes."

She inserted her key in her lock. "Yes."

"Good, then. I'll do the same and walk you back down, if you wish. That way, you can be certain we won't leave without you," he added teasingly.

"All right," Dana answered, hurrying inside to fetch her camera, cardigan, and the large canvas bag that was to serve as her purse throughout this trip. She groaned as she gathered all of this up, seconds later she headed back to the door. She hadn't realized until now just how much she'd stuffed into the bag!

Her family had always teased her about the many things she insisted on toting with her wherever she went. Conditioned by a decade of carrying a bulging backpack about the campus, she supposed. One could never be too safe, however, a voice within her defended. Canned goods, a machete, a pup tent—none of these struck her as being completely inappropriate, given Minnesota's often inclement weather.

But no, she hadn't resorted to such extremes just yet. In fact, she was firmly convinced that everything she was lugging to the corridor now was pretty much a necessity. She had a paperback novel, in case their guide had no narrating to do along the way or her fellow tourists proved unsociable. A hand-held tape recorder, in the event that someone presiding at one of the sites they were to visit began spouting historical details she didn't want to miss. Then there was a small umbrella to protect her from fair Erin's sudden rains, and, of course, her requisite canister of Mace for self-defense. Against whom, she wasn't entirely sure, however. Violent crime was said to be pretty rare in Ireland, and such a device was sure to prove worthless amidst anything as radical as an I.R.A. bombing.

Nevertheless, the canister was in there somewhere. Buried in the depths of this "beach bag," beneath layers of cosmetics, hair-care implements, and assorted date and address books, and Dana took her usual comfort in acknowledging its presence.

"Not one for eating breakfast, then?" Ian inquired, his ruddy face lit with a smirk as he stood just outside her room, awaiting her seconds later.

Dana could feel her cheeks flush a bit, as she finally made her exit and turned to lock her door behind her. First his impeccable recollection of what she did for a living and now this. My, but these Irish tour guides were attentive! She wasn't sure, however, whether she should feel annoyed or flattered. "No. I'm afraid not."

"Always dieting, you Americans," he noted, as they began walking to the elevator. "We call it 'slimming' here, but 'tis about the same thing. You shouldn't have to concern yourself with it, though. A lass as long and lean as you."

"Why, thank you, kind sir," she replied, again feeling entertained by his candor. "I'll keep that in mind the next time I get a craving for too much dessert."

"Well, if it's sweets you're wantin', there's a wonderful bakeshop not two streets down from here. I'll show you to it, if there's time enough when we get back."

"All right," Dana agreed, having no better plans in mind for the evening. He was just trying to be friendly, she told herself. What were tour guides for, after all, if not to help the single and stray members of their flocks to feel included?

"So do you speak Swedish or Norwegian, with this Scandinavian studies degree of yours, Dana?"

"A little of each. But it's Old Norse I'm most familiar with."

"I think you'll find that rather extinct these days. As out of use as our own poor Gaelic seems."

"Oh, yes. Well, I just meant that I can *read* it. You know, the Icelandic sagas, that sort of thing. There's not much call for speaking it, of course. Though I have been told by my instructors that my pronunciation is good. For what that's worth," she added with a laugh.

"Sweet Jesus, why would a pretty young lady like yourself want to clutter her mind with that old stuff?"

Dana smiled at the mystified knit of his dark brows,

as the crowded elevator finally opened to them and they stepped inside. "Because I'm Norwegian, Ian. All four of my grandparents came from Oslo."

"You know, I hear that so often from you Yanks. 'I'm German,' you'll say. Or 'I'm Italian.' But what you don't understand is that, to the rest of the world, if you were born and raised in the great U.S. of A., you're an *American* and there's an end to it! We couldn't care less where your old granny came from eighty-odd years ago and we're quite confused as to why you do."

Dana laughed with wonder at this. "Yes, well, I've never looked at it that way."

"Ah, you should start, if you ask me. America's still a fine country to hail from, even given all your problems with crime and such. I've been there three times now, countin' the trip the missus and I took to California last winter, and I have to tell you you've nothin' to be ashamed of. Except perhaps how few hours your bars are open on a Sunday," he concluded in a grumble.

Dana, catching sight of the thoroughly amused expression of a woman standing behind them—a lady she knew to be another American on their tour—bit the inside of her cheek in an effort to keep from laughing aloud at this criticism. He was kind of a nut, this Mr. Ian Preston. Refreshingly frank and droll, and a far more entertaining guide than she had, at first, imagined.

"Well, if it's old Norse annals you're after, lass, you've come to the right place. As you probably already know, there's enough Viking history in Dublin and the other coastal towns down here to fill an entire fleet of longships. I'll scare up some brochures on it for you when we return."

"Yes. Thanks," Dana replied. Something to read while she stuffed her face at the bakery to which he'd offered to take her, she thought flippantly.

"It's off to the Cork-Kerry stone circle then," he announced, as the elevator finally reached the lobby. "Those of you with Worldtrek Tours, starting in Dublin, will please follow me out to the coach."

A surprising number of the elevator's occupants did just that; and, within minutes, Dana was comfortably settled into a spacious double seat, which she had all to herself near the front of the huge bus.

Because all her grandparents came from Oslo, she thought critically. That was the stock response she gave whenever anyone asked why she had chosen to major in Scandinavian studies. Yet she realized now how evasive she was being in claiming so, since the real answer to this would never be that superficial or easy to articulate.

But, honestly, how could she begin to tell a stranger of an ancient dream that had, only that morning, visited her again? How, without coming across as a madwoman, could she explain to *anyone* that part of her felt as if it were literally entrenched in Viking times and that she often stood back from her twentieth-century existence, viewing it with a detachment that disturbed even her.

Yes, Mother, I'll survive this breakup with Steven, because I'll take refuge in some distant, murky past—

perhaps in some sort of psychosis *that always dulls the pain of such losses for me.*

But what was all this dwelling in the past truly about? she inwardly reproved. All this self-flagellation over some imagined future? One devoid of male companionship? The key to life, after all, was to focus on the present. Most of the great Eastern philosophers had said so; and, in truth, it was such a simple, indisputable determination that she couldn't figure out why it was always slipping her mind.

To hell with Steven and all of the other men who had broken her heart in the past! She was in Ireland now. Surrounded by interesting, affable people. Unlike those of her friends who were already tied down by marriage and motherhood, she could still afford such travel abroad; and she realized what a damned fool she'd be to continue brooding over the hapless love life she'd known up until now.

Heaving a refreshed sigh at this renewed resolution, she leaned against her seat back and watched as the last of her fellow tourists hurried onto the bus and the driver began pulling away from the hotel.

A whole new world was all about her, she acknowledged with a sense of joy she hadn't felt in weeks. There were quaint shopfronts, adorable little mixed-breed dogs, and rosy-cheeked pedestrians trotting along the walks. And she knew now that she didn't want to miss a moment of these distinctly Irish sights! God knew, there'd be plenty of time for moping when she got back to the States in a month or so.

Ian rose when they were just a couple blocks from the hotel and, with a microphone in hand, began to regale the group with sightseeing narrative and historical anecdotes that would entertain them all the way to the Cork-Kerry region.

To begin with, there was the "Barge," a widely known drinking establishment which had been set up on a long, unpowered boat anchored upon Dublin's Grand Canal. Because said barge was dutifully moved a few yards up- or downstream from time to time, it maintained immunity from the local laws restricting liquor-serving hours to which its land-based competitors were subject. A floating pub in essence—a testament to Irish ingenuity and love of alcohol—and everyone on the bus seemed quite amused to learn of it.

Ah, the "luck" of the Irish! What other people on earth could begin drinking at any hour of the morning and yet suffer so few mishaps on their streets and highways? Dana marveled, in fact, at the miraculously fortunate synchronism she witnessed all about her on the journey. Their poor bus driver was, at times, *beset* by the unexpected. The stray lamb or dog darting out from behind the hedgerows as another equally huge tour coach attempted to pass theirs on the single-lane roads and a nearly impossible-to-spot bicyclist fought to squeeze through the middle of it all!

Lord, Dana couldn't have been more right in choosing to let a tour company worry about the driving for a while! She was certain such hair-raising motoring experiences would, cumulatively, have shaved five to seven years off her life, were she playing an active part in them. And yet, through some divine intervention apparently granted solely to the Irish, every such encounter was ending without incident.

When, at last, Ian sat back down for a time, taking a short respite from his narration, Dana's attention drifted to some of those fellow tourists she'd already met.

The middle-aged married couple in the seat just in front of her were Sol and Barbara Goldfarb from New York City. They were charming *individually*. Their dark eyes had positively sparkled with interest as they'd chatted with others in the tour group at breakfast that morning and at the "welcome" gathering the afternoon before. The problem was, they seemed to abhor one another. When stuck together in the confines of a double bus seat, their conviviality had quickly turned to bickering, which they made no effort to hide. Dana was, therefore, hard pressed to figure out why such a couple would remain married, let alone do anything as seemingly optional as touring foreign countries together.

By comparison, the pair who sat just across the aisle from her were a breath of fresh air. White-haired sisters from Montana, they cooed at Ian's every utterance like a couple of winsome turtledoves. They'd apparently been lured into one of the airport gift shops just seconds after their flight had arrived, for everything they wore and carried now was covered with green and white shamrocks and trimmed with Irish lace. Dana had not seen such a tribute to "the wearing of the green" since her high-school class's production of *Finian's Rainbow!*

But they were sweet, no matter how ridiculous their apparel. They were the sort of well-meaning grandmas—seasoned and kindly listeners—who could save a person thousands in psychotherapy costs, if one cared to take advantage of their attention.

Ironically, however, the sisters' antithesis sat only one seat away from them. The tour group's know-it-all. She was the loathsome kind of creature who has plagued assemblages since the beginning of time. A person who, in no uncertain terms, has seen, done, and *been* it all!

This particular foremost-authority-on-everything was an elementary schoolteacher from Alabama, whose blaring voice and chattering had instantly warned Dana of her nature.

Gerta Jeffers was her name, and, though admittedly the day was young yet, she had already claimed she was present at the autopsy of John F. Kennedy, that she was an honored guest at the wedding of Charles and Di, and that she'd been the runner-up for Christa McAuliffe's place on the ill-fated space shuttle.

My, how the finger of destiny had mixed in old Gerta's life! It was rather amazing, given her incredible fortune thus far, that she hadn't also discovered she was the real Anastasia!

Poor Ian. What an earful he got each time he took a breather from his guide spiel! Gerta, doubtless having already stretched her credibility beyond all limits with the rest of the tourists, had planted herself in the seat just behind the Irishman, forcing him to nod periodically and at least appear to be listening to her.

But, experienced as he seemed at the tour-directing business, he'd surely find some way to free himself from Gerta, Dana assured herself.

Finally, at half past ten, they reached their first

destination. The coach came to a stop at a reception building situated several hundred yards off the highway on which they'd just been riding. They were about to visit a rather mysterious place, Ian informed them with an intriguing rise to his voice. A stone circle, much like the famous Stonehenge in England.

An excited buzz broke out among the coach's passengers, as they began rising and gathering up their cameras and such. Dana, on the other hand, found herself primarily excited about the chance to visit a restroom.

She graciously waited until several of the group's elderly pushed past in the bus's center aisle. Then, taking note of the direction in which Ian was leading the pack, she clutched her bag and sweater to her and went into the reception building.

Perhaps choosing to consume nothing more than a brimming cup of tea for breakfast hadn't been such a good idea, she silently admonished herself, wondering at the seemingly boundless bladders of the rest of her group.

When she rejoined her fellow sightseers minutes later, they were gathered about the center of the gravel-filled stone circle and Ian had ceded his narrating to a local guide. She was a tall, black-haired woman with rather severe features, and she spoke in a tone so commanding that it struck Dana as almost mesmeric.

Trying not to prove a distraction, Dana made her way stealthily about the outside of the circle, to the point where most of her companions were clustered.

Then, stepping through a gap between two wall stones, she made her way inside.

The guide was saying something about the heavens. Though there were no definite answers as to what purpose such Neolithic structures served, it seemed evident that they related somehow to the position of the sun and, perhaps, the locations of some planets. Maybe the circles had been used as an astronomical gauge of sorts, their alignment with the stars allowing the Stone-Age inhabitants of the British Isles to determine the beginning and end of the growing season.

Not familiar enough with such ancient sites to have formed an opinion on their functions, Dana simply listened. Experience had taught her that it was difficult enough to become expert on one period, let alone cluttering one's mind with facts on another.

But she was "leaving the headaches to Worldtrek Tours," she reminded herself—as she had promised her mother she'd do. So she supposed she shouldn't be too disappointed if she found some of the subject matter of little or no interest.

Feeling rather bored as the woman's commentary continued, Dana glanced down at her watch to see how near lunchtime it was. Her stomach was beginning to growl with such ferocity that she was certain everyone else could hear it. In the pauses between the guide's utterances, some portion of Dana's gastrointestinal tract was carrying on like a drain-cleaner commercial, and she tried, in vain, to silence it by sucking in her abdomen.

"It is thought that such sacred circles may have related somehow to a cult of the dead and the after-world," the brunette went on, "for graves have been found beneath many of them. And, of course, there is the presence of quartz in several of these sites, a stone believed, even today, to possess magical properties."

Maybe not so very magical, Dana thought, clucking as she noted that her quartz-crystal watch had stopped dead sometime between the present and when she'd last consulted it on the bus.

She glared down at its tiny octagonal face. One of her parents' gifts to her upon her receipt of her master's degree just a few years before, the timepiece certainly shouldn't have been malfunctioning so soon. Heaving an exasperated sigh, she gave her wrist several quick twists in the hope of reviving it. Then, though she realized the effort had probably been pointless with such new technology, she raised the watch to her ear to listen for any telltale ticking.

There was nothing to be heard, of course. Only the sound of her own astonished gasp as her eyes traveled upward once more and lit upon the figures who now stood all about her. To her amazement, these were no longer her fellow tourists, but a crowd of stern-faced strangers in voluminous white robes!

Chapter 3

She'd somehow died and gone to Heaven, Dana concluded, continuing to gape at the strange figures.

But, no. This wasn't the afterlife. There were no "pearly gates" here, only the circle of tall flat stones that had surrounded her just an instant before.

Yet, while the circle was still in focus, her new companions definitely were not. She saw them all through a strange haze, as though each was surrounded by some sort of aura. And, though the words they spoke were completely foreign, she could tell that their voices were out of sync as well . . . like the sounds of a record or tape that had somehow lapsed into a slow, slurring speed.

They were closing in around her, chanting a name she half knew was hers. She, on the other hand, couldn't seem to choke out even a syllable in response.

Priests! God help her, these were Druids, she realized. And the long, gleaming knife one of them clutched told her *she* was about to become a human sacrifice!

She wasn't quite sure how she knew all of this, except that it seemed apparent in their solemn, unwavering gazes—in the desperate yet furtive way in which one of them, a large elderly male at the front of the gathering, suddenly took hold of her wrist.

He was trying to gentle her, she acknowledged. His voice, his alien words were, all at once, hushed and soothing.

He pulled her forward, and, to her surprise, she moved along with him, not fighting him until . . . until the gathering of people before him finally parted to reveal the flat altar that stood just beyond, in the very center of the circle.

She recognized it! It was the *same* altar she'd come to know so intimately in her recurrent dream.

But this was no dream, she told herself. She was very much awake, and there wasn't a doubt in her mind that this was actually occurring!

She screamed, but, unable to pull her arm free of this would-be murderer, she had no choice but to drop to her knees and force him to drag her to that deadly destination. Across the well-trodden soil. Soil. . . . But, no. It wasn't simply a dirt surface anymore. Again it was the crushed rock–covered ground it had been as she'd tried to crunch her way, as unobtrusively as possible, back to her tour group earlier.

"Dana? *Ms. Swansen?*" someone whispered, and she looked up from the ground once more to find that she was at Ian Preston's feet. Without further hesitation, he bent down and helped her back up. Then he began moving her away from the rest of their group.

"Oh, Jesus, what happened?" she exclaimed, her

heart racing with terror. "What on earth just happened?"

"You screamed suddenly, then fainted, I think," he replied, his voice still quiet.

In that same instant, Sol Goldfarb, wearing a deeply concerned expression, approached them. "Need some help with her, Preston?"

Ian nodded. "Just in case she swoons again. You see to her left side, I'll take her right, and let's try to get her at least as far as the reception area, if we can."

At this, Goldfarb stepped up beside Dana and drew her left arm about his waist, causing her huge canvas purse to slide off her shoulder and collide with his bulbous posterior as he began trying to move her forward. "Good God! What has she got in that thing? An anchor?" he snarled, pushing it back up her arm.

"Who's to say?" Ian answered, flanking Dana as they walked in the direction of the bus. Then he raised his voice as he addressed her once more.

"Have you a medical condition we should know of, my dear?"

Dana shook her head, her alarm at the incident now becoming edged with embarrassment at having made such a scene. Lord, she was stuck with these people for at least five more days, and what a fool she'd already made of herself in front of them! "No. None that I'm aware of."

"Hmm," was her tour guide's only response, as they continued down the wide graveled path that led back to the entrance of the site.

"Could be a hypoglycemic attack," Sol suggested in his New York accent. "Barbara gets those sometimes in restaurants, when she's starved herself all day so she can eat a big meal. Just a half a glass of wine on an empty stomach is all it takes to make her pass out. I tell you, the first time it happened, I could've sworn she was having a heart attack!"

"I have *not* been drinking," Dana informed him somewhat indignantly.

"I didn't say you had, young lady, but you didn't eat anything at breakfast. Barbara and I were sitting right across from you, if you recall."

"That's true," Ian concurred. "I'm afraid your lack of appetite was a bit conspicuous, given all the food at the buffet table."

"Gentlemen, I hardly ever eat breakfast, and nothing like this has happened to me before. So why would it occur now?"

The pair of them exchanged mystified shrugs.

"Stress. That's what it is. Stress can do strange things to a person," Goldfarb suddenly declared. "Have you been under a lot of stress lately?"

That, sir, is none of your business, Dana wanted to snap. Given that he'd just gallantly come to her rescue, however, she decided against it. In spite of her still-ruffled state, she was keenly aware that she was going to need all of the allies she could get after the spectacle she'd just made of herself. "I don't know. No more than usual, I guess."

"Well, I say we take her into the reception building and buy her a Coke, Preston. Are there vending machines in there?"

"Aye."

"Good. Any sugary liquid will do. *Trust me,*" Sol

added, with the certainty of a New Yorker. "I've been through this dozens of times, so I should know."

Since Dana and Ian seemed unable to come up with any other theories on the subject, as they entered the shelter seconds later, "trusting" Goldfarb did seem the best idea.

So, in just a matter of seconds, Dana was firmly planted in a white plastic chair, before a large white plastic table, drinking Coca-Cola from an aluminum can.

"Do you want ice for that?" Ian asked, before settling down beside her at the table. "I know how you Yanks love ice in your drinks."

"No. Thanks. It's cold enough."

"Do you want me to stay with her so you can get back to the group?" Sol asked.

Ian's eyes traveled back to Dana's and flashed a subtle look that inquired as to whether or not such an arrangement would sit well with her.

She locked her gaze upon him and mouthed the word "no," so that only he could see.

"Um, I think not, Sol. It's probably best for me to stay here a few minutes more and have you go back to see that the rest return to the coach when they've finished with their picture-taking."

Goldfarb scratched his chin and shrugged in such a way that Dana felt almost guilty about not wanting him to remain. "O.K. See you back on the bus."

With that he was gone, leaving Dana and her Irish host to try to determine what strange force had come over her at the circle.

"God, I'm sorry, Ian. Your first morning out with

us and here you are having to play nursemaid to me!
I wouldn't blame you for dreading the rest of this
week." Dana dropped her gaze, choosing to stare
down at her cola can.

True to the code of the middle-aged Irish charmer,
Ian instantly cupped one of his warming palms over
the hand with which Dana held her beverage. "Ah,
that's all right, lass. It's just part of my job now, isn't
it? And, given the unemployment rate in this country
at present, I'm more than happy to have it. . . . So,
then, why don't you tell me what you think happened
back there? Could it just be the need for sugar, as Mr.
Goldfarb seemed to believe?"

Dana was teary-eyed as she looked up at him once
more, and she could see that he was surprised by it. So
was she, if the truth be told. She hadn't realized,
until Sol had left and let some silence fall over them,
just how traumatic the experience had been for her.
"No. I don't think so. I mean, I wish it were that
simple, but . . ."

"But?" the Irishman prompted with a gentle smile,
when she failed to finish her sentence.

Her nostrils began to sting with the effort to keep
from breaking down and weeping. "But it was more
than just fainting. . . . More like having a . . . a vision."
Her throat started to ache as she continued to fight her
emotion. "Do you understand? Oh, please say you
know what I'm talking about, so I don't have to go on
thinking I'm losing my mind!"

He was quiet for several seconds—obviously doing
his best to choose his next words carefully. "What sort
of 'vision' do you mean precisely, my dear?"

"Well, like . . . like a mirage. You know. Like what you see in the desert when you've gone too long without water."

"You mean, at first what you see is there and then it isn't?"

Dana couldn't help feeling heartened by this. Perhaps there really was some hope that he could be made to understand. "Exactly."

"So, what was it 'exactly' that you think you saw?"

She shook her head. "Oh, Jesus. I can't. I *can't* tell you. It's just so crazy!"

He gave her hand a squeeze. "No. I won't think you daft. I swear it." Then, lowering his voice as though not wishing to be overheard, he continued. "People have reported seeing many strange things in this place, so rest assured that you are by no means the first."

"Like what?" she inquired, suddenly feeling more at ease with this stranger, this foreigner, than she'd imagined possible.

"Like, say, a hundred-year-old Gypsy caravan driving along the roadway, clear as day. Then, in a flash, disappearing. Or a statue of the Virgin Mary, hovering above the hedgerow across the way, then gone in the blink of an eye."

A chill ran through Dana at the earnestness with which he related these examples. "Really?" she asked, her voice rising incredulously.

He clapped a palm to the level of his heart. "As God is my Maker. I've seen such things with my own eyes," he added in a whisper. "Though, if you tell anyone so, I'll emphatically deny it. Then I'll cut your tongue out," he exclaimed with a laugh. Seeing that he'd failed to amuse her with this comment, however, he reached out and patted her shoulder. "Just joking, of course, lass. But I really have seen some strange things, at this very site, so it's quite all right. You can tell me."

Dana looked up into his unblinking eyes. They seemed so compassionate, so filled with concern for her. "Druids," she blurted.

He drew his brows together, clearly in befuddlement. "What was that?"

"Druids, Ian. I saw people in long white robes coming after me with a knife."

He sat back in his chair and let his mouth drop open.

"You see?" Dana said tearfully. "You *do* think I'm crazy! I knew you would!"

He leaned forward again and shook his head slowly. "No. No. It's just that that's a new one, is all. I haven't heard of that before. But it stands to reason, doesn't it, though?" he went on. "I mean, that's probably who built the circle. Druids. Or their ancestors."

"So, are you saying you think I really saw what I saw?"

He nodded. "Yes. I don't doubt it. And, according to some physicists, there's a perfectly good reason why."

"There is?"

"Oh, aye. You see, I've made it my business to read up on such things, having experienced them once or twice myself," he added in an undertone. "And physicists say they're due to 'time-slips.' "

"What?"

" 'Time-slips' they're called. You know, where people's minds slip back to a time and event somewhere in the stone circle's past. Well, it needn't be a stone circle really. I've read that it can happen at any sacred site. Any place where there are mineral deposits such as there are here. Plutonium has something to do with it, if I recall correctly. Anyway, for an instant or two, there's what physicists call a 'macroscopic transient subatomic effect.' It's caused by the radioactivity's influence on the mind of the observer. And maybe that's why our ancient ancestors were moved to build their temples and altars in such places. Maybe they experienced these 'magical' properties too."

It was Dana who was agape now. "That's incredible. I've never heard of such a thing. How could I have been to so many archaeological digs and never have learned of this?"

Ian shrugged. "Not all dig sites are sacred, you know. Besides, I think this theory is fairly new among scientists. I mean, the books I've read on the subject are just a couple of years old. And, though time seems only to move forward, I guess they have proven in the new physics that electrons can actually travel backward in time."

Dana raised a halting palm to him. "Whoa. Don't get too technical with this, please. I've just had the scare of my life. And the horrible truth of the matter is, it wasn't really a new vision I saw, but like . . . I don't know. . . . Fragments, I guess. From a dream I've been having since I was very young."

He laughed, the outer corners of his eyes turning up as though he was quite intrigued by this disclosure. "You mean to tell me you dream of *Druids,* my dear?"

"Well, not voluntarily, mind you. And I don't think I realized they were Druids until the vision of them came to me just now. I mean, I had the dream again this morning, but I've never gotten a good look at the people in it. Not until now," she acknowledged again with an uneasy swallow.

"Why, there you have it, then. That dream had recently been in your thoughts and then you came here to this place with its mind-altering emanations and, faith and begorra, what else should appear to you? It's simply some sort of carryover. Don't you think?" he asked hopefully, consulting his watch and rising with an expression that said they were both due back on the bus.

"I suppose," she answered tentatively, realizing that, tour company itineraries being as tightly scheduled as they were, she simply couldn't take up any more of his time with the matter.

He smiled, as she got to her feet as well. Then he circled around her and wrapped a steadying arm about her waist. "Right, then. Let me help you back aboard. You aren't still feeling dizzy, are you?"

"No."

"Got your purse and whatever other belongings you brought along?"

She nodded and gave forth an awkward laugh.

"Listen, we needn't tell any of the others about this," he said softly, as they headed for the door. "I know how embarrassing these things can be, and I'm content to let them simply think your blood sugar was low, if you are."

"Sure," Dana agreed, though she sensed that he was

making this suggestion more out of a desire to avoid controversy than from real concern for her feelings.

"I shouldn't have told you all I did, I suppose. I somehow doubt my superiors would approve. It's just that I couldn't allow you to go on thinking you were alone in it. I mean, thinking you'd gone round the bend or something," he said.

They exited the reception building and began the short walk back to the waiting bus. "I know, Ian, and I greatly appreciate it."

"Well, it's just scientific conjecture is all. But I'll get you the titles of the books I've read on the subject when we're back in Dublin, if you'd like."

"I would. They sound fascinating."

"Aye. They are, until a time-slip happens to you firsthand, of course. Then it's all just plain frightening."

Dana laughed again weakly. "I'll say!"

He gave her waist a consoling pat. "Well, never you mind. It's over now. We'll be out of here in just a few minutes and on to a place you're sure to find much more soothing. An old monastery by the sea. There you should be feeling like yourself again."

Dana nodded, but in truth, she wasn't so sure. Her watch was still stopped, and now that she was back out in the sunlight, she noticed the same halolike outlines on things—the ones she'd seen about those Druids earlier.

It hadn't been just a vision she'd experienced in the stone circle but some sort of alternate reality. One in which she'd actually *felt* the strange priest's grip upon her, had *smelled* the odor of what, in retrospect, she

believed to be incense and burning animal flesh. It had
been far more than a mirage; it was very much like a
memory. Something that had affected several of her
senses.

Though she wanted, with all her heart, to believe
Ian's claim that it had been just an instantaneous illusion, she knew he was wrong in her case. Whatever it
was still seemed to be with her. As near as she could
tell, it was holding on tightly and quite unwilling to let
go.

Ian apparently had no narrating to do as they traveled to the monastery, so Dana put on the headphones
she carried in her purse and tried to immerse herself in
a Blues Brothers' cassette. The tape recorder she'd
brought along to record material for her research
would serve this alternate purpose today, she'd decided, since she seemed in desperate need of something
to anchor her to the present-day world.

The sunny morning had turned rather cloudy, and
by the time they reached their next destination, a kind
of thin fog had settled over the bay adjacent to it.

Dana turned and looked out of the left side of the
coach in order to scan the friary they were about to
enter. It had an arched stone entryway. This straddled
two huge earthen embankments, as though the passage had been dug, like a tunnel, clear down to the
valley where the compound itself was nestled. However hidden from view, though, this place was clearly
a monastery. Dana could see its circular bell tower as
clear as day hundreds of yards to the east. And,

though everything she looked at still possessed that odd glow which she'd somehow carried with her from the stone circle, she did hold some hope that Ian had been right in assuring her she'd find this place more enjoyable.

She shut off her recorder and stuffed it and her headphones back into her purse, only to have her ears instantly greeted by the Goldfarbs' conversation.

"Puff the magic dragon," Sol said to his wife, as the bus finally came to a full stop.

Dana turned toward the right window to see what he was pointing at and she spotted what appeared to be the serpent-headed stem of a Viking longship a good distance out upon the water.

"What is that?" Mrs. Goldfarb called out to Ian, as everyone was gathering up jackets and cameras to disembark.

Ian, now standing at the front of the coach, bent forward and peered out the window at the bay. "Oh, just the replica of a Norse warship. They keep it anchored out there sometimes for effect. The Vikings did so love raiding friaries."

"Why?" Sol inquired.

Ian gave this several seconds' thought, then shrugged. "Because the monks rarely fought back, I suppose. And, in such holy places, a person was sure to find plenty of golden icons and casks of wine to carry off. Ask Ms. Swansen there, behind you. Our Viking expert. She can tell you all about it, no doubt," he concluded, offering Dana a teasing wink.

With that Ian was gone, hurriedly descending the

coach steps in an effort to see the rest of the passengers safely down them.

"How are you feeling?" Sol asked, turning back to Dana. "Any better now that we've been sitting for a while?"

"Yes. Much. Thanks," Dana lied. Goldfarb and his wife were looking at her with such undivided attention that she just couldn't bear to say anything to deepen their obvious concern for her.

Barbara raised a questioning brow. "Is it true what he said? Are you really some sort of expert on the Vikings?"

Dana's cheeks warmed at the immodesty she would doubtless show if she answered honestly. "I guess so. I've studied them for nearly a decade, for what that's worth."

Sol entered the aisle, once all of the other passengers had gone by. Then he sidled into the opposite seat stall to wave both his wife and Dana out ahead of him.

"Barbara and I have a daughter about your age back home," he explained, as he stepped off the bus behind Dana seconds later. "I suppose that's why I was so worried about you earlier. A conditioned reflex, I'm afraid."

"Well, that's sweet," Dana replied, turning back to flash him a smile. "But I'm fine now. Really."

Mrs. Goldfarb's eyes narrowed, as they began walking, the three of them abreast, toward the friary's open front gate. "Did they kill the monks, do you know?"

"Who?"

She clucked impatiently. "The Vikings."

"Yes. Sometimes."

Barbara looked appalled at this. "Even though they were unarmed?"

"Yes. If they offered any resistance to the raid. But, oftentimes, the monks were simply taken captive and held on the Norse ships for a ransom from the local villagers."

"Good God, you *do* know all about this stuff, don't you? Kind of an odd college major, though, if you ask me," she noted critically.

Dana shook her head and tried to produce a diplomatic smile. "Oh, I don't know. It's just a history degree, and lots of people earn those every year."

To her surprise, Mrs. Goldfarb reached out and wrapped an arm about her shoulders. *"Sol,"* she blared to her husband who was now walking, several yards ahead of them. "Take a picture of me with this nice young lady before we go inside."

Her husband stopped and frowned back at her. "Why? She doesn't want to be in our pictures."

"Sure she does. She reminds me so much of our Janey. Let's just take a shot of her to show the family when we get back. . . . You don't mind, do you, lamb?" she asked Dana, her motherly embrace tightening.

Programmed by a lifetime of exposure to Scandinavian stoicism, Dana couldn't help tensing at her demonstrativeness. "No. I guess not."

At this, Barbara walked her to the mouth of the compound and stood by her side, against the left wall of the stone archway. "Hurry, Sol. Will you? Before it starts to rain. You know you can't get any decent shots with that thing once it clouds up."

"Damn it, woman, I'm coming! You'd think the world was about to end, the way you carry on!"

Dana smiled, as best she could, as the New Yorker snapped the picture seconds later. Heaven help her, she was being *adopted* by these two! When would people ever start treating her like the autonomous woman she knew herself to be? Was a wedding ring her only hope for achieving this?

"O.K. I've got it," Sol declared, putting his camera's lens cap back on. "Now let's catch up to the group, before I miss everything *this* tour guide has to say, too."

"Sol," Barbara snapped, at this obvious reference to his being called away at the stone circle by Dana's fainting spell.

"Yeah, well, no offense, young lady," he stammered, his face reddening. "I didn't mean that quite the way it must have sounded. We all know you couldn't help—"

His words broke off as his wife suddenly issued an excited gasp. "Oh, look, you two! It's not anchored. It's *moving*. It's coming this way!"

Goldfarb scowled confusedly and turned toward the seashore to see what she was pointing at. Dana looked past him to do the same. Barbara, meanwhile, pushed by the two of them, her high-heeled sandals and rattly gold bracelets clicking like mad as she bustled across the roadway and over to the waterfront.

"Look, Sol. The crew is even dressed as Vikings! Isn't this exciting?" she called back over her shoulder. "Quick, get over here and get a picture of the ship while the fog is breaking."

Mr. Goldfarb, rolling his eyes with what seemed irritable resignation, trudged after her, and Dana decided to follow as well. "I wonder why Ian didn't tell us this was a re-enactment village?" she asked Sol under her breath.

He raised the camera to his right eye as they walked, as though already checking to see if there was enough light on the gray misty bay for the shot. "Probably slipped his mind. But, boy, they look real through this zoom lens! Here, take a peek," he offered, lifting the strap up over his head and handing the camera to Dana. "Very impressive costuming, if you ask me."

Dana peered out through the magnifying lens as they continued to walk. "Wow! You're right. They do look pretty authentic. Must be some local college students with access to a theater costuming department or something."

"I guess they're planning on coming to shore, the way they're rowing," Mrs. Goldfarb said, as they finally reached her. She was shading her eyes with one hand and pointing at the vessel with the other. "I mean, they're moving awfully fast."

"Yes. They are," Dana agreed. "I hope they don't run the thing aground. It costs quite a bit to build longship replicas."

"Well, where are they going to dock it? That's what I want to know," Sol muttered. "There isn't a pier anywhere in sight."

"Oh, they'll just anchor it close and come in on rowboats," his wife replied with a surprising measure of certainty.

Dana, on the other hand, wasn't at all sure what the

crew had in mind. She simply stood and listened, as the rhythmic slaps of the longship's oars sounded with ever-increasing speed.

So *this* was what it was like to see Norse raiders approaching. After ten years of studying and teaching this very subject, she was amazed now at how little the textbooks had done to describe such an experience. She simply couldn't have imagined how ominous a dragon-headed bowsprit must have seemed to Erin's natives, as it cut through the sea mist as though propelled by some monstrous tail. How silent such a warrior-laden craft could be as it sneaked up on its unwitting prey! Indeed, in just a few seconds more, the longship would be within wading distance from the shore, and yet no one but Dana herself and the Goldfarbs were aware of its approach.

"Hello," Barbara shouted, once the vessel was in earshot. "Greetings from New York, New York, Vikings," she exclaimed with a laugh, waving her arms zealously over her head. "Are you getting this, Sol? I hope to God you're getting some good shots of this. What a great show these kids put on with that big creaky old thing! Hello, hello, fierce Vikings," she continued, turning back toward the ship.

Oddly, the crew of fair-haired young men didn't respond to her calls. Though they were looking toward shore and had finally stopped rowing, not one of them offered so much as a wave in return.

"Chilly, aren't they?" Barbara said out of the corner of her mouth.

"Ah, they're probably just staying in role," Sol replied. "You know how it is at these sightseeing spots. They're supposed to stay 'in character.' "

Barbara shook her head slightly. "Even so, it's kind of weird, isn't it. The way they're just staring at us. I know they can hear me, but they're not saying a thing back. They're not at all like the rest of the Irish people we've met. Such a friendly bunch on the whole."

"The *Vikings* weren't friendly, though. They were marauding bastards. Isn't that right, Miss Swansen?"

"Right," Dana confirmed.

"Still . . . there are some handsome young men on that boat. Such nice big arms and chests on them. It would be a shame if they didn't come to shore and let you have a better look, honey," Barbara whispered to Dana. "I bet you could find a husband out of the thirty or so of them. Don't you think?" she prompted, elbowing Dana with a laugh. "It only takes *one,* after all, to fill the bill. Finding a husband's like selling a house. That's what I always told our Janey before she got married. It only takes one interested party."

Sol waved her off. "Leave the poor girl alone, for God's sake, will you? I'm sure she hears enough of that from her own parents without getting it from you. Come on," he continued, giving his wife's right forearm a tug. "We'll never catch up to Preston and the rest at this rate."

Issuing an indignant puff, Mrs. Goldfarb set out after her husband in her high heels; and Dana, fighting a laugh at their incessant bickering, followed them back across the road.

"No loss in your not meeting them," Sol grumbled back to Dana, as they again walked toward the friary.

"If you ask me, they all looked a trifle like that killer who was in the news a few years back. That Jeffrey Dahmer. Wasn't that his name? You know, the one with all the body parts in his fridge."

Barbara glared back and let out a ferocious "Shush." "There you go again, opening your mouth before your brain has a chance to catch up," she went on. "He's from Minnesota, her home state, I hope you realize!"

"No, he isn't," Dana was quick to clarify. "I'm pretty sure he was from Milwaukee, Wisconsin."

Sol nodded. "That's right. You see, Barbara? Telling me to shut up when you're the one who's confused!"

Mrs. Goldfarb responded with nothing more than a cluck and kept walking.

"So, what do you think it is about Wisconsin that gives rise to such ghouls?" Sol continued, pausing until Dana flanked him. "Isn't that where that guy who inspired the movie *Psycho* came from?"

"Yeah. Ed Gein was his name. But, frankly, Mr. Goldfarb, I don't know that Wisconsin has had more than its share of wackos. Could be the long dreary winters get to some people, though. They've gotten to me some years. Then again, the only one they've ever moved me to want to kill is myself."

He arched a disapproving brow at her. "Oh, don't say that! A person your age. Why, you've got you're entire life ahead—"

For the second time in just a few minutes, his words broke off, and he and Dana both turned in alarm to

ee what was causing the racket they heard just a few
ards behind them.

To Dana's amazement, it was the "Viking" crew,
bout which they'd so recently been speaking. They
ad, as Mrs. Goldfarb predicted, gotten off their ship.
ut, rather than rowing to shore in any sort of ding-
ies, they'd apparently chosen to wade in, because
hey were soaked almost to their waists as they rushed
orward, their wooden shields and gleaming silver
words in hand.

"Dear God, I think they're going to run us down,"
Dana exclaimed, reflexively grabbing Sol's arm and
ulling him off to the right, just out of the range of the
nrush.

Barbara, now several feet ahead of them, turned on
er heel in that same instant with a glower. "What is
he matter with you people?" she demanded, gasping
nd clapping a palm to her chest. "Aren't you carrying
his a bit too far? You could have given me a heart
ttack! Racing up behind us that way! Don't think for
moment that this is going to go unreported to our
our guide, to say nothing of our travel agent!"

As though a bit taken aback by her words, the front
ow of "Norsemen" stopped in their tracks, causing
hose following them to come to a halt as well. Then
hey all simply stood staring at her, as if they consid-
red *her* the one who was out-of-line.

"I mean, I understand that you're just doing your
obs. Putting on a good show for the tourists and all,
ut *slow down,* for God's sake, before someone gets
urt! That's my advice," Barbara finished, shaking a
tern finger at them.

The "Vikings" were still for a second or two more.
Then, to Dana's astonishment, one of them stepped
forward and ran Mrs. Goldfarb through, just under
her rib cage, with his broadsword!

Chapter 4

Dana couldn't believe her eyes as the woman stood shuddering in agony for an instant, then fell forward, onto the graveled path that led to the monastery's gate.

Dear God, this is no enactment! a panicked voice within her shouted. All of this was *real!* Just as it had seemed to her back at the stone circle.

Still holding on to Sol's arm, Dana made a beeline for the friary. But he didn't come with her. Apparently choosing to stay behind with his wife, he jerked free of her grasp, and Dana was on her own as she raced away, through the arching entrance and down the long stone-lined passage that led to the compound.

Seconds later, she was well inside, her frantic footfalls leading her onto the path that encircled the monastery's graveyard. Here her fellow tourists were gathered in a huge haphazard circle, calmly listening to some woman speak about the friary's history.

"Run," Dana screeched to them, pausing just long enough to again catch sight of the circular bastion she'd spotted from the bus. "Run to the tower and save yourselves! There are Vikings coming!"

Her warning was greeted by several clucks of disbelief, as though this, coupled with her strange fainting spell at their last stop, was causing the group to conclude she'd taken leave of her senses.

Dana didn't stop to hear more, however. Mrs. Goldfarb's horrific end just seconds before was all the proof she needed that this Viking onrush was *real* and that she could very easily be the Norsemen's next victim if she didn't get herself to safety in a hurry!

Oh, how she wished this was just another "time-slip," which her beloved tour guide could stave off with a consoling chat and a Coke. But an innocent, unarmed woman had just been *run through* back there, and Dana was simply grateful that she herself possessed enough knowledge of places such as this to seek refuge where, in centuries past, monks had done so.

"The round tower," she shouted back over her shoulder at her fellow tourists, in the hope that some of them would finally take heed and follow.

They didn't seem to, however. Sadly, the only sounds she heard were those of her own feet, as she sprinted the remaining distance to the sky-high, spired shelter.

Her eyes focused upon the tower's door as she reached its base seconds later. It was ajar, thank Heavens, where it was situated the customary eight or more feet from the ground. But no ladder was propped beneath so she could climb to it!

"The ladder," she exclaimed, near hysterical now. "God, where's the ladder?"

Fighting back a sob, she circled about the tower, in rabid search of anything that might help her climb to its narrow entrance. Without some sort of ladder, she knew she'd be as powerless to get inside as this friary's ancient raiders must have been.

She'd marveled in her history classes at the ingenuity such bastions had reflected. But, now that it was *she* who was being warded off by the fortress, her wonder was turning to indignation—and the urge to kick the daylights out of the stony structure in a fit of panic and rage.

Fortunately, she was spared this painful act. Just as she came full circle back to the entrance side of the tower, she saw a tonsured head pop out of its doorway.

It was a monk. Or, perhaps, someone merely dressed as one. She couldn't be certain. But, whoever he was, he smiled at her. Then, to her great relief, he lowered the very ladder she'd been searching for and gestured for her to hurry up its rungs.

She didn't hesitate, of course. Though this was a total stranger to her, he appeared to be unarmed and she had to believe he couldn't pose as much of a threat to her as the raiders at the monastery's entrance.

Shoving her purse strap more securely up her right shoulder, she scrambled up the rickety device. Then she gladly accepted the "friar's" hand, as he bent to help her onto the wooden platform that served as a kind of first floor within.

"Oh, Lord, thank you. Thank you *so much*," she said in a gush, as she turned about to have a look at the tower's darkened interior.

He scowled at her, as though not understanding her words. Then, nodding and smiling once more, he reached back outside and pulled the ladder in after her.

"Oh, you might want to leave that down. There are others with me, you know. Other tourists."

Again he furrowed his brow, as if unable to make out what she was saying.

She pointed at the ladder, which he had only just set down beside him on the platform. Then she motioned toward the door. "The ladder. You might want to leave it down for a few minutes more, in case the others decide to take my advice and come up here."

Seeming to understand her gestures, he shook his head. Then he turned away from her once more and shut and bolted the tower's heavy wooden door.

"But you don't understand," she declared, grabbing one of his habit's long sleeves, a beseeching tone to her voice. "You obviously spotted the raiders from up in the loft of this thing. And I was outside the friary when they came to shore, so of course I know about them. But the others . . ." She paused and fought to finally catch her breath after her wild dash to safety. "The others only learned about it as I ran through the grave-yard a few seconds ago, and we can't just let them fall prey to the Vikings!"

His eyes lit up as though he finally understood one of her utterances. "Vikings. Aye. *Vikings!*" With that, he took hold of her as well, turned her around, and bustled her over to a rope ladder, which was suspended from a story far overhead. Then, handing her one of its lower rungs, he issued some sort of order in a language that sounded completely foreign to her.

"Dear Lord, you don't speak English, do you?" she acknowledged with dismay.

Seeming to have lost all patience with her, he uttered his strange command again, this time giving her rump a swat, as though he were trying to hasten a mule across a roadway.

Appalled, Dana reached out and dug her fingernails into the wrist of his offending limb. "You keep your hands to yourself, buster! I didn't race all the way here to be strong-armed by you! I've just seen an innocent woman struck down in midstride and I don't need you shaking me up any more than I already am!"

At this the holy man, snarling something in his odd tongue, jerked his wrist free of her, pushed her aside, and began ascending the ladder in her place.

Unsure of what to do in those seconds, Dana had a good look around her in an effort to assess what this lowest story of the tower had to offer. All she saw, however, was what appeared to be a water trough on the far side of the platform, and there was no way of knowing if its contents were drinkable.

What was more, the dreadful screams she was starting to hear, from the direction of the monastery's graveyard, were beginning to send chills through her.

"O.K. Wait a minute," she called after the monk. "Will I be safe down here, if they attack? Do I really have to climb all the way up there?"

He didn't answer, the nasty, unbathed beast! He simply kept climbing; and, fearing that he'd pull the ladder up after him once he reached the loft, Dana

decided she shouldn't risk being left behind. If she
really had "slipped" back in time to a Viking raiding
period, the monks would have several days' supply of
food and water stored on the uppermost floor of the
tower, and she knew she'd be a fool to cut herself off
from it.

She didn't receive a helping hand onto the loft, as
she reached it several seconds later. But, given what
she'd just done to her host's wrist, she knew she was
probably lucky he didn't cause her to fall backward to
her death!

She was about to try to apologize to him, in fact,
when she saw, from the light of the loft's single window, that they were not alone. Two of his fellow
monks were up there as well, apparently keeping
watch on the friary's front gate from this greatly ele-
vated viewpoint. They both turned about now and
looked her over from head to toe.

"Hello. I'm Dana," she greeted awkwardly, thinking it best to try to ingratiate herself with them.

They wanted nothing of her attempts at hand-
shakes, however, as she crossed to them an instant
later.

"Dana," one of them repeated, apparently to the
man who had facilitated her entry.

" 'Dana,' aye," he replied with a shrug; and that
seemed to be all any of them cared to say on the
subject.

Dana vaguely recalled being told once that her
name was of both Norse and Celtic origins, so perhaps
that was the reason they seemed to be accepting it so
readily. This didn't account for why they weren't

taken aback by her modern apparel. But, since they didn't appear to be questioning it, she surely wasn't going to prove foolish enough to try to offer an explanation.

The two who had been keeping watch turned back to stare down out of the window; and the one who had helped her inside withdrew a wineskin from a shelf built into the curved, stone wall and offered it to her.

Parched from her race across the monastery, Dana gladly accepted it from him. She removed its cap and took several swallows of its contents. It was wine, she realized. She had been hoping the skin held nothing stronger than water—nothing that might further muddle her thinking while these "Twilight Zone" experiences kept befalling her—but she somehow sensed that wine was all these men had to offer.

She resealed the skin and handed it back to him with as grateful a smile as she could muster. "Dana," she said again, pointing to herself. Then, raising a questioning brow, she pointed at him.

"Padraig," he answered flatly, apparently understanding her inquiry. "Padraig. Sruthan *agus* Leannan," he added, pointing, respectively, to the other men.

"Ah, yes. Thank you. Might I look out too?" she asked, motioning toward the window.

She wasn't sure if "Padraig" understood, but he waved her in that direction, so she decided it was safe to try to sneak a look.

Treading softly, she moved back over to where Sruthan *"agus"* Leannan stood. Then she went up on her toes in an effort to see past them.

She couldn't believe her eyes in the seconds that followed. The graveyard was no longer occupied by her fellow tourists, but strewn with the bodies of what looked to be newly fallen Erse villagers and monks! The cause of this was more than apparent, as the "Vikings" she'd seen earlier now plundered the place, hauling booty out of every hut and monastic building and slaying the few of the friary's residents who were still standing!

Dana's mouth fell open in horror! Where on earth had all of her compatriots gone? Where was that multicolored sea of windbreaker- and denim-clad people she'd dashed past only minutes earlier?

Though she didn't want to do anything that might further annoy her hosts, she couldn't help sidling in between them and poking her head out of the window. She needed to scan as much of the grounds as she could in order to convince herself that her American companions had somehow disappeared from the scene.

Several seconds of searching seemed to confirm this. There wasn't a sign of any of them. Not of the sweet old sisters from Montana. Nor the braggart schoolteacher from Alabama. Not even of Ian and the female guide who had been addressing the group in the graveyard.

It was as though all that was left of the twentieth century—her huge purse and her clothing—had retreated with her to this belfry.

"Jesus," she exclaimed, again feeling her eyes well with tears. "This can't be happening! This has to be some sort of awful dream!"

Without thinking, she shouted out Ian's name in a desperate attempt to locate him.

At this, the monk to her right, the one Padraig had called Leannan, clapped a hand over her mouth and jerked her away from the window. Then, scowling fiercely at this endangering action on her part, he cast her back toward the opposite wall of the tower. And the pain she felt as she hit the floor made her realize that she couldn't possibly be dreaming.

"Whisht!" Padraig hissed at her, raising a silencing finger to his lips as though he thought her deserving of execution for what she'd just done.

"Yes. Yes. I'm sorry," she whispered, sitting up slowly from her fall and wincing at the aching in her back. "I shouldn't have done that. I realize it now. I should have known better than to risk drawing the Vikings' attention to us. Again, I apologize."

Her repentance was of little use, however. Within a matter of seconds, she could hear some of the raiders racing up the path that led to the tower; and Padraig, still glowering at her, hurriedly crossed to raise the rope ladder they'd both climbed.

Thinking it best to stay out of everyone's way, Dana pressed herself more tightly up to the wall against which Leannan had thrown her. Then, drawing her arms and legs inward, she clutched her purse to her torso.

But the raiders can't get inside, she silently assured herself. The bolted door was too high up for the use of a battering-ram, and the two or three windows one found in such towers were virtually unreachable by any means. Hundreds of years of use had proven, in fact, that this sort of structure was impervious to anything except cannon shot and gunfire, and, if these really were Viking times she'd slipped back into, such weapons wouldn't appear in Europe for another five or six centuries.

The Norsemen could, however, shoot flaming arrows into the door of the shelter in the hopes of smoking the inhabitants out; and the scent of scorching wood that Dana smelled drifting up to the loft some twenty minutes later seemed to indicate that they had done just that.

Padraig, keeping watch of the entrance, responded to this with an infuriated huff. Then he strode over to the shelf from which he'd taken the wineskin, and pulled a large wooden bucket off it. Hanging the vessel, by its long braided handle, around his neck, he turned and kicked the rope ladder down once more. Then, still looking incensed at Dana's calling attention to them all, he climbed back down to the entrance floor of the tower.

Dana, knowing she'd be crazy to try to sneak any more peeks out the window, seized this opportunity to slip over to the edge of the loft and watch what transpired below.

It was predictable enough, she supposed. Once Padraig reached the platform, he disappeared into the back shadows of that story. Then, filling his bucket from the trough she'd spotted earlier, he proceeded to throw several rounds of water at the burning portal.

After a time, seeming satisfied that he'd extinguished any flame that might have gotten started on the other side of the door, he sank down to the floor, drew his knees up to his chest, and sat rocking and mumbling as if in prayer.

The canonical hours, Dana guessed as she went on watching him. She didn't know a great deal about ancient monastic life, but she recalled from her studies that they prayed at regular intervals. Maybe this was one of them, she thought, looking down at her watch.

The timepiece was still stopped, however, as stuck in this strange temporal plain as *she* seemed to be; and again, she found herself on the verge of tears as she recalled how she and Ian had sat pleasantly conversing only an hour or two before.

She suddenly felt empty, bereft. She'd spent almost her entire adult life studying her Norse ancestors, and now that a band of them was assembled just below her, she wanted nothing more than to slip back into the twentieth century and never read another word on Norse history.

She realized that she'd always viewed the Vikings from the luxury of a position no longer afforded her: a safe detachment had allowed her to romanticize their bravery in battle. But given the nightmarish carnage she'd just seen from the window and the hair-raising screams she'd heard, she was now forced to conclude that they were nothing more than shameless murderers. Indeed, Barbara Goldfarb's death was all the proof she'd needed of that.

"This attack is my fault, I think," she suddenly heard herself confessing.

The friars, her companions, turned from the window and stared at her as though half comprehending her words.

She shook her head remorsefully and made no effort to fight the tears that began streaming down her cheeks. "I know you can't understand me. The truth is this is all so complicated that even I don't understand what's going on. But I just have to tell you that I think *I'm* the one who caused it. I mean, some people lose their luggage when they travel abroad, but it's far worse for me. I've lost my century—probably my whole *millennium.* And somehow the three of you have gotten dragged into this mess along with me. . . . Something happened back there at the stone circle. My tour guide tried to tell me it was just a 'time-slip' or something temporary like that, but I knew better." She shook a fist at the heavens and clenched her teeth. "I didn't really get clear of whatever force came over me there, and, fool that I am, I brought it *here* with me. I should never have agreed to get back on that bus! That's where I made my mistake. I should have stayed at that damned stone circle until things returned to normal for me, then called a cab back to the hotel. But I didn't, and now look what's happened! Poor Mrs. Goldfarb has been stabbed to death, and God only knows what's happened to the rest of the group! I . . ." Her words broke off and she let her face fall into her upraised hands.

Lord, *what* had possessed her to start rambling like this in front of the monks? She wouldn't be the slightest bit surprised if they deemed her a lunatic and hurled her out the window to certain death below. God knew she'd been little more than trouble to them from the moment they'd granted her admittance.

She raised her eyes with a start, as she heard one of

them cross to her seconds later. To her great relief, however, he wasn't poised as though to seize her, but merely standing before her with a small round loaf of bread in his hand.

"For me?" she asked in disbelief, reaching up to dry her face with one of her sweat-shirt sleeves.

The monk, the one Padraig had called Sruthan offered her a pitying smile and held out the bread to her.

"Thanks! Wow, *thank you.* I'm absolutely famished. I skipped breakfast, like a fool, and I suppose you two have heard my stomach growling off and on."

She tore the loaf in half and tried to hand one of the pieces back up to him, but he shook his head in response.

"No. Take it, please. Come on, I feel guilty eating your food."

A soft smile tugged at one corner of his mouth, and he pointed over to a large cloth sack hidden in the shadows far to the right of the window. Several of the same sort of loaves were protruding from the top of it. It was clear that they'd laid in enough to have many to spare.

"All right," Dana agreed, lowering her hand and instantly popping a little piece of the bread into her mouth. "But I insist on giving you something in return. After the trouble I've caused, it's the least I can do." She set the loaf halves in her lap and began digging through her purse. "Here. Here they are," she declared after several seconds. "Some raisin and nut chocolate bars I bought in Dublin yesterday. You've probably never had candy before, but it's sweet like . . ." She searched her mind for a food with which he might be familiar. "Like honey. I think you'll like it."

Looking a trifle uneasy, Sruthan accepted it from her and stood watching the light from the window dance upon the gold foil underwrap that protruded at each of the bar's ends.

"Well, you have to open it first, of course."

He narrowed his eyes in obvious puzzlement.

She reached up to him once more. "Here. Give it back to me. I'll do it for you."

He returned it to her and watched with rapt attention, as she tore into the packaging and broke off several squares of the chocolate for him.

"There. Now, taste it," she directed, gesturing and handing it back.

He appeared rather skeptical at first—probably having precious few *edible* dark-brown substances to which to compare it. After a second or two of fingering the squares, however, he finally raised them to his nose to assess their smell. Evidently finding their aroma to his liking, he slipped them down to his teeth and took a bite.

Dana watched, smiling, as he chewed and swallowed the chocolate. "Good, right? Don't you think it's good?" Her family dog always had, after all, and he was a creature of an entirely different species; so she held every hope this man would like the candy as well. And while she didn't want to end up being the one responsible for introducing refined sugar to the human race, this was about all she had to offer the friars in return for the hospitality they were showing her.

Pressing his lips together, as though considering the

question, the monk emitted a whisper of a laugh and nodded. Then, with the wide-eyed enthusiasm of a small child, he walked over to the window and nudged his fellow friar into giving the candy a try.

The man who had shoved Dana out of the way when she'd called out for Ian seemed equally pleased with the offering. But, as though not wishing to allow her any gratification at this, he was quick to turn and scowl at her once more.

She had made a grave mistake when she'd revealed to the Vikings that there were more victims to be had up in the belfry, and she realized now that, no matter how anxious she might be to get back outside and look for her fellow tourists in the hours to come, she would have to follow the friars' lead in this. They, and they alone, would know when it was safe to leave the tower. If she truly wished to survive, she couldn't risk crossing them again.

Chapter 5

Dana was hopeful that the monks would think it safe to leave the tower by nightfall, but a flaming arrow, shot through one of its midsection windows just before sunset, indicated that this was out of the question. Tenacious buggers that the Vikings were known to be, they were still out there, and God only knew when they'd finally get bored with waiting about and leave.

Dana kept trying to remind herself that such raiders usually chose to withdraw fairly quickly, for fear that armed locals might close in upon them seeking revenge. But, if this happened to be the early tenth century she'd somehow "slipped" into, the prevalence of Norse rule in this region of Ireland might very well be serving to make this bunch bolder than usual.

Whatever the case, however, she drifted to sleep a few hours after darkness descended upon the monastery, and aside from being inadvertently wakened by the friars as they gathered to pray a couple of times during the night, she slept fairly soundly.

Dana's "prayer," of course, was that she'd wake to find everything she'd experienced since leaving the hotel the morning before was all just part of some awful dream. Sadly, though, the monks, the dim and musty loft, and her incredible confinement within it were all back in living color at dawn's light. And, though there wasn't a sound to indicate that the Vikings were still below in the hours that followed, her hosts made absolutely no effort to venture out of the shelter.

They did, however, allow Dana to quell her hunger periodically with the bread, cheese, and wine they had on hand, and she met her other bodily needs with a large bucket they'd left down near the door for such purposes.

Short of this, though, she found herself with nothing to do but take stealthy notes about her ancient companions in a small spiral notebook she'd brought along for her research.

Lord, she had *research* all right! More firsthand information than she'd ever imagined possible. But she knew in her heart that she'd trade every minute of it for the chance to return to her own time and country.

By midday sounds of life were again heard from somewhere near the base of the tower. To Dana's dismay, they weren't made by a rescuing force, but were a barrage of scathing shouts which she recognized as being distinctly Old Norse in nature.

Though the friars still seemed unwilling to let her near the loft's window, she did manage to slide up toward it upon her jean-clad posterior, and on closer earing, she was able to make out that the raider in question was calling them remorseless cowards for having taken refuge in such a bastion, rather than coming forth to help defend their compound. This accusation was, however, laced with so many unrepeatable expletives, that even if her companions could understand English, Dana knew she could never dream of subjecting their holy ears to an exact translation.

The monks must have gotten the gist of it, though, because after several minutes of this verbal assault, Padraig stormed down to the entrance floor of the tower, returned with their brimming bucket of excrement, and proceeded to fling its putrid contents out the window!

Judging from the bitter Norse sputterings that ensued—to say nothing of the triumphant laughter of Padraig's cohorts—Dana could only conclude that he'd hit his target.

This was indeed a victory for them, since Dana's studies had always stressed that there was nothing a Norseman hated more than being soiled in any way. The Vikings were religious bathers, always preferring hot baths to cold; and given all the work involved in gathering and heating water for such use, the warrior who had just been stupid enough to stand cursing beneath their window now surely had his work cut out for him.

"Oh, let me see! Can't I just have a quick look at him, too?" she entreated, clapping a hand over her mouth as though vowing to keep silent this time.

The monks, looking weak from their continuing

laughter, hesitantly parted enough to let her squeeze i
at the window, and still gagging herself with her palı
as a gesture of good faith, Dana stole a peek at tł
retreating raider. He was tall, blond, and dressed i
what looked to be a mail shirt, blue cloak, and brow
trousers. As Dana caught sight of him, he was flappin
his arms a bit, as if to shake free of the defilemen
Then, still cursing, he withdrew into a nearby thicke

"Thanks, gentlemen," she said, as she stepped awa
from the window once more. "It's just good to kno
that I could play some small part in driving one ‹
those monsters off."

Leif Ivar'sson braced himself as he saw his olde
brother, Booth, heading toward him. Though Le
wasn't close enough yet to be able to determine wha
had happened to the captain, he could tell that Booth
clothes were wet and there was a decidedly repulsiv
odor about him.

"What ho, brother?" Leif greeted cautiously. "D
you not think it time we left this place and returned ¹
our camp?"

"Silence," Booth snapped, continuing to hold h
arms in an odd outstretched position near his sides, a
he approached his second in command. "*I* shall decic
when we leave here, or even *speak* of it!"

Leif stopped walking and, in spite of himsel
pressed the back of his hand to his nostrils. The stenc
as he met up with his brother at the mouth of tł
friary's graveyard was enough to make him retch, bı

he knew he'd only evoke more of his sibling's wrath if he dared to say as much.

"By the gods, what has befallen you? You're all wet," he choked out, reflexively backing away from their crew's captain.

"What do you think?" Booth growled. "Those craven bastards in the tower threw their night soil down upon me, you fool! Did you suppose 'twas by cause of a very large bird?"

While such snideness on the part of his senior always rankled Leif, he knew that he could ill afford to let it show. Booth's murderous temper was renowned among the clan, and in point of fact, Leif had been sent along with him from Norway to see that he kept his insane rages in check.

Still fighting the urge to gag, Leif spoke again, this time employing the powers of persuasion he had honed throughout his many years of having to placate his hotheaded older brother. "Pray do not allow those Erse curs to shame you an instant longer, Captain. Go to the sea and free yourself of their droppings, and I shall lead a few of the men back to the tower to take up watch there for you. We all know such a vigil is beneath one of your high station, in any case. Go out and resume the loftier duties of command."

Booth, somewhat softened by this appeal, reached up to mop his wet hair with a dry end of his hip-length cape. Then he gave a slight nod. "Very well. Since I am likely needed back on the ship."

"Oh, indeed you are, sire," Leif assured him.

"All right, then," his brother said, and with a snort, he left, his sopped calfskin shoes making revolting

squishing sounds as he tracked off toward the monas
tery's front gate.

Though Leif knew he would have to follow Booth i
he was going to recruit some men to keep watch a
promised, he decided to linger for a few minutes mor
and draw in some fresh air. He'd felt on the verge o
losing his morning meal as he'd held his breath agains
his brother's stink, so he wanted Booth well sub
merged in the adjacent bay before he headed back ou
of the friary.

Leif utilized his solitude by leaning back against on
of the graveyard's headstones and staring at the dam
nable bastion that had caused his brother to mak
them tarry so long after their attack upon the friary
Were the decision up to him, he would have left th
place twenty-four hours before and gotten the crev
back to the safety of their base-camp. His long experi
ence at foraging had taught him that, short of some o
the Church's manuscripts and a small supply of food
such towers usually held little of worth to a Norseman
But Booth had taken it into his deranged mind tha
this particular belfry contained some sort of treasure
and there seemed to be no reasoning with him on th
subject.

Booth could be worn down by time, however. Jus
as the flame that burned most brightly, burned ou
most quickly, the commander would probably give u
this watch within the space of another twelve hours
So Leif would, once again, take the path of least resist
ance. He was sorrily aware that, given his sibling'
volatile nature, their men likely had more to fear from

Booth than from any local forces who might come to check upon the monastery in the next day or so.

Unlike his brother, however, Leif wouldn't prove stupid enough to let the tower's occupants know of his presence near its base. There were plenty of bushes and trees about the shelter behind which to hide, and it seemed more than apparent to him that the way to get mice to leave their hole was to trick them into believing the cat was long gone.

He would, therefore, persuade Booth to move their ship out of the tower's range of view and anchor it in wait for his band's return.

By the morning of their third day in the tower, Dana was beginning to believe she might go stark-raving mad if she had to spend even another hour in the darkened belfry. Now seeming to trust her more, the monks were allowing her occasional looks out of the loft window, and she knew they were as aware as she that the Viking ship had disappeared from their view on the afternoon of the previous day. Nevertheless, her companions still seemed reluctant to venture outside.

There were things she could be doing to make this confinement easier for them all, she supposed. She had a flashlight with which to illuminate the almost-immobilizing darkness that fell over them each evening. And she had her tape recorder and music cassettes with which to break up the monotony of the long hours. But, fearing the holy men might think her a witch if she brought forth such "magical" articles, she decided it was best to simply leave them buried in her purse. The chocolate bars had, she believed, been enough of a revelation.

Perhaps, given ample time to win the friars' full trust and to begin to understand some of their language, she could start to confide in them about her outlandish circumstances. But what she really hoped would happen, of course, was that she'd snap out of this "time-slip" and emerge from the round tower to find that her American companions had suddenly reappeared in the monastery's graveyard and were ready to head back to the coach and travel on to the next stop on their itinerary.

What exactly was that? Dana wondered, sadly searching her mind for some recollection of it. . . . Oh, yes! "Lunch at a Wexford pub."

How wonderful that sounded to her now! To have nothing more trying to deal with than choosing what to order off a modern-day menu. After the fairly tasteless fare the monks had been offering her for the past seventy hours, it was sheer heaven to simply sit back and fantasize about such delectable dishes as Irish potato salad and corned-beef sandwiches with spicy mustard.

God, if she ever got back to the twentieth century, she silently vowed, she would never again take such luxuries as a varied diet, hot showers, and electric lights for granted!

Never mind her heart-rending breakup with Steven, and to heck with having a love life! She'd gladly settle for the simple, everyday blessings henceforward. Even just receiving a phone call or postcard from her parents would seem nothing short of a miracle, she acknowledged, feeling tearful once more.

She wondered if her family knew of her disappearance yet. Given that those were not her fellow tourists' bodies scattered about the graveyard, could she assume that at least some of her companions had gotten safely out of the friary and gone off to inform the Irish authorities that she was missing from the group?

But, even if they had, how on earth would they ever be able to locate and rescue her? Time wasn't the same as space, after all. If it was, indeed, a thousand or more years that separated her from her loved ones now, who would know how to bridge them?

She bit her lower lip and did her best not to start weeping again. Maybe she had actually brought this nightmarish mess upon herself by so often burrowing into her studies of Viking times. Perhaps her wish to escape the misery of her splitup with Steven had been heard by some Higher Power and this was its cruel, albeit karmic, response.

Whatever the cause of her plight, however, nearly three days of wishing and praying to be returned to her own century had apparently done no good; so she was at a total loss as to what else she might try.

By midafternoon, though, it appeared that some relief was in sight. While nothing was being done about getting her back to the twentieth century, Padraig and the others did begin heading down the rope ladder as though to finally exit the tower. Craving light and fresh air, Dana gathered up her purse and cardigan, and eagerly made her way after them.

Once they all reached the entrance-level story, Pa-

draig unbolted the door. Then, when he and his comrades had each had a chance to pop their heads out of
the tower and make certain it was safe to exit, Padraig
cautiously lowered the wooden ladder to the ground.

Leannan was the first to go down. Then, once he'd
reached the ground and begun to pace about without
incident, the other two men slowly followed. Dana
was the last to step out of the safety of the tower, and
Sruthan reached up to steady the ladder for her as she
made her way down its rickety rungs.

"Jesus," Dana declared when her feet finally
touched the ground, and she turned about to cast an
eye over the surrounding shrubs. "The sunlight is almost blinding after all this time inside, isn't it?"

Her companions scowled at this. Apparently at her
unthinking use of their Savior's name, she realized,
and she covered her mouth in response.

"Sorry," she muttered. "I finally stumble upon a
word you guys understand and it had to be that one!
I really am sorry," she added sheepishly.

Issuing an exasperated cluck, Leannan turned away
from her and began perusing the bushes on either side
of them for any sign that the raiders had not, in fact,
left the place. Then, seeming satisfied that they were
out of danger, he led the way down the dirt path that
lay before them.

As they neared the graveyard, the fresh air, which
Dana had only just been relishing, became suddenly
very foul. It took her a second or two to figure out
what might be causing the stench, but as they neared
the site where she'd spotted so many slain Erse villagers and monks, the horrible reality became apparent.

The *bodies!* Dear God, she thought, covering her nose and mouth with one of her forearms, it might take days to bury or burn the dozens of corpses she'd spied; and never having had occasion to see a cadaver up close, she wasn't at all sure she had the stomach for such work.

She stopped in her tracks, letting the monks walk on for several paces, while she searched her purse for a scarf or kerchief to tie over the lower half of her face. None of the dead were even in sight yet, but already their stink was beginning to overwhelm her. And, though she hardly thought her circumstances could get much worse, she was wrong.

As she continued to press her nostrils to the back of her left hand, and rummage through the contents of her bag with her right, she felt someone grab her from behind!

One of the *raiders,* she deduced. Her friarly companions were all still within her view, so a Viking had hold of her! And, far from having to cover her nose against the reek of the fallen, she now wondered if she might smother beneath the huge hand that had just been clapped over her face.

There hadn't been time enough to cry out as the arms had clamped about her, and she found that all she could send forth now, from beneath this enormous palm, was a scream so muffled only her seizer could possibly hear it.

She still had one hand in her purse, however, and due to the training she'd received in a self-defense class she'd recently taken, she possessed the presence of mind to quickly locate and withdraw the tiny canister of Mace she always carried with her.

In the space of a heartbeat, she raised the container up over her head, and with its nozzle pointed backward, she depressed its sprayer button three times in rapid succession.

This was immediately greeted by a yelp from behind her, and to her great relief, her attacker withdrew his hands.

She should run away, she realized in those fateful seconds. That was what her self-defense instructor had drummed into her. Yet, a kind of morbid curiosity came into play, and she wheeled about to see a tall blond young man standing just inches from her.

Sucking several pained breaths in through his teeth, he was rubbing his eyes with his fists. Realizing just how well-aimed her blasts of the chemical mixture had been, Dana took the opportunity to do the ruffian further injury.

Before he even seemed aware that she had turned to face him, she kneed him in the crotch and stood watching as he gave forth a wail of agony.

"You big bullies," she growled, beginning to tremble with the rage she'd kept pent up for the past few days. "Cutting down all these defenseless people in such a holy place! You deserve to go blind! I hope the Mace *does* ruin your eyes!"

There were, to the best of her recollection, some instructions somewhere in her purse about how to wash the stuff from one's skin and eyes before any permanent harm was done, but she'd be damned if she'd bother digging them out for the likes of such a murderer!

Evidently in too much pain to continue standing after her blow to his privates, the raider dropped to one knee and began whimpering as though he were somehow aware of the great damage the Mace was capable of doing. Then, to Dana's surprise, he spoke in what she instantly recognized as Old Norse.

"Fire," he said.

Something about a "fiery rain," and she realized that he was referring to the Mace. This was his way of describing it.

Her breath caught in her throat, and she cautiously turned away from him to see that he really was explaining what had just befallen him to two other Vikings, who stood just three or four paces behind her.

Spotting the fear in their eyes, she raised the can in their direction. To her relief, they began to back away from her as though aware that she could inflict her "fiery rain" upon them faster than they could draw their swords and run her through.

They stopped, once they were a safe several yards away. Then an odd sort of standoff ensued, during which they simply studied her . . . as though far more aware than the monks had seemed that her clothing was not of their day and she was somehow very out of place.

Squinting fiercely, she stamped a foot to see if she could further ward them off. Short of a slight start on the part of the one closest to her, however, neither of them budged. They just went on staring as if thinking her some sort of a sorceress.

They seemed too afraid to approach her again, yet too wonder-stricken to retreat altogether.

Well, if it was sorcery they suspected, it was sorcery they'd get, Dana thought, using her free hand to again dig about in her purse. Her studies had taught her that, for all of their advances in everything from medicine to shipbuilding, the Vikings were as prone to fear of magic as any other ancient race, and she knew she'd be a fool not to take advantage of that vulnerability in them now.

She, therefore, snapped on her tape recorder as soon as her delving fingers came upon it, and because her headphones had been disconnected earlier, strains of the Blues Brothers' version of "Gimme Some Lovin' " came blasting out of her purse.

The raiders looked rather stunned by this at first. For several seconds they simply cocked their heads and listened, as if trying to determine how it was possible for male voices to be coming out of a bag. But, as Dana took a few steps in their direction and ordered them, in their own tongue, to leave the friary, their curiosity changed to unmitigated fear, and they turned and dashed away from her, down the path to the graveyard.

Though she was aware that she had saved herself from being slain for the time being, Dana knew her monkish companions were in trouble if she didn't do something to alert them to the raiders' continued presence. She, therefore, chased after the Norsemen, letting her recorder continue to blare at them and calling out the word "Vikings" repeatedly as she ran.

It was already too late for a warning, however. As

she came around the row of bushes that had blocked the cemetery from her view, she saw that her Erse friends had already been seized by three of the raiders who had apparently been lying in wait for them farther down the path.

"Dana!" Padraig exclaimed, as he spotted her once more. The rest of his utterance, being in his strange tongue, was lost to her. It was clear, however, that he was shocked at the fact that she was *chasing* two of the raiders and that her purse suddenly possessed such demonic capabilities.

" 'Dana'?" one of the Vikings she'd been pursuing echoed, stopping dead and turning to gaze upon her with a markedly reverent expression. "The *goddess* Dana?" he asked in Norse.

She shut off her tape player just in time to hear the tail end of this query. The "goddess," her frazzled mind quickly translated. But what on earth was he referring to? The "goddess"?

She stood completely still, searching her memory over the thundering of her racing heartbeat. "Dana?" . . . Dear heavens, he thought she was *the* Dana! The goddess of all goddesses in the Norse faith *Asatru*. The *mother* of *all* their deities!

She hadn't thought about the hallowed Dana in years. Upon reading about this matriarch of the gods for the first time, she had, of course, noted that she bore the same name, but this coincidence hadn't struck her as being significant. She couldn't possibly have guessed that it might one day save her life!

"Ja," she answered simply, raising her chin with a sudden queenliness. Though lying was not in her na-

ture, it seemed her only choice, given the circumstances.

Everyone froze in that instant, the Vikings out of obvious awe at this revelation and the monks at Dana's ability to converse with these outlanders.

"Where did you find her?" another of the raiders asked the one who had just questioned Dana.

"She came from the tower, after the friars," he explained.

"And she speaks our tongue?" he pursued in amazement.

"I do," Dana interjected. "And I commence you to throw down your weapons at once!"

To her dismay, they didn't respond to this. Dear God, they weren't going to be fooled by her after all!

" 'Commence?' " one of them finally repeated, as if perplexed.

Commence. Dana's mind raced. Damn it! Had she said "commence" instead of "command"? Lord, but her Norse was rusty!

"Command," she quickly amended, lifting her head and looking this inquirer squarely in the eye. "The . . . the language of mere mortals is unwieldy on the tongue of a god," she stammered with an indignant air. "Again I *command* you to throw down your weapons!"

She held her breath in the seconds that ensued, silently praying to her own deity that they'd obey her.

They did, thank heavens! After a moment, they took their knives from their captives' throats and tossed them to the ground. Then all of their swords, including the ones carried by the men who'd run from her, quickly followed.

"Now, let the Erse holy men come to me," she ordered, continuing to direct her imperious gaze at each of the Norsemen in turn.

The friars, still looking mystified, but nonetheless grateful at this unexplained turn of events, wasted no time in stepping away from their captors.

Not knowing any Gaelic, Dana could do nothing more than say their names and beckon them to her.

They came, of course. Not only did they cross to her, but obviously aware that she was far more influential than they in this situation, they actually stepped in back of her, like boys seeking refuge behind a mother's skirts.

Dana couldn't help turning back to them and chuckling a bit at this. After having spent three days with her and witnessing for themselves that she was as much a slave to every bodily function as any other mortal, she felt certain they couldn't be thinking of her as some sort of deity. As she returned her gaze to the Vikings, however, she saw why the monks were suddenly according her so much authority.

To her amazement, the raiders had not only disarmed themselves, but they'd actually dropped to their knees before her!

"Dear God," she exclaimed under her breath. She had certainly experienced many things in her twenty-eight years of life, but full-scale worship was altogether new to her.

Not unpleasant, she acknowledged, fighting a smirk. Just *new*.

But what, in God's name, should she do with them now? Short of the occasional brown-nosing college student, she'd never had anyone at her command, so she decided to step forward and collect their weapons, while she gave this question further thought.

As she lifted the hilt of the first broadsword she reached, however, its surprising heaviness made her realize what an onerous task she'd undertaken, and she gestured for the monks to come and help her get the arms out of their enemies' reach.

"Where is your ship?" she asked the Norsemen sternly.

"Hidden just up the coast," one of them replied, only daring to look up at her for the instant it took him to answer.

Not as proficient at speaking Norse as she'd always been at reading and writing it, Dana required several seconds to decipher this and formulate a response.

They'd purposely hidden their vessel from the tower's range of view, she realized. All to trick her and her companions into finally coming out—the scoundrels!

"And when will they return for you?" she pursued in an icy tone.

"Just before sunset," that same man answered.

Heaven help her, what could she possibly do with them until then?

She could . . . put them to work burying those they'd slaughtered! *Yes.* That seemed the perfect task for them, she concluded, again becoming aware of the awful odor of decay all about her.

"You will bury those you have murdered," she sud-

denly declared in a booming voice. "Then, when your
ship comes back, the lot of you will leave here, never
to return!"

"*Ja*, Great One," a warrior replied, and looking as
though they feared she might strike them down with a
bolt of lightning if they disobeyed, the Vikings all
slowly got back to their feet.

A chill ran through Dana in those seconds. What
power! What ineffable joy to finally be in such total
control of the situation, after three days of having
fallen victim to forces she might never comprehend.

But, just as she was beginning to glow with this
newfound sense of conquest, one of her Norse worshippers said a word that she knew she had no hope of
understanding. Not without the well-worn Old-Norse-
to-English dictionary she'd left on her desk at the
University of Minnesota.

Despite her efforts to fight it, she did flash the man
a puzzled look. Supreme goddesses weren't supposed
to have to wrestle with vocabulary problems, she realized; but she could hardly reply when she didn't have
a clue as to what she had just been asked.

He repeated the word, his tone again sounding questioning. But this time, fortunately, he made a couple of
gestures as he said it—the movements of digging with
a shovel.

Shovels. Yes, of course. That was it! As dastardly as
their deeds of the past few days had been, they probably couldn't be expected to dig graves with their bare
hands.

"Go and find what you need on your own. You

raided this place, so you must know where everything
is," she snapped.

Continuing to kowtow like a pack of toadies, the
took their leave of her, each heading in a differen
direction, as though to go off in search of the tool
they sought.

All except one. And he, looking very sheepish b
this point, didn't even dare glance up at her as h
lingered just long enough to address her once more
"But, Your Greatness, why does our brave warrin
here anger you so? Is it not the will of your belove
son, Odin?"

Perhaps she was only imagining it, given how
shaken she still was by this unlikely development, bu
he actually appeared to be trembling slightly as h
made this inquiry.

You dare question me? she wanted to rage in return
To her credit, however, she somehow found the pres
ence of mind to stop herself. This might, after all, b
her only opportunity to preach more compassionat
ways to these savages.

"There is nothing brave in slaying those who bea
no arms. See to it you choose your battles more wisel
henceforth."

Had she used the right words to say this? she won
dered. What if she'd again revealed her fallibility b
choosing an incorrect term or two? Maybe she woul
just be better off keeping her mouth shut.

Fortunately, though, it appeared that her ques
tioner found this response satisfactory. He nodde
quite penitently and headed off toward one of th
nearby monastery buildings without another word.

Dana heaved a sigh of relief at this. All the Old Norse her professors had drilled into her throughout the years was finally being put to a more practical use than she and her skeptical family had ever dreamed possible! It might, in fact, have just saved her life and those of her Erse companions.

"Worth all that tuition money, Mom and Dad?" a pointed voice within her queried, as she stood trying to gather her wits. Oh, there was no question about it!

Chapter 6

In the minutes that followed the strange woman's attack upon him, Leif got back to his feet and staggered into the adjacent bushes to retrieve a skin of water he'd left there during their long wait for the Ersemen's emergence from the tower.

He didn't know if anything on earth could quell the incredible burning in his eyes, but if it was indeed some sort of liquid *fire* that vixen had sprayed at him, fresh cool water seemed his only resort. He squinted fiercely, as he finally took his hands from his face. Everything around him was a blur seen through two smarting slits, and he nearly tripped over a large rock as his horribly distorted gaze at last lit upon his drinking vessel.

With his fingers trembling at his continuing pain, he pounced, like a wounded animal, upon the water bag. Then he quickly poured its contents over his half-opened eyes.

It stung at first, the falling fluid feeling like speeding gravel against the raw skin of his eyelids. But then, fortunately, the burning began to subside, and he sank to his knees and buried his face in the thick grass at the edge of the copse.

There was no question that his eyes felt better when they were covered. It was as though they craved protection from the very air around him. But then, too, so did his lungs and throat it seemed; for now that the pain in his eyes was abating, the other areas that she-wolf had affected were screaming for equal remedy. Most notably, his still-aching groin, he acknowledged with a moan.

Who the *Hel* was she, anyway? That fair-haired Ersewoman in blue *trousers* so formfitting no one could possibly have mistaken her for a man? Erin's females weren't often known to fight back during such attacks, let alone to speak Norse to their attackers! Yet this one had done both and amazingly well at that.

By Odin! Leif silently raged, clenching his teeth and rolling onto his back to again try facing the sunlight. Why hadn't his men slain her the instant they'd seen her gaining the advantage with him?

Instead, he had heard them back away from her, and at the odd blaring voices she'd somehow produced, they'd actually turned tail!

By Thunder, what had his tortured eyes missed of the scene that might now help him understand how she could have changed two of his bravest warriors into frightened rabbits? And where, in the name of *Valhöll,* were they all now, that he should be left here to suffer alone?

With a determined growl, Leif pushed back up to his feet, drew his sword, and found his way out of the bushes and back onto the path that led to the grave-yard. There was something very strange afoot here, and he had every intention of getting to the bottom of it!

Dana was helping the monks haul the last of the raiders' weapons into a nearby hut when the Viking who had grabbed her earlier finally came around the bend from the tower.

"Where are my men?" he demanded in his native tongue.

Dana turned and looked at him. His sword was drawn, so she knew he must be handled with caution.

"Stay where you are," she said in Norse. "I am the great goddess, Dana, mother to all those you worship, and this I demand of you!"

To her relief, he remained still.

"Dana?" he replied skeptically. "You dwell *here,* upon the holy ground of the Erse?"

"Ja. You must know that one as mighty as I can be at once in many places."

Leif was silent for a moment, his burning eyes continuing to tear as he endeavored to grasp her claim. Even to his terribly fuzzy vision, however, she didn't look much like a halo-enveloped goddess. She was on the scrawny side and had definitely felt like a mere mortal, as she had struggled in his grip earlier.

On the other hand, how else could one explain her rare abilities? The blasts of fiery rain she'd delivered, her lightning quick blow to his privates, and that deafening chorus of male voices she had somehow brought forth as she'd chased his men away.

"If you be the mother of Odin and Thor, why do you side with these outlanders now?" he asked quizzically.

"Because they are right and you are wrong!"

"In what way are we wrong, pray, Goddess?" he inquired, with an edge to his voice that was just cheeky enough to make Dana's palms start to sweat.

He isn't buying this claim, a panicky voice within her noted. He was, apparently, the commander of this Norse band, because he seemed to be proving a much tougher customer than the others.

She paused for a few seconds more before answering. She couldn't allow his tenaciousness to rattle her into marring her reply with incorrect word choices. "You are wrong because only cowards kill those without weapons. Such is not the path to *Valhöll.*"

Leif swallowed dryly at this reproof. He wanted to point out that it was only by order of his evil-tempered brother that the men chose to slay their Erse victims rather than take them prisoner. He stopped himself, however. If this female really was the great goddess Dana, her powers of all-knowingness would already have made her aware of their captain's cruel ways.

"It was not by my command that these people were slain, but by my brother's," he said simply.

"Then," the skinny "goddess" retorted, "your brother was wrong. Now go and find a . . ." She paused as though searching for a word. "A *shovel* with which to help bury those you have murdered."

While Leif wasn't sure it was the wisest tack, given

the frightening powers she'd already displayed, he pressed the point of his sword into the ground before him and leaned forward, putting much of his weight upon the weapon. "And if I refuse?"

Dana swallowed uneasily. "Then I shall come and spray you again with my . . . 'fiery rain' and see to it you go blind this time."

Leif drew in a deep breath and straightened a bit at this. He'd never had occasion to deal firsthand with a deity, or anyone claiming to be one, and he was not at all sure how to proceed. Yet, as the woman withdrew the tiny vial and he recalled all too well his previous encounter with her, he sensed that he had no choice but to do as she asked or flee like a coward. Because he was the third-born son of a Norse earl, the latter was out of the question.

"Very well," he agreed. "But what do you intend to do with us, when the digging is through?"

"Your ship will return for you at sunset?" she inquired. Given her presumed clairvoyance, this was, of course, more a statement than a question.

"Ja."

"Then you and your men will reboard it. And you shall sail away and never return to this place."

While this sounded like a just enough arrangement, given a deity's ability to strike them all dead instead, Leif simply couldn't bring himself to pass up this opportunity to ask questions. It stood to reason, after all, that, if the gods liked to be worshipped, they also liked being praised. So that was the strategy he took with her.

"What, dear Goddess? Would you send us away

with no further chance to question you and learn from
your infinite wisdom, as your own son Odin would do
in our places?"

Lord, Dana thought, this is a wily one! In the Norse
religion, the god Odin would risk his very life in his
pursuit of wisdom. So what better way to win his
so-called mother's favor than to insist upon following
his example? But, good grief, that was *all* Dana needed
now, some Viking catechizing her about the inner
workings of the universe!

"As I have said, I am angry with you and your men
for your deeds here, and I've no will to act as your
teacher today!"

To Dana's surprise, this troublemaker actually
dropped to one knee before her as he spoke again.
"Then perhaps *tomorrow* you might say me yea, sweet
Dana?"

She glared at him, noticing for the first time just how
large and entreating his red-rimmed eyes were capable
of becoming.

Mr. Goldfarb had been wrong about this bunch.
Not *all* of them looked like serial killers. On the contrary, this one actually possessed a touchingly boyish
appeal. In spite of herself, Dana began to feel cap-
tivated by it, her expression starting to betray the fact
that she had almost as much interest in questioning
him as he seemed to have in querying her.

What a priceless opportunity, after all! If she did
succeed in getting back to her own century, would she
ever again have the chance to interview a *real* Viking
about his life and feelings?

Good heavens, if she got out her tape recorder, she

could even capture his answers in his own words and voice!

But, *no,* some sobering side of her countered. This situation was far too dangerous for her to run the risk of continuing to spar with him. He was, despite any appearances to the contrary, still a murderer. Indeed, the gruesome-smelling evidence of this was all about her, and she knew she didn't dare show her queasy susceptibleness until this precipitant devotee was out of her sight.

"Go and dig, you worm, before I set you aflame," she blared.

Leif tried to wipe the smirk off his face as she snapped at him once more. He truly didn't wish to anger the deity further; it was simply that the twinkle of curiosity he'd just spotted in her eyes made his heart sing. She, a *goddess,* was actually interested in him, intrigued enough to stand studying him as though trying to commit every detail of his form and features to her cosmic memory!

The truth was he felt moved to drop to *both* knees now and completely prostrate himself to her. But, given that that didn't seem to be her divine will, he thought it best to simply obey her, for the time being, and go off in search of a shovel.

To Dana's great relief, the big galoot finally appeared to be taking her warning seriously. Letting his gaze fall, he got back to his feet and began heading away, toward the monastery's vegetable garden.

"As you wish, Goddess," he called back to her with another slight genuflection. And, though he was clearly complying with her order now, the come-hither

look he flashed her in parting made her cluck with
indignation.

She nevertheless kept her eyes fixed on him as he
strode away. Cocky bastard! How dare he stand there
and grill her, when his companions had shown the
humility to simply do as they'd been told?

Who did he think he was? But, by the same token,
who did *she* think she was! She was just lucky she'd
been able to keep up this sham for as long as she had,
she reminded herself. If and when the Norsemen discovered she wasn't a goddess, they were sure to show
even less mercy to her and her companions than they'd
intended to in the first place. So, the best course of
action was for her and the monks to seal themselves
back up in the tower, while these intruders did the
work of interring their dead.

Dana saw to it that the Vikings' surrendered weapons were placed in a large sea chest and hauled to the
round tower. Then she and the monks all climbed back
inside it and rebolted the door behind them.

While the friars now appeared rather wary of her,
they did seem most grateful for her remarkable ability
to tame their foe. And, in spite of their language barrier, it was evident that they were inclined to attribute
her "magical" powers to the forces of good, rather
than evil.

The Norsemen were surprisingly hard workers—
given that burying those they'd killed wasn't a volun-
tary task—and by late afternoon, they'd inhumed a
surprising number of bodies.

Dana watched them toil from the loft window, taking in all she could of their movements and conversation. And, once again, she found herself wishing it was possible to study them at closer range.

In spite of their barbarism, there was so much she wanted to learn about them. So many details of their day-to-day lives no historian had ever recorded.

But she didn't belong here, she reminded herself. While she might be in the right place, she was definitely in the wrong time; and she knew that her only goal now should be to wait in the safety of the belfry until the Vikings left as ordered, then to emerge and go in search of her twentieth-century comrades.

With an uneasy sensation in the pit of his stomach, Leif left the friary and went to greet Booth, as he spotted the rowboat heading to shore.

"So, where are the heads of those who dared to defile me?" his brother called from the craft's bow, as one of his freemen oared him to land.

Leif waited until they were in fairly shallow water, then waded out to help pull the boat to shore. "Have I your word that you will listen calmly while I tell you what came to pass?" he asked. He was careful to keep his eyes locked upon Booth's as he spoke, so that he could better gauge his brother's response.

His sibling narrowed his eyes, as if in warning. "You do. But be brief, little brother, for I have not yet had my supper and I want my business here settled forthwith."

"Very well, Captain. While we have no heads or

treasure for you, I am happy to tell that we have come upon something far better."

Booth scowled, as he finally rose and stepped ashore. "And what could that possibly be?"

"A *goddess*. The very queen of the goddesses. Dana!"

The senior Norseman's jaw dropped. "Dana?"

Leif nodded and smiled. *"Ja."*

Booth lowered his voice and leaned forward, so that only his brother could hear as he spoke again. "I fear 'tis *you* who hath taken leave of your senses on this occasion, Leif."

"Neinn. 'Tis true. I saw her with my own eyes."

"Here? In Erin?"

"Ja. Locked away in the very tower you bade us watch."

"Ah, nonsense!"

Leif reached out and grabbed his forearm. *"Neinn.* 'Tis true, I tell you. I not only saw her, but she worked a wonder or two for us as well."

"What manner of wonder?"

"Well, when I tried to lay hold of her, she rained liquid fire into my eyes, and I swear to thee, it nearly claimed my sight! Then she brought forth a chorus of men's voices and strange-sounding instruments from a cloth bag she carried."

Booth pursed his lips and squinted again, as if still doubting his brother's sanity. Then, after several seconds, he spoke once more. "Hmmm. And where is she now, this 'goddess'? Take me to her that I might judge her powers for myself."

"She has gone back into the tower, I'm afraid," Leif

confessed. "I am sorry, brother, but it seemed not to be her will to dwell among us. She said she was angry at our having slain those who were not armed here. Then she commanded us to bury the dead and leave this shore, once you returned for us."

Booth, accustomed to being the only one in charge of his men, bristled at this. Then he perched upon the starboard gunnel of the rowboat, as if to give the matter further thought.

"A Norse goddess in Erin, you say? Did you not question her on this?"

"I did, and she told me that one with her divine abilities can be in many places at once."

"*Ja.* But why would she choose to dwell with outlanders on foreign soil? Is she not *our* goddess?"

Leif nodded.

"Hmmm," Booth said again, this time scratching his bearded chin, as though thoroughly considering the situation.

Leif meanwhile, exhaled a stealthy sigh of relief at the fact that his brother seemed to be accepting this account of what had happened.

"Perchance she tests us," Booth suggested after a moment.

"Tests?"

"*Ja.* To see if our devotion to her is strong enough that we would risk going against her supposed wishes and carry her back to her rightful home in Norway."

"*Ja.* Perchance. But do you not think her able to achieve such passage on her own? I mean, a being who can bring forth both fiery rain and men's voices from a mere bag?"

"You're afraid of her," Booth accused. " 'Tis not out of awe but cowardice that you obeyed her!"

"Neinn," Leif quickly denied. " 'Twas just that never before hath a god come to me in mortal form, and for the sake of my band, I thought it best not to cross her. She is capable of great wrath, mark my words. And 'twas I who bore the worst of it," he added. "You are indeed fortunate that she chose simply to see you splattered with night soil. It could have been far more torturous, I assure you!"

"I've no fear of her," his brother retorted. "I shall don my bearskin, taking the form of a beast, as her son Odin so often does, and I will, thereby, lure her down to tend to me as the mother she is to him."

It was Leif whose jaw dropped now, astounded as he was at the ingenuity his unbalanced sibling sometimes displayed. *"Neinn,* Booth. I think that design, though clever, most unwise. She could, I've no doubt, destroy every one of us, if she discerns that you are trying to deceive her. You know all too well how unpredictable a female's wrath can be."

Booth arched a brow at him, a glint of philandering mischief in his eye. "I also know how much more easily a female can be swayed. . . . But be not confused, brother," he continued, his voice becoming steely as usual. "No matter what face she shows us, I will not leave here without her!"

Though he didn't wish to cause an argument in front of their crewman, Leif gave forth a slight groan at this. If Booth succeeded in this hairbrained plan, it was altogether possible Leif would find himself with not one but two hotheads to keep in check!

* * *

A short time later, Dana was leaning back against one of the loft walls, filing her fingernails. She wouldn't, even twenty-four hours earlier, have risked revealing such a modern-day implement as an emery board to the monks. But, given that they'd already learned of some of her other "miraculous" belongings, she thought it was probably safe to produce one more. After so many days without any attention, her nails had, quite naturally, fallen into an awful state.

She would, of course, have far preferred a shower and shampoo to this short-form manicure, but until the Viking ship sailed away, these seemed beyond the bounds of possibility. So she was trying to make the most of what she could achieve now.

As the Norse chanting began below, however, she realized that the luxury of leaving the tower was still a long time off.

"Ah, damn it!" she exclaimed, tucking her file back into her purse and getting up to cross to where the friars were keeping watch. "Are they still here?"

Indeed they were, she discovered, as the monks made room for her at the window. Even though she'd seen what looked to be all of the raiders leave the compound at least half an hour earlier, they, sorrily, were back again and in even greater number! What was more, they were all carrying shimmering gold and silver icons and they were being led by someone who was wearing what appeared to be a bearskin!

Discouraged, she shook her head, then let her face fall into her upraised hands. "Dear Lord, it's back-

fired," she said in an undertone. "They haven't gone as
I ordered, but have come back to *worship* me, for
God's sake! What are we going to do now?" she asked,
raising her face and turning to search her companions'
eyes for any glimmer of a suggestion.

Unfortunately there was none. While the trio of
holy men looked happy to see that some of the riches
the raiders had, doubtless, stolen from them were
being so graciously returned, they seemed totally at a
loss as to how to get rid of the culprits. So it appeared
that Dana was once again on her own in this intermi-
nable nightmare.

Losing patience with the situation, she turned back
to the window and began shouting down at the Norsemen. They, meanwhile, had formed a semicircle about
the base of the tower and, having stopped their chanting, were staring up at her as though she possessed all
the power in the universe.

"Simply set your offerings down and go," she bel-
lowed. "I ask nothing of any of you but that you leave
this place, never to return! Are you deaf that I must so
command you a second time?"

Though they did begin dropping to their knees and
bowing their heads at this outburst, not one of them
moved to take his leave in those seconds, and Dana
was forced to roar at them once more.

"Be gone now, before my son Thor strikes you
down with one of his lightning bolts! I shall not warn
you again," she screeched. Having made herself almost hoarse with this final utterance, she pushed away
from the window and went to resume her place on the
opposite side of the loft.

"Well, that's *it*," she said to the friars, throwing up her hands as she sank back down against the wall. "I've done everything I can think of to get them out of here, the bastards! They're like dog do on a shoe, for heaven's sake! I mean, you just can't get rid of them! So, I guess we're stuck up here again until they finally get tired of waiting and leave."

She shook her head, near frustrated tears. She knew perfectly well that the monks couldn't understand a word she was saying, yet she was just too aggravated to keep her mouth shut.

"Now, don't look at me that way," she began again, suddenly catching sight of Padraig's beseeching expression. "In spite of how it must seem, I probably have no more power over that mob than you do. Just because I speak Old Norse, doesn't mean I know how to control them, and I really don't think it's fair of you to expect it! So," she continued, taking off her cardigan and rolling it into a makeshift pillow, "I'm going to sleep now. Some guys I know have been waking me up with their praying at all hours of the night, so I really could use a nap. And since we've already learned that the Vikings can't break into this thing, I suggest the rest of you just kick back and do the same."

With that, she set the rolled-up garment upon the straw-littered loft floor. Then, curling into the fetal position, she lay down and planted her head upon it.

Sadly, however, her respite didn't last long. Within just a few minutes, a wrenching round of high-pitched screams came from below, and she knew she had no other choice, with the monks unable to speak English, but to get up again and find out for herself what was happening.

As she reached the window, and saw what was taking place below, she wished with all her heart that she hadn't looked out.

They were *skinning a live hare,* she realized after several seconds, craning her neck in an effort to make out precisely what was happening.

Good God almighty, they were no longer content to simply leave treasure at the foot of her spiring retreat, but had actually resorted to sacrificing this poor, helpless creature to her!

Being a devout animal lover, Dana knew she had to put a stop to this at once! It simply wasn't in her nature to stand by while someone or something was being tortured for her supposed benefit.

"All right, that's the last straw," she exclaimed, beginning to tremble with fury as she crossed to gather up her purse and sweater. In a blur of motion, she tied her cardigan's sleeves about her neck, slung her purse over her right shoulder, and kicked the rope ladder down once more. "I won't put up with another minute of this! Frigging extortionists," she snarled in parting, as she quickly descended to the tower's first story.

Her Erse cohorts came to observe her in those seconds. Abandoning their watch at the window, they poked their tonsured heads out over the loft's edge to witness her courageous departure. And, while they couldn't have deciphered her angry comments as she reached this decision, the expressions of mingled admiration and concern on their faces said they understood all too well why she'd been driven to this desperate egress.

They clearly didn't intend to join her, however. The instant she stepped off the rope ladder and her hands released it, Leannan pulled it back up hand over fist.

"Great, guys. Thanks for standing behind me on this," Dana grumbled up at them. She was trying to look tough, even though she knew how dwarfed and pathetic she must have appeared to them from their aerial view. "You're a brave bunch, you are. No wonder the Viking raids went on for so long in this country!"

She was greeted by reverent gasps, as she unbolted the door and swung it open a second or two later. Still hearing the rending cries of the rabbit, her first impulse was to storm right out of the bastion, but fortunately she stopped herself in the nick of time.

The ladder! She moved back a pace and scanned this darkened first story for the wooden device. Surely it wouldn't do much for her godlike image, if she proved witless enough to just step out of the tower and fall several feet to the bone-shattering stone path below.

During the seeming eternity that ensued, she did manage to locate and lift the unwieldy thing. Then, as she began lowering it from the threshold, she was relieved to have several of her Norse worshippers rush forward to aid her in climbing down.

Chivalry, she thought with wonder in those precarious seconds. The very beginnings of medieval chivalry were suddenly all about her; yet she wasn't swayed by that for very long. Once her feet reached the ground, she pushed her way through the gathering and hurried around to the windowed side of the belfry to put an end to the ghastly act that had called her outside.

Nothing in the world brought her blood to a boil like the sadistic treatment of an animal; and no sooner did the sacrificer and his victim come into her view, than she dashed over to them and tore the big brute's hunting knife from his hand. Then, steadying the hare on the large stone upon which it had been laid, she put the poor creature out of its misery by lopping off its head.

"And who's next?" she queried in Norse, her teeth still clenched as she turned and faced the crowd of Vikings. It wasn't, she realized, so much courage she was displaying now as rage. Boundless, heedless fury that really had put her in a mind to *kill* anyone who dared to provoke her further.

As she could have predicted, though, not one of the raiders stepped forward to volunteer for such a fate. In spite of their worshipfulness toward her, human sacrifice was a very limited practice among the Norse. It was regulated by such factors as holy days and one's station in life. So it was clear that, if Dana truly wanted to lop off a man's head this evening, she'd have to force the issue.

"Ah, you're disgusting," she spat out, throwing down the knife. "All of you. Thinking for one moment I would be *appeased* by such cruelty to a little animal!"

"Then what will appease you, dear Goddess?" the man who had grabbed her earlier asked in an imploring tone.

He was still down on his knees, as were most of the

rest of his countrymen, and again Dana found herself being tugged by his large blue eyes.

There was suddenly an odd little ache in her throat, and for a moment, she felt relieved that he could still see, that her Mace hadn't succeeded in blinding him. It would have been a terrible shame, she thought with a sigh. His were such engaging eyes. . . . She'd really had no idea that a man of these ancient times could be so good-looking.

But *no,* a voice within her scolded as it had earlier in the graveyard. She simply couldn't let herself forget what a threat he and his men posed to her. She had to get back to safety at once.

"Just go," she replied in a soft, weary voice, her gaze fixed solely upon him. "Leave your treasures here and sail away from this place, as I asked you to this afternoon. Neither the monks nor I wish you to stay."

"But we won't try to harm any of you. Will we, my lord?" he inquired of the towering fellow in the bearskin. The one from whom Dana had just snatched the hare.

My lord? Dana's mind echoed. This jerk draped in animal fur was their *captain?*

"Neinn," the man in question quickly agreed.

Dana shifted her gaze to him and jabbed an admonishing finger in his direction. "You had better not! That is all I have to say to you, you hare *torturer,"* she shot back in the most threatening tone she could muster. Inwardly, however, she was tremendously relieved to have their word that they would not turn on her and the friars—a Viking could almost always be counted upon to keep his promises—yet she'd be damned if she'd allow her relief at this pledge to show.

"Now go, for good and all, as I have ordered," she concluded. But, as she turned on her heel to walk back to the tower door, she suddenly found herself unable to bring her right foot forward. Someone had hold of her pantleg, and she wheeled back to see that it was her previous assailant once more.

"That is twice you have dared touch me today, you fool! Do you wish to see yourself turned to ashes where you kneel?"

The Norseman recoiled a bit at her hissing and took his hand from her. *"Neinn,* sweet Goddess, but neither do I wish to see you go back inside. Prithee, since the treasures we offer have not brought a smile to your lips and our sacrifice brought only your wrath, might you stay here just long enough to tell how we might better serve you?"

Lord, what persistence, Dana marveled. She hadn't met with such dogged entreatment since a phone solicitor had gotten hold of her regarding a so-called long-distance "savings" plan!

She heaved a worn-down sigh. "Very well. You want to 'serve' me, gentle men, then this is what I require. A hot meal, a hot bath, and your chief's soft bed on which to sleep tonight. And, pray, young man, since you insist upon continuing to speak to me, refresh my memory. What is it you're called? I fear there are far too many of you mortals for one goddess to stay mindful of all your names."

"I am Leif, son of Ivar," he replied, a whisper of a smile appearing on his face.

He was surprised at the commonplaceness of her requests. She could see it in his eyes.

"Leif. *Ja,* that is right," she returned, nodding as though this fact had simply slipped her mind. "Well, you and your men go off now, Leif, and bring me all I've requested."

"And you will stay down here?" he asked gingerly. "You will not lock yourself away in the tower against our return?"

Dana shook her head. Not on a bet, mister, she thought, fighting a smirk. The truth was, if they brought her even one of the amenities she'd just named, she was fairly sure she'd be back out of the belfry in a flash.

"And to eat?" Leif inquired.

She wanted to laugh in that instant; he sounded so much like a waiter at a Norwegian restaurant she'd once frequented.

"Chicken, I think," she answered after several seconds. "I have never tasted rabbit or I would agree to eat the one your 'bear' friend brought along. But *ja,* a roasted chicken will do just fine, if you can find one at this hour."

"We can," her self-appointed servant answered, smiling broadly.

"Oh, and do get back to digging graves, once you have finished bringing forth what I've asked. The monks and I would like to see the rest of the dead buried by morning."

"As you wish, Your Greatness," Leif replied; and Dana sensed that her decision to come out and confront this mob hadn't been so ill considered after all.

They could prove wily enough to poison the food she'd requested, she supposed. That seemed a pretty good way to test a deity's immortality. But, then again, the Norse gods weren't like most others. Everything she'd read about them had indicated that they bled and suffered at physical attacks just like humans. They were, in that sense, rather more like the Greek heroes than divine beings, and this, she was quickly realizing, was most fortunate for her.

Short of producing the occasional twentieth-century "miracle" with the stuff she'd brought along in her purse, she probably wouldn't be called upon to do anything too herculean. So it was fairly likely that she could maintain this ruse for quite some time, if need be. But she hoped it wouldn't be necessary for too much longer.

Meanwhile, though, why not make the most of the raiders' insistence upon serving her? It would beat holing up in this dark musty tower for another three days. . . . And, while she was about it, she might even go so far as to ask the Vikings to heat some bathwater for her flea-bitten Erse friends as well!

Chapter 7

"She does not seem a goddess to me," Booth grumbled, as he and Leif were rowing the requested bed frame and bathing tub to shore a short time later.

"You are merely vexed at having to grant her the use of your bed," Leif retorted, beginning to feel quite winded at the work of conveying such a heavy load to land.

Booth, who had abandoned his attempt at passing for Odin as a bear, shook his head and continued to hold their unwieldy cargo in place as the longboat glided along. *"Neinn.* I've had plenty of women in my bed through the years, and I can assure you it has never vexed me."

A smile tugged at one corner of Leif's lips. "I don't think she intends to have you join her in it."

The commander, clearly not sharing his sibling's amusement with this, simply responded with a loud "Humph."

"Well, if she is not our goddess Dana, as you seem

to allege, how do you suppose she knows so much about us?"

Booth shrugged. "What does she know that speaks of clairvoyance?"

"She knew to ask for *your* bed, did she not? She knew that only the captain of a Norse ship is afforded the luxury of bringing his bed along on such raiding trips."

Again Booth raised his shoulders with an air of indifference. "We have come to these shores for many generations now. So, word of how we live on our ships and in our camps must surely have spread among the Erse by this time."

"But that's just it. I don't believe she's of Erin."

"Why not?"

"She speaks our tongue too well. And I have yet to hear her say a word to her Erse companions. You may notice this as well, if those cravenly monks dare to come down from the tower once we return to her. Then, too, we must wonder why she was not afraid to confront us, when the men with whom she'd taken refuge remained at the window, far up in their loft. You have to admit she is brave beyond measure for a female."

Booth paused to ponder this. "*Ja,* but extraordinary bravery does not make her a goddess."

"*Neinn,* but the other feats I've told you of seem to."

"Hearing of is hardly the same as seeing for one's self," Booth maintained.

"Then I shall entreat her to work another wonder tonight, for your sake."

"Pray, do," Booth said with a chilly edge to his

voice. Then an awkward silence fell between them. "And, if she is who you claim, well . . . we cannot simply leave her here, you know," he added in an ominous undertone.

"Are you again suggesting we *steal* her away with us?"

Booth clenched his teeth and stood up just long enough to rebalance the huge leaning headboard of his bed. *"Ja,* if she won't come along of her own will."

Leif's heartbeat sped up at the very idea of such an abduction. He had only told Booth of this purported goddess in order to justify not having killed her and the other occupants of the tower. It simply hadn't occurred to him that his brother would prove foolish enough to insist upon making off with her. "But why?"

"Because, if she is, forsooth, the great Dana, she belongs with us, not a trio of cowardly outlanders."

"But should we not permit her to choose for herself whose company she wishes to keep? She is, after all, a divine being, and she somehow brought herself to this place of her own accord."

"That she is 'divine,' as you say, remains to be seen."

"Just . . . just do not anger her, Booth, I pray thee," Leif said gingerly. "I tell you she possesses powers that you and I cannot even imagine."

That was *all* Leif needed! A full-scale battle breaking out between two such spitfires! One of whom he had promised his father he would see home safe and sound at the end of this summer's raiding.

Booth shook his head and smirked. "How you do

fret, little brother. I shall rein myself with her, you may
be sure."

"*Ja,* you *must* now, for we gave her our word we
would not do her or the monks any harm."

Booth arched a brow and fixed his jaw in that pig-
headed expression Leif had come to know all too well
in his twenty-odd years of life. "True. But, mind you,
giving her passage back to the land whence she arose
is hardly doing 'harm.' "

"*Ja,* but she has, no doubt, come unto us that we
might gain some sacred wisdom from her, and that
should remain *our* aim in all of this as well."

"Um-hmm," Booth replied absently, turning to
look back at their second longboat, which carried his
bed's mattress, linens, and the caldron in which they
would heat Dana's bathwater. As was his habit, he'd
long since stopped listening to the voice of reason his
younger sibling was sent along on such journeys to
provide. So Leif sensed that Booth was once again
about to gain his "sacred wisdom" the hard way.

While waiting for the Norsemen to return from their
ship with the things she'd requested, Dana called out
and gestured for the friars to come down and help her
carry some of the treasure they'd left behind into the
tower. But, looking as though they feared it was simply another trick on the part of the Vikings, the friars
refused to leave the loft. So Dana, certain that at least
some of the gold and silver icons scattered about the
bastion belonged to this monastery, busied herself
with carrying many of them inside on her own.

She wasn't alone for long, however. Within just a few minutes, three of the Norsemen returned to her with a dead and thoroughly plucked chicken and asked if this particular bird met with her approval. She said it did, and seeming pleased with this, they went off to one of the nearby monastery buildings, apparently to cook the thing over an Erse hearth.

Roughly twenty minutes later, they came back to her, carrying a small table and three stools. These they placed close to the door of the tower, and before again taking their leave, they motioned for Dana to seat herself as if to dine.

When they returned again minutes later, Dana's mouth began to water at what they set before her. In addition to the monkish fare of bread, cheese, and wine, there was a large bowl of cooked vegetables in some sort of white sauce. Peas, carrots, and onions swimming in a blend of cream, butter, salt, and garlic, Dana deduced, as she used the wooden spoon they provided to take her first taste of the dish. After over three days of little more than bread and wine, it struck her as one of the most delicious concoctions she'd ever eaten.

"Oh, this is *wonderful,*" she praised in Old Norse, taking another mouthful.

Her servers looked almost embarrassed at the compliment. Their cheeks bore that odd splotchy blush that Dana had sometimes seen on peach skins, and she couldn't help noticing at such close range how very young they were. She doubted that any of them were out of their teens, in fact. But then again, this shouldn't have surprised her. She'd read that Viking lads often began joining their fathers and older brothers on such raids as early as age twelve.

"Sit," she invited, still feeling delighted at this culinary treat. "Why don't you join me?"

"Oh, *neinn,* Your Greatness," one of them quickly replied. "The other two stools are not for us, but for our captain and his brother Leif. They should be here to dine with you, once the chicken is cooked."

"Ja, 'Leif,' " she repeated with a nod, reaching out to break a piece of bread from the round loaf they'd brought to her. She used it to soak up some of the delectably buttery vegetable sauce before popping it into her mouth. "The one I spoke to earlier. Pray tell me, as mortals, how it is to serve under his command."

They appeared nonplussed by the question, one of them turning and cocking his head in amazement at the other two.

"What do you mean, prithee?" the oldest-looking of them asked.

She took a swallow of wine. "Is he a cruel commander or is he kind?"

"But he is not our commander, Goddess. His brother is."

"Ja, I know. But when Leif is, when he leads a band of you to watch a tower as he did here, how is he?"

One of them seemed to be fighting a laugh at this mystifying line of questioning. "Well, he's kindly, I suppose."

"Much more so than his brother Booth," another put in, rolling his eyes.

This, for some reason, caused him to be elbowed sharply by the lad who stood just to his right.

Dana, however, couldn't help but pounce upon this revelation. It did, in fact, seem to jibe with what Leif had said to her earlier—that it had not been he but his brother who had ordered that the monastery's occupants be slain rather than taken as slaves. "Ah, *ja,* so Booth is the more cruel of the two," she acknowledged. "I thought as much. . . . And they are both husbands and fathers, are they?" she continued, trying to make it sound as though she was simply making polite small talk. "I only ask, you see, because I have been so long away from your land that my memory of it sometimes fails me."

"Oh, *neinn.* Neither of them have yet married."

"Whyever not?" Dana again looked up from her dining, her eyes scanning all of theirs in turn.

Unfortunately, however, the only responses she got were shrugs and sheepish expressions. Perhaps because they really were little more than boys. Or maybe there was something they preferred not to reveal. Whatever the case, though, they didn't seem to want to discuss the subject further, and they all looked very relieved as a procession of their countrymen interrupted the conversation by returning to the tower—with everything from bed linens to a wooden bathtub in tow.

"But where is the chicken?" Leif queried, as he and the man who'd formerly been draped in a bearskin leaned the elaborately carved headboard up against the tower's base.

"Still cooking, cousin," one of the servers blurted nervously.

Leif clapped his hands twice, as if in command. "Well, go and get it, boy. It must be done by now."

At this, the three lads were off, and Leif turned to face Dana with a warm smile. "They have kept you entertained I trust, Goddess."

She smirked. "They have."

"Good. My brother and I will join you at table, and the water for your bath is already beginning to be heated in a caldron in the cookery. 'A hot meal, a hot bath, and your chief's soft bed.' This *is* what you requested, in that order, *ja?*" he inquired, offering her a slight bow.

She sat back on her stool, studying this charmer as intently as any she'd ever met at a singles' bar. "It is."

She *liked* him, damn it! His face seemed one she'd known forever. The attraction was undeniable, and she sensed that, in spite of their rather rocky first encounter, he felt the same way.

"So, you enjoy vegetables," Booth suddenly observed, planting himself on the stool to her right and propping his elbows on the table. "Now I would have thought ambrosia far more suitable for a deity."

Dana, scowling at this rude interruption of her silent exchange with his brother, turned to Booth. "Oh, have you ambrosia here for me? I was not aware of that, pilgrim."

Booth, clearly taken aback by this shrewd retort, swallowed uneasily and removed his arms from the table. "Well, *neinn. Neinn* . . . Goddess," he stammered.

"Then it would not be at all wise of you to offer it to me. You could be searching this region for days trying to gather the makings for such, couldn't you?"

He pursed his lips before dropping his gaze as if unable to think of an apt response.

Not overly bright, Dana silently noted. *Mean and dumb*—a dangerous combination, or so history had proven.

"I think what Her Greatness means, Booth, is that she eats as mortals do, when she takes on such form. Is that not so, my lady?" Leif interjected, crossing to the table and seating himself at it as well.

"I know what she meant, dullard," Booth snapped. "And don't you dare speak to me as if I were a child!"

A terrible silence fell upon them, as the two males locked angry gazes.

"Gentle men," Dana began again. "I would have you leave me if you are about to fight. For that does not suit the place where one dines. The great hall of the dead is filled only with laughter and merriment, after all. For this is where a man finally knows his warring days are behind him."

Dana inwardly scolded herself. Why on earth had she attempted to say so much, to express such a deep thought, when her spoken Norse was still so rusty? What if she'd again used a wrong word or two?

Fortunately, however, it didn't appear that she had. In fact, both Booth and his brother now looked quite moved by this rather poetic reproof. But the contemplative quiet that fell over them was, sadly, short-lived.

"So where the *Hel* is that chicken?" Booth demanded, pushing back up to his feet.

Leif offered him an unruffled smile. "Pray go and see if you might hasten it, brother."

With a cluck, Booth stomped off, apparently to do just that.

"As you must know, Goddess, he has a bit of a temper," Leif whispered over to her, when his sibling was well out of earshot.

"Ja," she returned with a soft laugh.

"Prithee, do not take offense, though. He sometimes forgets himself, but I think, at heart, he means no disrespect."

"I'm sure not," she replied, reaching out to give his right forearm a quick pat.

Leif's breath caught in his throat at the gesture, and he felt an odd tingly warmth on the patch of skin she'd touched. She, *the goddess of all goddesses,* had just deigned to make such consoling contact with him, and he couldn't help being profoundly affected by it.

How lovely she was, he acknowledged. His stricken eyes hadn't allowed him to get a very good look at her when they'd first met, but now, his vision almost back to normal, he couldn't help drinking in her remarkable raiment and comely features.

Her long flaxen-colored hair was caught up at the back of her head in a strange, shiny circlet of some kind. What an outlandish ornament it was, he thought, wanting very much to reach out and touch it. And such an unusual, yet lovely hue to boot. It reminded him of the purplish color he'd sometimes seen within the iridescent inner coating of an oyster shell: a measure of pink blended with an equal amount of light blue.

Piercing the lobes of her ears were rings of much the same color. Then again the shade was repeated in the pear-shaped pendant that hung from the delicate, woven silver chain about her neck.

If only she would permit him to simply tap a finger-nail upon one of these unearthly adornments.

But *neinn.* She wasn't like other women, he sternly reminded himself. If he proved too forward with this one, she might very well set his loins afire with a mere glance. And, having already experienced her wrath, that was not a risk he cared to run.

But perhaps he was already doing so, he realized, as he caught himself staring at her chest. He swallowed uneasily and, with much reluctance, forced his gaze back up to her face.

It wasn't that her well-covered breasts had appeared to be anything but average in size and shape; it was just that they were so *erect,* as if they were being held aloft by some fashioning.

But these thoughts had to stop, a voice within him warned. What if she was capable of reading his mind? He doubted she'd find its present contents very flatter-ing, in spite of the fact that he had the best of inten-tions toward her.

The truth was he'd already concluded that, beneath all of her alien trappings, she was the very embodiment of Norse maidenhood. Like a daisy against the crisp blue of a Norwegian sky, her soft, blond hair and azure eyes brought him inexplicable comfort. She was, in this mortal form, as innocuous as a lass from a neighboring farmstead. A disarmingly simple and clean-scrubbed beauty whom—had he not seen and *felt* the evidence of it for himself?—he would never have suspected of being a deity. . . . Which brought

him to the secret request he knew he must make before
Booth returned.

"Dear . . . dear Goddess."

She looked somewhat surprised at his sudden uneasiness. *"Ja?"*

"It is not that I wish to trouble you, mind. Not for
the world, most especially after my unforgivable attack upon you earlier. But, pray, could I ask that you
work just one more wonder for my brother's sake
tonight?"

" 'Wonder'?"

"You know," he continued to whisper. "As you did
with your 'fiery rain' and 'singing bag' earlier. Might
I entreat you to show such powers to our captain?"

"But why? Does he not believe I'm Dana?"

Fortunately, her voice was even as she asked this,
but Leif realized that, given the precarious natures of
females, particularly this one, he probably wasn't out
of the meshes yet. "Well, I know he *wishes* to. With all
his heart, Your Greatness. 'Tis just that he feels a bit
cogged, I think, at not having been here to witness
your divine works for himself."

She sat back on her stool, as though giving the
matter some thought. "Very well. If you are certain
'twill satisfy him."

A relieved smile spread across Leif's face and he
nodded. Then, to his surprise, the deity raised a mischievous brow at him.

"Shall I squirt him in the eyes, as I did you?"

Leif lifted a cautioning palm. "Oh, *neinn.* Prithee,
don't do that or he will make the rest of us mortals just

as miserable, I'm afraid. Just . . . just a bit of song from your bag, my lady. I am sure that will do."

She nodded. "All right. And then will you go?"

"Go?"

"You and your crew, will you all leave here as I requested?"

Leif couldn't seem to hide his hurt at this. "But I thought you wanted us to finish burying the fallen."

"After that, I mean. Will you go then, as I've asked?"

"*Ja.* I suppose. If you're certain you want nothing more from us. . . . But"—he went on, somehow finding the courage to reach out and touch her arm as she had his—"will you not feel lonely? Here with a trine of monks who could not possibly worship you as we do? That is to say, we could prove most pleasing to you, in ways that such *chaste* men cannot."

Dana's gaze flew from his stroking fingers up to his eyes in that instant. Dear God! He seemed to be offering her *sexual* services! Of all the bloody gall!

Part of her wanted to slap him. Yet another, more progressive part, aware that what he was proposing was probably no different from the favors a male deity would be given in her place, knew she shouldn't take offense.

"Stay ye mindful, Norseman," she began again in a growl, being careful to lock gazes with him for effect, "that when I want aught from you, I will ask for it."

"Oh, of course, my lady. . . . But I notice," he added, narrowing his eyes at her shrewdly, "that you have yet to pull your arm away from my caress."

With an embarrassed blush, Dana instantly did so,

dismayed at how the wonderful feel of his whisper-light touch had lulled her into letting him continue it. Lord, it really *had* been too long since she'd been with a man! Steven had left her more affection-starved than she'd thought.

Leif dipped his head conspiratorially toward her. "Why did you do that?" he murmured. "The others weren't watching."

She lowered her voice to a hiss. "Well, just see that they don't! You horrible beast, killing my friends like that! What makes you think I want such favors from you?"

"Your 'friends,' Goddess?" he echoed.

Dana bit her lip, realizing the mistake she'd made in having blurted out so much. She must try to remember that this man was a product of his times. Viking nobles were expected to pillage and kill for a living. Choosing instead to focus upon peaceful pursuits, like farming and commerce, would have been considered beneath them. "Oh, forget it. I cannot expect you to understand," she concluded.

"You can if you explain it to me," he replied, once again offering her that entreating look she'd found so irresistible earlier.

"*Ja.* I can, can't I?" she responded under her breath. "You're very clever, indeed. I can see it in your eyes." It was she who leaned in toward him now. "So, tell me, why is it that you are not the captain of your crew? Why do you take second stead to a man such as your brother?"

"Because he is older than I, my lady. By one and

one-half years. Surely you know he is the one who must command."

Her blue eyes seemed to look right through him. "But it is, none the less, *you* who commands, is it not?"

Leif dropped his gaze somewhat abashedly. He just wasn't aware until now how much this simple truth must have shown. "Dear Dana, prithee do not ask that I disparage my own blood for you. My father—"

"Oh, *ja,* your father," she repeated, giving him a knowing nod. "Now there is the lord you *really* serve."

"Does not every son?"

"Ja. Until he is a man himself, which you, verily, have erenow come to be." He was probably in his late twenties, Dana surmised, studying his rugged, yet appealing features in those seconds. Maybe a year or two younger than she, and, yet, in the temporal scheme of things, it was likely that he was centuries older. Perhaps he was even a very distant ancestor. But, having witnessed the aftermath of the attack he and his men had carried out against this holy place, she preferred not to go on entertaining such a possibility.

Heavy footsteps were suddenly heard upon the winding path that led from the graveyard, and Leif, looking relieved to have their conversation about his relative manhood thusly interrupted, spoke again. " 'Tis probably Booth returning, Goddess. So, pray, remember your promise to show him a wonder before the evening is through."

"Oh, *ja.* I'll need my bag for that, won't I? Let me go get it. I left it in the tower." She got quickly to her feet and, relieved that the monks hadn't dared to come down and shut the door behind her, stepped over to the ladder and hurried up its rungs.

Once inside the belfry, she saw that her purse was precisely where she'd left it, not far from the threshold. She instantly began digging about within it in search of a blank tape to put in the recorder. When she found one, she switched it with the Blues Brothers' cassette she'd left in the player; and, now armed for the feat that lay ahead of her, she shoved the recorder back into the bag, slung the straps up over her shoulder, and went back outside.

When she made her winded return a moment or two later, Booth had, indeed, come back and was setting a platter full of well-browned chicken pieces in the center of the table.

"Those dolts," he grumbled. "They barely had the damnable fire built, so 'tis not surprising the roasting took so long! I knew we should have left them at home with their mothers."

"Mind you, we were young once, too," Leif replied in a patient tone, obviously wishing to stress forbearance to his quick-tempered sibling.

Dana seized their hushed yet heated exchange as an opportunity in which to slip her huge purse under the table and reach down to press the "record" button on her cassette player. Then, taking an instant more to make certain the apparatus was running, she sat back down on her stool.

That would be Booth's "wonder," she'd decided during her quick trip to fetch her bag. After a few minutes of recording their supper conversation, she would press "rewind," then "play" and pray to God the machine had functioned properly.

"What is that, Goddess?" Booth inquired, as she returned her attention to the table and began helping herself to some of the chicken.

She looked up at him blankly. "What?"

He reached out and tapped the glass-covered face of her wrist watch. "That."

She froze, unable to think of a way to explain it. Even if it had struck her as wise to disclose much about twentieth-century technology to these barbarians, she doubted that she could find the words to put such ideas across.

"Merely a . . . a bracelet," she said at last. "You have seen bracelets, have you not?"

His eyes narrowed, as he continued to peruse the watch. "Never one such as that. Never one with such writing within. May I have a better look?" he asked with the intrigued grin of a schoolboy.

Dana nodded and extended her wrist to him. He, in turn, gave the face of the timepiece two taps with the nail of his right forefinger. Then he issued an amazed laugh.

"Touch it, Leif," he urged, pulling Dana's wrist over toward his brother.

Leif rose and bent across the table to do so. "Shielded by a piece of clear ice!" he exclaimed. "But not cold. How is this possible, Goddess?"

Clear ice? a voice within Dana echoed. Evidently this glass looked quite different from the kinds these Vikings had probably seen—even seized—on their raids.

She shrugged, continuing to think it best not to do too much explaining. "I know not."

"But didn't you make it?" Booth queried, cocking his head.

"Neinn. 'Twas a gift."

"From whom?" Leif chimed in.

"My father," she replied, unable to think of another answer.

Booth's mouth dropped open. "You have a father?"

She gave forth a soft laugh. *"Ja.* Of course."

The captain appeared indignant now, like a scholar who'd just found a scroll of history that had heretofore been kept hidden from him. "Then why have we never heard of him? What was his name?"

"Jim . . . James, actually," Dana faltered, fearing that she'd once again said too much to these dangerous men.

Leif donned a faint smile. "James, *ja.* This is a name I have heard before, I think."

"Ja. 'Tis a very old name, indeed," Dana assured him.

An awkward silence ensued, as the two Vikings continued to study her watch, and Dana let a subtle sigh of relief escape through her teeth. Thank God they'd expected no more of an answer than this, because she somehow sensed that "James Andrew Swansen, D.D.S." would prove ridiculously difficult to try to translate.

"And what doth the writing within it mean?" Booth pursued.

Dana looked down at the watch herself now, seeing the brand name and the digital display, which still read ten-thirty, as it had when it stopped running a few days before at the stone circle. "I . . . I know not."

"Oh, but you must, my lady, since you wear it," Booth insisted.

"Neinn. 'Tis not important, pilgrim, that any of us understand the language of the 'Great Void,' the time before Creation."

To Dana's relief, neither of them made an attempt to argue with this. They just went on staring at the timepiece as though finding it enthralling.

"I want it," Booth suddenly declared, lifting his gaze to look her squarely in the eye.

"By the gods," Leif hissed. "You are mad! 'Twas a gift from her father!"

In spite of his brother's acidic tone, Booth kept his regard fixed upon Dana. "But that does not mean that she can't be persuaded to give it to me. Or would some manner of bartering be more to your liking, Goddess?"

Dana was tempted, in those seconds, to let him have the watch in exchange for his vow that he and his crew would leave the monastery and sail far away, once they had finished the work of interring the dead. She remembered, however, the part the watch had seemed to play in her "time-slip" experience at the stone circle; and, thinking it might somehow be needed for her return to her own century, she sensed it was best not to give it away.

"Neinn," she answered, doing her best to sound unflappable. "It is mine. A gift, as your brother has reminded you, and I will not part with it."

Another tense silence fell over them, and Dana's

heart began to pound for fear that the volatile captain would lash out at her. Leif, too, looked quite uneasy, as if afraid that the scene might end in his brother nearly being blinded by her "fiery rain" as well.

Then, finally, Booth withdrew his gaze from her and plopped back down upon his stool with a childish groan of disappointment. "Ah, very well," he snorted, snatching up a large piece of the chicken and beginning at once to devour it.

How amazingly infantile he is, Dana thought, offering Leif a relieved smile.

Leif, looking equally grateful that matters hadn't come to a head, also returned to a sitting position and helped himself to some of the poultry as well. "Eat, prithee, Goddess," he urged, "for soon, as darkness falls, it will grow too cold for your bath."

"Ja," Dana agreed, taking a couple of hurried bites from the drumstick she'd selected and then washing them down with a gulp of wine. She'd never been a big fan of alcoholic beverages, but she certainly understood now how a man as dangerously unpredictable as Booth could drive one to imbibing them.

"I . . . I've a wonder for you though, Captain, in my bracelet's stead," she announced, reaching stealthily under the table to press "rewind."

Again his expression was that of a little boy. He appeared somewhat disgruntled still, yet hopeful that she would tender sufficient remedy. *"Ja?"*

"Ja. . . . Here. Listen," she directed a few seconds later, pulling the bag up onto her lap and again reaching into it, this time to press "play."

What followed was, of course, an exact reproduction of the conversation they'd had since Booth had returned with the chicken. Dana watched, fighting a smile, as the two men sat gaping at this hauntingly familiar exchange, which arose from beneath the table.

"Why, that is *my* voice," Booth exclaimed.

She nodded. *"Ja.* And your brother's and mine. Speaking every word again, precisely as first spoken."

The two men continued to listen intently, until the recording had played all the way through. Then Dana slipped her hand back into her bag and shut the player off as quietly as possible.

"But 'tis nothing more than echo," Booth said, sitting back with a critical sniff after several seconds. "The echo one could find in any fjord while passing through."

"The echo of a word or two, *ja,* brother, that I would say is no miracle. But the echo of so much discourse, heard many minutes after it was spoken, now this is truly wondrous."

"Hmmm," Booth replied, continuing to sound skeptical. "Tell me, Goddess, could we hear it again?"

Dana met his challenging regard by raising a brow of her own. "Most certainly. And again and *again* after that, until you are driven mad by it repeating in your brain! I'm yet roiled by your hurting that poor hare, mind, so do not tempt me," she concluded through clenched teeth.

Booth drew away from her once more, his eyes having widened with each syllable of this threat, as if he'd had no idea such torment was possible. *"Neinn,* then," he answered with a dry swallow. "Thank you anyway."

"Your bathwater, my lady," Leif suddenly reminded her. "Let us get you to the kitchen, while it is
still hot enough."

Dana, sensing that Booth's next request would be to
have a look through her "wonder-filled" purse, knew
it was best to take his brother's advice. It was quite
clear to her now that the more time she spent in the
cantankerous captain's presence, the more likely she
was to lock horns with him.

Moreover, Booth was not particularly pleasant dinner company. Unlike his princely-looking brother's,
his face had a brutish quality, his brows so wide and
bushy that they simply became one over the bridge of
his nose, as though he were some sort of Neanderthal.

"Very well," Dana replied, hurriedly taking a few
more bites of the poultry. Given how hungry she still
was, she was tempted to make a little sandwich that
she could eat en route to her bath. Some roasted
chicken and a slice of cheese between two slabs of the
monks' wheat bread would have been just the thing to
satiate her. Remembering, however, that John Mon-
tagu, fourth earl of Sandwich wouldn't give rise to
such a creation for at least another eight hundred
years, she thought it best not to inadvertently teach
folk as imitative as the Vikings about it.

She'd read somewhere that a time traveler who
somehow altered the course of history might never
come to be born in his own age, and she sensed it best
not to run such a risk, if she could avoid it.

"But, pray, bring me two slices of buttered bread,
once I am in the bath, will you?" she added to Leif, as

she rose and slipped her purse straps up onto her right shoulder once more.

"Of course," he agreed, getting up and extending an arm to her, as though to usher her to wherever they'd taken that wooden tub she'd seen earlier.

"Was that 'wonder' enough for him, do you think?" she whispered to Leif, once they'd made their way to the graveyard.

"Ja. I think so. It should satisfy him for a while anyway. We will simply let him continue to stuff himself and ponder it all. It is his habit to eat and drink mightily in evening, then fall into a heavy sleep. So I doubt you will hear aught more from him tonight."

"Good. I can't say I wish to. And just where are you leading me?"

"To the friary's kitchen. The Erse don't have bathhouses, as you must know, so this seemed the only other place for you, since there is a great hearth within to keep you warm." He stopped walking, causing her to do the same. Then he turned to her with a concerned expression. "Prithee, is there somewhere else you have been bathing since you came here? I am sorry that I did not think to ask."

"Neinn. I've chosen no other place, for I have not been here long."

He began leading her along again, this time wrapping an arm about her shoulders. "May I touch you thus, Goddess?"

"Ja," Dana answered, actually grateful for his guidance and steadying grip. It had already grown dark enough that she was having some trouble seeing the stone-strewn path. And, because she was unfamiliar

with the monastery's buildings—save for its round tower, of course—she knew she probably had no choice for the time being but to put her faith in him.

Their bodies were a "match"—a fact that could not possibly have been escaping Leif's notice. He seemed precisely the right height for Dana, their forms coming into a natural alignment which made a tingle run through her. There was simply no denying that the heat and subtle scent of him pulled at her like a magnet.

They felt so right together, and yet it was all so terribly wrong, she reminded herself, letting her gaze drift for an instant or two up to the starry evening sky. The air was so clear, the heavens so different now, that she was once again forced to conclude she truly had been swept back at least a millenium in time.

Yet here, right at her very side, was a perfect "fit," the terribly rare sort of man who could make her go hopelessly weak in the knees by simply extending an arm around her. She shuddered to think, in fact, what might happen to her, if they ever had occasion to slow-dance together. What a pathetic pool of melted gelatin she'd become! And how utterly defenseless!

But, a voice within her hastened to warn, she shouldn't let the feel of this Norseman and his slow, respectful gait fool her. He was not at all like any of the twentieth-century males she'd known. She'd seen with her own eyes that he and his comrades were cold-blooded murderers. Evidence of it was all around her, as his men continued to dig graves about the friary by the flickering light of the lanterns they'd apparently brought from their ship. And, no matter how protective Leif seemed toward her, Dana knew she shouldn't let her guard down.

If it wasn't murder she had to fear from him, then it was rape. She, of all people, knew how notorious the Vikings were for committing *that* crime. So she simply couldn't allow him to discover what a seductive effect he had upon her. Or, like a deer mesmerized by the lights of an oncoming car, she was sure to become his for the taking!

Chapter 8

There was indeed a warm glow to the little building into which Leif led her a moment or two later. The kitchen's long hearth was lit at one end by the hot coals over which the Norsemen had obviously cooked her dinner and heated her bathwater, and the chamber was also illuminated by four flaming torches, which rested in wall brackets. Appearing to be made entirely of light-colored stone, rather than the wattle and daub that Dana had seen so much of from the tower while viewing the compound, the cookery could, evidently, withstand such exposure to fire.

"Here, Your Greatness, is your bathing tub," Leif declared, leading her to the large wooden vessel, where it had been placed just beyond the far end of the hearth.

He'd been quite right in promising her a hot bath, for, even in the dim light of the chamber, Dana could see steam rising from the tub.

"From our ship we brought you two towels, a cake of soap, and a change of raiment. I mean, if you wish it, my lady," he explained, pointing to a small pile of fabric which rested on the stone floor, beside the bath.

"A change of raiment?" Dana repeated curiously.

He stepped over to the mound of cloth and, bending down, pulled a long lustrous gown out from beneath the towels. It had flared, wrist-length sleeves and the duck-tailed sort of back hem Dana had seen depicted on many ancient Norse tapestries and engravings.

"Heavens, it shines in this light as though made of real gold," she noted, marveling.

"Oh, but it is, Goddess. 'Twas woven with golden threads. It belongs to one of my sisters. But, when she heard you were here, she insisted it be given to you. I know it is, forsooth, the frock of a mere mortal, but I'm afraid 'tis the best we can offer you at present."

Dana crossed to him and ran a hand over the glistening gown. How incredible it was to actually see such a garment firsthand, let alone be given this opportunity to don it! "Oh, *neinn.* Do not apologize, for it pleases me greatly."

"Then you will change into it from those trousers you wear?" he asked charily.

She gave forth a soft laugh. "You're not accustomed to seeing females in pants, are you."

"Oh, I meant no offense, Your Greatness. Indeed, yours is a form that would prove winsome in any manner of dress. It is just that—"

"Just that they need laundering—don't they?— these rank old pants and my shirt," she finished for him. "Isn't it amazing what so many days without plumbing will do?" she added under her breath in English.

"What was that?"

"Nothing, good pilgrim. I was merely thinking aloud."

"Was that Erse you spoke just now? It sounded a bit like it."

"*Neinn.* It . . . it was my own language. I suppose you might say the tongue of the gods," she lied.

He appeared intrigued. "Oh? And might you teach it to me? A few words of it, anyway?"

"Perhaps," she answered tentatively, again fearing that such disclosure might somehow change the face of history.

"*Ja,* very well," she agreed, when he continued to simply stand staring at her. The stress of the past few days, coupled with the wine she'd drunk at supper, seemed to be catching up with her, and all she wanted now was to finally be allowed the privacy to undress and lower herself into the heavenly-looking tub of hot water. "Here is one word of it for you. *Scram!*"

" 'Scram'?"

"*Ja.* It means 'Leave the kitchen now, so I can bathe in peace.' "

Though it was clear that he was wounded by the order, it was also apparent that he was trying not to show it. "And all of this you can say with a single word?"

She fought the urge to smile at his boyishness. "*Ja.*"

"Well, then, 'tis indeed a wondrous tongue. But you want me to go now, don't you?"

"*Ja,*" she answered without hesitation.

"I thought, however, that I might stay and guard you from intruders. 'Tis not that my companions would walk in upon you by design, mind. 'Tis just that some of them may not know you are in here."

"Very well, then. Go and guard me from *outside* the door."

Somehow sensing that this was her final word on the subject, he gave her a nod and took his leave, closing the cookery's door behind him. And, for the first time in over three days, she was completely alone and deeply grateful for it.

The foremost order of business was to take off her wrist watch and stow it in her purse. Then she began to disrobe. There were no shutters on the windows, so she took care to drape one of the towels in front of her, as she did so. She hurriedly stepped out of her espadrilles. Then, holding one end of the towel in her teeth, she let it conceal her, as she hurriedly removed cardigan, pants, and top. The towel wrapped securely about her, she slipped off her undergarments. Then she dipped a toe into the bathwater to make sure it wasn't too hot.

Fortunately, it was just the right temperature, as much to her liking as any she'd ever drawn for herself. She wasted no time, therefore, in dropping her towel and lowering her body into the tub.

God, it was *marvelous,* she acknowledged with a blissful sigh, reclining until her neck came to rest upon the vessel's back ledge. She hadn't realized how wonderful a hot bath could be until now, having been denied one for so many days. And, were she not acutely aware that the building she occupied was still surrounded by a pack of murderous barbarians, she was certain she would simply have drifted off to sleep.

For all of their faults as a race, however, she had to give the Norse credit for their love of bathing. After several days of sharing tight quarters with a group of Ersemen who smelled as if soap and water had never touched their bodies, the Vikings' relative devotion to cleanliness was an absolute godsend. They were, indeed, an oft-washed, if savage, bunch.

She shut her eyes and allowed herself to simply soak for several seconds, trying to imagine that she hadn't been swept back in time but was still in the safety of the large bath in her Dublin hotel room.

It worked for a moment or two. For at least that long anyway, she managed to convince herself that she didn't have a care in the world. Then, as a chilly breeze suddenly passed through the kitchen's side windows, causing goose bumps to form on her neck and shoulders, she again became aware that this was no twentieth-century tub, which she could replenish with the turn of a wrist; and she realized that she should start washing herself, before her bathwater turned cold.

She slowly sat up and reached down beside the tub for the large towel she'd deposited there. Using it to shield her nakedness once more, she rose and stepped out of the water. Then, with all of the speed that the brisk evening air could inspire, she hurried to where the Norsemen had left the soap, bent to pick it up, and returned to the enveloping warmth of her bath.

Pure lye, she thought, raising the cake of soap to her nostrils and drawing in a good whiff of it. There were, of course, in this concoction none of the sweet fragrances and softeners that she'd come to expect from soaps and shampoos, and she couldn't help shuddering to think what it might do to her heretofore pampered skin.

She really had no choice in the matter, however. Her huge purse contained many things, but soap was not one of them; so it was either this or the risk of becoming lice infested.

With a groan, she ran the soap over her body and sank down in the water to rinse a bit. Then, taking the plastic clip from her hair, she arched back and drenched her blond mane. With any luck, she told herself with a bolstering swallow, she'd find a way back to her own time soon, and this would be the last of such baths she'd have to take. She did, in any case, have a large tube of hand cream in her bag. This she could apply to her skin if the soap proved as drying as she suspected.

She was just beginning to work up a bit of a lather in her hair, when, to her horror, she heard the cookery door swing open. Her upraised hands reflexively dropped to cover her breasts, and, with stinging streams of soapy water dripping into her eyes, she turned to glower at the intruder.

" 'Tis only I," Leif said in a wavering voice, hurriedly stepping inside and closing the door behind him. "I thought perhaps you would want that buttered bread you requested earlier. So I went back to the table to fetch a couple of slices for you, along with more wine. You are yet hungry, *ja?*"

"By all that is sacred, Leif," she exclaimed, "I told you to stay out of here!"

He appeared, in her slightly blurred vision, to be puzzled by this scolding.

"Pray pardon me, Goddess. I thought your concern was that none of the others were to enter."

"Turn around," she growled, no longer able to bear the smarting in her eyes and sensing he wasn't going to be as easy to get rid of this time as the last.

Fortunately, he seemed willing to obey this request, and, as he and his platter and pitcher turned away, she quickly dunked her head back into the water and rinsed the soap from her hair. Then, snatching up the towel once more, she tented it over the tub and slid down in the bath, until only her neck and shoulders were visible over its rim.

"All right, damn it all, just set the bread over here, where I can reach it, and leave."

"But I can't."

Perplexed, she raised a brow at him. "Can't?"

" 'Leave,' " he clarified.

"Why not?"

"Because 'tis the Norse way to attend our highborn as they bathe. Thus, had I not agreed to come back in and do so, our captain would have appeared in my stead. I felt certain that would not please you."

"Indeed it wouldn't. Accursed rabbit killer! I don't want him anywhere near me!"

"Well, then, 'tis I who will have to see to you," Leif declared, a slight smile coming to his lips as he crossed to her and set the platter and pitcher down to the right of the tub.

"And what is it precisely you think you'll be 'seeing to'?"

"Why, anything. What do you wish, Your Greatness? That I pour you some wine? That I rub your shoulders and back? We mortals enjoy massages in our bathhouses. *Whate'er* you wish," he concluded with an insouciant shrug.

"I wish you would leave."

Again he looked a bit hurt by this request. "And risk letting you come to blows with my ill-natured brother? *Neinn.* I should never agree to that. You would surely end by killing him, and I gave my father my word that I would see Booth home alive within just a fortnight or two."

"Oh, all right," she replied, heaving an exasperated sigh. "Pour me some wine then, since you seem so bent upon serving me."

Smiling once more, he dropped to one knee beside the tub and filled the silver cup he'd brought in. Then he handed the brimming container to her.

Not wishing to reveal any more of her body to him, Dana lifted one of her hands out from under the draping towel, just high enough to grasp the cup and raise it to her lips. She took a couple of deep swallows of the wine. She needed them to steady her nerves.

"Here," she said, handing the half-emptied cup back to him. "Now go. You have done all I wish to ask of you."

Instead of looking dejected this time, he simply chuckled as he accepted the cup and returned it to the platter. "Ah, nonsense, my lady. It appears you could use a great deal more."

With the silence of a snake, he slipped behind her in that instant, and the next thing Dana knew, he had pushed her wet hair aside and his fingers were rubbing the tenseness from the back of her neck with a dexterity that took her breath away.

She should object, a voice within her warned. She'd had enough self-defense training to realize that she had already let this stranger get far too close to her. God knew those huge hands of his could reach forward and strangle her at any moment!

Yet, choking her seemed to be the last thing his kneading fingers would do. In fact, his touch was so gentle and soothing that she was beginning to believe he had some sort of healing ability.

"Should I stop?" he whispered, careful to lean forward, so that his hot breath streamed directly into her right ear with every syllable of the question.

To Dana's dismay, his fervent utterance didn't stop there, however, but traveled all the way down to her loins.

Feeling too transfixed to answer, she merely gave her head a slight shake.

Lord, she'd never experienced anything like it! He somehow took possession of her in those seconds, as though the flesh and muscles of her neck and shoulders were clay in his sculpting palms.

In spite of herself, she closed her eyes and began to lean into his massaging like an affection-starved house cat. Let him go ahead and strangle her, if he wished to! To her exhausted and wine-clouded mind, it now seemed a far preferable end to those that had befallen the poor Ersemen his companions were burying.

"Does this please you?" he murmured after a moment, his confident tone saying he knew full well it did.

He is a smooth one, Dana acknowledged. A man

clearly accustomed to winning his way with the opposite sex, and, with him believing that she was a deity, his charm was obviously tiptop.

"If it did not, I would most certainly tell you to stop," she replied, in as detached a tone as she could seem to produce.

"Would you?" His voice was still a murmur, yet strangely sportive now, as he instantly followed the query by pressing his lips to a point just below her ear.

Dear God, now what? Dana thought.

He seemed content to let his mouth freeze there for several seconds, giving her plenty of time to consider how to respond. Then, as she felt his lips pucker and push away from her neck ever so slightly, only to repeat the action just an inch or so below that, she knew beyond a doubt that matters were getting out of hand and it was time to object.

"You are kissing me," she declared, doing her best to sound repulsed as she drew away from him.

"Neinn, my lady. Simply offering thanks."

Again covering her chest with her arms, she turned to scowl at him. "Thanks for what?"

"For working that wonder for my brother earlier. It was most impressive."

"Oh . . . good. Good," she stammered, swallowing as she dropped her gaze and tried to collect herself. He mustn't be allowed to see how this hint of amorousness had aroused her. She was supposed to be a goddess, after all. Immune to such carnal stirrings.

It was already too late, however, she acknowledged, as she looked back at him again. The glint in his eye was so knowing that she instantly realized nothing she

could say or do would make him believe she hadn't
enjoyed it.

"You have never made love with a mortal before,
have you?"

It was far more a statement than an inquiry, so she
didn't bother to answer. Indeed, she might as well have
been a vestal virgin for the patronizing expression he
wore in those seconds.

" 'Tis all right," he assured, reaching out to brush a
lock of wet hair from her forehead. "For I have never
made love to a goddess either."

"And just what makes you think you ever will?" she
asked, pulling the tub-draping towel more securely to
her cleavage.

"Oh, I will, dear Dana," he answered softly, a trace
of a cocky smirk playing upon his lips as he slipped
back to her right side and knelt there. "For you are, in
some way, my destiny, and I, for reasons I may never
understand, am yours."

She couldn't seem to argue with him, because he
was, quite simply, the most handsome, well-built male
she'd ever met. His broad, muscular shoulders and
neck—bespeaking summer upon summer of longship
rowing and farm work—were somewhat visible now,
beneath his water-splattered tunic. And his blue eyes
shone like jewels in the chamber's flickering torch
light.

"Listen, Leif, I . . ." Her next words seemed to catch
in her throat.

He cocked his head slightly and offered her a soft
smile. *"Ja?"*

I don't belong here, was what she wanted to say. By

tomorrow's light I'll have your men searching high and low for my tour guide and the rest, and, once they're found, I'm out of here and back to the comforts of my own century!

But he would never understand. She could hardly comprehend any of it herself. So, unable to think of anything else to say, she simply ended by asking him for a razor, with which she planned to shave her legs and underarms.

"A 'razor'?" he echoed.

"Ja."

He issued a soft laugh. "But women do not use razors."

"I do."

"For what purpose, pray?"

"For my own personal purposes. Now, prithee, do go off and find me one before this bath gets too cold for me to stay in it."

Still looking mystified, he slowly pushed back up to his feet. "You do not mean to harm yourself or me with it, do you?" he asked cautiously.

It was she who laughed now. *"Neinn."*

"All right then. Whatever you wish, Goddess. I am sure that, unkempt as the Erse are, we can find a razor without having to row back to our ship."

He was right, as it turned out. Within just a few minutes, he slipped back into the cookery, again carefully closing its door behind him; and, immediately catching sight of a silver glint in one of his hands, Dana knew he'd found what she'd requested.

Continuing to look perplexed as he reached the tub,

he extended the straight razor to her, handle first. "Do take care, my lady, for this is very sharp."

She clucked. "Well, *ja*. It should be, shouldn't it? Are not most razors sharp? Now, prithee, go away or turn about or something, since I don't believe I can do this without getting out of the tub."

Though still appearing wary, Leif obliged her by walking over to the hearth's stony ledge and leaning heavily against it, his back to her.

He heard a slight splash and the dripping of streaming water as she apparently rose an instant later. And, half fearing that she might slip up from behind him and cut his throat, he sneaked a peek at her.

His mouth dropped open at what he saw. She'd wrapped the large towel about her and, having made her left armpit soapy, was now shaving it with her right hand.

By Thunder, what was she doing? What would prompt a female to do such a thing? Leif had always been taught that only men needed to shave and certainly nothing more than their faces!

He wanted to go on watching this curious ritual, but, worried that she might catch him at it, he returned his gaze to the bed of smoldering coals before him.

It wasn't until he heard her give forth a distinctly pained sound seconds later, that he turned about to face her fully.

The towel was still wrapped around her, but she and the razor had apparently moved on to her legs, for she was resting her right foot upon the tub's rim as she bent to shave her calf.

"You cut yourself," he acknowledged with a gasp.

"Yes!" she exclaimed in English, wincing. Then, re-membering who she was addressing, she returned to Old Norse. *"Ja.* And down to the bone it appears."

"Oh, *neinn,* my lady," he said with obvious concern. He hurried to her, despite her request that he stay away. The blood she'd drawn came instantly into view for him, as he stepped over to retrieve the second towel they'd brought from the ship. "And, with that soap all about it, it must burn like fire."

Dana nodded and bit her lip against the pain. "It does," she replied, lowering her calf back into the bathwater in the hopes of rinsing it off.

He returned to her and stooped at her side. "Here. Give it to me, that I might stop the bleeding. Having been in battle so many times, I'm far more practiced at this than you, I wager. I warned you of the blade's sharpness, did I not?"

"Ja. Of course you did," she snapped, lifting her leg out of the tub once more and turning about to perch upon its edge.

He wasted no time in moving even closer to her and tying the towel about her lacerated shin. "What would possess you to shave your legs in any case?"

"Quite simply, pilgrim, they *itch* if I do not."

"But our women don't complain of itchy legs."

"Likely 'tis because they never shave them."

His only response to this warped logic was to knit his brows, as he continued to stare up at her.

"Goddesses should have smooth, shaven legs. And there's an end to it," she declared, suddenly near tears at both the pain of the deep cut and the torrent of emotions the past few days had caused her to endure.

But goddesses shouldn't cry, a voice within Leif wanted to counter. He stopped himself, however. What, in very sooth, did he know of goddesses, anyway? As a man, he was most familiar with the teachings about the male deities in his religion. Perhaps he had missed a point or two about the fairer of *Asatru's* divine beings. Yet, as this lady's eyes began to drip now, with the tears they could no longer seem to contain at her injury, he couldn't help feeling something was amiss with her claim that she was the great Dana.

"My . . . my hand slipped," she offered weakly, as though in her own defense. "It was wet with soap and water and . . ." Her words broke off, and, to Leif's great dismay, she actually began to sob!

I'm used to *safety* razors, for God's sake, Dana inwardly protested. Coming from a time of waxing and electrolysis, she'd just never been exposed to anything as lethally sharp as what he'd brought her; and she wished, with all her heart, that there was some way to explain this to him. She wasn't sure that it would have done any good, however. The expression he wore said that, while a Nordic god might be allowed to bleed on occasion, weeping was pretty much out of the question.

"Oh, Jesus," she wailed in English. "I've blown it altogether, haven't I? I'm dead meat now!"

She thought she'd done enough crying up in the tower to have completely relieved herself of all the stress and fear this horrible time-slip experience had caused her. But she'd been wrong, unfortunately, and now God only knew what this savage would do with her and the monks!

Leif narrowed his eyes, as he continued to study her in those harrowing seconds. He'd comforted a Norse maiden or two through the years, but consoling a deity struck him as a nearly impossible task, and, for the life of him, he didn't know what to say.

Mortals weren't supposed to offer solace to gods, after all. He was almost certain, in fact, that it should have been the other way around.

But perhaps this one was testing him for some reason. Maybe she was checking to see if he was quick-witted enough to handle some daring deed that he would later be asked to carry out. . . . And, all at once, the answer seemed to come to him.

"Your legs itch and your hand slipped with the razor because you are not accustomed to being in mortal form, Goddess. *That* is it, is it not? That is the answer to the riddle you have set before me," he concluded triumphantly.

Dana looked up from her precipitous cry and wiped her eyes with the back of her hand. "What?"

"Well, your weeping and your bleeding. 'Tis all because you are not yet accustomed to being in the flesh."

She nodded, seeing no other way out of the precarious spot in which her unexpected show of emotion had placed her. *"Ja. Ja,* I suppose that is right."

"Ah, poor soul," he cooed, looking at her with genuine sympathy. Then, to her utter amazement, he rose and hugged her to him.

"Dear little Goddess," he continued, "bearing such adversity just so you might dwell among us and teach us more of what we need to know. . . . Let me finish the shaving for you. I am quite practiced with such blades. Then I shall see you to my brother's bed and let you sleep in peace."

"All right," Dana agreed after a moment, sniffling and doing her best to quiet herself. It needed doing, and he certainly couldn't be any worse with the primitive razor than she had proved to be. "But mind the leg I cut, prithee. That towel you've wrapped about it is all that stands betwixt me and agony now."

He offered her a gentle smile as he pulled away seconds later. Then, dropping to his knees once more, he refilled the wine chalice and handed it to her. "So drink, Your Greatness. 'Tis the only balm we have with us, I'm afraid, and 'twill also help you sleep."

Thinking this pretty sound advice, under the circumstances, Dana took several sips of the sweet beverage as Leif went about the task of lathering up her other leg and shaving it.

He was, as he'd promised, adept with the razor. She felt little more than the blade's chilliness, in fact, as he ran it over each side of her calf. But, once he'd traversed the bony terrain of her knee and headed all the way up to where her cloaking towel ended, high on her thigh, she knew she had to make it clear that he had gone far enough.

Her hand dropped down to catch his wrist, as his fingers moved to push the towel upward. "That will do," she said firmly.

His large, innocent eyes traveled up to meet hers. "Did I cut you, pray?"

"Neinn. 'Tis just that I wish for the shaving to stop there."

Again, *blast him,* a roguish smirk played upon his lips. "Are you certain? I mean, that nothing else itches?"

"Ja," she snapped, but she couldn't help being inwardly amused at this juvenile attempt on his part to see more of her. Men! How little they had changed through the ages!

"Very well," he replied, making no effort to hide his disappointment. "But, you will tell me, won't you, if any more shaving is needed?"

She bit her lower lip, fighting a laugh. Perhaps it was all the wine she was consuming—the chalice he'd brought her seemed to hold an amazing amount of it—but she wasn't feeling nearly the pain of a minute or two before. And she couldn't help believing that his amusing ways had something to do with this.

What a wag he was! Yet, at the same time—given his easy manipulation of both her and his volatile brother—what a diplomat. How altogether lovable he was beginning to seem; and she took another gulp of the wine, as she again realized that her time with him would probably prove far too short for her to allow herself to become attached to him.

Research, she told herself dutifully. This was an opportunity to research an ancient Norseman that was more golden than any she could have imagined. And, as he carefully began the task of shaving *around* the makeshift bandage he had applied to her right calf, she started to question him accordingly.

"Refresh my memory, prithee, pilgrim. How many brothers and sisters have you?"

He did not look up, but wisely chose to keep his

attention focussed upon the razor. "Four brothers and three sisters. I am the third-born."

"And have you your own farmstead back in Norway?"

"Neinn. Such land is scarce, as you must know. And, forsooth, I will not need it until I wed."

"When will that be?"

He looked up at her just long enough to laugh at the question. Then he again reached behind her and rinsed the straight razor off in the bathwater. "Why, that is for you to answer, is it not? I thought you gods able to tell the future. . . . You *can,* can't you?" he added pointedly.

She nodded, realizing this was not altogether untrue. She could, indeed, tell him much about the future; but she knew perfectly well that this wasn't the time span to which he was referring. "We don't choose what is in a man's heart, though, Leif. We merely bless or forsake the unions you mortals arrange."

"Then you've naught to bless or forsake in my case, Your Greatness, for there is no beloved in my heart, and I doubt there soon will be."

"Why not?"

He pulled a crumpled kerchief out from under his belt-strap and used it to rebandage her cut calf. Then he dipped one end of the towel into the bathwater and knelt at her feet once more to begin rinsing her now-shaven legs with it.

"Prithee do not trifle with me, my lady," he replied, flashing her a look that was half-scowl. "You know full well why I have asked for no woman's hand. And again I beseech thee not to force me to disparage my own blood."

Dana swallowed uneasily and sat back a bit on the tub's rim. She didn't have the faintest idea what he meant by this, but she sensed it was wisest not to press him on it.

"So, you yet live on your father's farmstead?"

"Ja."

"Tell me of it."

" 'Tis a farmstead. What else is there to tell, pray?"

"Well, describe your family's longhouse to me. All that is within it."

"I would weary you with such talk."

"Neinn. You would not."

With a sigh that said he thought she was growing a bit giddy from the wine, he slowly rose and began unbrooching his cape. "Very well, Goddess. If 'tis a bedtime tale you seek, let me first lead you next door to our captain's warm accommodations."

Not bothering to ask her permission, he extended an arm about her and eased her onto her feet. Then he wrapped his cape around her. "You haven't long been mortal, have you," he said under his breath, "to have grown tipsy from so little wine."

"It seemed a good enough share to me," she retorted, doing her best to return to a sober demeanor.

"Well, come along next door, pray. I think you will find lying down less taxing than walking, in any case." With that he led her over to where she'd left her belongings; but, as he bent to pick up her purse, she rushed forward and grabbed it before he could.

"Oh, *neinn,* pilgrim," she gasped. "On pain of death, ye must never, *never* touch my bag!"

He looked dumbfounded by this. "But why not?"

"Well, because . . . because 'tis from the place from which I came and it could be most perilous in your hands or those of your men."

"It could kill us, you mean?"

She nodded, realizing she had no other choice. From the start, her very survival with these barbarians, and that of the monks, had clearly hung upon her "wonder"-producing purse. She knew she couldn't risk having its twentieth-century contents fall into the Vikings' hands.

To her relief, he seemed to accept this warning as truth and he offered no argument. "Your raiment, though, my lady. May I touch that?"

Dana nodded, and he stopped once more to gather up her clothing. As he did so, however, her brassiere slipped out from where she'd left it, hidden between her jeans and her shirt; and, after gazing upon the undergarment for a few seconds, he looked up at her with one comically raised brow.

" 'Tis nothing," she blurted, snatching it up and hurriedly stuffing it into her purse. " 'Tis merely something I wear under my clothes."

"Ja. I gathered as much, Goddess, since this is the first I have seen of it." The fashioning that holds her breasts high, Leif instantly deduced. But his Norse sense of decorum would not allow him to try to confirm this with her.

"Well, let us go, then," she began again crisply,

slipping the bag's straps up onto her right shoulder and closing his cloak more tightly about her.

"All right," Leif replied, wrapping an arm around her waist in order to brace her against the night's chill. He then led her out of the cookery and over to another stone building, which was just a few paces away.

"Our men placed the bed in here, my lady, because they were told not to intrude as you bathed," he explained, as they entered the second dwelling. "It is not as warmed as the kitchen, I fear, for its hearth-fire was just built. But I am sure you will find the furs on Booth's bed enough to stave off the cold."

Even as he was speaking these words, Dana's eyes lit upon the huge bedstead, where it was situated in the far right corner of the chamber. She couldn't help hurrying forward to get a better look at it in the dim firelight.

Its headboard was exquisite! More intricately carved than any reproduction she'd seen, and she instantly ran a hand over one of its serpent-headed posts, as she reached it. "How beautiful!"

Leif looked a trifle caught off guard by the compliment. "*Ja,* well. 'Tis new, you see. Wrought for Booth, when our father stopped raiding two summers ago."

"Oh, I shall like sleeping here," she declared, setting her purse on the floor and pulling back the bed's covers so that she could climb onto its mattress. Though it was on the hard side, this was, indisputably, the most comfortable piece of furniture Dana had set eyes upon in over three days, and she knew she'd be a fool to do anything but sing its praises.

As if to underscore this, another of the evening's

brisk winds swept through the open windows of the dwelling, and she wasted no time in pulling the captain's large fur blanket all the way up to her neck.

Leif couldn't help smiling at her girlishness, as he watched her wriggle in under the covers. How childlike she was, this deity! And this only seemed to bear out his deduction that she was very newly born to mortal form.

"I will go back for your wine and the platter of buttered bread, if you wish, Your Greatness."

"Oh, *ja*. Prithee do," she replied, sitting up once more and leaning back against the bed's broad headboard.

As he turned and left, Dana reached down to her purse and pulled it up onto her lap. Within a second or two, she was able to locate her comb amidst its contents, and she withdrew that and began running it through her wet hair.

Lotion! she suddenly thought. If she hurried, she might be able to apply a fair amount of it to her bath-dried skin before the Viking returned. God only knew when he'd leave her alone again, after all. But, considering how savage some of Leif's fellow Norsemen had shown themselves to be, she wasn't sure it was safe to go unguarded by him for any length of time.

Though it was fairly dark inside this second dwelling, her fingers managed to close about what felt to be her large tube of lotion within her purse, and she immediately dredged it out and began applying it to her feet and legs.

Leif proved too quick for her, however. He was

back with her clothing and after-supper snack before she even got to the unmentionable terrain beneath her bath towel, and she knew she would simply have to settle for lubricating her arms and neck area now and let it go at that.

"What have you there?" he inquired, crossing to her and setting the platter and pitcher down on the floor beside the bed.

She hurriedly recapped the tube and slipped it under the linens. "Nothing."

He gave forth a whisper of a laugh. "Nonsense, my lady. You had something white in your hand as I entered. Something small, yet long. Prithee, might I see it once more?"

" 'Twas nothing, I tell you. Simply a kind of oil for my skin."

He nodded. "Oh, *ja*. Perfumed oil, was it not? I can yet smell its sweet scent in the air. Our lord did bring my mother such a gift from a land far to the south once. And she, too, applied it after her baths. . . . Pray, let me put it on your back for you, for no one's arms can reach that far," he concluded, extending an open palm to her as though he didn't intend to take no for an answer.

He was right, of course, Dana realized. In what could well have been over a thousand years, human-kind still hadn't come up with any effective ways for a person to accomplish this simple task alone. And, since he already knew of such amenities as perfumed oil, there seemed no real danger in letting him see and touch the lotion.

She slowly withdrew the tube from the bedclothes and handed it to him.

He seemed spellbound by it for several seconds. Wrapping his fingers around it, he moved it about in his right palm, as though fascinated by both its feel and the way the firelight danced upon its reflective plastic surface. Then, to Dana's surprise, he lifted the sealed bottom edge of it to his mouth and bit down upon it slightly.

"What manner of casing is this, Goddess?" he asked, sinking down on the edge of the bed and looking at her with an intrigued smile. " 'Tis like a wine skin, yet colder and firmer. And it shines as sunlight upon snow."

Plastic, Dana thought. She really *was* getting drunk, if she'd been foolish enough to think that the lotion's container wouldn't provoke questions from him.

"I know not how, or of precisely what, it is made," she replied, realizing that she was being at least ninety-nine percent honest with this answer. The truth was she'd never taken the time to learn the composition of various plastics or how they were formed.

"Well, where did you get it, pray?"

"Out of my bag."

"You mean to say you can just wish for a thing and you will find it in your bag?"

"Well, 'tis not, forsooth, quite as simple as that, pilgrim." There were, after all, a few little details like shopping trips and money to be considered in such acquisitions. However, she knew better than to try explaining any further. "But, *ja,* if I need something, it can, more often than not, be found there."

"By the Heavens, what an awesome power to possess!"

"Ja, well, it is not without its . . ." She searched for an appropriate Norse word, amazed that her limited vocabulary had held out so far. "Its *thorns,"* she finished after several seconds. "So might we just proceed with putting the 'oil' on my back?"

He returned his gaze to the tube. "How does it open, pray?"

She reached out and flipped its hinged cap upward. "There. Then you just squeeze it and the 'oil' comes out."

He gave forth a delighted laugh, as he followed her instructions, and a drop of the white substance spewed from the strange little tube—only to slip back down into the tiny hole from which it had come.

"Hmmm," he said with a roguish expression. "I dare not say what it does remind me of! Not in a lady's presence, anyway. This was most certainly crafted by a *male,* though, Goddess."

Dana clucked at this randy observation and again took the tube from him. "Here," she declared, turning one of his palms up and squirting a liberal amount of the cream into it. "Is it your will to aid me in this or not?"

"It is," he replied, sobering, even though his eyes, with a child's fascination, were still fixed upon the substance. "Turn around."

Moving her purse to the other side of her, well out of his reach, Dana did as he asked.

Leif couldn't help lifting the strange white "oil" to his nostrils before spreading it upon her. It smelled faintly of roses, and it felt surprisingly waxy. Then, not wishing to annoy her further with his diversions, he pulled the bed's covers away from her and rubbed the stuff upon her shoulders and upper back.

"Your towel, my lady. Prithee, let it fall," he whispered laughingly into her right ear, when he had finished with all that was exposed of her back. "How like a virgin you act . . . for one who hath borne so many gods and goddesses."

"I am *not* a virgin," she countered, turning back to flash him an indignant look.

His tone became strangely challenging. "Well then, do stop conducting yourself as one, pray. I cannot oil your skin through a towel, you know. And, clairvoyant as you are, you must have sensed by now that you can trust me in so innocent an effort as this."

She turned away from him once more and, unfolding the towel at her cleavage, pushed it all the way down to her hips.

He was right, of course. If she was going to succeed in keeping him and his countrymen believing that she was a vastly experienced and all-knowing being, she would have to stop acting as though she feared she was about to be raped at any moment.

Despite this stoic resolve, however, she couldn't help letting a tiny yelp escape her, as she felt him deposit a chilly dab of lotion at the base of her spine.

"Cold?" he inquired.

"A little."

"*Ja.* Odd stuff, this 'oil' of yours. I have never seen its like. . . . But you know, Goddess, not all of the sensations of the flesh need be unpleasant."

"What does that mean exactly?" she asked, her voice reflecting her continuing suspiciousness.

"Only that I hope the bite of a razor and the chilliness of the night will not numb you to what pleasures can be found in mortal form."

His broad, warm palm seemed to span the width of her back, as he continued to lubricate her skin. "The joys of the flesh, though few, can be very nice indeed," he continued, letting his fingers slip around to the side of one of her breasts. "And you needn't go about with the ache of a broken heart either," he added, leaning up against her and resting his chin on her right shoulder, very near her ear.

Dana's breath caught in her throat, but she tried to tell herself she wasn't in the least affected by how good it felt to be touched this way by him.

Yet, never before had she been so close to a man as handsome and well built as he. Never had she felt as though the shoulder span of a lover was formidable enough to stand between her and any force that might threaten. Indeed, the only thing that had been formidable about Steven and all of her other egghead boyfriends was their earning potentials. And that sort of thing certainly didn't matter much now—in this ancient world of warriors and heroes, in which she seemed to be stuck.

"I . . . I'm not heartbroken," she replied.

At this, his hand traveled up to her shoulder, and, in the space of an instant, he had her pinned, facing upward, to his brother's firm mattress.

She reflexively pulled the blanket up to cover her breasts. But, in truth, it didn't seem to matter, for his eyes were fixed solely upon hers—his blue orbs plumbing her own, as though he were searching a well. "You are, I think. There is, forsooth, an emptiness within you that seems, for all the world, like that of a spurned lover."

"You killed my friends here," she hissed. "Is that not cause enough for what you think you see in me?"

"Neinn. And, by all that is just, Goddess, I tell you again that we did *not* know that the Erse villagers and monks here were friends of yours."

"You mean to say that none of those you slew were dressed as I was? Not even when you first came to shore?"

He shook his head emphatically. "Not one."

Dana swallowed dryly. While she was inclined to believe him, this was very mixed news for her, since it seemed to indicate that she had, indeed, slipped out of the reach of her twentieth-century companions.

"Besides," Leif began again softly, "what I see in you is a far more private grief than that. One which has long been with you. . . . Pray, Goddess, if you would only tell me who it was that hurt you so, I would go forth and see him dead this very night," he added in an urgent whisper.

She shut her eyes and gave forth a bitter laugh. "Much as I wish you could, 'twould be impossible for you to reach him."

"He is that far up in the Heavens?"

He is that far *forward in time,* she wanted to reply, but she caught herself. "Listen, Leif," she continued, opening her eyes and again meeting his gaze. "Just go away from here in the morning, as I have asked. That is all I truly wish from you."

"But I cannot now. Never could I do such a thing."

"Why not?"

"Because I've seen how vulnerable you are, my lady. How unprotected in the cruel realm of men, and I do not want any more pain to befall you. Fortune hath sent you onto my path, and it is my duty to guard and to *please* you until it returns for you."

" 'Please'?"

"Ja, please. Which now means finishing the task of rubbing oil upon you." He took his pinioning grip from her and, with a gallant air, eased the fur blanket down and away from her neck and shoulders.

She did not stop him as he resumed the work of lotioning her skin. She did not even protest, as his large warm hand slipped down, beneath the linens, to pay similar attention to her breasts and stomach. And, when his fingers slid even farther downward, stopping at the secret vee between her legs, she still made no effort to object. His eyes were simply too adoring, too filled with the desire to satisfy the longing he perceived in her, for her to resist.

He must have been reading her expression too in those seconds. Her face must have conveyed her consent, for, without further hesitation, two of his stout fingers, still lubricated with lotion, slid deeply up into her and began working to bring her the most ineffable pleasure she'd ever experienced.

He somehow knew precisely where and how to touch her. Indeed, he seemed, in those fevered moments, to know how to make the very Earth shake!

And, when she tried to muffle her enraptured outcries by biting down upon the bed's linens as she climaxed, he took the liberty of replacing this makeshift hush-cloth with a penetrating kiss.

After a decade of study, Dana had thought she'd learned virtually everything about the Vikings. She'd been wrong, however, for nowhere had she read how skilled they could be at loveplay!

Chapter 9

Dana woke with the light of morning shining in her face. She looked down to see that she was lying on her left side, clutching her purse. She also saw, to her sudden dismay, that someone was clutching *her* in much the same manner!

An arm—the most muscular male forearm she had ever set eyes upon—was wrapped about her. And she turned back with a start to see a huge blond man snuggled up next to her.

Leif! she instantly recalled. This enormous, snoring Norseman had befriended her, and she, sorrily, still seemed to be caught in Viking times.

Her first impulse was to pull away from him, to slip out from beneath his heavy limb and get as far from him as possible. But, remembering how tender he'd been with her the night before, how attentive to both her feelings and her physical needs, she remained in his warm embrace. It seemed like a lifetime since she'd awakened with a man in her bed, and she wanted to savor it for a few minutes longer.

She turned to face him more fully, and she lay studying his features. How boyish he looked as he slept. So defenseless and unaware of his surroundings. Yet he was, she reminded herself, the most manly male she had ever met. More capable of defending himself and *her* than anyone she'd known. Why, the blush-provoking memory of what he'd done to her just before she'd fallen asleep should have been enough to make her recall that he was anything *but* a child!

There had, of course, been incredible progress made in many areas during the centuries that apparently separated their respective times. But, Dana thought with a soft, coquettish smile tugging at one corner of her lips, *foreplay* wasn't one of them, apparently. Indeed, all of the twentieth-century men with whom she'd been intimate could have benefited greatly under the tutelage of this longhaired raider.

Still smiling to herself, Dana leaned over and pressed an affectionate kiss to the Viking's temple. "I want to stay in bed," she whispered in English, "but I have to go look for my friends. I just . . . just don't belong here," she added sadly.

With that, she rolled back onto her left side and eased herself and her purse out of his hold and off the wide mattress.

It was very early. Perhaps just after dawn, judging from the reddish tone and low angle of the sunlight coming through the east window of the dwelling. So, not wishing to wake Leif, she tiptoed around the end of the bed and found her clothes, where he'd left them hours before.

Searching first for her underpants, she pulled her

jeans from the top of the pile and draped them over the bed's footboard. Just beneath them was her shirt, and after that, to her surprise, was the shimmering gold gown Leif had brought her.

Smiling once more, she pulled it off the floor and held it up to herself in an effort to judge its length. It looked to be a pretty good fit, actually. Except for its trailing back hem, which was the style of the day, it appeared she could wear it without having to do any alterations.

What a glorious "find" it was, she thought, extending one of its long, flared sleeves against her outstretched arm and feeling how heavy the dress's metallic thread made it. Next to a coat of mail, it had to be the most weighty of Old Norse garments; and, with Leif still asleep and everything so quiet outside the dwelling, she just couldn't pass up this opportunity to try it on.

She hurriedly pulled its hem up over her head. Then, unbrooching the cape Leif had lent her, she let the gown slip down over her tall curving form as her arms found their way into its sleeves.

"This is incredible," she gasped, stepping out of the nest that the fallen cloak had formed at her feet. She began to pirouette about the little stone building, her arms flung out at her sides. The golden threads of the garment were cold, as any metal, against her bare skin, and she felt invigorated by it, as though she'd been lowered into a vat of decongestant vaporizing ointment.

Ordinarily, she didn't like feeling cold, but, for some reason, it seemed wonderful now. And she couldn't help moving toward the east window and continuing to pivot on the balls of her feet, as she watched the sun's orange rays play upon the gown's glistening fibers.

Dear God, what a priceless specimen from Viking times! How she wished she could return to her own era, wearing it in place of her clothes.

But that was probably impossible, she told herself glumly. And, even if she were able to pull off such a feat, who on earth would believe that the dress was between eight hundred and a thousand years old? It was simply in too pristine a state for such a claim to be credible.

Letting her arms drop back down to her sides, she walked solemnly over to the window to take a look outdoors. The truth was, she'd had all the flights of fancy she could stand in the past few days, and it was time to begin her effort to return to her own century in earnest.

Leif's eyes fluttered open and he focussed upon the most heavenly sight he'd ever seen. The Goddess of all goddesses was no longer nestled at his side, but standing before an arched window, bathed in the golden light of the celestial domain to which she must surely have longed to return.

If anyone among his crew harbored doubts that she was a goddess, he need only have seen her now, Leif thought with a dry, awe-stricken swallow. He sat up slowly, quietly in his brother's bed, wanting to get a better look at her but, as with a doe in the forest, not wishing to startle her in any way.

He remembered how she'd let him touch her the night before, and he couldn't help smiling a bit. True mortal form was a very different thing from a deity's version of it apparently, for how else could one explain how tight, how virginal this mother of so many Norse gods had felt to him?

But then again, what possible explanation could there have been for his being fortunate enough to have spent an entire night with her? While he had always fought bravely on raids and followed Nordic law pretty much to the letter, he just couldn't imagine what feat he could have performed to be worthy of so sacred an encounter. And he could only assume it was some sort of undeserved miracle.

The truth was that he hadn't simply pleasured her hours before in the darkness, he had *worshipped* her. And, though part of him knew that it would go against all of the precepts of the universe for her to remain in fleshly form forevermore, another part was already aware that it would be shattered at her leaving him.

"Goddess?" he said softly.

She turned back to face him with a gentle smile, her long, blond hair taking on a reddish cast in the dawn's glow.

"So, you will wear my sister's gown today? I am pleased."

To his surprise, her smile suddenly faded. *"Neinn.* Beautiful as it is, Leif, I must again don my own unwashed raiment and go in search of my friends."

"But I have erenow told you that we saw naught of them as we raided this place."

She continued to sound consolatory. "I know. But that does not mean that they aren't out there somewhere. And now that daylight has finally returned, I must do my best to find them."

"Very well," he replied resignedly, sitting up more fully against the headboard. "How might I aid you in this?"

"Well, first, I wish to go out to the shore. I saw a female friend slain just beyond the friary's front gate, and I want to know if her body might yet be found there."

Leif furrowed his brow, having absolutely no recollection of anyone, apart from the compound's Erse peasants and monks, being killed during the raid. Not wanting to argue with the deity, however, he decided against voicing this once more. "As you wish, then, my lady," he said, hauling himself off the mattress with a sigh and retrieving his tunic from where he'd left it at the foot of the bed. He put it back on, then bent to pick up the cape he'd loaned her. "I shall see you to the shore. Will you yet be needing this, pray?" he asked, holding up the cape.

"Neinn. Thank you."

He, accordingly, draped the garment over his back and brooched it at his shoulder.

Dana, feeling fairly sure of her ability to get dressed beneath the voluminous skirt of the gown, crossed wordlessly to the end of the bed. After removing the kerchief Leif had used to bandage her cut leg, she began to slip into her clothing as well.

"Do you want some breakfast, Goddess?"

She shook her head, having already managed to put on her panties and jeans without revealing much of herself to him. "I've lost a lot of time already, I'm afraid . . . holed up in that tower with the monks. Heaven alone knows how far my friends might have gotten from here by now."

"Oh? Why would they flee from you?"

"They were not fleeing from me, they were fleeing from *you!* You and that pack of sword-wielding wolves out there. How many times must I tell you that?"

He looked, for an instant, chagrined by her outburst. Then, assuming a more offensive posture, he spoke again. "I don't suppose it would serve any purpose to tell thee once more that I do not recall any among the fallen who were arrayed as you were."

"Neinn," she answered flatly. " 'Tis time for me to see for myself what is out there, pilgrim."

Her resoluteness as she said this made him realize that no amount of cajoling *or* intimate servicing on his part would ever mitigate the headstrong quality in her. He couldn't help letting her know, though, how puzzled he was by her need to cloak herself under his sister's gown as she changed. "Why do you hide from me thus? I mean, after what came to pass betwixt us last night."

It was she who looked chagrined now, as she withdrew her arms from the gown's sleeves and worked to don her odd, cupped undergarment beneath it.

"Be-because," she stammered, clearly lost for a better reply.

"But do you truly think there is aught I might see of you that I have not already felt? For, in truth, ye have nothing to be ashamed of. I have never set eyes upon a body more gracile than yours as you stood before the window just now."

While flattered by the praise, Dana was much too preoccupied with the hope of being reunited with her fellow tourists to respond in the way he evidently wished. "I think, Leif, that I do not want to speak of such matters at present," she replied, sighing with relief at finally getting her shirt back on and at last being able to free herself of the tenting gown.

She honestly believed this curt response would put an end to his line of questioning. To her surprise, however, he came and planted his towering form smack-dab in front of her, as she bent to gather up her purse.

"So what of us, my lady?" he asked, the inquiry half entreaty, half demand.

Dana couldn't help gulping a bit, as she stepped back and stared up into his face. " 'What' of us?"

"Am I to be embraced only in darkness? Or will you confess to such gentler feelings in the light of day as well?"

Oh, God! she inwardly exclaimed—the great beast seemed to be seeking a good-morning hug or some such thing!

"What . . . what do you want of me?" she choked out, thinking it best not to anger him, if he could be easily obliged. He was, after all, proving to be her closest ally in this dreadful set of circumstances.

"A kiss," he answered simply.

"All right." She went up on her toes in that instant and, taking hold of his shoulders, pressed her lips to one of his cheeks.

"Fie, how you torture me," he said in a barely audible growl; and, the next thing Dana knew, she was slung back in his arms with him kissing the daylights out of her in an all-out dip!

"Dear Lord," she gasped in English, when he finally, mercifully, brought her back to an upright position and gave her a chance to catch her breath. "You Vikings don't do anything nice and easy, do you?"

A satisfied smile spread across his face at having gotten what he'd obviously sought. "More of your 'godly' tongue?"

He meant her use of English, she realized after several seconds—a wave of relief washing over her. *"Ja."*

"Your words were complimentary, I hope."

She smiled slightly as well. "More or less."

"Would I make a satisfactory lover for you, do you think, Goddess? I mean, if you yet choose to dwell among us here on earth?"

She reached out and gave his hand a tender squeeze, her eyes again locking upon his. In view of the kindness he'd shown her, she owed him at least this much sincerity. *"Ja,* Leif. Most satisfactory, I assure you. Now, pray, let me pass so I can go forth in search of my friends."

"And, if you find them, you will leave here, won't you?" he said, his tone strangely knowing.

Dana felt a lump forming in her throat at the dejected waver in his voice. "Umm . . . I don't know the answer to that. I'm sorry, but I honestly don't." This was the truth, after all, she acknowledged, for, even if she did succeed in finding some of her fellow tourists still alive, there was no guarantee that they hadn't been swept back in time right along with her.

"Why not?"

"Well, 'tis all so terribly complicated, pilgrim. I fear you would never understand."

"I understand, though, that a man who has passed an entire night with you in his arms deserves more than to have you go on calling him 'pilgrim.' "

"Very well, then. I apologize if it offends thee, Leif. *Now,* might we go?" she concluded, inwardly shuddering at how possessive he suddenly seemed.

Blast it all! Why had she let herself get so damnably intoxicated on that wine the night before? If she had only tried a bit harder to maintain some sort of godly distance from him, she felt certain she wouldn't be having to deal with his puppy-love antics now!

"Ja," he agreed, though his expression said that he was still quite reluctant to let her go off in search of her companions. Returning to his gentlemanly self, however, he escorted her to the door.

The monastery was quiet as they made their way toward its entrance several seconds later.

"Did your men return to your ship?" Dana asked. "Or are they sleeping in some of these dwellings?"

"They passed the night here, I've no doubt, my lady. They would not hazard leaving us open to an Erse attack. *Ja,* they are most certainly yet here, though it appears they have finished the work of burying the dead."

"Ja," she replied, daring to draw in a deep breath

now. "The air is not filled with as much stench, is it?"

Leif shook his head.

"And what of Booth? Do you suppose he stayed as well?"

"Oh, no need to worry about him, Your Greatness. He shall be upon us soon enough, I warrant. His first task each morning seems to be finding cause to come and bellow at me."

"You don't like him," Dana observed.

Leif looked nonplussed, as they continued to walk. It was as though he had never even considered his feelings for his sibling. "Verily, what matter does it make what one feels for one's kin? Save for one's spouse, they do remain kin, hated or loved, do they not?"

Dana couldn't help laughing a bit at this. There was such a comical indisputableness about it. *"Ja.* I'm afraid they do." All sense of levity left her a second or two later, however, as they finally drew near the compound's entrance and she saw for herself that Barbara Goldfarb was no longer lying where she'd been run through four days earlier.

"She was there," Dana declared, hurrying forward, through the friary's front gate and over to a large circle of dried blood in the dirt. "One of your men stabbed her in this very spot."

"If you say so, Goddess. Clearly *someone* was slain here. But, as you can see, whoever it was has likely been buried."

"Ja, but whichever of your men took her from here can tell me, can he not?"

"Tell you what?"

"Whether she was dressed as I am. If she wore sandals with high, pointed heels and many gold bracelets on her arm."

He continued to look doubtful about such a possibility. *"Ja.* Whoever buried her would surely remember such oddities as you describe."

"Good. Find him, prithee," Dana replied, turning toward the bay and suddenly noticing that the single-lane highway, upon which their tour bus was parked when she arrived, was no longer there. Only a stretch of rocky beach remained in its place.

Due to the trees and shrubs, which were growing about the front of the monastery, she hadn't been able to get a view of the terrain beyond the entrance from the tower. So this was the first geographical proof she'd come upon that she really had slipped back in time, and she couldn't help reaching out and taking hold of Leif's shoulder in an effort to steady herself.

"What is it?" he asked with great concern.

"Nothing. Oh, Lord . . . nothing," she faltered, knowing she couldn't possibly explain.

Without another word, she let go of him and dashed down to the bay. As she reached the tideland seconds later, she turned around and froze at what she saw from this greatly broadened perspective.

Her worst fear was instantly confirmed. There was nothing but woodland for as far as the eye could see in either direction! The modern dwellings she remembered spotting in the hills beyond the friary had vanished, and the entire shoreline looked untouched by humankind. Except for the monastery, in fact, it appeared as virginal and untamed as the Boundary Waters of her native Minnesota.

Dana sank to her knees in the wet sand and let her face drop into her upraised hands. "I'm stranded here! Dear God, *stranded!*"

Chapter 10

"What is it, my lady?" Dana heard Leif ask seconds later, and it was clear that he was standing just inches from her once more. "What troubles thee so? And what is this word 'stranded,' which I heard you cry out?"

She lifted her face and looked at him forlornly. "It . . it means I am trapped here, Leif. Against my will."

He furrowed his brow. "*Asgardhr* has banished thee?"

"*Neinn*," she answered wearily. " 'Tis just that. . . . Oh, you can't understand."

She thought he might become indignant at this. But, to her surprise, he dropped to his knees as well, so he could look her in the face. "I shall," he insisted, his blue eyes twinkling with determination.

Dana sincerely doubted this, yet he seemed so bent upon trying to share her grief, that she couldn't refuse him. "All right. 'Tis just that . . . that nothing of my time remains here."

Indeed he didn't understand. That much was evi-

dent from his blank expression. "Nothing?" he re
peated nevertheless, as though to console her.

She shook her head glumly. "Nothing."

"Of your time?" he continued to reiterate.

"Right. Nothing."

"Remains *here?* Is that not what you said?"

"It is."

"Then, per chance, my lady, 'tis somewhere else yo
must look."

She was on the verge of again telling him that h
could not possibly comprehend her predicamen
when it suddenly dawned upon her that this suggestio
was not as nonsensical as it seemed. "Oh, God, o
course. *Of course.* You're right!" she exclaimed, half i
her tongue and half in his.

She reached out to him and, planting a hand on hi
shoulder, pulled herself back up to her feet. "The *stor
circle!* It has to be there now because the guide said
dated all the way back to the Neolithic Age. That's i
Leif! I must find it again and see if this time-slip thin
can be lifted there! Wow, you're a genius," she de
clared, pulling him to her and kissing his cheek as h
rose as well.

He couldn't have understood anything she'd jus
said in English, of course; but he did look ampl
pleased by her sudden show of gratitude. In fact, h
threw his arms about her and kissed her full on th
mouth with the same breath-stopping fervor he'd ex
hibited back in her sleeping chamber.

His tongue was so delving in those seconds, his hol
so heartfelt, that Dana couldn't help getting swept u
in the emotion of it. As hot arousal shot down to he

loins, she knew she'd have to pull away or risk sinking
to the sand with him in a passionate tangle of lovemaking.

"Neinn, neinn now," she whispered, finally freeing
her lips from his. "Much as I wish to celebrate, let us
rein ourselves out here in this plain view. Your crew
may not accept such feelings in a goddess."

"Very well," he grumbled. Then, looking in desperate need of a cold shower, he opened his arms and let
her step away from him. "But, pray, tell me what it is
we would be 'celebrating.'"

"Again 'twill be hard for you to understand, but
there is somewhere I wish to have you take me."

He smiled. *"Ja?* Where?"

"'Tis a . . . a sacred place. An Erse stone circle to
the southwest of here."

"A stone circle?"

"Ja. Have you not seen any of them? Large rings of
tall flat stones where the Erse worshipped, before they
became Christians."

"I believe I have heard tell of them, Your Greatness.
But I have never seen one. Pray, why must you go
there?"

Again she had to search for an answer, stammering
all the while. "To . . . to make matters right again
. . . betwixt *Asgardhr* and me."

"Then you will leave this mortal form?" he asked,
his eyes large with apprehension.

"Forsooth, I don't know. I wish I could tell you
with certainty. But, *ja,* that could well be."

"And you are asking that I take you there?"

"I am. For it was you who said just last night that

I'm too vulnerable to dwell without you in this realm
of men. You *would* protect me during my journey
there, would you not?"

"I would have you stay with me, my lady. I would
have you come with us to our base-camp and then
safely back to our homeland before summer's end."

"Oh, *neinn,* Leif. I cannot travel that far. I must stay
in Erin."

"For how long?"

"Forever, mayhap."

He looked crushed at this news. "And how far from
here is this circle of stones you seek?"

She tried to do a quick calculation in her head.
Though that first morning of the tour had, admittedly,
turned nightmarish for her, she seemed to remember
the bus ride from the stone circle to the monastery
being about two hours long. Nevertheless, distance
was hard to gauge by travel time in a country like
Ireland, she reminded herself. The roads weren't good
for the most part, the highways often single-lane. And,
too, there had been several delays along the way, due
to the congestion caused by traffic and pedestrians in
the many small towns through which they'd passed. "I
don't know. One hundred miles, perhaps."

" 'Miles'? " he repeated, obviously mystified.

"Oh, God," Dana said under her breath. "I do not
know your word for this . . . this measure of distance.
I'm sorry."

"Well, how long would it take for us to ride on
mounts to it?"

On horseback? This was something Dana hadn't
considered. She hadn't done much riding, but she'd

once heard that a horse could usually travel eight miles per hour at a running walk. So, what was that? She squinted, searching for the answer. "Thirteen hours, maybe. Perhaps more."

"A little over a day's ride, then?"

"Ja. I believe so."

"And it is due southwest of here, you say?"

Again she hesitated. Now *this* was the question that would truly prove her stumbling block. She'd been so shaken up at the time, that she hadn't paid much attention to what course the coach had taken to reach the friary. So, unless she could find a sightseeing pamphlet map of the region, buried somewhere in the depths of her handbag, she would probably become terribly lost out in the wilderness that now lay before her. "I don't know for certain. But I will try to find out."

A wet shore was no place for searching through a purse, however. So, taking hold of Leif's hand, she began heading back toward the monastery.

As they reached the friary's front gate a few minutes later, Booth was waiting for them, and, seeing the furious expression he wore, Leif knew he had better try to deal with his brother alone.

"Go inside, prithee, Goddess," Leif whispered to Dana, easing his hand out of hers as they walked. "I believe our captain craves a word with me."

She stopped and turned to flash him a questioning expression. It was as though she was worried for his safety.

" 'Tis all right," he assured her. "Pray go ahead now
and I shall rejoin you in your bed chamber anon."

Though she still looked hesitant, she did resume her
quick pace, slowing only to offer Booth a "Good
morn," as she passed him.

Booth muttered something resembling a greeting in
return. Then, when the deity seemed far enough down
the entrance passageway to be out of earshot, he
stormed to where Leif still stood at its mouth.

"Why did you *kiss* her out there?" he demanded. "I
saw it with mine own two eyes, so do not try to deny
it!"

Acutely aware of how dangerous his brother's outbursts could become, Leif took a step or two backward. " 'Twas *she* who kissed me."

Booth pursed his lips until they paled with his rage.
Then he closed the space between them once more and
clamped his hands to Leif's shoulders with a numbing
tightness. "Do not lie to me, brother, for I have greater
sway here than I have erenow brought against thee! I
saw it all and she merely kissed your cheek. 'Twas *you*,
forsooth, who took her into your arms as a lover
would!"

Leif could almost feel the color draining from his
face. He and Booth had certainly come to blows
before, but never over anything as menacing as a female, let alone aught as coveted as a goddess. He was,
therefore, tongue-tied, his well-known diplomacy failing him for some reason.

It was not so much for himself he was afraid now,
as for the rest of their crew. While Booth would never
risk alienating their father by killing Leif or any other

member of their immediate family, he had been known, on a few occasions, to lash out at others under his command; and Leif knew he couldn't live with the guilt of causing a shipmate's demise.

He should have guessed that Booth would become jealous, given the circumstances, a voice within him chided. He should have anticipated such a confrontation and taken measures to forestall it. Yet, he'd been so bedazzled by the prospect of serving as the great Dana's consort, even if only for a few days, that he hadn't exercised nearly the caution he ordinarily would have.

"You lay with her last evening as I slept, didn't you?" Booth accused, his eyes narrowing venomously.

"Neinn, Captain. I merely guarded her."

At this the commander's virulent gaze became all the more exacting. "So you two did not swive? You swear it?"

"By the blood of our kinsmen," Leif answered honestly.

Booth's eyes continued to search his for a few seconds longer. Then, finally seeming satisfied that Leif was telling the truth, he released him with a slight shove backward. "Well, see that you don't, little brother, for she is *mine!* 'Twas *my* crew that found her, and I alone hold the right to possess her." With that, he turned and began thundering back into the friary.

"Pardon me," Leif called out, hurrying forward to flank him, "but deities, by their very natures, cannot be possessed by any man, Captain."

Booth, seeming unfazed by this retort, kept moving down the passageway. "Well, this one will be, if she remains with us. And she shall, save that she has means in that bag of hers to escape."

"But you can't take her captive, Booth. Why, the very Heavens might open and crush us all for such an offense!"

"And what else do you propose we do with her, pray? For I am not leaving such a treasure here to be wasted on the doltish Erse!"

"She wishes to be taken to a circle of stones to the southwest."

Booth stopped walking and turned to his sibling with a suspicious look. "How do you know this?"

"She told me so."

"When?"

"Just now. On the beach."

"A circle of stones?"

"*Ja.* Very large stones, at which she claims the Erse once worshipped."

"But I thought she was a Norse goddess."

"She is."

"Then why would she wish to go to such a place?"

"I know not. I only know that she says 'tis little more than a day's ride from here and she seems bent upon going, whether we agree to accompany her or not."

"So, did you tell her that our base-camp is to the southwest as well?"

"*Neinn.* I am sorry, but we merely spoke of traveling to this place on horseback. Journeying as the crow flies, it would seem to me she could reach the circle more swiftly by land."

"Did she agree?"

"Neinn. Not really. I do not believe such mortal calculations hold much interest for her."

"Well, if she be the divine creature you claim, why can she not simply *will* herself to this sacred site? Why would she need to travel as we 'mere mortals' do?"

Leif shrugged. "Again I know not, Captain. But 'tis fortunate she seems to seek our aid in it, don't you think? I mean, since you wish to keep her with us for as long as possible."

"Ja. I suppose. But she must be made to understand that none of us will take her to this place solely by mount. If it is, indeed, southwest of here, she will have to make much of the journey in our ship."

"But 'tis inland, I believe, this circle of stones, else she would surely have told me 'twas on the coast."

"Where'er it be, brother, we shall take her the first part of it by water," Booth declared impatiently. " 'Tis indisputably safer for all concerned, if we travel most of the way by sea, then ride the rest. She must be aware of how the local kings' men outnumber our own."

He was right, Leif realized. Though he would hardly have believed his sibling capable of such calm, reasonable thought a few minutes before at the gate, Booth seemed invincible now, and Leif knew he'd be a fool to argue with him.

"Ja," he answered simply.

"Good. Go within and tell her as much," Booth directed, giving him the goading slap on the back that always accompanied his orders. "And inform her, too, that we shall depart forthwith."

*   *   *

Dana had just finished searching through the contents of her purse, and was putting everything back into it, when Leif entered her bed chamber several minutes later. Though she hadn't been left alone long, she had managed to steal into one of the neighboring stone buildings, wherein she'd found what looked to be freshly penned manuscript pages bearing the date "anno Domini 916." So now at least, though she couldn't pinpoint where she was, she was pretty sure she knew *when* she was.

The tenth century A.D., Heaven help her! But it was probably better than the ninth, she told herself wryly.

"Do I interrupt?" Leif asked gingerly, as he spotted her leaning over his brother's bed, rushing to refill her mysterious bag with all manner of strange-looking objects.

"Neinn. But avert your eyes for just a moment, will you?"

Not wanting to annoy her, in view of the officious message he had to deliver, he turned around and kept his gaze fixed upon the chamber's open door until she told him he could look her way once more.

"What is it, Leif? Why did your brother appear so rankled as we entered?"

He crossed to her and answered in a barely audible voice. "He umm . . . he did not like my kissing you, Your Greatness."

"You mean he saw us out on the beach?"

Leif nodded.

"Nosy bastard," Dana sputtered in English.

"What?"

"Nothing. I simply wish to know what business it is of his who kisses me!"

Leif cleared his throat and directed his gaze downward for an instant. "He is, forsooth, commander of our crew, my lady."

"Well, he's not *my* commander. Let me make that plain."

"Ja, Goddess. That is true. He does, however, offer you the safest possible passage to this circle of stones you seek."

"But I didn't ask him to take me there. I asked you."

Leif couldn't help smiling a bit at the praise implicit in this. "I know, dear Dana. And rest ye assured I shall be with you as well, for we will set sail for the southwest within the hour, if it be your will to join us. Our base-camp is also in that direction, you see."

She sat down upon the bed and pondered this news. "Hmmm. I thought you were planning on taking me to the circle on horseback."

"Well, that is one way to reach it. But, in very sooth, 'tis not at all the safest, given both the Erse raiders and the standing armies we might encounter along the way."

"But this circle is not near the sea, Leif. Though, I don't quite recall its location, I can tell you that much."

"Then we shall ride mounts the rest of the way, my lady. But, of course, the less time spent traveling on land, the better. I'm sure you understand."

She was silent for several seconds, simply staring down at her lap as though deep in thought. Then, to the Viking's relief, she looked up at him again and nodded.

"Ah, good. Then you have no objection to departing with us soon?"

"None, I suppose," she answered evenly. "But I do think it best to warn you that I won't be doing your brother's bidding, even if it is his ship."

Leif swallowed dryly and drew closer to her. "Oh, he intends no offense, Your Greatness. 'Tis just that 'twould shame him before our crew if you appeared more fond of me than of him. So I must ask that any further shows of affection betwixt us be made only when we are alone."

"Alone?" Dana repeated with a surprised laugh. "Where, pray, would we find ourselves alone on a longship?"

"Well, we likely won't of course. I simply meant that, once we reach our camp, I've a tent, as does our captain. . . . But, *neinn, neinn,* I must not mislead you, Goddess," he continued, suddenly looking very ill at ease. "The truth is that, if any man shall keep you company—"

" 'Company'?" she interrupted pointedly.

His face flushed a bit with embarrassment. *"Ja.* You know, as I did last night."

A hint of a smile played upon her lips. *"Ja?"*

"Well, 'twill have to be Booth."

"Oh, fie. How repulsive! I won't let him near me," she replied, her voice suddenly so steely that it sent a chill up Leif's spine.

"Very well, then, Your Greatness," he began again in his most allaying tone. "Just let him appear to the rest of our men to have won you, pray." With a be-seeching expression, he stepped over to the bed and, wrapping an arm about her, sat down at her side. "Merely for the sake of a peaceful journey to our camp ... prithee," he added, directing a melting whisper into her ear.

His charms had worked on her the night before, so he could only hope they might still hold some magic now, in the stark light of day. "Pray believe me when I tell you that you do not want to hazard making such a trip by land from here."

Dana fought the tingles that ran through her at his murmuring. "Oh, very well," she consented after several seconds. "But I warn you that I won't let him lie with me as I did you, Leif. And he had better not even attempt it!"

He drew away from her slightly, and, for the first time, Dana noticed the pained, almost tearful expression he wore. It was as if he believed he had already lost her somehow—as though he truly thought all hell would break loose if he was seen even sitting this near to her again.

"Then tell him as much if he makes such advances, my lady. But, for the good of all of us, I pray thee, do so only when you are alone with him. You should not, under any circumstances, cause him to lose face before our men."

"Why not?" she shot back, turning more fully to him.

"By cause of his rages, of course. Now, prithee, don't force me to say more." To Dana's surprise, he abruptly rose and began heading toward the door.

"Goddess, is there aught you need from this place before we depart?" he asked, turning back to her before taking his leave.

His suddenly stolid manner caused her to draw a blank for several seconds. "I . . . well, I yet wish to know about the woman who was slain in that spot before the gate. And the monks in the tower, I want to bid them fare well, since they showed me such kindness."

He offered her the shadow of a contrite smile in parting. "That you must do on your own, I fear, for 'tis certain they will not come down from their loft at the call of a Norseman."

Leif was right, as it turned out. The three friars didn't even dare to descend at Dana's call. So, with their rope ladder still lifted, she had no other choice but to shout up her farewell in English and hope they caught the gist of it.

She, of course, had some reservations about leaving them. There was no question, after all, that they were a far less dangerous bunch than the Vikings. And, too, the monastery was the last place she had seen her fellow tourists, so she felt somewhat pulled to remain.

On the other hand, she and the raiders had one very important thing in common: the Norse language. And that, coupled with their seeming willingness to take her back to the stone circle where the time-slip had first occurred, struck her as reason enough to run the risk of sailing off with them.

Though it surprised her, she'd already come to trust

Leif. No one could have convinced her, back when the bloody raid was taking place a few days earlier, that she would ever put her faith in any of the barbarians outside the tower . . . but, strangely, she did now. Or at least some part of her wanted to believe she did. And, unless she was willing to see a body exhumed—which she wasn't—she had no choice but to believe two of his crewmen's claims that the woman, whom they had found slain in the spot where she'd seen Mrs. Goldfarb killed, was not wearing sandals with "high, pointed heels" and "many gold bracelets."

Everything and everyone Dana had known of the twentieth century had vanished, she told herself stoically, as she and Booth's disassembled bed were rowed out to the anchored longship a short time later. The only wise course now was to move on to the stone circle and take her chances there.

As she boarded the Viking ship, she was greeted by the same awe-struck kowtowing the Norsemen had performed the evening before outside the tower. Though she was almost certain Leif had told her that he and his men had taken no prisoners during their raid upon the friary, she scanned the crowd of worshippers before her on the off chance she'd spot one of her fellow tourists among them. No such luck, however, and, after just a few seconds more, Booth wrapped an arm about her shoulders and informed his crew that their goddess had likely had her fill of such sentimental displays. He went on to claim that she now sought only the privacy of the tent they had erected for his use on board. Then, before Dana could offer a word of argument, the captain bustled her off to his striped quarters, where he said she'd be out of both the wind and sun.

Once inside, she was given a goblet of wine and seated upon a bench at what appeared to be a small dining table. Leif sat to her right, and his brother planted himself just across from her.

"Leif has told me of your wish to go to a circle of stones, Goddess," Booth began soberly.

She nodded and took an uneasy swallow of her wine. *"Ja."*

"Why, pray, do you want this?"

" 'Twould, as I told him, be hard for you mortals to understand, I fear, Captain."

"Why?" he asked, continuing to sound utterly humorless.

"Be-because there are matters that only *Asgardhr* fathoms, forsooth. Believe me when I tell thee that even I do not comprehend all that might come to pass in such a place."

"Then why would you wish to go there?"

Dana couldn't help tensing at his catechizing. Her palms were growing moist, her throat dry, and she realized that she hadn't felt so on the spot since she'd undergone the oral exams for her master's degree. "I simply . . . feel called to it. I am sorry that I can tell you no more than this."

"Our captain requires no more," Leif chimed in, slanting him a stern look. "Do you?"

"Neinn. I suppose not," Booth conceded grudgingly.

"In very sooth," Leif continued, "my brother invites you to share both his accommodations here on

the ship and those at our camp, once we reach it, my
lady. He has decreed that a feast be held in your honor
this eventide and that you accept this heartfelt gift
from him." Leif extended to her a knotted silken scarf,
which appeared to have come from the Orient.

"Why, thank you," Dana replied, accepting it, but
raising a skeptical brow at Leif.

Booth made a shooing motion with the back of his
hand. "Well, open it," he said, scarcely concealing his
natural gruffness.

Dana gave forth an awkward laugh and looked
down at the crimson offering once more. "Oh, my.
There *is* something inside, isn't there?"

Her fingers were trembling so that she was forced to
set the gift down on the table as she continued to try
untying it. When, at last, she succeeded, she found a
gold ring within, resting upon a tiny pillow. "Oh, my,"
she said again.

"She hates it," Booth snarled, glaring at his brother.

Dana shook her head. *"Neinn.* I don't, Captain. Not
at all."

"Then put it on."

"Ja, put it on, prithee, my lady. Booth troubled
greatly to find one among our treasures that might fit
your gracile fingers."

"All gold," the commander hastened to add.

"I've no doubt," Dana assured him, trying to smile.

Again, however, a scowl darkened the captain's features. "Ye've countless rings just like it in *Asgardhr*,
haven't you? I told you, Leif, we'd have naught of
interest to offer her!"

"*Neinn,* now. I truly haven't another like it," she declared.

Booth's face reddened all the more, and he looked as though one of the veins visible at his temples was about to rupture. "Then, by Thunder, put it on."

Though still a bit shaky at his irascible manner, Dana managed to slip the ring onto the third finger of her right hand.

A growl came from somewhere deep within the Norse commander. "*Neinn,* woman! On your other hand."

Dana looked up at him with a furrowed brow. "But that finger is reserved for betrothal."

"*Ja.*"

"Well, I am not agreeing to wed you, Captain. What would give you such a notion?"

Booth slammed his fists down upon the table, causing his two close-quarter companions to flinch. "There, little brother! Is that not precisely what I told you she would say?"

With that he stormed out of the shelter, leaving Dana to stare at Leif in perplexity.

"What was that about?" she whispered.

Leif looked duly sheepish. "He wishes to woo you. Is it not clear?"

" 'Woo' me? Are you crazed? I just told you, back at the friary, that I don't want this kind of attention from him."

"Never the less, Goddess, 'tis what he wishes to give. And I'm afraid I was forced to counsel him in it."

"Then counsel him to stop!"

"I daren't."

"Why not?"

"Because, when you have known Booth as long as I have, you come to realize that, no matter how distasteful you might find it, 'tis a far better thing to have him wooing than scorning you. Hence, I would suggest that you humor him as much as you can, my lady. In very sooth, he means no harm."

"No harm? Wasn't he just seeking to become betrothed to me?"

"Well, in some measure, I suppose. But you are a goddess, after all, so none among us would take such a pretense to heart."

"Leif, I don't like this," Dana confessed, lowering her voice all the more and feeling a slight wave of panic run through her.

"Like what?"

"The way matters have been since Booth met us at the friary gate earlier. His possessive manner with me and the way you have . . ." She stopped and bit her lip, realizing that one of her supposed omnipotence probably shouldn't be expressing the sort of emotional need that, even now, was causing the back of her throat to ache.

"I have what?" he pursued.

"Oh, forget it."

"Neinn, pray tell me, Goddess, for I truly have no wish to displease you."

Even this claim stabbed at Dana now, because of the polite, yet detached tone with which it was delivered. It was *courteous.* Almost patronizingly so. . . . Just as Steven and several of her other lovers had been when they'd broken up with her.

All at once, she found herself fighting tears. Pain she thought she had long buried seemed to be bubbling up from somewhere deep within her.

She'd be damned if she'd reveal it to yet *another* man, however! Especially one who was laboring under the assumption that she was some sort of immortal.

" 'Tis nothing, as I said. I simply think I should warn you not to leave me alone with that sot you call a brother henceforth, no matter how much he might claim to want to woo me. For I've curses far worse than 'fiery rain' to inflict upon him, if I see call to do so!" She locked eyes with Leif, determined not to let anything, except her almost murderous desire to free herself from Booth, show.

To her relief, the Norseman looked amply chastened by this warning. "Very well," he said in an undertone.

Good, Dana thought. Without disclosing the true extent of her vulnerability, she had managed to secure his promise that he would play the buffer between her and his loathsome sibling. What was more, she knew this meant that she could count on having Leif keep her company, at least some of the time, in the days to come.

And, after only one night with him, one evening of having him massage her, hold her, *worship* her, she'd already come to value his companionship greatly. Far more than she had realized.

In a time that was not her own, speaking a tongue that also wasn't hers, she knew that Leif's affection was probably the only comfort she could hope for.

"I must leave you for a short time now, however,"

he declared, rising and moving toward the door of the shelter. "There is much to be done outside, as we row out to sea. But I promise to return if I see Booth come in."

"Rest assured I shall summon you, if you don't," she said, in as threatening a tone as she could muster.

He turned and left, all trace of his former amorousness seeming to have gone.

God, how little men really had changed in the ten centuries which now separated Dana from her own! How was it possible for a person to be as adoring as Leif had been toward her just an hour before, only to have him turn into some frightened robot whose sole concern seemed to be maintaining the peace?

Was he really that afraid of his own brother? And, if so, *why?* Surely fear of the occasional fit of anger couldn't have been the only factor in Leif's sudden about-face.

But, with any luck, maybe they would get her to the stone circle quickly enough so that she could "slip" back into her own time without becoming more entangled in their puzzling lives.

She'd have to hope so anyway, she thought, crossing her forearms on the table before her and letting her head come to rest upon them.

"Anno Domini nine hundred and sixteen." She searched her memory, decade upon decade of Norse history and raids, and she managed to dredge up only one string of information about that year: the battle at Confey, "wherein the Erse were defeated by the Vikings and the Norse would, by such battles, later come to hold great sections of Ireland for the next half century."

Well, that was the quote, more or less. And, to her dismay, she was smack-dab in the middle of this tumultuous period.

Leif had, in any case, been right about avoiding travel by land. As peaceful as this particular shoreline had seemed to her as she'd scanned it earlier, there was no question that Erin was currently swarming with clashing armies and raiders of at least three different nationalities. And Dana could only hope that her search for the Cork-Kerry stone circle didn't cause her to cross the paths of men who were even more volatile than Booth seemed to be!

Chapter 11

It took until nearly sunset to reach the Viking base-camp; and, though most of the crew seemed to think her rather daft for it, Dana chose to be "above deck," outside of Booth's shelter for much of the journey.

Not knowing how much longer she would remain in these times, she wanted to take in as many of the details about the ship and its steerage as possible. The wind seemed to be coming from the northeast fortunately. So, though Booth's twenty-eight rowers were in place upon their sea chests at the sides of the vessel, they were frequently afforded the luxury of lifting their oars from the water and bantering and laughing with one another, as the ship's sail caused it to glide along.

Wanting to avoid Booth, who was overseeing the helm, Dana stayed up near the serpent-headed bow-sprit. She stood, the wind in her long blond hair, studying the magnificently crafted stem with its border of grapevinelike spirals. And, as she watched it cut through the water with such silent grace, she felt, for the first time in days, proud of her Nordic heritage.

So often through the years, she had pictured herself, a fair Scandinavian maiden, at sea upon just such a majestic craft; and now that it was actually happening, she was almost numb with awe.

"The Heavens would give us naught but mild weather with you at our bow, dear Dana," she heard someone say.

She turned to see Leif standing just a foot or two behind her.

"The wind, as if by magic, carries us precisely on course," he continued. "And, with thee aboard, we have no fear of your son Odin's wrath or Thor's oft-times perilous storms. Why, every nobleman in Norway will bid a fortune to take ownership of this vessel, once word that *you* were upon her reaches our land. Prithee believe me when I tell you that our captain is very greatly pleased by this."

She pursed her lips, then offered him a biting smile which said she couldn't care less how his older brother felt. "With me remaining behind in Erin, what proof will he have that I was on this ship?"

"Only the words of all of those with us now, Your Greatness. But, if ye've some way for more evidence to be offered, I would pray thee make it known."

"I will, if aught comes to mind. But you may be sure, *pilgrim,* that, if I do so, 'twill be solely as a favor to you, not Booth."

As she'd hoped, he winced a bit at hearing her revert to calling him "pilgrim." Given how he'd withdrawn from her since they'd left the monastery, however, she felt it was fitting retribution.

He swallowed dryly, and she could tell he was stung

by it. True to his stoic warrior code, though, he braced himself with a deep breath. Then he took a step backward and resumed the businesslike tone he'd used upon her earlier. "I thank thee, Goddess, regardless of whom such a gift is meant to favor."

In that instant she felt strangely compelled to slap him for having been so openly desirous of her, then suddenly freezing her out. But deities were probably expected to be above such human displays of indignation. So, still feeling most of the crew's eyes upon her, she simply turned her back to him once more.

Leif stood behind her for several seconds, part of him longing to go on talking to her. But, knowing Booth would disapprove of his having prolonged exchanges with her henceforward, he finally turned and made his way past the multitude of scattered wooden shields and barrels that cluttered his path back to the helm.

As promised, a feast was held in Dana's honor that evening at their camp. And, though it took place out on a beach, rather than in a Norwegian longhouse, Dana could see that it was very much like the revels described in so many Old Norse writings.

The camp was strategically hidden from view of the adjacent bay and, within that same gap between two sea-cliffs, three long makeshift tables had been set with wooden dishes and serving platters filled with everything from fish to venison. A recent raid of a wellstocked Erse ring-fort was very much in evidence, for Dana had never seen such an array of breads, vegetables, wines, and cheeses.

At both Booth and Leif's insistence, she had agreed

to forfeit her own clothes for laundering and to wear their sister's splendid golden gown to the festivities. And, once Dana saw the lengths to which the camp's inhabitants had gone to make such a spread possible, she knew she'd been right to oblige this wardrobe request.

After nearly two days of it, she still wasn't sure she'd gotten the knack of being worshipped. She'd always assumed that mass veneration would be a pleasant experience, one that would make a person feel greatly uplifted. But, given the precarious nature of this ruse, she found it largely unsettling. There was simply no way to have anticipated what it was like having dozens of eyes watching her every move, listening for each of her utterances; and she was, at last, beginning to understand the great strain that England's Princess Diana had often referred to in speaking of her life as such a public figure.

Diana's circumstances weren't quite as dire as Dana's however, she acknowledged, for being a "royal" could not have been as demanding as playing the role of a deity. Dana, after all, could only *guess* what these very distant ancestors of hers would believe to be acceptable behavior from her. All of her reading about the Norse religion had seemed to indicate that precious little was known about the Goddess "Dana," so she was really winging it. She had to assume that the penalty for being discovered at such an imposture would be death. She could only hope, therefore, that she'd find her way back to both the stone circle and her own century before that fate befell her.

Despite her protests about the betrothal ring Booth

had offered her earlier, she was tacitly, but quite obviously, paired with him again now. Side by side, they occupied the two places of honor at what was clearly the head feasting table. Fortunately, however, Leif was sitting on Dana's right, so she did have someone with whom to converse each time Booth turned his odious profile to her.

Indeed, the commander seemed to feel little or no obligation to make dinner chat with anyone. Short of the gluttonous grunts he issued while devouring the food he'd mounded before him, nothing left his lips. And, when the meal was finally coming to a close and his wine-merry crewmen and women began banging their drinking horns on the tables, calling for him to pay homage to their goddess by dancing with her to the tune being played by their pan-piper, he slammed his fists down on either side of his plate and flatly refused.

An uneasy silence ensued, during which even the music came to a halt. Then Leif, again assuming the role of placater, leaned back behind Dana and whispered a request to Booth that he be permitted to dance with her instead.

The captain, seeming already a bit clouded by all of the wine and mead he'd consumed with the meal, was slow to respond. When, after several seconds, he did so, his answer sounded to Dana like half *"ja"* and half belch.

Leif straightened and, directing a soft smile at Dana, rose and took one of her hands in his.

Their eyes met, and, while she hoped hers would convey the fact that she wanted very much to dance with him, her misgivings about it must also have shown. Short of seeing some of the folk dancing that had made its diluted way down through the ages to such modern Scandinavian-American celebrations as *Svenskarnas Dag,* she was absolutely lost as to how to move to this music. She couldn't help beginning to tremble, therefore, as Leif led her out to the stagelike center space created by the U-shaped formation of tables.

"Our captain does not know how to dance," he explained to her under his breath.

Neither do I, she wanted to add—loud and clear—before she humiliated herself in front of all these people. She managed to hold her tongue, however.

Her eyes would probably get the message across, in any case. She knew full well they now reflected her apprehension at not knowing how to proceed.

Leif donned a subtle yet perceptive smile in response. Then, to her great relief, he closed the gap between their two bodies by taking her into his arms and starting to slow dance with her.

Slow dancing, she thought, giving forth a slight laugh as her chin came to rest upon his right shoulder. Of course. What else would they be able to do to the almost waltzlike tune that the piper was presently playing? . . . Given how romantic it was, historians would have been crazy to think such dancing hadn't been around since the beginning of time.

"What amuses thee?" he whispered, his smile still apparent in his voice.

"Nothing. I just didn't think this was the sort of dancing you had in mind."

"It displeases you, Your Greatness?"

"Oh, *neinn*. Forsooth, I could not be more pleased."

"Good," he murmured, letting one of his hands slip down to her posterior and draw her more tightly up against him.

In that instant, as she felt her loins pulled forward to meet his, she couldn't repress a desirous sigh. It was as if their bodies had been made expressly for each other—as though she had *always* known this moment in time and had spent her whole life simply waiting for it to arrive. It was half memory, half destiny for her somehow; and she couldn't help recalling Leif's claim the night before that they were, in some way, one another's destiny.

But how could they be? With Booth having put the kibosh on their sharing any prolonged time alone—to say nothing of her resolve to find the Cork-Kerry stone circle and get back to her own century—how could they hope to end up together?

Leif must have heard the amorous sigh that had escaped her. His right ear was just inches from her lips, after all. Yet, still stubbornly stolid, he didn't make a sound to indicate that he was feeling the same intense need for her.

His body was quick to betray him, however. Though Dana was fairly sure it wasn't what he wanted to have happen, his hard arousal was rising between their swaying forms, and her loosely woven gown was doing little to shield her from its heat.

Her arms tightened around him as well, and, as he continued to lead her about to the dulcet music, she took in the sights that surrounded her. By turns, her gaze lit upon the silvery twilight that played on the nearby sea waves, the orange flames and black smoke of the pole torches that illuminated the feasting area, and, of course, the starry sky.

She'd been growing a bit cold in her clingy Norse garment at the table; but, now, in Leif's embrace, she felt inexplicably warmed from head to toe.

This heat, this excitement in him, was merely his *body* speaking, however, she acknowledged again. She'd certainly been through enough failed relationships with men to have learned that their physical desires weren't always indicative of true emotional need.

And, as the musician's languorous tune finally came to a close and Leif brought their dancing to a gradual halt and eased away from her, she could see in his eyes how right she was in reminding herself of this sorry truth.

"With regret, my lady, I must repair to my brother's tent now."

"You said you wouldn't leave me alone with him," she objected, trying to keep her words equally hushed.

"But you won't be. There are scores of my kinsmen all about you. Besides," he continued, lowering his voice all the more, "I go within that you will not find yourself alone with him later."

"I don't understand."

"You will," he assured, giving her hand a parting squeeze. Then, without another word, he turned and strode off down the beach toward the captain's quarters.

Heaving a discouraged sigh, Dana made her way

reluctantly back to the table and resumed her place at Booth's side.

She was growing colder as night continued to descend, and, were this surly Norseman Leif, she would not have hesitated to ask for his cloak. But, given Booth's unpredictable nature—coupled with the fact that he was presently engaged in a rowdy drinking contest that had caused him to spill what looked to be an entire flagon of wine down his gray tunic—she was given ample pause.

Fortunately, however, she wasn't subjected to the evening's chill or her host's nauseating revelry for too much longer. Within a few minutes, he turned to her, his speech now slurred with inebriation, and declared that he felt it was time they retire for the night.

Dana, of course, did not hesitate to take him up on this. Though she shuddered to think what might happen between them once they reached his tent, the prospect of finally being able to warm herself beneath the fur covers of his bed was all too enticing.

Nodding her agreement, she reached under the table and retrieved her purse. Though she'd warned Leif not to go into it, she wasn't sure if Booth and the rest had been informed of its supposedly deadly contents; so she knew she must take it with her wherever she went.

Slipping the bag's straps up over her right shoulder, she rose with Booth and followed him down the shore to his dimly lit shelter. Lacking his brother's courtliness entirely, he made no effort to slow his pace for her as they walked. Though it hardly seemed possible, he was oblivious to how her trailing gown and ill-fitting Viking shoes hindered her progress upon the shifting

sands. And he was already seated on one of his sea
chests, with an uncapped wineskin in hand, by the time
she reached the tent.

"A swallow?" he asked, extending the skin to her as
she entered.

"Neinn. Thank you all the same, Captain."

To her relief, she caught sight of Leif's slumbering
form in that instant. As promised, he had, indeed,
slipped into Booth's tent, and, now almost completely
submerged in a sleeping bag of sorts, he lay with his
back to them in the far right corner of the shelter.

But he was only pretending to be asleep, Dana tried
to tell herself. Surely, given her divine standing in his
eyes, he would keep his word and snap to her defense,
should his cantankerous brother get out of hand.

Not wanting to call Booth's attention to him, of
course, she instantly took her gaze from where he lay.
Unfortunately, however, it was already too late.
Though glazed from drink, Booth's eyes managed to
follow hers, and he craned his neck to stare back at his
sibling.

"Milksop," the commander grumbled, waving his
brother off with a caustic laugh. "He never could hold
his mead."

Look who's talking, Dana wanted to retort; but,
relieved that he didn't seem inclined to chase his sibling out of the tent, she merely smiled and nodded.

"Has Leif warned you never to touch my bag?" she
inquired, crossing to the makeshift table upon which
the dwelling's only light source, an oil lamp, rested.
She sat down on the adjacent bench and slipped her
purse under it.

Booth took another long drink from the skin. *"Ja.* He said that I would die, if I did," he answered with an insouciant smile.

Dana, unnerved by his nonchalance on the subject, addressed him sternly. " 'Tis true. You will, Captain."

He stared at her, his neck and head continuing to wobble as though he was about to lose his balance upon the chest. "Ah, but you are assuming that I *care* whether or not I die, when, forsooth, I don't."

His eyes seemed vacuous, completely unreadable in those seconds, and Dana was filled with the chilling realization that he was being honest. "Oh, but you must. For, even if you've no fear of death, the way in which it claims you must be of some concern. And do believe me when I tell you that my bag holds the most ghastly ways of all."

He looked, for an instant, almost intrigued by this threat. Then, fortunately, he grew more solemn. "I shall not go near the accursed thing, if 'tis so important to you, Goddess."

"Good. 'Tis for the best, I assure you," she replied, making no effort to hide her relief.

It was sadly short-lived, however. Within an instant or two, he sat back on the trunk and donned a smirk that was brazenly lustful. "So, tell me, Your Greatness, did my brother warm you up for me with his dancing?"

Though Dana was fairly certain she knew what he meant by this, she wouldn't have dreamed of saving him the trouble and embarrassment of having to explain. " 'Warm me up'?" she echoed.

"Ja. So you will be wet and ready for me in my bed now."

She wanted to storm over and slap him across the face, but, not wishing to set him off, she simply threw back her head and issued a dry laugh. "Oh, *neinn.* I assure you, pilgrim, *no one* is capable of making me 'ready' for you."

His lascivious smile sank into a glower and his eyes seemed to shoot daggers at her. "Then, hallowed wench," he growled, "I shall take you *dry."*

She was frightened by his determined tone, but knew she couldn't afford to let it show. Rather, she sat forward on the bench and fixed him with an equally dauntless glare. "You, you bearded lout, shall not set a finger upon me!"

To her surprise, this retort caused him to lean back on his chest. "But I only wish to offer you pleasure, Goddess. Is that not what is expected of a host?"

"Not necessarily, for 'tis for me, your guest, to decide what will be pleasing and what will not."

He arched a devilish brow at her. "But how can you know this for certain, save that ye've had a taste? For, verily, many is the maid who returns to sit astride this 'bearded' face. I can promise you an exquisite blend of pleasure and pain, if you will only give it a try."

Though inwardly shocked at this invitation, Dana kept her voice even as she answered him. "Again, thank you all the same, Captain, but I shall decline."

"You shall not," he suddenly thundered. "I grow cross now at your many rebuffs." With that, to Dana's amazement, he sprang to his feet and lunged toward her.

Everything became a panicked blur for her in those seconds. He was rushing headlong at her. And the next thing she knew, her self-defense training kicked in and she was bringing the side of her right hand down upon an artery in his neck with what seemed enough force to split a brick!

Suddenly his eyes rolled back and he sank to the floor of the tent with a thud.

"By Thunder, ye've killed him," Dana heard someone exclaim, and it seemed to jolt her back to the present moment.

Her gaze shifted to Leif, who was now sitting bolt upright.

"Neinn," she said breathlessly. "He is only unconscious, I think."

With a fiercely furrowed brow, Leif hurried out of his sleeping bag and crossed to kneel beside his brother. "Are you certain?"

"Ja. If you can still feel his heart beating."

He clapped his hand to Booth's chest. "Ah, *ja.* Thank the Heavens, I can."

"Good. Then he'll live, the cur," she snarled, and, with a disgusted huff, she stepped back to the bench and sank down upon it once more.

Leif looked up at her, his eyes wide with awe. "Whatever did you do to render him thus?"

" 'Tis for mortals to merely guess at, I'm afraid. And, while we are asking questions, pilgrim, what exactly were you busied with when he came rushing at me? I thought you said you would protect me from him! 'Twould serve you both right if he were dead!"

"But it all came to pass so swiftly, Goddess. I am

sorry, but, even though I was awake all the while with the intent to aid you in such a case, you simply struck before I could get to him."

"Well, that was fortunate, wasn't it? Given that he might well have raped me before you got both legs out of that bag of yours!"

Though still furious with Leif, Dana was gratified to see that his concern was finally centered upon her, rather than his wretched brother. "Oh, I don't believe it was in his mind to rape you, Your Greatness. I think he merely felt he was offering you a favor."

"Are you crazed? That was the most revolting proposition I have ever heard! Why, I shall surely be sick, if I dare think on it a moment longer!"

Leif didn't reply. Fighting a smile, as though he somehow knew she wouldn't have been so quick to refuse such servicing had the offer come from him, he simply returned his gaze to his brother's still form.

"All right, that is *it,*" she roared. "I want both of you out of here at once! This bed is mine again tonight, so I want you to haul that swine off with you to your tent and make certain he remains there until morning!"

He looked deeply wounded by this demand. "But Goddess—"

"Do not question me," she interrupted, "lest I do to you what I did to him!"

Clearly scared by this threat, Leif hurriedly circled around to slip his hands under his brother's arms and turn him about so he could drag him out of the shelter.

"You chose to honor his wishes over mine, so you

deserve him, you lackey," she couldn't help sputtering after him.

"What was that?"

"Nothing."

"Neinn, my lady. You said something to me, and I very much wish to know what it was."

Dana swallowed dryly, doing her best to keep the hurt of his sudden coolness toward her from showing. " 'Twas nothing, I say. I merely feel that your devotion to your detestable captain is foolheaded at best. He is naught but a bully and a churl. Why, he should have been drowned at birth like an undesirable whelp. And *you* are, therefore, the worst kind of coward for choosing to serve him!"

"You're jealous," he acknowledged in a whisper, his tone filled with amazement.

She turned her face away from him and stared at the oil lamp's flame. "I am not."

Leif, having already succeeded in wheeling his brother about so his head was pointed toward the door of the dwelling, set Booth's torso down and rose to walk over to her. *"Ja.* You are."

"Get out of here, I say, or I shall cast my fiery rain upon you again. I swear it!"

While she didn't dare look his way, she could feel him kneeling at her side seconds later, and, to her chagrin, he boldly reached out and took one of her hands in his.

"Neinn. You shan't, dear Dana. For we both know that 'tis not disdain you truly feel for me, but fondness."

"You're mad!"

"Am I?" he murmured, raising her hand to his lips and beginning to kiss it. The sporadic use of his tongue as he did this seemed to indicate that he was as eager to taste of her as she was of him.

She couldn't keep her voice from wavering as she answered. "I thought Booth forbade you to pay such attentions to me."

"He is not awake to know now, is he?"

"But he will be soon enough, mark my words. Such blows never keep a man down for long."

"Then I will take him to my tent and return to simply massage your neck and shoulders as I did last night. Surely he will have no objection to aught as innocent as that. And, if fortune smiles upon us, all of the spirited drink he swilled at the festivities will take over where your blow left off."

Dana looked back at him and offered an indifferent shrug. Then she got up and walked over to the bed to finally seek the warmth she craved beneath its fur covers. "Suit yourself. This is your brother's tent, forsooth, so I suppose I cannot stop you from coming back to it."

Again his expression was aggravatingly knowing, as she watched him back out of the shelter with Booth's limp body in tow a moment later. Their slow dance must have betrayed her desire for him, for there seemed no way to convince him now that she wasn't covetous of the devotion he was showing to his brother.

She slipped in beneath the blankets and rolled away from him, listening as he made his laborious exit. Why on earth *should* he believe her claims that she wanted nothing more from him than protection from his ill-tempered sibling? The truth of the matter was that she was beginning to suspect she'd never wished to make love to any man more. He was tall, handsome, incredibly well built, charming as any prince, brimming with knowledge on the very subject to which she'd dedicated the last decade of her life, and there wasn't a chance in the world that he was HIV positive!

What more could a woman ask, for heaven's sake? He was a veritable godsend, and she was starting to realize that she'd be an absolute fool not to take full advantage of his "services" before she found her way back to her own time.

Shameless lust! Wow. It seemed like ages since she'd experienced it, and she had to admit to herself, as she nestled in under the bedclothes, that it felt marvelous. She wanted his mouth upon hers, her arms about his waist—the warmth, the entire length of him deeply within her.

But, all of a sudden, reality reared its ugly head once more and she sat up against the headboard with a troubled gasp. She hadn't been taking her birth control pills! Though they were still in her purse, she'd been so shaken up by her time-slip that she hadn't thought to keep up with her dosage in over four days!

With another gasp, she scrambled off the mattress, crossed to where she'd left her bag, and dug the plastic dispenser pack out of one of its side zipper pockets. Then she went back to the bed, stowed the purse beneath it, and rose again to scout around for something with which to wash the pill down.

There appeared to be nothing but Booth's wineskin.

So, with a repulsed groan, she popped out two of the tablets and walked over to the sea chest upon which he'd left it.

She couldn't remember exactly what her doctor had told her about catching up on missed pills. She thought it might be advisable, however, to simply double up on them for the next four nights and hope for the best.

But what if she depleted her supply before she got back to the twentieth century? What if she did manage to kindle a clandestine love affair with Leif, only to find herself running the same risk of pregnancy that had plagued womankind since the beginning of time?

God knew her family had been more than accepting of the often odd choices she'd made in her adult life; but returning home carrying a *one-thousand-year-old* fetus would probably be pushing things too far!

Perhaps she'd be best off rationing the tablets from now on. Only taking them on those days when she really felt she was apt to need them. And, though she wasn't sure this reasoning was altogether sound, she went back to the bed and returned one of the pills to that outside pocket.

"Your Greatness seeks something?" Leif inquired softly from the mouth of the tent.

Dana started with surprise. Then she hurriedly rose and turned to him. "Oh, just something to drink, I guess."

He stepped inside and reached back to tie the door flap behind him. Then his eyes locked upon her with a hooded look that was palpably seductive.

She, in response, surreptitiously slipped the remaining pill in her mouth and swallowed it with a nervous gulp.

"There is a skin of water in one of Booth's chests, my lady. Shall I get it for you?"

"Oh, *neinn.* Thank you, anyway, but I suppose I should simply retire for the evening now."

"Go to sleep, you mean?"

She feighed a yawn and stretched her arms up over her head. *"Ja."*

He scowled slightly, his expression reflecting hurt and just a hint of anger.

He was right to be annoyed with her coyness, she silently acknowledged. Her eyes, her swaying body as they'd danced, had virtually shouted "come hither" to him. Yet, now that they were finally able to steal a little time alone, her sudden fear of pregnancy was making her act like a frightened schoolgirl.

"Then you do not want a massage?"

"Well, I suppose that would be all right, Leif. But, prithee, as we've discussed, nothing more."

"Very well. I would not betray my brother, in any case."

"I've every certainty," she replied, slipping into bed and turning her back to him, so he could begin at once to rub the day's tensions from her shoulders and neck.

She heard him cross to her an instant later, but, to her surprise, it was he who issued an order now.

"Move more toward the center of the bed," he said in a murmur.

"Why?"

"So I might climb on behind you. Surely you cannot want me to stand or kneel all the while, can you?"

"Oh, *neinn.* Of course not," she quickly agreed, obliging him. She'd already caused him enough trouble for one day, she supposed, without expecting him to stand while attending to her, like a mere serf. Yet, as he joined her on the mattress and his legs came to rest snugly on either side of her, she began to think she'd made a mistake in consenting to such an arrangement.

He was aroused again. And he seemed to want her to know it, as he wrapped his arms about her and slid her more tightly into the vee of his lap.

In spite of herself, she couldn't help letting a gasp slip from her lips at this highly suggestive contact.

"What?" he asked in a teasing whisper, brushing her long hair aside and starting to rub her neck.

"I think you know what."

He gave forth a soft laugh and slipped his hands forward to caress her own tellingly erect nipples. *"Neinn,* Goddess. Pray explain."

With a cluck of fake disgust, she took hold of his forearms and pushed backward upon them. "My neck, pilgrim. I thought we agreed that was what you would rub."

His fingers dutifully returned to the work of kneading her nape. "Oh, *ja.* How forgetful of me," he replied with a smile in his voice.

"So, Booth is still out cold?"

"Ja."

"Good. Do you, umm . . . do you think he will seek retribution against me when he wakes?"

"If he is wise, he will be properly afeared of you and never attempt to touch you again."

"And, if he is not wise? For, in very sooth, Leif, he does strike me as none too much so."

"I know not, my lady. I only know that I shall be here to protect you, no matter what may come."

"Really?" she asked pointedly. "So would you kill him in my defense?"

She could feel him freeze at this question. "Let us hope I will not find need to."

"But if you do?"

"Pray, Goddess. There are many ways to stop a man, short of slaying him. Why, you yourself proved that just a few minutes ago. So, believe me when I tell you I would find means without forsaking our sire's faith in me. 'Tis my duty to see Booth home alive in a few weeks, remember?"

"*Ja.* So it is. But, if you'll forgive me for saying so, I do think your father a fool for not appointing you the captain of this crew. For, while Booth may possess the courage and skill with weapons to serve as commander, he has not the wisdom and wit to steward negotiations as is also required of Norse leaders. You, on the other hand, seem to. It is you who acts as captain to these men most days, I believe. Thus I cannot imagine why you don't feel you deserve recognition for it. . . . Save, of course, that 'tis *cowardice* that keeps you from claiming your due," she added, still wanting to vex him a bit for having turned his attentions from her since they'd left the friary.

His hands seemed to reflect his anger, as they moved down and tightened upon her shoulders. "Prithee, tell me, Your Greatness," he said through clenched teeth, "can you assure me my place in *Valhöll?* For that, as you must know all too well, is what I stand to lose if I prove disloyal to my sire and Booth.

"So can you?" he demanded, when she wasn't quick enough to respond.

"Well, *neinn,*" she conceded after a moment.

"Then, pray, let me hear no more of my superiority to our captain, for 'tis my very soul at stake if I disobey our father."

She bit her lip and sank into a sheepish silence. How could she have forgotten the sacredness of a Norseman's bond with his lord? Why, a Viking without a chieftain or earl to serve, was, to the Nordic way of thinking, like a ship without oars or a sail. He was in a kind of exile, over which death was always considered preferable. And Dana was rapidly discovering that the last thing she wanted was to see Leif die.

"When will we depart in search of the stone circle?" she asked, her voice brightening with this change of subject.

"By first light, if you wish."

"I do," she answered simply. Though the thought of slipping back into her own time and leaving Leif behind saddened her, she told herself it was for the best.

"Have you any more notion where it is, pray?"

"Ja. I found a kind of map to it in my bag, but I am not sure I understand it."

"Might I see it, then?"

Dana pulled away from him and, turning back toward the right side of the mattress, flopped onto her stomach to reach under the bed and retrieve it. Not wishing to have to go digging for the map a second time, after she'd finally found it in her purse at the monastery, she had been careful to store it in the same side pocket in which she'd left her birth-control pills. So she was able to withdraw it very quickly now.

"Here," she said, reaching back to hand it to him. She knew that the little pamphlet, which contained the map, would provoke questions from him with its bright colors and glossy finish; but, being none too skilled at such things, she saw no other way than to let him try to help her decipher it.

He gasped as he received it from her. "By Heaven, 'tis unlike aught I have ever set eyes upon. So small and shiny and with more hues than even the scrivenings of the Erse monks!"

She rolled onto her right side, propped her chin on her upraised hand, and smiled at him. *"Ja."*

"So where is this map you speak of?"

"On the inside panel. Open it."

He did so, then sat studying it for several seconds. "I need more light," he grumbled, wheeling himself about on the bed and getting up and going over to the oil lamp on the table.

"This writing on it, Goddess, is it in your tongue? For 'tis not a language I have erenow seen."

Dana climbed off the bed as well and walked over to confer with him. *"Ja.* This crosslike symbol stands for north, south, east, and west, you see. To give you your bearings. And these words are 'Cork' and 'Kerry.' They are places here in Erin. Pray, have you heard tell of them?" she asked anxiously.

To her dismay, he shook his head.

"Well, no matter," she replied, drawing in a bolstering breath. "We shall find the circle, none the less. . . . This is the route, by land, to the monastery whence we just came, I believe," she continued. But, as she reached out to point to the part of the map in question, she couldn't help flinching at the horrible howling that suddenly emanated from just outside the tent.

"Oh, my God," she exclaimed. Before she could say a thing more, however, Leif took hold of her shoulders and pulled her back behind him.

"What is it?" she demanded in a hiss.

He shushed her fiercely. Then, taking his knife from his belt-strap, he began moving toward the entrance of the shelter.

"Are there wild animals in Erin? I had no idea—" Her words broke off at what she saw in that instant. As though unhampered by the tent's tied door flap, whatever was outside simply ripped the shelter open with two huge, fur-covered hands!

Then, as Leif moved up close enough to push the creature away, those same mitts grabbed him and pulled him out into the darkness with such ferocity that Dana simply stood frozen with shock for several seconds.

A voice within her told her to go and get the Mace from her purse, then search Booth's sea chest for any weapons he might have left therein.

Her mind was directing her to do these things on some rational level. Yet, on a far more basic one, she was simply paralyzed with terror.

In spite of her own good counsel, she stepped forward in an effort to see what was happening outside.

It was horrible! An absolute nightmare! The large

hairy beast, at least Leif's match in size, was rolling about in the sand with him—clawing and biting him, as though rabid.

A *bear,* she realized. Heaven help them, it appeared to be some sort of cross between a Neanderthal and a bear!

Cringing at this mauling, she stepped away from the door and finally found the presence of mind to hurry over to her purse. Though the shelter was very poorly lit, her delving hand found its way to the tiny canister of Mace within seconds. Then, before returning to the grisly scene outside, it occurred to her to snatch up the oil lamp as well.

For the third time in just two days, her self-defense training was coming to the fore; and, though it took a few seconds for her to find the safest possible angle for such a feat, she managed to pour the lamp's hot oil, along with its flaming wick, over the beast's head.

Instantly stopping its attack upon Leif, the creature sat up with a bloodcurdling snarl. Then, as it pulled away from the Norseman some more, Dana was able to reach down and spray it squarely in the eyes with Mace.

At this it reared up, coming to its full height upon its hind legs. And, with the back of its head now afire from the lamp, it dashed off toward the adjacent bay.

To Dana's relief, Leif was uninjured enough to get back to his feet in those seconds. But, rather than expressing thanks for her daring rescue, he began railing at her.

"Accursed *Hel!* What have ye done?"

"Saved you. I was saving you from the bear," she blurted, near tears at this unexpected reproof.

"But that's no bear, Goddess. 'Tis Booth! Don' you see?"

"Booth?"

"Ja," he snapped. "His freeman mistakenly delivered one of his chests to my tent, upon our return this afternoon, and he must have dug his bearskins out of it. I thought you would show the good sense to stay inside; that is why I put you behind me earlier," he concluded. Then, still fuming, he pushed past her and headed after his sibling, leaving her to contemplate it all in mystified silence.

His *brother?*

But of course! That explained why she'd heard howling, rather than a bear's roar, when the attack began. It also accounted for why Leif hadn't used his knife to defend himself.

There were still a lot of questions to be answered, however. Why, for instance, had Booth chosen to dress in a bearskin again tonight? It hadn't struck her as an unusual thing to do, when he'd been worshipping her the evening before and attempting an animal sacrifice. But, short of engaging in battle or religious practices, she couldn't imagine why the captain would want to costume himself in such a way.

Unless, of course. . . . But, no, she told herself with a horrified swallow. Berserkers were really rather rare among the Vikings, and no chieftain in his right mind would appoint one to command the dozens of men and women in a Norse crew.

Berserkers were psychopaths, after all. They were

madmen, who, while stupendous warriors upon foreign soil, couldn't always be trusted to dwell peacefully among their own countrymen.

"Howling as though he were a wolf, the berserker was impervious to pain and often unstoppable in battle. Once he reached his opponent, he frequently chose to tear him limb from limb, as a wild animal might." This was yet another quote from one of the history books Dana had all but memorized during her academic career. If the truth be told, however, she'd never dedicated much thought to such passages. Just as with reading about the Romans feeding the early Christians to lions, these images were simply too hideous to even be fully imaginable.

Yet, seeing how clawed and bitten Leif's face and neck were just now, she knew that the reality of such atrocities was finally right in front of her; and she was suddenly seized by such a chill in the cold night air that she wanted to go and hide herself under the captain's bed and never come out!

"Leif," she suddenly shouted, "I *pray* thee, come back up here before he attacks again!"

The full moon was bright enough that, even from where she still stood, she could see her imploring was in vain. Not only was Leif not keeping his distance from his dangerously insane brother, he was actually cradling him in his lap!

Having sunk into the splashing waters of the bay in order to relieve himself of the burning from both the oil lamp and the Mace, Booth had finally chosen to sprawl on his back. And now, Leif—the lunatic!—was sitting in the water with him, holding his head and torso and speaking in the same hushed, tranquilizing tones a mother would use on a babe.

Dana bit her lip, realizing how wrong she'd been in accusing Leif of being a coward. It wasn't fear he felt most when it came to his older brother; it was pity. The sort of enabling sympathy that had allowed abusive men to prey upon their kin from the beginning of time.

What a pathetic display, she thought, feeling herself growing a bit misty-eyed. And she knew, without being told, that the biggest favor she could do Leif was to go back inside the tent and pretend the attack had never taken place.

Indeed it had, however. And, as she reentered the now unlit shelter, she knew she'd somehow have to come to terms with the fact that she was not only in the keeping of a barbarian, but the most dangerous kind of all!

Chapter 12

Dana was on the verge of sleep when Leif returned to the tent a short time later.

"I brought you another lamp, Goddess," he said softly, as he entered.

She sat up in a panic, clapping the bedclothes to the dipping neckline of her gown.

Leif, having set the light on the table, turned to her with an apologetic smile. " 'Tis only I, my lady. You needn't fear Booth's wrath again tonight."

She sighed with relief and slipped back under the covers, letting her head come to rest on one of the pillows once more. "Why? What have you done to him?"

He crossed to her and sat down at her side on the edge of the bed. "Trussed him," he answered; and, perhaps it was only Dana's imagination, but his face seemed to flush with embarrassment.

Again she sat up a bit, her features drawing together in puzzlement. " 'Trussed' him?"

"Ja. 'Tis his wish at such times, Your Greatness. It doth help him save face, you understand."

She reached out and, to his obvious surprise, sympathetically placed a hand upon one of his. *"Neinn.* I fear I haven't understood from the first, Leif, and for that I apologize. I was wrong to assume you were simply a coward where your brother is concerned."

"But, being all-knowing, I thought you were aware he was a . . ." His words broke off, and she could tell how difficult it was for him to give voice to the ugly truth about his sibling.

"A berserker?" she finished for him.

He nodded and dropped his gaze.

"Neinn. The truth is none of us gods can know everything about all of you mortals. You greatly outnumber us, of course."

Seeming encouraged by this admission of imperfection on her part, he cautiously lifted his eyes once more and dared to look squarely at her. The relief that showed in his features, as the corners of her mouth turned up to form a soft, empathetic smile, warmed her heart. It seemed in that instant that she'd always known his face and he'd always known hers.

"Anyway," he continued, "I feel certain Booth forgives you for burning him earlier. 'Twas only his bearskin that caught fire, fortunately."

She pulled back from him in amazement. "Forgives me, you say? Forgives *me!* Fie, you're *both* madmen! How can you possibly see me as the culprit, after what he did to you?"

"Oh, 'twas nothing."

"Nothing? Why, just look at you, Leif. You're covered with scratches and bites!"

He waved her off. "Ah, it has happened many times before. No harm done verily."

"But human bites can be among the most baneful. You really must let me have a look at you in better light," she declared, determined now to talk some sense into him.

Shoving aside the blankets, she climbed out of bed and bent to pull her purse out from under it. "Now, let me see. I should have some antiseptic in here somewhere."

"What?"

Her cheeks grew warm as she realized she'd slipped into speaking English again. "Nothing. 'Tis just that I think I have a liquid in here that will keep your wounds from growing peccant. . . . Oh, *ja*. Here it is," she announced, withdrawing a little plastic squirt bottle of Bactine and a packet of facial tissues, then shoving the bag back under the bed.

She took hold of one of his hands and tugged on it. "Come along now. Over to the light, so I might attend to you."

Still looking reluctant, he slowly rose and followed her.

Once they were seated on one of the table's benches, she pulled the oil lamp up close to them and began applying the antiseptic to the many punctures and claw marks on his face and neck.

"It stings a bit at first, then numbs you like . . ." She hesitated, searching for a substance with which he would be familiar. "Like ice does."

He nodded, the trust he displayed in letting her nurse him this way again touching her heart.

"Ja. Then what does it do? Will the bites disappear, pray?"

"Neinn. They will still need time to heal. 'Tis just that this liquid will keep them from becoming peccant, as I said."

"Ja, ja. That's right. . . . But how?" he queried after several seconds.

Dana inwardly groaned, knowing it definitely wasn't her place to try explaining the destruction of microorganisms to a tenth-century warrior. "Oh, prithee, do not ask. Forsooth, 'tis not wisdom I am permitted to share with you."

"Very well," he said glumly.

"So, do tell me why it was, given Booth's howling earlier, that none of your fellow countrymen came to our aid."

"Well, their merrymaking yet goes on, my lady. So, perhaps they did not hear."

"They heard. Everyone within a league of here heard, save that he or she be deaf."

Again he looked embarrassed by the subject. "They . . . umm. Well, you must remember, Goddess, that they are, for the most part, my kinsmen, and 'tis not pleasant for any of us to acknowledge that we have a man such as Booth in our clan. *Neinn,* verily, even *leading us."*

"Then why on earth did your father allow him to take command? What could possibly have been in his mind?"

"Well, Booth is not like most of his kind. He truly

regrets such shows of anger. Why, by the morrow, I wager he will have fallen into silence with you, ashamed beyond words of what he did tonight."

"And you believe his being ashamed somehow exonerates him?"

"Perhaps not fully. But I must say, to his credit, that he has yet to slay a Norseman or woman. And many of his kind cannot make that claim, as you likely well know."

She narrowed her eyes and sat staring at him dumbfoundedly for several seconds. "Leif, you dear man, don't you realize he attacked you? Even as a mad dog might! Why, if I had not been here to distract him, I believe he would have killed you."

He shook his head. "Oh, *neinn*. Not his own brother. And 'tis no matter now, for he is amply trussed, as I have told you."

"Well, mayhap, trussed is how he should be at *all* times."

"Neinn. 'Twould not be necessary, I assure you, for he has been known to go for longer than a fortnight without such slips into madness, my lady."

She studied his neck and face more closely by the lamp's light and noticed, for the first time, the scattering of tiny scars upon them. "And you . . . just look at yourself, covered with the evidence of his past fits. Alas, you're as crazed as he for abiding it!"

"But he is my blood."

"Neinn. He is your nemesis. And 'tis high time you awoke and realized it!"

He scowled, suddenly seeming as incensed by the topic as she. "Can you guarantee a place in *Valhöll* to me, Goddess? For earlier I thought I heard you say you could not."

"Neinn. Of course I can't."

"Then fault me no more where my brother is concerned," he thundered, "for I would rather lose my life here on earth to him in honor than lose my soul in betrayal!"

Dana couldn't help recoiling slightly at this outburst. Then, fearing she'd lose her temper with him in return, she recapped the antiseptic, gathered it up, along with her unused tissues, and went back to the bed to put them away.

He was over to her before she could even restow her purse and, as she rose from the task, he wrapped his large, muscular arms about her waist and squeezed her up against him, while drawing a savoring breath in through his teeth. "Alas, I am sorry, dear Dana. 'Tis not for me to lose my patience with you, when you, by troth, have shown such forbearance with Booth and me."

She swallowed dryly at this moving apology and raised a defensive shoulder to her right ear, never having been able to resist such heated whispering from a male.

Then, in spite of his firm hold upon her, she managed to turn about in his arms and stare up into his azure eyes. " 'Tis just that I shall never understand how you became the keeper of such a beast!"

He drew another deep breath and, letting go of her, turned and sank down upon the bed. "Come and join me, prithee," he invited, extending a hand to her. "For 'tis a long tale, indeed."

She obliged him, and they both reclined, lying across the width of the mattress. The flickering lamp light caught their gazes as it cast eerie shadows upon the tent's pointed ceiling overhead.

"Do you know of the passage to manhood we in Norway observe?"

"Neinn," Dana answered. The truth was, though, that she thought she remembered reading of such a thing in twentieth-century Iceland, and she'd wondered if it had its roots in ancient Scandinavia. She was, at last, about to find out, however, so she wouldn't have dreamt of dissuading this disclosure from him.

"Well, 'tis a rite in which each lad of twelve years dresses in bearskins before his first raid. It is believed that becoming akin to the great bear helps young warriors to be braver in battle. Thus we practice our spear throwing, swordplay, and wrestling in such guise for many weeks before sailing away upon our fathers' warships. And, for most of us, this practice is enough to brand the image of our animal fierceness upon our minds evermore. For others, however—those very few like Booth—a kind of possession sets in and *being* berserk stands in the stead of merely *acting* thus." Sighing as though the topic was still most uncomfortable for him, he rolled away from her, onto his stomach. " 'Tis not fear of battle that causes them to become this way, mind, Goddess. Not at all. For I have fought and raided at Booth's side for ten summers now, and I can truly tell ye that he is the bravest warrior I shall ever know. He fears nothing, it seems. Not pain or wounds. Not even death."

"Ja. He told me that earlier, remember? While you were pretending to be asleep here."

" 'Tis true. And that is what makes him so dangerous at times, I suppose."

"So, if he does not fear death, how do you rein him?"

Leif laughed to himself as though a bit amazed at this question. "How little you really *do* know about us, Your Greatness."

She clucked with impatience. "Well? My question yet stands."

"He fears dishonor, of course. In his sane moments, he is afraid of bringing shame upon our clan, and, so far, that is what has saved us all from having to pay blood-money in his name."

Oh, yes! Blood-money, a voice within Dana reminded. It was the Viking-law penalty for all family members of anyone found guilty of having killed a fellow Norseman. The fines for such an offense could be terribly high. Enough to make every kinsman in a clan fear the loss of his very hearth and home. So, naturally, great measures were taken to make certain no berserker got out of hand with his own crew or countrymen.

Abroad their murderous rampages were seen as undiluted valor, but in the Vikings' own land they were considered criminal. Therefore, much effort must have gone into maintaining this differentiation.

Wow, Dana inwardly exclaimed. The age-old mystery of the berserker unraveled for her in just a few short minutes!

On the surface the word seemed simple enough:

berserkr, the Old Norse term for bear's skin. To dress
in a bearlike costume. But, somewhere during the millennium that had once separated a historian like Dana
from men like Leif, something had gotten lost in the
translation. Had it really been some sort of rite of
passage that had led Nordic men to wearing such skins
into battle? Or was this link between "bear shirts" and
insanity, "berserk," related somehow to the widespread werewolf myth in ancient Europe—as some
scholars had surmised?

Now, however, Dana seemed to have the answer.
Indeed, she'd come upon firsthand knowledge which
many of her contemporaries would have paid any
price to acquire!

"Pray, Leif, these rages of your brother's, is there
aught he eats or drinks that seems to call them forth?"
she queried, remembering the debate in her field over
whether or not naturally occurring hallucinogens
could have been at the root of them.

"Neinn. Booth is overly fond of mead and wine, of
course, as you have seen. But that is true of most of us
and such outbursts do not follow."

"Is he always drunk when they come to pass?"

He nodded tentatively. *"Ja.* I suppose so."

This rang true for Dana, since everything she had
read on the subject had seemed to indicate that berserker behavior was at least somewhat related to alcohol consumption. "Then, could you not prevent him
from drinking? Could you not try to convince him that
the Loki that possesses him at such times comes from
within his wineskins?"

Suddenly looking pensive, Leif sat up on the bed. "Forsooth, I have never thought of such a course."

"Well, mayhap it will help. 'Tis worth a try in any case. Don't you agree?"

"*Ja,* Goddess." He offered her a soft smile. "And, by tomorrow's light, you have my word that I shall suggest this to our captain . . . I do not hold great hope that he will follow this counsel, however," he added, "as spirited drink hath been his first love for many years."

Dana raised a discerning brow at him. "Since he was *twelve?*"

"Right. You see? You are more all-knowing than you admit," he replied with a weary laugh.

"And *you* have a right to a life apart from attending to your older brother. You are strong and comely. A fine warrior, I've no doubt, and there must be many a Norse maiden who would pledge herself to thee. Booth is the reason you have not taken a bride, is he not?"

"*Ja.* He is. And I assumed you knew as much back at the monastery. In very sooth, however, dear Dana, even if your counsel to him doth avail, I could not return to Norway and court a maid."

"But why not?"

He stared down into her face, his eyes suddenly glistening with emotion. "Because I've met you."

Dana's breath caught in her throat at this, and, to her surprise, she felt a bit tearful, too. "Oh, Leif," she choked. "I . . . I cannot stay with you. You must know that by now."

"I know that you seek this ancient worshipping

place of the Erse, and that you likely hope it will somehow take you back to *Asgardhr*. But, if it shouldn't, Goddess, and, if Booth will permit it, I would seek you as my consort."

Though she believed she was doing a pretty good job of not letting it show, Dana couldn't help melting at this. His murmurs were just so soft, so low that they seemed to travel all the way up her spine, sending shivers of desire through every part of her.

Never, in the course of her twentieth-century life, had she received such a proposal—let alone from such a man as this. And keeping her enthusiasm about him to herself now was proving one of the hardest things she'd ever had to do.

Thinking it best to put some distance between them, she sat up and pulled away. Then she deposited herself on the other side of the bed, her head coming to rest on the far pillow. "Alas, pilgrim, 'tis all so complicated," she declared with an uneasy sigh, again focussing on the lamp's light as it danced upon the tent's ceiling.

To her dismay, however, she didn't get the chance to say a thing more. In the space of a heartbeat, he was upon her, pinning the sides of her gown to the mattress with a threatening whisper. "Fie, do not ever call me 'pilgrim,' again! I have shared with you, in only two days, my deepest secrets. I have told you the cause of the scars my body bears. And yet you, who are so clearly scarred within, will reveal naught of how you came to be so heartbroken, so bereft of kith and kin in this realm!"

Though she was afraid of his anger in those sec-

onds—of his great physical strength—she did her best
to seem unruffled. "And you would wrest it from me
with such snarling?"

His manner softened. "I would hope that one who
is so concerned about my not having a mate would at
least admit to having known ill fortune in that sphere
as well."

"All right, so my heart can be broken."

"*Has* been broken," he corrected.

"Has been broken. So, what of it? What possible
good can come from my telling you the particulars?"

"I could comfort you, of course. I could help you to
forget him. Whoever he be. This villain you once
trusted with your love."

She donned a subtle smile. She had no doubt that he
could help her forget—especially given what she'd felt
as he'd pulled her between his legs earlier. Held up
against such brawn, such prowess, the memory of
Steven's often marginal lovemaking was sure to pale
considerably.

"Why do you smile?"

"Because I am pleased with you."

He grinned as well. "Pleased as a goddess or pleased
as a woman?"

"Both."

His smile broadened, and there was suddenly a look
in his eye that was so confident, so sure of her willingness to make love with him that she couldn't help
issuing a slight gasp in response.

She could almost hear his mind asking, as though
they were playing an Old Norse board game; Well, is
it your move or mine, my dear?

"Later," she found herself saying aloud.

"Later?" he echoed, his expression turning roguish.

"*Ja.* I mean, what you really want is for me to tell you of the man who left me, right?"

He gave forth a discouraged sigh and lifted himself off her, again looking markedly annoyed at her reluctance to let matters take their course between them. "Right," he answered, flopping onto his back.

"Well, he had dark, *thinning* hair. I sometimes told him he was going bald, but he preferred to say that he was simply 'thinning.'"

"A god losing his hair?" Leif asked with a skeptical rise to his voice.

"Oh, he wasn't a god. I mean, *he* may have considered himself one," she added with a biting laugh. "But he definitely was not."

"But I thought you told me back at the friary that you have never made love with a mortal."

"*Neinn.* You were the one who said that and I simply failed to offer any argument."

Seeming encouraged by this news, Leif rolled onto his right side, propped himself up on his elbow and smiled at her once more. "All right, then. So you *have* made love with a mere human."

"Oh, *ja.* Many times."

"And, pray, how do we compare with gods in that way, Your Greatness?"

"Well, it depends on the man in question, of course."

"And this human lover of yours, what was his name, prithee?"

"Steven."

"Ah, *ja.* 'Tis like our name 'Stefan,' right?"

"Right."

"So he was a Norseman?"

"Neinn."

"Erse?"

"Neinn."

"What then?"

She shrugged. "A blend of races, Leif. I . . . I am not sure how to answer this."

He clucked with impatience. "Well, was he tall?"

Again unable to translate measurements for him, she thought and said, "I believe you are about a head taller than he."

The Norseman seemed thoroughly pleased with this news.

"And broader? Am I broader than he through the shoulders and back?"

"Oh, *ja.* Infinitely," she answered, offering him an approving smile.

"So, I could slay him for you with little trouble, could I not?"

She laughed to herself. "I've no doubt."

"Then why won't you allow it?"

"Oh, Leif, 'tis not a question of gaining my permission. 'Tis just that he is very, very far away from here."

"I shall cross all the seas to reach him then!"

"Neinn. Forsooth, no one hath built a ship that can carry you that far. What's more, I'm not sure I want him dead."

He looked dumbfounded at this. "He broke your heart, the maggot, and you do not want him dispatched?"

"Neinn." She assumed a mischievous smirk as she continued to hold his gaze. "I think I would rather see him maimed."

"That is good, too," he agreed, nodding. "I have done my share of that through the years as well."

"I'm certain you have."

"Then why, with the fiery rain and other scourges at your command, Goddess, did you not maim him yourself, pray?"

Dana's mind flashed back to the 1993 indictment of Lorena Bobbitt, and she bit her lower lip as a sudden wave of wickedness ran through her. While the rest of the world had asked at the time how such an atrocity as a woman's cutting off her husband's penis could happen, Dana had wondered—given the general insensitivity of so many males—why it didn't happen *more often!*

To her credit, however, she was managing to remain fairly straight-faced now, as she considered it all—all of the heartless things Steven had said and done during their years together. "I don't know. Perhaps I was simply too hurt to do aught in retaliation."

She sobered all the more, knowing their little game of "what if" regarding Steven was destined to remain just that. "I suppose his greatest offense was simply failing to love me as much as I loved him."

Leif's eyes widened with obvious wonder and he reached out and ran his fingers through her hair. "But how is this possible? Did he never gaze upon your loveliness and want it solely to himself for an eternity? For any wise man would. I certainly do."

Oh, God help me! a voice within Dana exclaimed.

She was going to slide right into his arms, like a help-less mound of mud, if she didn't get herself off the bed at once!

"I would possess you as a field of wild flowers on my family's farmstead. I would lay claim to you thus and never let you go," he continued in a winning whisper.

Oh, it was tough being worshipped! Dana had simply never realized that complete adoration could be so irresistible!

"Listen, Leif, I—"

"I know," he interrupted. "You cannot stay with me. You do not belong here. You have erenow told me all of this. 'Tis just that, until you must leave, sweet Goddess, what possible harm could there be in your lying with me as you did that cur of a mortal? That 'Stefan' or whate'er he was called."

"Steven."

"Right," he retorted with a sniff; and the blatant jealousy he showed in that instant warmed her through and through.

It had been so long since she was confident of *one* man's love, that the very idea of having two males come to blows over her made her spirit soar. She, therefore, did not resist Leif now as his fingers, still intertwined in her hair, drew her face over to his.

He kissed her with a fervor as their lips met, and she couldn't help kissing him back. His tongue played about the edges of her mouth, then plunged deeply to interact with hers, the underlying similarities to what he obviously wanted to do to another part of her causing her to gasp with anticipation.

She arched up to him slightly as he moved to lie over her, her chest heaving.

With a sigh of unmistakable appreciation, he slid the sleeves of her gown down her shoulders and bared her breasts to his large hot palms.

To his relief, she wasn't wearing that cupped contrivance tonight, and his hands were instantly able to close about the soft pink crests of these marvelous appendages.

She was simply warm flesh and blood, he tried to tell himself in those heated moments—no different really from any other maid with whom he'd found gratification through the years. Yet, the knowledge that she was, at the same time, a deity, forsooth the mother of all whom the Norse held dear, seemed to rein him. It compelled him to slow down and make certain he pleasured her in every way he could, rather than simply taking her in a heedless rush, as his mortal form longed to do.

Dana, sensing the sudden masterfulness in him, which was only natural for such a primitive male to assume in bed, simply allowed him to continue to lead her through this exquisite seduction. She feared this might be their last night alone together, that Booth or their trip to the stone circle would prevent them from fully expressing the passion that had been smoldering between them. So she made no effort to stop him as his lips left her now whisker-chafed mouth and traveled down, with a trail of wet kisses, to close upon the tip of her right breast.

His tongue teased and flickered upon her nipple

with superb adroitness. Then, to her amazement, she felt him *bite* it ever so slightly.

She couldn't help giving forth a tiny yelp, yet she instantly realized that this was much more out of a sense of apprehension than pain.

He lifted his mouth from her, his eyes darting up to meet her gaze with gentle reassurance. "Be at ease, love. I am not like my brother, so you need have no fear of me." His fingers replaced his lips upon the tender peak, and he caressed it as though to atone for his playful transgression.

"But why—"

He saved her the embarrassment of having to finish the question. "Because I want you to think of me by the morrow. As we set off for the circle of stones and hazard Booth's wrath each time we so much as look at one another, I want you to still feel my touch, my mouth upon you. Forgive me, dear Dana. I will not risk hurting you again," he vowed, looking duly repentant.

"Well, it was not so much pain I felt as surprise," she admitted.

He smiled softly, his eyes shining with a sweet expression that said he knew they were still very much in accord.

He slipped his arms under her and, with a whisper of a laugh, rolled onto his back, causing her to follow and end by lying over him. Then he slid down beneath her, and, when his face was again level with her chest, he began tenderly licking the part of her which he'd offended.

Drawing in a deep, relishing breath, he pulled down

on her shoulders until his stubbly cheeks were surrounded by the wonderful softness of her pendulant breasts. "By the Heavens, smother me in your flesh thus and I shall die the gladdest of men!"

With that he slipped one of her nipples into his mouth and began sucking upon it like a babe.

Dana sighed with pleasure, throwing her head back, as the warmth and wetness of it, the relentless downward tugging sent waves of torturous arousal all the way to her loins.

It was really such an easy, natural position for a pair of lovers to assume, yet she'd never tried it in quite this way before. She'd never thought to suspend this sensitive part of herself over a man's face; and, again, she had to give this simple Norseman credit for teaching her more about foreplay than she'd learned in the supposedly sophisticated world from which she'd come.

She let it continue for a moment or two more: the subtle abrasion of his bristly cheeks and jaw upon her alabaster skin, the gentle pinches of his lips and teeth, the tickling of his tongue. First upon the breast on which he'd inflicted his love bite, then upon its twin.

And, when she felt she could no longer bear the almost explosive excitement it was causing in the lower half of her, she pulled away, coming to a sitting position upon him with a tiny whimper.

He wanted her as much as she did him. Not only did the somewhat abandoned expression in his eyes tell her this in those seconds, but so did the hard swelling she felt just behind her, as she sat more upright upon him.

"Prithee, my lady, bid me leave you this instant, if this is not what you truly want. For, in any other case, 'twill be torment for me to stay."

The look he wore wrenched her, and she knew that, in spite of any concern she might have about birth control, the two of them could not possibly part now. There was simply too much longing between them, too much love for one another's company.

Having him leave at this point would have been so much like being dashed in the face with a bucket of cold water, that she realized she simply couldn't withstand it.

" 'Tis what I want," she whispered, letting her torso slip back down over his and her lips drop to his right ear.

"Are you sure?" he asked, his voice wavering.

"*Ja.* I shall hate myself forever if I don't make love to you at least this once."

His tone said that he couldn't believe his good fortune in this. "Very well."

Dana was already straddling him, but she knew she needed to lift herself enough to pull up the skirt of her gown. As she did so, he wasted no time in reaching down to the waist of his trousers and baring himself as well.

His deep-blue eyes were both adoring and daring a moment later, as it seemed to become incumbent upon her to initiate their coupling.

Her breath caught in her throat. She'd certainly made love this way before, but never with a man so well endowed. Never with a towering, two-hundred-bound Viking! And, in this moment of truth, she couldn't help feeling some misgiving.

" 'Tis all right, love," he murmured, seeming to sense her uneasiness. He drew her face down to his once more and pressed his lips to her cheek. "There is no need to rush."

He kissed her mouth a second or two later, and she felt his fingers slip up between her legs at the same time. With surprising gentleness, two of them parted her lower lips and eased their way inside her, their agile stroking helping to prepare her for what was to come.

He was right, Dana acknowledged with a rapturous sigh. Not all tenth-century raiders were ruthless animals like Booth, for this one seemed to know, without being told, that this was not the most painless position in which to enter a woman.

She closed her eyes and continued to coo at his intimate manipulation. It felt even more wonderful than it had the night before, and she could almost have contented herself with it, were it not for all the yearning she had seen in his gaze just a minute or two earlier.

So, determined to give him some of the pleasure he was bringing her, she reached down and pulled his fingers from her. Then she slowly replaced them with his long erection.

In spite of how he'd readied her, it did hurt a little at first. Something to remember him by, come the morrow, she thought, wincing a bit. Yet, as she finally took all of him inside, a warm, satisfied sensation filled her, and her ears were likewise filled with his impassioned moan.

She did not begin to move at first, but simply lay holding him, silently savoring the feel of it, of having an honest-to-God Norse warrior so deep within her. It was a sensation meant only for a woman, a claim that the often pompous male scholars in her field simply could never make—even if a time-slip had befallen one of them. More importantly, however, it was sheer heaven!

After several seconds of remaining still, she lowered her lips to the side of his neck and wet it with several French kisses, meanwhile causing her secret recesses to open and close about his hardness several times.

"Fie, do not tease me," he responded, with a provocative growl. And, before Dana had the chance to reply, he rolled her, still joined with him, onto her back and began moving in and out of her with breath-stopping fervor.

Dear God, she wouldn't have dreamed of protesting. It was utter bliss! Every thrust more sublime than the one before it!

Perhaps she'd been too long removed from the joys of lovemaking, but she couldn't remember ever having experienced anything as earthshaking!

She didn't want it to end. Yet, as it continued for several minutes more, part of her feared she might be driven mad by the flood of ecstatic sensations it was causing within her. Then, too, there was her nagging concern about an accidental pregnancy; and, as the Norseman's climax obviously neared, she found herself pulling away—trying to uncouple from him.

He wouldn't allow it, however. Clenching his teeth as though half crazed by their feverish act, he held her fast for its culmination, driving into her with relentless rapidity now as he drew her hips down to meet each of his thrusts.

She actually screamed in those seconds. Not caring who might hear, she cried out with abandon—until his ravaging lips and tongue managed to quiet her with another heated kiss.

"By Thunder, how I love you," he whispered into her ear, his voice filled with more ardor than she'd ever heard from a man.

"I think I love you, too," she replied. But she hated herself, even as she said it, for sounding almost as tentative as any of the males who had dumped her through the years.

Chapter 13

"I failed to satisfy you," Leif said dejectedly, slipping out of her and rolling onto his back.

Dana, hearing her own heartbreak in his voice, immediately turned to comfort him. "Nonsense," she declared, wrapping an arm about his left shoulder and pressing her naked torso up against his massive back. Given his size, she felt almost as though she were trying to comfort a Brahman bull. She'd just never realized she could have such a crushing effect upon anyone so large. "Did you not hear me cry out in rapture? Can you possibly think that happens every time I'm with a man?"

Though his tone was slightly brighter, he still sounded hurt. "I do not know."

She pushed up and kissed the side of his neck. "Well I'm telling you it does not, my sweet, so prithee believe me!"

He slowly rolled over and turned to meet her gaze. "Are you certain?"

She nodded resolutely, recalling many a flaccid eve-

ning with Steven and his out-of-shape predecessors.
"Oh, *ja*. By troth, I must tell you that you are the best
lover I've ever had."

Even in the dim lamp light, Dana could see the
boyish glow return to his face. "Verily?"

A reassuring smile came to her lips, and she looked
him squarely in the eye. "By all the Heavens I swear
it."

"Then why did you try to pull away in the midst of
it?"

Her smile faded. "Well, 'tis hard to explain."

"Pray, do try," he insisted, giving her a look that
said he felt she owed him at least that much.

"Well, I . . . I feared having your seed go into me."

He furrowed his brow as though this were the last
thing he expected her to say. "But why?"

"Because I'm in mortal form now. I could beget a
child with you, and, forgive me, but 'tis not what I
wish at present."

His mouth dropped open. "You mean to say you
could bear a babe with a human? I did not think this
possible."

"Oh, but it is. And, while I find you quite comely
and noble as a warrior, love, you must try to understand when I tell you that I do not wish to bear *any*
mortal's child."

"I shall try," he replied with a pensive swallow.
"But I would think a goddess able to stave off such a
conception."

"Usually I can, but I've . . . I've too little of my
magic potion with me, I'm afraid."

Though he appeared to be fighting it, a roguish grin

played on his lips. "I would like a son who is half god," he confessed, reaching down and running his fingers over her stomach.

"*Neinn,* Leif, believe me, you would not, for he would soon gain the advantage with you, don't you think?"

He frowned and his fingers moved up to stroke her long blond hair. "I suppose."

"And every lord deserves his child's respect, at least until such time as that child becomes a lord or lady as well."

He nodded, continuing to look discouraged. "*Ja.* . . . We cannot be consorts, can we?"

"Oh, now, I didn't say that," she purred, running the back of her right hand over his now-spent manhood with the whisper of a smile. "In very sooth, I would be crushed if you didn't wish to lie with me again. 'Tis just that I truly do not know how much more time we will have together, love, and I don't wish to see us both hurt at my departure from this realm."

" 'Tis already too late to stop me from it, for, as I hope you heard, I just confessed my love to you."

She gave one of his hands a squeeze. "*Ja.* I heard. And I thank you deeply for it, my dear."

"So thanks is all I can hope for in return?" he asked, his voice edged with pain and indignation.

"For now, Leif, *ja.* I'm sorry. But 'twould be unfair of me to promise you aught more at this time."

"So when will you know for certain what more you might pledge?"

She shrugged. "When we reach the stone circle. If we find it and it fails to work its magic upon me, I'll know 'tis my fate to remain with you and your clan."

"I shall pray it fails then," he said in a reverent whisper, leaning forward and kissing her lips.

They lay in each other's arms for several minutes, a satisfied, yet slightly worry-filled silence falling over them. Then, fearing he might doze off and be caught in bed with her in the morning, Leif slowly sat up.

"I must go sleep outside now, Goddess, lest we hazard enraging my brother once more by being found this way come morning. Fear not, though, for I shall be nearby through the night to protect you."

"Very well," Dana said glumly, sitting up as he rose from the bed. Though she knew her circumstances wouldn't allow her to promise him anything more than she already had, she was greatly saddened now at having him leave her. And she had to conclude, from all he'd said, that he felt the same way—for Heaven only knew if they'd be able to steal any more time alone together.

She reached out and gave his hand a wistful squeeze, as he stood beside the bed. "Prithee kiss me again before you go."

The shadow of a sad smile came to his lips, and he bent to oblige her. Their mouths and tongues rejoined as though unwilling to pay any heed to the higher purposes of which their minds were all too aware.

As he broke the kiss off seconds later, Dana let her eyes fall shamelessly to his nakedness: his muscle-bound chest, his narrow midriff and hips, and, of course, the part of him that had brought her such ecstasy only minutes earlier. His body looked bronzed and shadowy in the warm glow of the lamp's light, and, again, she felt terribly heavy-hearted as he pulled his trousers back up to his waist, then closed and rebelted them.

What a splendid example of maleness he was! Part of her couldn't help but ache at the realization that he would probably agree to marry her and make himself all hers right then and there . . . if she could only do the same.

But it just wouldn't be fair to him, she silently admonished herself. Given that she knew so little about her future, it simply wasn't right to try to make guarantees.

One thing was certain, though: she would definitely feel his touch upon her "by the morrow," as he had wished. Her breasts still ached from his fervent attentions to them. The depths of her positively throbbed with the lingering sensation of his fierce thrusts. And she was actually filled with gratitude that his love for her had moved him to be anything but gentle toward the end of their coupling.

Along with these mementos, however, was her awareness of the menacing liquid now streaming out of her. Warm and sticky, it settled into the bedclothes beneath where she sat, and she was again worried about what might come of such an unprotected encounter.

Time alone would have to tell about that, too, a voice within her noted dolefully. And she found that all she could offer, as Leif gathered up his primitive sleeping bag and crossed to the door to take his leave a moment later, was a weak "Good night."

* * *

Leif's legs felt heavy, as, minutes later, he made his way across the beach to his nearby tent to check on Booth before retiring. The sand kept shifting under his feet and he was worn out from having made such vehement love to their eminent guest.

Though lying with Dana had been the most thrilling experience of his life, part of him wanted to be angry with her for remaining so noncommittal. He knew, however, that this would just be wasted emotion, given her seeming inability to predict her own future.

But there was something else on his mind as well now. Something that had been troubling him for most of the day. It was the box. The tiny black boxlike object which he'd found upon Booth's bed, when he'd been disassembling it back at the friary.

The contrivance was unlike anything he'd ever seen. The look, the feel, the smell of it were all so unearthly that he'd simply had to conclude that it belonged to his dear Dana and that it must have been among the things she had emptied from her bag, when she'd returned to her bed chamber that morning. She'd obviously failed to recover it at the time, though; and, not spotting it until she was off attempting to converse with the monks in the tower, Leif had hidden it under his belt-strap so it wouldn't fall into anyone else's hands. He'd kept it there during the passage back to their camp, then stowed it in his tent upon their return.

Due to the goddess's chilling warning about the contents of her divine bag, Leif had been quite hesitant to touch the box at first. But, because his hand had brushed against it without incident as he'd rushed to strip the bed of its linens, he had decided to hazard stashing it on his person and keeping it until such time as he could return it to Dana in private.

That time had simply not arrived during the course of the day or the evening. In fact, it had only been in the past half hour that he knew he could give it back to her without fear of Booth walking in on them. But now Leif had to admit to himself that his curiosity about it was finally getting the best of him.

Dana was *so* mysterious, after all. Such an enigma to him and everyone else in the crew, that, given the love and devotion he'd just demonstrated to her, he felt almost entitled to whatever additional information he could glean about her and her godly abilities. In view of her aggravating tendency to answer so many of his questions with a patronizing "I fear you would not understand," he was beginning to think he'd be a damned fool not to help himself to at least a little more knowledge. And, considering that the device had now been in his possession for over fifteen hours and it had yet to cause him even the slightest bodily harm, he couldn't help but conclude that a bit of tinkering with it would probably prove fairly safe as well.

As he stepped into his tent, he saw that Booth was dead asleep where he'd been left trussed upon his bed earlier. So, taking up the shelter's lit lamp, Leif withdrew his precious find from where he'd hidden it in his sea chest, and exited as quickly as he'd entered.

With the moment of decision now upon him, he vacillated just outside the door for several seconds. Then he chose to head off to the unoccupied side of the beach—well away from where Dana or any of his companions could hear or see what was to transpire.

He walked several hundred yards to a small dune, behind which he could hide, and, once he reached its other side, he sank down upon the sand and began studying the contraption by flickering lamp light.

It had a kind of window on one side of it. This was an ice-clear surface, like the one Booth had spotted on the goddess's bracelet the night before. And, peering through it, Leif could see a little yellow wheel of sorts with what appeared to be a black axle at its center.

To the right of this window were many rows of needle-sized holes. Leif ran a fingertip over them and felt that they were indeed as recessed as they looked to be in the dim light.

So far, so good, he told himself, with a brave swallow. He hadn't yet been turned to ash by the strange little device, so he decided to continue examining it.

There was alien scrivening here and there upon it. It was in white ink and very uniformly rendered. And most of it was located at one end of the box, where there were four tiny protuberances. Drawing in a deep bolstering breath, he began fingering the first of these, and nothing happened.

Finally, after much fumbling, he succeeded in pushing it inward, toward the center of the box. To his astoundment, the thing began making a barely audible hissing sound, and what looked to be a hard red bead at the adjacent side of the contrivance instantly became illuminated!

Terrified, he tossed it to the ground and pushed away.

Nothing else happened in those suspenseful seconds, however. And, regaining his courage, he leaned forward and picked the box up once more.

What a gloriously bright color, he thought, feeling almost mesmerized by the glowing crimson droplet. Its light emanated from within it somehow, like a minuscule lamp draped with some sort of bloodstained membrane. Or like the clearest of rubies held up to the sun, he concluded, comforted by the fact that he'd finally thought of some naturally occurring substance to which he could compare it.

Encouraged by this, he moved on to the next protuberance and pressed it inward as well. To his amazement, this caused the first one to pop back out at him and, all at once, he noticed that the box's hissing had become louder.

Considering this a warning of some sort, he instantly lowered the next push-button, and, to his relief, the ominous noise stopped. But then, not half a second later, the box actually began *talking* to him, and, again, he dropped it in a panic.

He was about to bolt to his feet and run away, when, to his astonishment, he realized that the voice he was hearing was his own! Followed by Dana's! Then Booth's!

By Thunder, this was the "echoing" the goddess had produced from her bag the night before! This was the very wonder she had wrought to help convince Booth of her omnipotence.

But why, if it really was some sort of miracle, was it happening again now at a mere mortal's hand?

Leif continued to listen, until the conversation finally ended and that odd hissing began anew. Then, after several more seconds of poking at the row of buttons, he managed to quiet the box completely and the red light at its side was somehow extinguished.

He'd just worked a wonder, he noted triumphantly. Deep within him he knew, however, that, given what it seemed to indicate about his beloved Dana and her supposed abilities, this was not a favorable turn of events.

Chapter 14

A joggling at her shoulder woke Dana a short time later, and she opened her eyes to see Leif standing beside the bed with her little tape recorder dangling from his fingers by its wrist strap.

With a gasp, she quickly sat up and reached out to take it from him. She was too slow, however. Shaking his head, he whisked it away from her grasp and perched upon the mattress with a shrewd squint.

"Your 'echo' box, my lady, is it not?"

Her heart sank at this, for it meant that he'd already fiddled with the thing enough to know its function. *"Ja,"* she answered, trying to keep her voice even. Then she leaned forward and snatched at it again.

This was to no avail, however. Employing his quick, warrior reflexes, he had it well away, on the far side of him, in a flash.

"Leif, *prithee!* 'Tis not a plaything, I hope you realize—"

"I know," he interrupted in a mocking monotone. "Only 'on pain of death' should I be touching it. Yet,

'Goddess,' in spite of your warning, it seems to me I have touched it in every possible way since finding it upon this very bed at the monastery this morning, and, forsooth, here I sit before you alive and well."

"So deem yourself fortunate and return it to me at once," she exclaimed, not wanting to believe that this taunting bastard was the same ardent lover who'd held her in his arms just a short time earlier.

"Not before you tell me more," he countered. "Such as why it is that I, a mere human, was able to make the box echo as it did from within your bag last evening. Without so much as a sorcerer's incantation, I worked a wonder which you would have me believe only a deity could."

Caught completely off-guard by this confrontation and still a bit drowsy, Dana found herself lost for a plausible answer.

"Leif," she began again finally, her voice cracking with trepidation, "you claimed earlier that you love me. So, if that be true, I beg you to give the box back!"

For an instant he seemed quite moved by this appeal. His strong feelings for her shone in his eyes like a ship appearing through a brief break in a sea fog. Then, in a twinkling, the look was gone, and, to Dana's dismay, his expression became stony once more.

"Answer me," he demanded in an ominous whisper. "Lest you'd prefer to explain it to our captain in the morning."

She gave forth an unnerved sigh and leaned back against the bed's headrest. "Oh, verily, what does it matter *who* can work a wonder with the thing, as long as it was *I* who brought it here from *Asgardhr?*"

"You're not the Goddess Dana, are you?" he gritted out, his tone saying there was no point in her continuing to insist that she was.

She swallowed uneasily. Having seen so much of his gentler side, she scarcely believed he was capable of striking such terror in her heart now. "And, if I'm not, what, pray, will you do to me?"

Again his eyes narrowed as he obviously gave the question consideration. "I . . . I would likely keep it to myself, since I have, as I've told you, a fondness for you, Dana. Or whate'er it is you're called," he added testily; and it was clear that part of him absolutely bristled at having to make such a colossal concession on her behalf.

She couldn't help exhaling a long relieved breath. *"Ja.* That is what I'm called, forsooth. My name truly is Dana."

"But not the Dana you led us to believe you were yesterday afternoon." This was much more a statement than a question.

Her voice became pleading. "Leif, the monks and I were so weak against you that, when one of your men heard the friars call me Dana and he assumed I was a goddess, I'd have been a fool to argue." Her eyes locked upon his, searching them for further compassion. "You would have done the same in my stead, believe me!"

He leaned back a bit. *"Ja.* I wager so."

The corners of her mouth wavered as she tried to don a comforted smile.

"But, now that we have established that you are not *the* Dana, mother of our gods, *who,* in the name of all that is sacred, are you? For, in very sooth, you are not like any Ersewoman I have encountered!"

She gave forth a soft laugh, feeling a great deal more at ease now that he'd informed her he intended to keep the truth about her a secret. *"Neinn.* I'm not Erse."

"I thought not. You are a bit too fair haired and your command of our tongue far too good."

"Why, thank you, love. I have long studied to make it so."

"Studied?" he echoed incredulously.

"Ja. In places of learning, such as the Christian Church has built in this land."

He shook his head. "The Church has never taught Norse to its flock, you may be sure of that!"

"Well, I didn't mean that I studied your language in a friary exactly. I simply meant I did so in such a place of learning."

He continued to look nonplussed. "In what land, prithee? Certainly none that I have heard tell of."

"Oh, but your people shall," she replied, arching a spirited brow at him. "It has yet to be discovered, I admit. But 'tis a place very far to the west of here, to which a Norseman will sail nearly a century hence. And he will call it 'Vinland.' "

"But, if you are truly not a deity, how can you know what will come to pass one hundred years in the future?"

"Because I have studied that as well."

Deep furrows of confusion formed in his forehead. She reached out and placed a hand upon one of his shoulders, wanting to brace him for the overwhelming disclosure she was about to make. "The truth is I am not so much from a distant place as from a distant *time*. Pray, have you seen in the writings of the monks here that they deem this to be the year of their Lord nine hundred and sixteen?"

He nodded.

"Well, I come from the year *nineteen* hundred and ninety-four of that same count."

His jaw dropped open, and she gave his shoulder several consoling pats, praying all the while that he would not simply conclude she was a lunatic.

"But how . . . how is this possible?"

"Believe me, I am as lost for an answer to this as you are."

"Well, you must know something about how it came to pass."

"Neinn. Only that it befell me at the stone circle to which I have asked you to take me."

"Then, how did you come to be at the friary?"

"I traveled there later, half in your time and half in mine, I think . . . Alas, Leif, I wish to Heaven I could tell you more, but that is all I know of it."

He was silent for several seconds, clearly needing some time to try to grasp this unavoidably vague explanation. Then, handing the tape recorder back to her, he got up and began pacing pensively beside the bed.

"The year nineteen hundred and . . . ." he broke off, obviously not remembering exactly what she'd said.

"Nineteen hundred and ninety-four," she finished for him with a cautious expression.

"By Thunder! 'Tis a dizzying number, isn't it?"

"Ja."

"Well, pray pardon me for asking, but could it be that the gods sought to punish you by casting you back so many centuries?"

Dana shrugged, then donned a sheepish look. "Per chance. But I do not believe in your gods, forsooth. I am, rather, a Christian, like the monks here. And I truly don't remember doing aught for which anyone would want to chasten me."

"Hmmm. You are a Christian, you say?"

"Ja."

"You mean, this Jesus will yet have a flock one thousand years hence? I can hardly believe it possible!"

"Oh, *ja,*" she confirmed. "A 'flock,' indeed, and millions upon millions strong to boot."

He shook his head in wonder. "Such cravenly teachings in that faith," he muttered. "Who in all the world could believe in them?"

She was about to inform him that virtually all of his own race would turn to Christianity within the coming century; but, given the opinion he'd just voiced, she decided this would be unnecessarily cruel.

"Come sit down again, love, for I've much more to explain," she urged, feeling, in view of how his face had paled in the past few minutes, that this was safer than his continuing to stand.

To her relief, he took her up on the invitation, first sitting, then choosing to flop back upon the mattress, his legs draped down its side. " 'Tis simply too fanciful a tale to be aught but the truth," he concluded, shaking his head once more.

Dana smiled and reached out to run her fingers through his hair. "I am glad beyond words that you realize that."

"And this place from which you hail is named 'Vinland'?"

"Neinn. Not anymore. 'Tis 'America' in my time."

"So what is your race called then?"

" 'Americans.' "

"And you say we Norse settled this land and that is why you are flaxen-haired like our women?"

She gave forth another laugh, realizing how much more there truly was to tell. *"Neinn.* America is filled with people of all races, Leif. I am blond and my eyes are blue by cause of my parents' parents coming from Norway, as you do."

A gentle smile settled upon his lips. "Oh, I am mightily pleased to hear that."

"I thought you would be. 'Tis comforting, isn't it? To know for certain that your kind shall yet be upon the earth a thousand years hence."

He nodded. "And to know, too, that they will keep our tongue alive."

Dana didn't have the heart to tell him that Old Norse was hardly a language with which the average American was familiar, so she decided upon a softer course. "Well, it is not dead, in any case."

"So your echo box and fiery rain, they are not wonders, but merely the inventions of your time?"

"Right."

"And the blow you used to fell Booth, how was that possible?"

" 'Tis simply a form of hand-to-hand combat known in my time as well."

"And anyone can learn it?"

"Ja."

He slanted her a discerning look. "Then you are, indeed, as vulnerable in the realm of men as I sensed you to be last night?"

"Ja," she answered, her voice quavering at having to make such a jeopardizing admission.

"Hmmm."

He continued to study her, and she felt suddenly uneasy once more.

"And you age as any other mortal doth?"

She nodded.

His eyes narrowed. "You look to be roughly of the same number of years as I."

"And what is that, pray?"

"Twenty and two," he replied.

She bit her lip, doing her best to hide her surprise. Though she, of all people, was aware of the hardships of life in Viking times, it was still rather shocking to see the hard evidence of this before her very eyes.

"So you are about the same then?"

"Neinn. I'm nearly thirty," she admitted with a blush.

He sat up and took a better look at her. "But this cannot be! How is it possible? For I have seen you, even in the harshest light of day, and you haven't a single sign of so many years upon your face."

Her smile broadened considerably. "You know, I

grow more fond of you with each moment that passes."

"But you still have not answered me. How is it possible for you to look so young?"

She shrugged. "I know not, save to tell you that, in my time, we have many 'oils,' like the one you spread upon me last night, and these seem to keep us in our youth. Then, too, the living is much easier in my century. Our homes are very well heated against the long winters and cooled against the summer sun."

"So this is sometimes a cold place—'America'?"

" 'Tis, forsooth, so large a land, love, that it is, at once, both hot and cold."

He looked perplexed, and she, in turn, issued a light laugh.

"Well, 'tis quite cold in the part from which I come, for it's in the north." She rolled her eyes and issued a weary cluck. "My Norse ancestors would not have it any other way, of course."

"So you live in longhouses there?"

"Oh, *neinn*. I have what is called an 'apartment.' 'Tis hard to explain, but it is like a small portion of a very large and tall house in which many people live."

"Many?"

"Hundreds sometimes."

"It must be enormous then."

"Ja. Much more so than a warship, for instance."

His eyes widened with amazement. "This century sounds as though 'tis very desirable, indeed."

She nodded, feeling for the first time sorry at his fate of being born so early in history. Here, but by the grace of God, could she have ended up as well. And the thought of having never known such luxuries as running water and contraceptives—of having so little control over nature—made her feel terribly homesick once more.

"Pray, are you betrothed or wed in this time in which you live?" he asked gingerly, his tone telling her he would be shattered if she said yes to either of these.

She offered him a receptive smile. *"Neinn."*

"Good! Then I shall go with you to it when you return," he declared.

She was stunned at this suggestion. "Oh, *neinn*, Leif. Much as I might wish it could be so, I do not think it possible."

"Why not?"

"Well, first of all, I'm not even certain that *I* can find my way back to it. And, secondly, you would likely alter events, if you went there with me, and that could be very dangerous."

"Why?"

"Because I've been told that time is like . . ." She paused to search for an analogy he might understand. "Like a loosely woven cloak. If a stitch in any of the rows is dropped or cut, the whole garment may begin to come apart, making it so I, or someone of much greater import in the vast scheme of things, might never be born."

"I don't understand."

She shook her head. "Alas, neither do I, love. But 'tis crucial that we try to abide by this rule. Forsooth, I must even ask that you not tell anyone of my land or the ways in which life is different in my time, for such foreknowledge could change how the future unfolds."

He donned a wry smile. "You can rest assured I will not speak of it, my lady, for my brother will likely *kill* you, if he learns you are not a goddess."

She gave forth a nervous laugh. "Well, that's a good reason, too, isn't it?"

His smile became more compassionate, and he reached out and took one of her hands in his. "I think so."

"Will you . . . will you love me any less, now that I have told you the truth about me?"

He gazed into her eyes. "I know not. 'Tis all so hard to grasp, I'm afraid."

"*Ja.* I feel the same way. It has been nigh onto a week since I slipped into this time, and I still cannot believe it."

"One thing is certain though, my dear," he said after several seconds.

"And what is that?"

"We had better find that stone circle and get you out of our captain's hands before you say or do aught that will make him realize you are only human. For, if such should come to pass, I cannot promise that I will be able to save you. Many things provoke his anger, but deceptions seem to enrage him most, and yours is the greatest deception I have ever known!"

Chapter 15

Though Leif felt more certain of Dana's love for him than before, his dreams were filled with nightmarish images as he slept just outside the door of her tent. He could only conclude that, because her "slip" from her time had befallen her at this stone circle she spoke of, it was the product of some sort of Erse sorcery—which he'd been told was once very potent in this land.

But what diabolical mischief! Devising a way to hurl total strangers back ten centuries! There had been slaves from Erin upon his family's farmstead since his earliest memory, yet he'd never guessed they were capable of such spitefulness! And he had to admit that he found it very disturbing. In fact, there was no doubt in his mind now that, though Dana had sworn him to secrecy, he would have to find some way to warn his father of this magic, once he returned home.

As he lay mulling all of it over, he heard Dana calling out for him from within, and he instantly got out of his sleeping bag and went into the tent to see what she wanted.

"Ah, good, you're still there," she declared in greeting. "I was worried you wouldn't be."

He scowled at her strange words.

"Oh, sorry," she began again, returning to his language. "I just woke and did slip into speaking my own tongue."

He smiled as he crossed to her and sat down upon the bed. "Oh, *ja*. The 'language of the gods,' or so you wished to have me believe, when first I heard you use it."

She nodded and gave forth an embarrassed laugh. "But *neinn*. 'Tis merely the tongue of America."

"So Norse is not spoken in your land?"

"Well, *neinn*," she confessed. "We speak 'English.' It comes from the huge island to the east of here."

"Oh, *ja*. We Vikings journey there as well."

She smiled, her eyes suddenly filled with pride in her Norse ancestors. "I know you do."

He patted his lap, reciprocating her smile. "Pray, rest your head here, that I might stroke your lovely hair."

She obliged him, and he sat running his fingers over her crown. "There are some more questions I wish to ask you, Dana, before the sun comes up and my kinsmen begin to stir."

"All right."

"Well, if you come from America, what are you doing in Erin? Did you journey here to raid per chance?"

She laughed. *"Neinn.* Forsooth, 'tis, in the main, against the law of my century to go raiding."

"But why?"

"Because each land is a kind of kingdom unto itself, and we believe that its sovereignty must be defended by the rest of the earth's kingdoms." This was an oversimplification, of course. Dana knew very well that the world she'd left was filled with instances of one government infringing upon another. But, given how deadeningly early in the morning it was, this abridged answer was about all she could manage.

"Then how, pray, do your people amass their holdings?"

"By trading. The way you do in towns like Hedeby."

"And that is enough to sustain you all in every season?"

"So far, thank the Heavens. And we pray daily that this remains true."

He shook his head. "I cannot imagine a world without raiding. How is it possible, then, for your men to prove their strength and daring?"

"Oh, there are ways, believe me. We have games and competitions, such as your wrestling. And there are many branches of trade in which men can rise to the top and make pawns of all who work beneath them," she added bitterly. "But, to be just to your gender, I must admit that there are some women who do the same."

His eyes shone with intrigue. "Oh? And are you one of those?"

She smiled up at him. *"Neinn.* Much as I think my parents would have me be, I have shown little interest in aught but the Norse studies I told you of last night."

"Hmmm. Fancy a *female* devoting herself to such

matters. 'Tis like the work of our skalds in some ways, *ja?*"

"I suppose."

"I admire this," he declared, giving her head a couple of pats.

"Why, thank you, kind sire. Though you now know I'm not a goddess, I was hoping you would still revere me for something."

He lifted her chin so her gaze would meet his as he continued to stare down at her. "You have my *love,* Dana, and I believe that is far more important."

She swallowed dryly, amazed at how moved she felt in that instant.

He bent to punctuate this poignant declaration with a long kiss, and she, of course, did not resist him.

"You have mine, too, Leif," she replied, when he finally let them both come up for air. And the resoluteness with which she did so surprised even her.

She knew, in her heart, that she wasn't simply saying this in order to keep him loyal to her. She actually felt it. She was finally coming to the realization that, with him, she experienced a sense of wholeness she hadn't known with any other man.

"Why did you ask if I came here to raid? Did I look like a raider to you, when first you saw me at the friary?"

He laughed. *"Neinn.* You looked like a slip of a maiden with fire in her bag."

"Then why did you ask that just now?"

"Because I thought perhaps you did something which might have provoked the Erse at this circle of stones. For it is said that the magic of their forefathers is very strong indeed."

She nodded. *"Ja.* I think you are right about that, love. But, I swear to you that I do not recall doing aught to provoke *anyone.* All I know is that, since I was a child, I have had dreams about such a place and about the ancient priests of the Erse, the ones who came before the Christian sort."

"Dreams of them?"

"Ja."

"And what comes to pass in these?"

" 'Tis . . . 'tis embarrassing to tell, I'm afraid."

"Why?"

"Well, by cause of the fact that 'tis like what you and I did last night."

He raised an incredulous eyebrow. "The Erse priests made love to you?"

"Not the priests, but a villager, I think. And he did so upon some sort of altar."

Leif drew an audible breath in through his teeth, as though in sympathy. "Before the priests?"

"Ja. Alas, love, I would rather not speak of it further."

"I understand," he whispered, again stroking her hair. " 'Tis odd though, is it not, having the same dream for that many years? And one so far removed from your own time."

She nodded.

"Does it frighten you, what happens in it? Or does it simply shame you?"

"Oh, both, I suppose. But, verily, the most fearsome part is that I am killed in the dream."

"Killed?"

"Ja. By one of the priests."

"But why?"

"I'm not certain. But I do not think it by cause of any offense. I simply believe they mean to sacrifice me to one of their gods."

"Hmmm. Then this dream must indeed take place in an ancient time, if 'tis before Christians arose on these shores."

"Ja. 'Tis likely some past life of mine come back to haunt me for some reason."

He knit his brow. "A past life? You mean to say the people of your time live more than once?"

A subtle smile pulled at one corner of her lips. "I don't know. There are many who think it possible."

"Odin help us! 'Tis difficult enough earning one's way into *Valhöll once,* without having to do so many times!"

She smiled more fully and gave his left hand a squeeze. "Well, according to your faith, there are two ways to such immortality, are there not? The first through courage in battle and the second through devotion in love. And I would have you choose the latter course with the loyalty you shall be called upon to show me until I can find my way back to my own time."

To her surprise, he did not return her smile, but looked suddenly sullen, as though the weight of the world had been lowered onto his shoulders.

"What is it, love?" she inquired, her voice barely audible.

" 'Tis simply that you know not what you ask.

While drink makes our captain dull-witted each night, you must never forget that he is perilously sharp in the light of day and 'tis crucial you do *nothing* that might cause him to suspect you are aught but the goddess you claimed."

She sat up slowly. "Well, of course, I won't. I realize my life hangs upon it."

He hugged her to him, as though about to see her off to a war. "Oh, Heaven help me . . . the feel of you," he murmured, his tone quite helpless. Then, seeming to steel himself, he pulled away from her and got off the bed. "I must go now, before we're found together this way."

"But—"

He shushed her. *"Neinn.* Not another word, I pray thee. By day you must *be* the deity you led us all to believe you were, and I must play the part of second in command. Not one look or sigh can be allowed to betray our feelings for one another."

She gulped and sat more upright against the headboard. "All right."

"Your raiment. 'Tis likely laundered by now, so I shall fetch it for you. I think it best you wear it as we travel, since that golden gown might draw Ersemen to us with the sun shining upon it."

"Very well," she replied, feeling heartbroken all over again at having him resume such a detached air.

Don't cut me off this way, part of her wanted to plead. To her credit, however, she managed to stay silent. Trying desperately to tell herself that he was only acting distant in order to protect her, she simply bit her lip.

"The map," he said, beginning to scan the tent for it.

"Map?" she repeated numbly.

He clucked with impatience. *"Ja.* The one you were showing me last night. The one you think leads to the circle of stones."

"On the table."

He rushed over to it and stashed it in his belt-strap. Then he turned to leave.

"Leif?" she whispered after him.

He scowled over at her.

"What if we find the stone circle today? What if this is the last of our time alone together?"

His voice was edged with bitterness. " 'Tis *you* who wish to leave here and return to your own time."

"Ja. I do," she conceded. "But how shall I say good-bye to you? How can I tell you I love you, if others be about when I depart?"

"I suppose I will know you mean to say these things," he retorted, his resentment still thinly veiled.

"Neinn. We need a sign, you and I. We need a way to speak to one another without anyone hearing."

"Dana," he beseeched in a hiss. "I must return to my tent at once. I can hear my kinsmen starting to wake!"

"I've got it," she declared, moving toward the foot of the bed and hauling its linens along with her. "I shall wink at you. I shall close one eye thus, and, in this way, you shall understand what I am saying."

"By the gods, woman, *very well,"* he snarled. "I shall do the same then, if 'twill satisfy thee!"

"Good," she replied. But he was already gone. She

could hear his heavy footfalls in the sand as he trudged off in the direction of his own shelter. And, again, as always seemed to happen when they parted company, she was filled with an awful sadness.

Painfully familiar with the symptoms of Booth's hangovers, Leif tried to be as quiet as possible as he entered his tent a few minutes later. He was hoping he'd find his sibling still asleep, but to no avail. The poor devil's eyes were wide open, where he still lay, trussed at his wrists and ankles, upon the bed.

"Untie me, ye bastard," he growled. "I have been awake for half an hour, awaiting your return! So where in *Hel* have you been?"

Leif hurried over to the bed and began at once to free him. "I . . . I was seeing to the Goddess's raiment, Captain. It needed laundering, and I asked also that she provide us with a map to the stone circle she seeks. Which, I am glad to tell, she did."

When Leif finished untrussing his brother, he withdrew the colorful pamphlet from his belt-strap and tossed it onto Booth's lap.

The commander sat up slowly and took hold of it. But, rather than beginning to study the thing, he pressed it to his forehead with a moan.

"By Thunder, she burnt me last night, didn't she? That witch!"

"Keep your voice down! She's just a few paces away in your tent, remember? Do you truly wish to anger her afresh?"

" 'Anger' her? Fie, I would tear her limb from

limb—if I thought for a moment it would not cause her to bring the full wrath of *Asgardhr* down upon us!"

Leif sat on the end of the bed, doing his best to douse his brother's fuming with his own coolheaded manner. "But you suffered another of your spells last night. You attacked me. So what was she to do, pray?"

"That is precisely it. I attacked *you,* not that she-wolf! So what possible call did she have to set me afire?"

"She thought you would kill me. She was merely coming to my defense, as she surely would yours, had you been in my stead."

Booth's expression fell until he was regarding Leif through hooded and very skeptical-looking eyes. "I think not, little brother. I honestly think not."

"But why? She likes you well enough, I wager. 'Tis just that you scare her a bit."

Booth gave forth a caustic laugh. "And repulse her even more."

"Whatever makes you say that?"

Booth rolled his eyes. "Did you not see what came to pass betwixt us, when I crossed to kiss her in my tent? Why, she struck the side of my neck with such a blow that it caused me to drop right where I stood! And this I think doth not bode well for me as a potential suitor, you dimwit!"

Leif bit the inside of his cheek and let his gaze fall, in an effort to keep his amusement at this sarcasm from showing. "Very well, then. Perhaps 'twould be best if we bring both of our tents along on the journey to the stone circle, so you won't have to share your quarters with her again, Captain."

"And seem to be rebuffed by her before my crew? Never!"

"Well then, begin the evenings in her company. Appear to retire with her to your tent after supper. Then sneak off to mine, once darkness falls. Our men will be not one wit the wiser."

Booth was silent for several seconds, as though pondering this suggestion. "Ah, to the nether regions with her! Let her make her way to these damnable stones on her own! I've no wish to go searching for them, and I'll not let you or any of my men do so either."

It was Leif who fell silent now. Though he was no more enthused than his brother about running the risks of such overland travel, he knew Dana couldn't keep up her precarious ruse forever. Sooner or later, Booth or someone else in the crew was sure to see through her.

"Captain, I do entreat you to reconsider," he began again evenly. "For she has confided in me that she seeks these stones in order to return to *Asgardhr*. And, once she finds her way back to it, there is no further danger of her snubbing you before the others. You will be safely rid of her, and it cannot be said that she refused you. Rather it will be believed that she sought only to return to her own realm, having had her little adventure among us."

Issuing another moan, Booth dropped the map, clapped his hands to his ears, and slid back down to a reclining position. "And, if I don't take her there, but rather allow you and your freemen to do so, it might also appear as though she has rejected me."

"Um . . . *ja,*" Leif hesitantly agreed. While there was

nothing he would have liked better than being entrusted with transporting Dana on his own, his higher duty to his brother forced him to concur.

"Ah, fie. Very well," Booth said through clenched teeth after several seconds. "But see to it our horses carry twice the ration of mead we would need for a few nights. I shall not survive this ridiculous quest without it!"

Leif's first impulse was to deliver Dana's warning that spirited drink might be the cause of Booth's berserker episodes. He stopped himself, however. Given that his brother's states of drunken senselessness would likely afford him the only privacy he might have with Dana while on this pilgrimage, he knew better than to offer one word of argument now.

Chapter 16

After Leif left, Dana seized her solitude in order to take pictures of the Viking artifacts that surrounded her. Finding her camera in the depths of her purse, she crept out of Booth's tent and hurried down to the bay to photograph the longships, before the camp's occupants woke and could spot her doing so.

The dawn's light was marginal at best, and she couldn't be certain that any of the shots she took would turn out well. But, knowing that this would be her only opportunity to get the vessels on film, without being seen by their curious crews in the process, she realized it simply had to be done.

Upon her return to the tent, she replaced her telescopic lens with the wide-angle variety; and, now using a flash, she took several pictures of Booth's carved headboard, his sea chest, its contents, and the makeshift table, with the soapstone oil lamp that rested upon it.

Then, with this photographic evidence procured, she stowed her camera back in her purse and proceeded to make a lengthy entry in her research note-book. She listed everything she could remember about the feast the Vikings had given in her honor and all that Leif had told her about the berserker tradition.

It had occurred to her, while he was elaborating on this the night before, to try to get it on tape surrepti-tiously. She'd been rather angry with herself at the time, in fact, for not doing so. But, now that she'd learned this would have been an impossibility, since he'd intercepted her recorder hours earlier, she allayed herself with the realization that she'd probably gath-ered as much audio and visual proof of her slip into Viking times as her limited opportunities had permit-ted.

And, perhaps, if she and Leif could steal a bit more time alone together, she might be able to persuade him to describe his family's longhouse and farmstead in detail, so she could capture that on tape. In view of the fact that he'd already discovered the recorder could do him no harm, she would probably find him agreeable.

He returned from Booth's tent half an hour after leaving her; and, as promised, he gave her back her now-laundered jeans and sweat shirt. But, as they were preparing to depart in search of the stone circle a short time later, trouble struck once more.

The stallion, which Dana was given to ride, seemed to sense her uneasiness with horses, and the beast began rearing each time she attempted to climb into the saddle. Naturally, the more the creature acted up, the more Dana was made to look like a bumbling, anxiety-ridden fool. And, after her second pratfall, Leif was again forced to come to her rescue.

"What is the matter?" he asked under his breath. He was being careful to keep his back to Booth in those seconds, so as to prevent his brother from witnessing any more of the "goddess's" vulnerability than he already had.

"I'm afraid of horses," she confessed in a whisper.

He scowled. "Well, could ye not have told me as much before now, so that our men could have built you a wain in which to ride?"

"I . . . I just thought I had conquered it, Leif. I thought, since this is the only way for me to get back to the circle, I would somehow find the mettle to ride. But, alas, I haven't. I was thrown from a horse as a child, and I've never had a way with them since."

"My dear lady, *every* youngster is thrown sooner or later, and most manage to master riding none the less."

She lowered her voice all the more. *"Ja.* Perhaps in your times, but not mine, forsooth. We no longer use horses for travel for the most part."

"But how can this be?"

At this point in their heated, if hushed, exchange, Dana couldn't help noticing that virtually every eye in the camp had fixed upon them. She, therefore, tried to offer the gathering a smile before returning her gaze to Leif. "Can you truly believe this is the best of times for me to be trying to answer that?" she queried out of the side of her mouth.

Fortunately, Leif seemed to become aware of their silent audience as well, and, without saying anything more to Dana, he walked off to the front of their caravan to have a word with Booth.

The captain, looking more surly than ever in his hung-over state, glowered as his brother spoke to him in low tones. Then, after several seconds, he snorted and waved Leif off, as though giving his consent to whatever had been requested.

To Dana's relief, the younger Norseman returned to her and announced that she would be riding with him on his steed. So, she and her overloaded handbag were mounted with Leif upon the poor creature minutes later.

"Is there aught *else* you fear, pray?" Leif snapped, as they finally began riding out of the camp. "I think you should give me the entire list, before my brother comes to suspect us both of some manner of conspiracy!"

The "list" seemed endless, now that Dana thought about it. She feared everything from field mice to drive-by shootings. But, given Leif's peevishness at present, she'd be damned if she'd fuel his apparent suspicion that she was some sort of sissy!

She might not have been a goddess, as she'd originally led him to believe, and she'd obviously had very little firsthand experience with the pitfalls of day-to-day life in the tenth century. But these shortcomings certainly didn't seem cause enough for him to start treating her like a second-class citizen!

"There's naught else," she replied in a hiss near his ear. She somehow sensed in that instant, however, that it was not so much the inconvenience she was causing him, as his resentment of her decision to return to her own time, that was making him act this way.

* * *

By late afternoon, Leif and Booth weren't the only ones who seemed annoyed with having to make this pilgrimage on Dana's account. Indeed, after over ten hours of journeying in search of a circle of stones, which Dana had initially estimated was no more than half a day's ride from their base-camp, even the Viking freemen seemed irritated.

It hadn't helped, of course, that they'd been forced to outride a pack of Erse archers around midday and that one of their horses had been unfortunate enough to take an arrow in its right thigh. That had certainly put everyone on edge. But now, as sunset approached and the tired and hungry band faced the prospect of having to set up camp deep within enemy territory, they were becoming more vocal about their disgruntlement.

"By Thunder, I shall strangle her if she comes too near!" Booth whispered to Leif, as they again stopped to water their horses. "So *you* take her aside and tell her we don't believe we will find this accursed circle she speaks of and we now wish to return to our base."

"But I . . . I can't, Captain."

"Why not?"

"Well, she claims 'tis at *Asgardhr's* bidding that she seeks this place, and who am I—verily, who are any of us?—to counter such a will?"

Booth's eyes narrowed to two venomous slits, and he seized Leif by the tie of his cape. "Go and *try,*" he ordered in a growl, his expression saying that he was dangerously close to having another of his fits.

"Very well," Leif retorted, jerking out of his grasp. "Very well, indeed. But, if aught should betide me by cause of this, brother, let it be on your head!" he concluded, shaking a finger at him.

Fortunately for all concerned, Leif managed to compose himself by the time he reached Dana, where she was reclining in the shade of a nearby oak tree.

"I crave a word with thee, my lady," he declared, reaching down and extending a hand to help her to her feet. "Away from here, you understand," he added, trying even harder to sweeten his tone.

She looked skeptical; but, to his relief, she did allow him to aid her in rising.

"What is it?" she asked in a barely audible voice, as they began walking away from the others.

"This stone circle of yours is not turning up, and Booth is, naturally, growing impatient."

"Well, what do you mean to say? Doth he wish to return to your camp?"

"Precisely."

"But we can't! I'll never get back to my own time without the circle. I'm convinced of it now."

"So? You will stay with us then."

"Leif, we have erenow discussed all of this. I can't stay here!"

"But why not?"

"Because I belong in my own century, of course. I have parents and siblings and friends there, and 'twould not be fair for me to simply vanish from their lives without making every effort to get back to them."

He suddenly stopped walking. Then, reaching out and taking hold of her hand, he turned her to face him.

"But you've no betrothed there. You have told me as much. And, even with all of the wondrous contrivances, which you claim make life so much easier in your time, I should not think it any more joyful without that kind of love and companionship."

Dana bit her lower lip at this. Then she let her gaze fall, as the unavoidable truth of his words began to sink in for her.

Easier, yes. The twentieth century was indisputably that when compared to these ancient times. But happier? . . . Well, she would have been a fool to make such a declaration.

"Prithee, love," he went on in the most entreating manner he could seem to muster. "Prithee, understand how perilous it is for all of us out here in this foreign wilderness. We could perish at any time, should another band of Ersemen descend upon us. And, in spite of your good intentions, we both know that there is naught your fiery rain or hand-to-hand combat could do to save us then."

Dana was silent for a few seconds more, her chin beginning to quiver with the realization that her map was proving of no use now and that she would be continuing to put so many lives at stake, if she insisted upon searching for the circle much longer.

"How much more time will Booth give me in this?"

Leif exhaled a weary breath. "I know not. Another day, perhaps. But likely no more."

Her eyes started to well with tears, and she kept her face directed downward. The prospect of never seeing her family again was beginning to have its full impact upon her and she suddenly felt as though she were being torn apart. But, given these feelings, how could she go on asking Leif and his fellow Norsemen to continue running the risk of not being able to return to *their* kin?

"Another day, you say?" she queried, reaching up to blot her eyes with the cuff of her sweat shirt.

He nodded.

"Pray, go and tell your captain, then, that I am amenable to this."

Leif did so, and, to his relief, Booth grudgingly granted Dana an additional twenty-four hours.

She seemed so glum throughout their supper of dried fish and bread, however, that Leif took her aside once more and offered to help her continue searching for the stone circle yet that very night.

Her mouth dropped open and she again became tearful. "But 'twould be so dangerous for you. Indeed for us both, Leif, going out on our own in the darkness."

"Oh? And can you honestly think it any safer by day, with six more of us along?"

"Neinn. I suppose not."

"Well, there you have it. 'Tis not so crazed a suggestion then."

She turned more fully to him, her eyes glistening as they locked upon his. "But you don't even want me to find the circle. You have made it plain from the first that you wish to have me stay in this time with you."

His voice quavered with emotion as he spoke again. "But I have also made it plain that I love you," he murmured, "and I would rather you go back to what pleases you than stay where you will be miserable and endangered."

She choked up at this, and she realized that, no matter how many men she dated in the twentieth century, she would never, ever find one who would care enough to be willing to place himself in such jeopardy for her.

"I wish to Heaven I could hug you right now," she exclaimed in a whisper.

A trace of a smile played upon his lips, and he shook his head. *"Neinn.* You wouldn't be that foolish with the others watching."

She dropped her gaze to her feet. *"Neinn."*

"But, later. When I have persuaded Booth to let us go and make the most of the time remaining to us on this quest, we can do a great deal more than hug, if you wish."

"Indeed I do," she answered in a tremulous voice, her eyes making love with his, as they continued to stand there beside the brook next to which the freemen had staked their tents. And, for the first time, Dana truly began to believe that her push to get back to her modern-day life might be a mistake.

By the light of the full moon, Leif and Dana rode due northwest for what she guessed to be half an hour or so. Directing their horse along the edges of the woods they passed en route, Leif managed to keep them in the shadows most of the way; and, fortunately, they did not come upon any forts or settlements from which the Erse could catch sight of them.

Dana had borrowed one of the freemen's heavy capes to keep her warm in the night air, and, after closing it more tightly about her, she returned both of her arms to Leif's waist as she sat behind him on his steed.

"Are you certain there was naught distinctive about the land upon which this stone circle was built?"

Dana leaned farther forward and spoke into his ear. *"Neinn.* Nothing, as I've told you. 'Twas neither on particularly high nor low land, as I recall. And, alas, the only things that might help me spot it are of my own century. There was what we call a 'highway' very nearby and a 'reception building.' But these could not possibly be here now."

"You are not making this easy for me, you know, Dana."

She hugged him more tightly and pressed the side of her head to his back. "I would if I could, love."

"You said this morning that your people no longer travel by mount much."

"Right."

"Pray, how is this possible? What could you use in a horse's stead?"

"Oh, verily, I should not be telling you such things, Leif. Your learning of them could unravel the order of time and events, as I explained last night."

His tone was resentful when he spoke again. "I have kept your most important secret so far, have I not?"

"Well, *ja.* Of course. 'Tis just that you must promise me you will not dwell upon the inventions I tell you of. Prithee, swear that my talk of them will simply slip into one of your ears and out the other."

He chuckled at this saying, apparently never having heard it. "I swear so."

"All right, then." She began again hesitantly, "We have what you might call 'wains.' You know, with four wheels?"

"Ja."

"Only they need no horses to pull them. They are enclosed. Rather like covered wagons, and they transport people and things with a power that is borne within them."

Dana clucked, knowing she wasn't doing a very good job of explaining what a car was, but feeling unable to be more specific, given her limited command of Old Norse and his meager understanding of anything beyond wind and fire power.

He issued a skeptical "humph" and shook his head.

"Well, believe me, it is so. Of course, 'tis a very advanced thing, the 'car.' Even in my time, it has been known to us for little more than a century. And, just as a horse needs hay and oats for energy, the 'car' needs a fuel we call 'gasoline.' "

"It eats this?"

"In a manner of speaking. It 'burns' it, more precisely."

"And where do you find such fuel?"

"Far down in the ground."

"You must dig for it?"

"Oh, *ja*. Very deeply, in fact."

"Is that not a great deal of work?"

"Indeed."

"Then in what way are these 'cars' better than mounts?"

"Well, they are much faster, to start with."

"I can think of nothing more fleet of foot than a horse, my dear."

"That is because you have not ridden in a 'car.' But, since you are pressing on this subject, I will tell you that a car can go many times farther in an hour than the average horse."

"How many times farther?"

She shrugged. "Thirteen maybe."

"Impossible!"

"Neinn. Not in my century."

He was silent for several seconds, obviously trying to grasp what she'd just said. *"Ja,* well, per chance it *is* far better than the present, this time of yours."

"But maybe not in every way," she conceded.

There was an intrigued rise to his voice. "Oh?"

"Ja. For, you see, they have cut down nearly all of Erin's woods."

"Who has? Not the Erse surely!"

"Well, *neinn.* 'Twas more by cause of the English. You know, the people on the island to the east of here, who gave us our language?"

"But why would they want to do such a thing?"

"To clear land for farming, I suppose. For Erin will one day run out of space for crops, as you have in Norway."

"Hmm. Enterprising traders, these 'English.' Taking one people's trees and giving another their tongue! No doubt you 'Americans' are more fond of them than the Erse."

"How true!"

"But what of the creatures of these woods? The deer and the birds and such? What became of them?"

"Many of them perished, I am sorry to tell."

"So, the Erse live solely upon livestock and fish in your century?"

"*Ja.* They seem to, as do most of us in other lands. But I was told that the people of Erin can eat nothing from the Irish Sea in my time."

"The what?"

"Oh, I forgot. That name means naught to you, does it? The sea next to the friary where you found me."

"What came to pass? Pray, do not tell me the 'English' claimed all of the fish along with the trees!"

"Well, *ja.* Sadly, they did, after a fashion."

"But how is this possible?"

"Umm. . . . 'Tis very hard to explain, forsooth."

"Dana," he suddenly snarled, "if you say that to me one more time, I swear I shall be moved to thresh you!"

"Well, then," she began with a gulp, "let me try to put it into your words. You see, in my century, we have a special, yet very deadly, sort of force, which lights and cools our homes and cooks our food. 'Tis called 'electricity,' and the creation of it involves a thing we've named 'nuclear power.' And this nuclear power, if spilt into the bodies of water or land near which 'tis stored, can poison them for many, many thousands of years."

"And these infernal 'English' spilt such into Erin's sea?" he inquired, his voice growing louder with his obvious ire.

"Ja. But 'twas not done by design, mind. It was an accident, a 'nuclear' accident."

" 'Twas an outrage, more rightly," he declared through clenched teeth, "for many is the time I have bathed in those warm aqua waters, and my heart grows sick to think they could ever be so tainted! I ask thee, what manner of poison could spread so far and wide? . . . Verily, it sounds to be a deplorable time, this century to which you wish to return!"

Dana fell silent, unable to think of a thing to say that might counter this. For the first time in her life, she really understood how insane it was to simply accept such atrocious mishaps as being unavoidable; and, all at once, she had to agree with Leif's conclusion. Try as modern man might to flatter himself regarding his accomplishments, nineteen hundred and ninety-four was not really so rich a time in which to live. And, perhaps, trading such conveniences as cars and microwave ovens for clean water, and the gorgeous ivy-covered forests through which Dana and the Norsemen had been traveling all day, was truly the rational course.

She was silent for a moment or two longer, wistfully contemplating all of this, when Leif spoke again. "Perhaps, if you do go back to this time of yours, your first task should be seeing that all of these 'English' are put to death!"

She couldn't help laughing under her breath. "Oh, Leif. I wish it were that simple. But, alas, the English are not the only ones having such accidents. In very sooth, the leaders of my own land are to blame for much of the same kind of damage. To say nothing of the kingdoms far to the northeast of here. By troth, nearly every sovereignty I can call to mind is gradually poisoning its people in one way or another."

"Well, there's an end to it, then," he growled, suddenly reining back on their horse.

"What?"

"We are done searching for this damnable 'circle' of yours. I love you far too much to return you to such a depraved time, and I'll hear naught more about it!" With that, he steered the stallion about and they began heading back in the direction from which they'd come.

"Oh, *neinn*, Leif, you misunderstood," she blurted out anxiously. "I said we were being poisoned *gradually*. I am not likely to die from it, if I go back to my century. And, to my people's credit, we are taking some measures to see such damage prevented. Even, in some cases, repaired. . . . Pray, stop," she beseeched, as the horse continued to gallop.

Heaving a thoroughly exasperated sigh, Leif again slowed the mount. "But we should head back to the others now, in any case, my dear, for I gave Booth my word we would take no longer than an hour or two for this trip. And, after that time, he will likely grow concerned and come looking for us."

"All right then, if we must," she replied with a discouraged sigh. "But, pray, at least agree to take us to those far woods," she continued, pointing across the adjacent clearing, "so that we might scan new ground en route. For we now know the stone circle is not to be found along the path we've just taken."

Exhaling loudly, Leif obliged this request, directing the horse into the moonlit field and through the woods on its other side. Then, when they reached the far edge of them, he caused the stallion to turn and begin heading southeast once more.

"Thank you," Dana whispered, again leaning forward and speaking into his ear.

"Humph! Choosing such a century over staying with me. I should push you from this steed, woman, and strand you here!"

"Oh, but you won't," she cooed, nibbling affectionately upon the side of his neck, "for we haven't yet made love, as we agreed we would while away tonight."

A part of Leif wanted to bristle at this presumptuous coquettishness. But another—very aroused by the fact that she was neither the cowering slave girl nor the inexperienced Norse maiden he'd likely be stuck with under any other circumstances—would not have dreamed of doing anything now that would make her less than receptive to the carnal suggestions he had in mind. In fact, if she could only be persuaded to do to certain other parts of him what she had just done to his neck, he felt sure he would end the evening deeply satisfied.

Dana couldn't help smiling to herself as the horse was once again brought to a tellingly slow pace. "Here?" she asked.

He shrugged, then turned his profile to her, revealing a roguish grin. "Why not? 'Tis as good a spot as any for what we have in mind."

She swallowed apprehensively, suddenly realizing that, in spite of her many years of dating, she'd never before made love outdoors. And, though there was probably no one within miles of them, she couldn't help feeling rather self-conscious at the prospect of it.

Before she could fret about this any further, however, Leif reined them to a halt, got down from the stallion, and reached up to help her out of the saddle as well.

"Come along," he murmured, kissing the back of her hand. "We've a millennium to bridge once more."

In view of all he'd done for her, the good faith he'd shown in running the risk of riding this far afield alone in search of the stone circle, she knew she could hardly refuse him now. So, swallowing her misgivings, she lifted herself from the horse, brought both legs around to the right side of the animal, and dropped into Leif's upraised hands.

His long fingers nearly encircled her slim waist, and, as her feet touched the ground, his lips were already upon hers—kissing her with such abandon that it was almost frightening.

The stallion whinnied a complaint and stepped away, as Leif's passionate pressure upon Dana pushed her farther and farther into the creature's side.

The Norseman responded with a soft laugh. "He wants no part of this, I wager," he said, finally ending their kiss. "And that is wise, for he is likely more tame than you and I are about to be. I shall tie him to a tree and return anon," he pledged in a seductive whisper, slowly relinquishing his hold upon her and stepping forward to lead the mount away.

"*Ja,*" Dana mumbled, trying to catch her breath and regain her footing after their electrifying exchange.

As she gazed out at the clearing that lay beside them in those seconds, she noticed that a mass of fog was settling upon it. And, though she feared it might hamper their trip back to the others if it proved too widespread, she was strangely grateful for its cloaking now. It would, no doubt, soften the blow of having to disrobe right out in the open.

"Fog," she noted, pointing to the field, when Leif finally returned to her.

He cast a hasty eye over it, only to turn back to her and bury his devouring lips and tongue in the flesh of her throat. This time, there was no polite fingering of her breasts, none of the courteous tentativeness of the night before. Rather, his hands closed over her chest with a possessiveness that was unmistakable.

"By Thunder, teach me of your advanced century now, my sweet," he murmured, sliding one of his rough, unshaven cheeks up the side of her face. "Surely, in the course of one thousand years, you ladies have learned a thing or two more about bringing pleasure to a man."

Though she found his suddenly wolfish tone exciting, Dana had to admit to herself that this contrast to the way he'd been the night before truly surprised her.

"Leif?" she queried, her voice rising more with disbelief than questioning.

He didn't pull away, but kept his mouth pressed to her flesh, softly biting and lapping at her neck in turn. "What?"

"You're so different this evening."

"You mean from when I still believed you were a goddess?"

"Ja."

"Well, is it not better now that we can forgo the niceties and simply be two mortals rolling around in the grass? I have always felt that worrying about manners reins passion too greatly, haven't you?" he asked, clenching his teeth and suddenly pushing down upon the waist of her jeans with such force that her posterior began to burn from the chafing of the material.

"Neinn. They 'unzip,' you see? In front," she quavered, beginning to wonder if she'd made a mistake in agreeing to ride off to the middle of nowhere with him. They had, after all, only known each other for a couple of days, and he'd been so gentlemanly until now, that she simply wouldn't have guessed he possessed such a fiery side.

"Well, pray, see to it at once," he ordered from somewhere deep in his throat, "for I grow impatient with waiting for what I crave!"

Fearful that he'd do the jeans irreparable damage if she didn't act quickly, she reached down and opened them to him with trembling fingers.

In a heartbeat, his right hand was inside them—his stout digits finding their way up into her with a stinging dryness that made her poor recesses grow wet in their own defense.

She groaned and threw her head back in those seconds, the pain and pleasure of it making her far too weak in the knees to go on standing.

"I . . . I can't do this," she stammered breathlessly.

"You can and you shall," he declared, nipping at the lobe of her right ear, as his fingers continued their feverish movement far below. "I've hazarded far too much to let you slip back into your own time without making love to me at least once more!"

"*Neinn.* I meant I can't do this standing any longer. Prithee, might we lie down?"

He issued a husky laugh. "Oh, but of course, my dear."

With the smoothness and speed of the most practiced playboy, he slipped his hand from her jeans and swept her up in his arms. Then, carrying her several yards into the adjacent field, he set her down in the thick grass with amazing gentleness.

This was terribly short-lived, however. As soon as he was reclining as well, he began kissing her with a delving fierceness that said her mouth was hardly the *only* orifice he wished to explore.

"Leif, you're scaring me," she admitted in a wavering voice, when he finally lifted his lips from hers.

He smiled and tossed back the strands of long blond hair that had fallen into his eyes. "Why? Because I'm no longer treating you as a goddess? Ah, what rubbish! I am never at my best as a lover when on my best behavior. We're sure to have much more sport and merriment together as equals. . . . Here," he began again, a mischievous look in his eyes, "let me show you what I mean."

Before she could object, he raised her sweat shirt to the level of her shoulders and began blowing raspberries into her bared stomach.

It tickled unbearably, and she started squirming beneath him, laughing until her eyes watered. "Lord, stop it! Stop," she exclaimed. "You've lost your mind, hauling me all the way out here to do that!"

He frowned. "Indeed. You are right. This is not at all the response I wished to evoke from you. My mouth is much too high up. I can see that now. Forsooth, I think I meant to do something to you *here,*" he declared, sliding all the way down to her lap and pushing her jeans down with him.

He was correct in this assessment, for, an instant later, she was moaning with ecstasy as his fingers opened her lower lips to his eager tongue and teeth.

She'd never experienced anything like it! It was as if one hundred alternating sensations were overloading her brain! His bristly chin scratched the intimate folds of her, while his tongue was deftly stroking some pleasure point hidden deeply within.

She whimpered a bit at the overwhelming feel of it. But, when she tried to pull away, she discovered that his hands had slipped beneath her and were holding her in place. What was more, they were actually raising this secret part of her up to his rapacious mouth.

"Ah, let me taste the honey I have set astir in you," he whispered up to her, during his only pause in this lusty act. And, just hearing this and the hunger with which it was spoken, made Dana grow limp all over again.

"Oh, stop! I pray thee, *stop,*" she pleaded after several seconds more. His frenzied motions had already caused her to climax, and she found that the only thing she wanted now was an actual coupling with him.

"Only if you promise to do the same to me," he replied, bending down once more and letting his teeth close slowly over the quivering love knob that she knew had grown swollen with his merciless attentions to it.

"*Ja. Ja.* You have my word," she gasped.

At this, his mouth dropped open and he pressed a soothing kiss to that same spot.

"Ah, Jesus," she exclaimed in English, as he finally let her ease away from him and sit up. "I suppose this is some sort of Viking version of 'angry sex'!"

"What?" he asked with a waggish smirk. "I think you have slipped into speaking your language again."

" 'Tis nothing," she replied, arching her bottom skyward and pulling her jeans and panties back up to her waist. "I was merely commenting on your prowess as a lover."

He looked very pleased to hear this. "Well then, my dear, do give me this opportunity to do the same for you," he retorted, rolling onto his back and lowering his own trousers with shameless rapidity.

Though she didn't want to embarrass him by staring, she couldn't help letting her eyes lock upon his huge erection. It seemed she hadn't gotten as good a look at it in the darkened tent the night before as in the bright moonlight of this moment; and she had to admit to herself that it held a fascination for her.

She wasn't sure whether the Vikings usually circumcised their sons, but this particular male hadn't been—and that, doubtless, was contributing to his surprisingly large size.

"Come now, love," he prompted playfully, when her eyes remained fixed upon his male organ for several seconds more. "Don't tell me the men of your time no longer have such appendages!"

She laughed under her breath, her cheeks warming at being caught gawking. "Oh, *ja*. Of course they do. Else how could we beget children?"

"I know not. I'm simply glad to hear that the 'English' have not devised some way to snatch up all of these as well!"

She chuckled again, then pursed her lips at realizing what a dry wit this primitive man possessed.

The truth was that, given the breakthroughs in reproductive technology in the 1990's, she wasn't altogether sure such organs really were necessary to the furtherance of humankind anymore. But, again, she knew this wasn't information she should be disclosing, so she kept it to herself.

More importantly, this was hardly the time to be slipping into thoughts of such technicalities. This dear and very sexy man had just laid himself open—and naked—to her, and she knew her only urge should now be to give him some of the pleasure he had, so repeatedly, given her.

Without further delay, therefore, she slipped on top of him and, with a provocative purr, sat up and removed her cape.

"Lift your head," she directed in her most gracious tone.

He knit his brow in confusion.

"A pillow," she explained, bunching the cloak up in her hands.

He smiled. "Oh."

As he raised himself from the ground an instant later, she slipped the cushioning garment under his neck and head, and he gave forth such a satisfied sigh

Ashland Price

that she felt certain she was about to perform loveplay for her most appreciative recipient yet!

"Such a sacrifice, my lady! The warmth of a cloak exchanged merely to cradle my head," he noted with an admiring grin.

She smiled as well. " 'Tis the least I could do."

He arched a sportive brow at her. "Oh, *ja?* And what, pray, would be the most?"

He'd been right about them having more fun together on this "equal" basis. Indeed, his amorousness was proving intoxicating to her now. She was positively giddy, in fact, as she pulled off her sweat shirt and let the chill of the evening air fall over her. For the first time since her freshman year in college, she felt as though she could truly throw inhibition to the winds.

Leif was so young and impetuous, so full of an untamed energy she hadn't known in any of the older men she'd dated, that she felt very youthful and adventurous again, too. It was almost as though he had led her mind back to a time before she had suffered even one of her heartbreaks, and she was, all at once, infinitely grateful to him for it.

The way he looked at her now, the sparkle in his eyes that said he found her so beautiful, so exciting, as she unfastened the front of her bra and let her breasts spill forward to merge with his own ample chest—all of it made her believe that she was one of the most desirable women in the world and that those who'd jilted her through the years had been crazy for doing so.

She was finally realizing that Leif hadn't fallen in love with her simply because he believed she was a goddess. He'd done so because he found her attractive. Because he liked the look, the feel, the scent of her— and would probably always crave them.

It seemed impossible to her. An incredible dream come true. Yet, in light of her astonishing slip backward through ten centuries, who was she to question what was possible and what wasn't?

She leaned forward and pressed a tiny rosebud of a kiss to his lips. Then, with a vamp's laugh, she threw her head back and gave her blond mane a fetching shake.

With a longing groan, Leif reached up and ran his hands over the sides of her breasts. But, wagging a finger at him, Dana eased them out of his grasp and slid down to caress his manhood with them.

He watched as she slipped the erection into her cleavage and closed her bosoms firmly about it. Then, as she began rubbing slowly up and down over him, her eyes rising to lock upon his with each forward surge, he issued a helpless sigh and let his head fall back upon his makeshift pillow.

"That's it, my darling," he encouraged in a murmur. "That strange century of yours is starting to look better to me all the time. But, whate'er else you do, pray *don't* be gentle!"

Teeth, she realized in that instant. He'd seemed quite fond of using his on her—having nibbled every part of her in the past couple of days, from her ear lobes to certain unmentionables far to the south. And *that* was, no doubt, what he wanted from her now as well.

With this in mind, she slid farther down upon him,

letting her mouth replace her chest, and she began at once to tease the most sensitive portion of him with her lips and tongue.

Seeming immediately enraptured, he mindlessly let his fingers slip down and tangle in her hair. And his moans, as she proceeded to alternate her strong sucking with several rounds of tiny nips upon the tip of him, told her that she was succeeding in driving him as mad with bliss as he had her.

It made her feel strangely powerful: this newly found ability to extract such sounds from so stalwart a man. And she would gladly have seen this servicing through to its explosive end, had he not reached down with both hands and firmly stilled her.

"Will you let me enter you again?" he whispered. "I mean, given your fear of my seed?"

She swallowed dryly, caught off-guard by the request. "I shouldn't. But I will, love, if you wish it."

"Don't you?"

"Of course. I can think of naught I want more."

He grinned. "Then who am I to deny it to you?"

She slipped back up to kiss him, and, as she did so, he sat up slowly and began unbrooching his cape.

She eased her mouth away from his and smiled. "What are you doing?"

Arching upward, he pulled the long garment out from beneath him and brought it around to drape over her back. "Covering you, you daft thing! Out in this chill without a stitch on your upper half! What's to become of you?"

Still holding the ends of the cape, he used it to pull

her more snugly up against him. "I shall see you thoroughly warmed now, though. Have no fear."

She wrapped her arms about him and was on the verge of kissing him again, when something far beyond his right shoulder caught her eye.

She froze. The fog had lifted slightly, since they'd been engaged in their dalliance, and now, to her amazement, she could see what looked to be a giant set of gaping teeth, not thirty yards from them.

"Leif," she gasped, her eyes widening.

He was too enthralled now with kissing her neck to respond much. "What? What is it?" he asked absently.

"Look! Back there. Behind you."

He finally snapped to attention, probably fearing she was going to tell him they were about to be attacked by Ersemen.

"What?" he demanded, wheeling them both around in a hurried effort to direct his gaze to where she was pointing.

He scowled as his eyes fixed upon the odd structure as well. "A ring-fort? *Neinn.* It cannot be. 'Tis too small and scantly built."

She pulled away from him and, closing his heavy cape over the front of her, got slowly to her feet. *"Neinn.* Don't you see? 'Tis the stone circle! Holy buckets, I can't believe it! We've *found* it," she exclaimed, slipping back into English.

Chapter 17

Leif felt as though he'd been dropped, naked, into a half-frozen lake. Not only had he been interrupted while on the verge of making love to the most comely female he had ever known, but now she was hurrying toward a collection of tall flat stones which threatened to hurl her one thousand years out of his reach!

"Dana," he hissed, springing to his feet as well. "Don't go too near it! You've no way of knowing, forsooth, *which* century 'twill cast you into this time!"

He overtook her an instant later and, catching hold of the cape he'd given her, jerked her back into his arms. "Stop, I say! You must approach a thing such as this slowly, if at all!"

"But it's the right one," she countered, her voice high with excitement. "I recognize the stones! They are taller and wider now, I admit, but I'm quite certain they're the same ones."

He continued to hold her fast. "But how could you know this?"

"Well, I stood within them for several minutes,

while our. . . . Oh, I don't know what to call her in Norse. Our 'guide,' I suppose. She was our guide to this place, and she told us of the circle's origins and long history. And there, you see?" she asked, pointing. "There in its center is the flat stone which the ancient Erse priests used as an altar of sorts."

Leif swallowed uneasily and took a couple of steps backward, forcing her to retreat with him. "Well, I do not like the looks of the thing. It smacks of sorcery, and I think we would both be best off staying well away!"

She pulled free of his grasp and began moving toward the circle once more. "Oh, don't be silly. 'Tis simply the place where the Erse once worshipped the sun and such. It can't hurt us."

"Huh! Behold what it did to you! And with no provocation, I hasten to remind thee!"

She turned and smiled back at him, again clutching his cape about her nakedness. "I'm fine, am I not? I haven't been killed or maimed or rendered ill, have I? I'm simply . . . simply in the wrong century. And, perhaps, that is more easily set right than we think." With that, to Leif's horror, she moved right up to one of the towering stones and ran her palm over the back of it.

"You see? 'Tis safe enough," she concluded.

He continued to look unconvinced. "You crazed wench! Don't you dare set one toe in there until we have tossed a rock or stick in to test it!"

She laughed a bit under her breath. He reminded her so much of her overly cautious father, and of all the admonitions he'd issued through the years, that she couldn't help feeling rather warmed by his protective sternness now.

"Here," she replied, bending to pick up the biggest stone she could spot nearby. Without hesitation, she threw it into the center of the circle, where it landed with a light thud against the hard ground.

"It was filled with white chippings," she explained. "In my time, they have filled it with what we call 'gravel.' "

Leif took a hesitant step forward, finally seeming to accept the fact that the structure hadn't done her any harm so far. "Why?"

She shrugged. "By cause of rain, I suppose. People's shoes don't get as muddy when they are walking on chipped rock, you see."

He nodded, the Norse appreciation of cleanliness being boundless.

"And also, in my century, love, many thousands of travelers can visit such a site in just the course of one summer, and this begins to wear away at the ground and the footpaths. So I suppose the 'gravel' is there to shield all of that as well."

"Why on earth would such a multitude come to visit a jumble of stones?"

Again she fought a laugh at his pragmatism. "Because 'tis very old, to begin with. 'Twas built many millennia before your time, in fact, and the people of my century are just naturally drawn to aught that is so ancient."

"That they might 'study' it, as you told me last night?"

"Right. To gather information about it and write it in our books and tell it to our children."

"But don't you 'Americans' have circles this old to visit in your land?"

"We don't have such circles at all."

"Why not?"

"Because our kingdom is much younger and we have never had Erse priests on our shores. . . . Now, look," she continued, pointing to the rock she'd thrown inside. " 'Tis yet there, is it not?"

"Ja," he reluctantly agreed.

"And still in one piece?"

He peered at it. "It seems so."

"Well then, what danger could there be in my stepping inside?"

"Neinn. Now, blast it, woman! You stay right where you are, or I shall rush over and knock you into a very deep sleep! There is a world of difference betwixt a rock and a living being, I hope you realize!"

"All right then. Go and fetch your horse. And, if he can walk into the circle with no evil befalling him, we will know 'tis likely harmless for me as well."

He scowled. "Are you mad? How would we get back to the others, if the thing sends him off through the ages? You can't, by troth, wish to *walk* all that distance in such a hostile land!"

"If he's sent to another time, we'll simply step inside and follow him."

Leif crossed his arms over his chest. *"Neinn."*

She narrowed her eyes at him incisively. "You see? 'Tis not so easy, this leaving your own century behind, is it?"

She moved around to the opposite side of the circle and stepped between the two stones that were separated by the widest gap.

"What are you doing?" he gasped.

"This is the space through which I entered, when the time-slip first happened, and I shall do so again now. Unless, of course, you prefer to send the mount in first."

"Dana, I *pray* thee, don't do this!"

Her expression became genuinely questioning. "Why not?"

"Be-because," he stammered, obviously fighting great emotion. "This is an *evil* place."

"But you've known, almost from the start, that I intended to come here and try to find my way back to whence I came. Indeed, last night you even said you wanted to join me."

"*Ja.* But that was before you told me that the people of your time are poisoning the land and water and cutting down all of the trees."

She extended a hand to him, her voice suddenly filled with warmth. "So, come there with me and you and I shall help to see the earth saved from that fate. Many are joined in that very cause already, in fact."

He shook his head. "I can't."

"But why not?"

"Because I, too, know these stones. For I have also seen them in a dream. And it was, forsooth, one of evil portent. One from which I woke wet with the sweat of great fear," he admitted, his voice cracking. And, for the first time since they'd spotted the circle, Dana realized how truly terrified he was of it.

"Why did you not say so erenow?"

"Because I didn't know what it was in my dream. Your telling of this place was too vague for me to realize I had seen it once in my sleep, too."

"But how do you know 'tis evil?"

"Someone in the dream died. Someone I loved with all my heart."

"Who?"

Chills ran through Leif at the eerie recollection of it, and he found he could do nothing more than shrug.

"Well, was it a man or a woman?"

"I do not know," he snapped. "Isn't it enough that I loved whoever it was?" With that, he turned his back to her and abruptly began walking away.

Dana was unsure what to do in those tense seconds. She wanted to step into the circle and explore its abilities to get her back to her own time, but she knew she couldn't risk leaving him in such a state. He had simply come to mean too much to her for their farewell to be so cold and filled with resentment.

She hurried back around the outside of the ring and went after him. "Leif, prithee, do not let it end this way betwixt us! I've had some time to think on it, and I truly want you to come forward to my century with me, if that be possible. So pray, don't let me go into the circle alone now," she beseeched.

He stopped and simply stood staring down at the grass beneath them, its long breeze-blown blades and tiny meadow flowers looking, in the deep-blue moonlight, like the flowing vegetation on the floor of a sea. "At least one of us will die in there, my love. I do not know how, forsooth. But I do recall now that both a

male and a female perished therein. It was a woman I
loved, I distinctly remember that much. And, by all
that is sacred," he added, sounding near tears as he
turned and took hold of her shoulders with a breath-
stopping firmness, *"you* are the only maid I have ever
had such feelings for. I will not stand by and watch
you die!"

She looked up and searched his eyes. "But what's to
become of me if I stay? Your commander has proven
himself insanely jealous of my attentions to you. We
must steal every kiss, every longing look so that he
does not see. And, when the time comes that he somehow learns I am not a goddess, and we both know
that, sooner or later, he shall, what will he do to me?
Burn me at the stake for being a witch, mayhap? See
me poisoned or 'accidentally' killed by one of his freemen when your back is turned? By Thunder, if I am to
die in this time, I would prefer that the circle killed me
than I spend the rest of my days wondering when your
brother will! For you may believe that his rages will
never claim anyone save your enemies in battle, but I,
in very sooth, do not!"

Leif swallowed loudly, uneasily, knowing she was
speaking sense to him—knowing he was deluding himself if he thought the two of them could have a future
together while Booth still drew breath. This place
might have scared him with its haunting resemblance
to a nightmare he'd all but forgotten until just a few
minutes before, but it obviously held no such fear-
someness for Dana. And, if it was honestly her will to
enter it and do her best to return to her own century,

he knew he must find the nerve to go back and watch this gut-wrenching wonder take place.

He was a Norse warrior, after all; so he should, at the very least, show the courage this slender maiden was demonstrating.

Yet, though he knew it was only right to see her back to the circle and kiss her good-bye, he just couldn't seem to bring himself to turn around. It felt so much like the time when he'd had to kill a badly injured steed on his father's farmstead that memories of that harrowing event, that day when he'd been forced to take the life of a creature he'd held dear for over a decade, welled in him now, almost leaving him paralyzed.

Nevertheless, he reminded himself, helping to end the poor horse's suffering had been the most merciful and loving thing to do. And there was no doubt in his mind now that love, in its most intense form, was what he had come to feel for Dana as well.

"So be it," he said in a barely audible voice, letting her take his hand and lead him back to the site.

But may the gods, if, indeed, they have any power in such an alien domain, have mercy upon us, he thought, biting his lip in an effort to keep his continuing trepidation to himself.

The chilliness of his hand and his suddenly stiff gait surprised Dana. It was hard for her to believe that a man as large and strong as he could be afraid of such a thing. She would have guessed nothing could scare him to this degree—let alone an arrangement of stones which, she was sorrily aware, had only sporadic ability to affect those who entered it.

" 'Twill be all right," she assured Leif, giving his huge palm a squeeze and managing a bit of a smile. Then, as they finally reached the far side of the circle and she brought them to a halt before the portal she remembered entering several days earlier, she turned and threw her arms around him.

He hugged her back, of course. Stifling what sounded like a sob against the crown of her head, he stood holding, and rocking, her as though he might never let go.

"We *could* enter it together, you know," she whispered. "Perhaps, that way we won't be forced to part.

"Honestly. Everything will be fine, love," she continued, when he failed to reply. "Just as you have looked after me in this time, I will do the same for you in mine. I am paid well enough to provide for you, too. You simply have to trust me, Leif, as I have come to trust in you."

He eased away from her just enough to take her face in his hands and stare down into it.

If Dana had any doubt that he'd become tearful, she didn't now as she looked up and met his eyes.

"But what will become of my brother? Who will look out for him if I leave with you?"

She clucked with deep aggravation and pulled free of his hold. "Him again?" she exclaimed. "Do you believe for one moment that he ever gives a thought to your needs or feelings?"

"In very sooth, he is not obligated to, for he is my senior, not the other way around. And it is, of course, truly my father I serve in attending to him, not Booth himself."

"But that is just it," she snarled, losing all patience on the subject. "This is your golden opportunity to rid yourself of all of that, don't you see? You disappear with me now, into another century, and what can your crew and kinsmen conclude but that you died in honor, serving the mother of all of your goddesses in her quest for some divine site? *When,* I ask you, will you ever again get such a chance to escape your bondage to that madman?"

He was silent for several seconds, biting his lower lip and narrowing his eyes as though giving this proposal serious thought.

"You're right, of course," he said after a moment. "By the gods, I never realized how miserable I have been in my station until this very moment!"

She offered him a soft, knowing smile. "Being a dutiful son, you've simply never allowed yourself to, I wager."

He gave forth a surprised laugh. "Huh! I am now, though, am I not?"

She reached out and took his hand once more. *"Ja.* So, why tarry? Why don't we just step inside and see what awaits us?"

Again, to Dana's dismay, he looked as though he had reservations. *"Ja,* but what of the question I asked earlier? What if the circle takes us to a time other than yours? What will we do then?"

"I don't think that can happen. I mean, as it was explained to me, these time-slips always return you whence you came." They should only last for an instant or two, as well, a voice within her silently added. But, having become as attached to Leif as she was now, she had no intention of telling him the many ways in which her time-travel experience had differed from those Ian had recounted.

A silence fell between them once more, and Leif let go of her hand and began pacing anxiously before the portal. "The horse," he said finally. "We cannot just slip off and leave him tied to a tree. He might starve to death out here alone."

"Well, go and get him, then. Set him free or bring him in with us. Whatever you wish. But, pray, let's get on with this, before Booth comes looking for us!"

"Very well. Do you want to remain here?" he asked, before heading back toward the woods.

"Ja," Dana replied, closing his cape more tightly about her. She was suddenly realizing that she should go and collect her bra and sweat shirt from where she'd left them in the nearby grass. It wouldn't do, after all, to return to the twentieth century *topless.* She was sure she would have plenty of explaining to do about her odd disappearance as it was!

"All right," Leif called back, as he moved off into the darkness. "But, pray, do not go in without me."

He was already too far away for her to be able to tell whether there was a hint of sarcasm in his tone as he made this request. Nevertheless, she answered him soberly.

"Oh, I wouldn't dream of it, love. Never fear." She stood there for several seconds longer, marveling at how strange it was to come upon the stone circle again in such unkempt, overgrown surroundings. Yet, in spite of the fact that there was nothing here to herald its presence, no well-trimmed grass, designated walk-

ways, or reception buildings, she recognized enough of
its features to know beyond a doubt that this was the
same one. And, with that firmly in mind, she hurried
off to retrieve the rest of her clothing and put it back
on.

Fortunately, Leif was prompt in returning. His obvious misgivings about entering the circle were starting
to ruffle Dana as well, and she sensed that it would be
best for them both to simply get on with their plan.

Dropping the horse's reins as he neared, as though
he intended to leave the animal behind and simply let
him graze, Leif made his way slowly back to the opening before which they'd been standing just a few minutes earlier.

"Are you ready?" Dana queried, again taking hold
of his hand as he reached her. She felt her tone was
commendably heartening, given her own uncertain-
ties.

"Of course not, my dear. I know of no man who
could amply prepare himself for the kind of journey
you've described."

She looked up into his eyes. "It does not hurt, in any
case. I mean, if 'tis a comfort to you, all I felt when the
slip befell me was some dizziness."

He shook his head. "Ah, pain is the least of my cares
at present. I have been wounded far too often in battle
to fear aught as simple as that."

An admiring smile played upon her lips. "Then you
should fare very well in my time, for few men there can
make such a brave claim."

Again he looked markedly skeptical about her century. "Hmm."

"Come on," she urged, her smile broadening. " 'Tis not so bad. You'll see."

Leif wasn't sure he wanted to "see," however. It was one thing to be shaken from one's era like a flea from a blanket, as Dana apparently had been. But to simply walk into another time of one's own free will—as if choosing to take that fateful last step down the face of a cliff—struck him as sheer madness.

Nevertheless, it was probably the only way to be free of Booth, as she had pointed out. And that seemed reason enough to try it.

As she led him forward an instant later, though—as they both went inside and the stones they'd passed seemed to form an invisible barrier behind them— nothing, absolutely *nothing* happened.

The trees and sky all about the circle remained the same. The horse they'd brought from their camp was still quite visible where it continued to graze in the adjoining field. And none of the chipped white rocks which had filled the ring in Dana's time appeared at their feet.

"Damn it all," she barked, leading them both farther into the circle. "This just *has* to work!"

"Perhaps it requires more time," he suggested. "Didn't you tell me earlier that you stood herein for several minutes, listening to your 'guide' speak?"

Dana, feeling a mix of discouragement and perplexity, let go of his hand and walked over to sit down upon the low flat altar in the circle's center. *"Ja.* That's true."

Drawing more confidence from his companion's obvious lack of fear now, Leif crossed to the altar and sat down beside her. "Then we shall simply wait here for a while and see what comes to pass," he declared, wrapping a consoling arm about her shoulders.

She exhaled a long ragged breath as she again realized that she might truly be trapped in the tenth century for good.

"Pray, what else did you do here? Save listening to your guide, I mean?"

She furrowed her brow, trying to recall the details of those harrowing moments. "I don't remember doing aught else."

"So you were just standing herein, looking at your guide?"

She snapped her fingers. *"Neinn.* You're right. There *was* something else! My 'watch.' "

"Your what?"

"That bracelet about which your brother was questioning me back at the friary."

"Ja?"

"Well, in my century, we call them 'watches,' and they are used to tell us the time, the hour. You know, as a sundial does."

"Oh, *ja?* But how is this possible with something so small?"

"It just is, love. Believe me. It not only tells you the hour, but the number of minutes since it passed. And I remember now that I chanced to look down at it as the guide spoke, and I noticed that it had stopped dead."

"It was no longer working?"

"Right."

"So then what did you do?"

"Nothing. I just looked up once more, and suddenly the time-slip came over me."

"Then perhaps you need this 'watch' to make it happen again."

She sprang to her feet. *"Ja.* Maybe I do. I shall go fetch it from my bag. . . . Oh, Lord, Leif," she gasped. "My *bag!* I forgot all about it! 'Tis still tied to the saddle on the horse. I might very well have slipped back to my own time and left it behind, if you hadn't reminded me of it!"

"So what harm would there have been in that?"

"Well, don't you see? My fiery rain, my echo box. All of my things from the twentieth century. If your people or the Erse had gotten hold of them, who is to say how much events betwixt your time and mine might have been changed? No wonder the circle won't take me back! It has been trying to tell me that everything will be too greatly altered if I do not retrieve what is mine. You are wise beyond measure," she concluded gleefully, bending to press a grateful kiss to his cheek.

"Hold a moment," he ordered, rising as she turned and began hurrying back toward the portal through which they'd entered. "Don't leave me in here *alone!* Have you lost your wits? I want naught of your accursed century without you!"

She stopped and turned back to him, extending a hand in his direction with a sheepish laugh. "Oops. Sorry, darling! Come along with me then."

He did so; and, when they returned to the circle, they went and sank down on the altar once more, with Dana's bulging purse placed between them.

Though it took several seconds in the shadowy moonlight, she did manage to find her wrist watch in the depths of the overloaded bag; and she brought it forth now and sat staring at its still-frozen digital display.

Leif leaned toward her and studied it as well. "What hour does it herald?"

"Thirty minutes past ten."

"Ah, blather! 'Tis not even nigh ten of the clock!"

"Neinn. Not ten at night. Ten in the morning. For that is when it stopped working."

"And it hath not moved even a moment forward since then?"

"It does not appear so."

" 'Tis odd."

"What?"

"That this 'watch' should stop in its count of time just before you were cast backward fully ten centuries through it."

"Ja," she agreed.

"Do you think the secret lies in our making it work again?"

"I certainly hope not, love, for I do not know the first thing about fixing watches."

"Well, what causes it to count? Gears, per chance? For I must confess," he said sheepishly, "I have some skill at repairing things."

"Spoken like the son of a true nobleman," she replied with a teasing laugh, knowing how the Norse aristocracy avoided anything that smacked of manual labor. "Unfortunately, however, *I* must confess to having no notion as to what makes it 'count,' as you put it. I'm hopeless when it comes to measures and machinery."

He smiled as though rather embarrassed for her. *"Ja.* I gathered as much when you tried to estimate the distance betwixt the monastery and here. Prithee, why don't you hand the contrivance to me, that I might study it more closely."

For the first time since she'd pulled the watch out, Dana took her eyes from its tiny octagonal face, and, still not feeling a hint of the dizziness that accompanied her first time-slip, she gave it to Leif with a forlorn sigh.

Guardedly, he accepted it from her. "And you are certain this is all it does, mark time? It does not also spit liquid fire like that other device of yours?"

Dana smiled. *"Neinn.* Of course. 'Tis perfectly safe."

"Very well."

As he sat tinkering with the timepiece, Dana pushed her purse back behind them and let her head come to rest heavily upon his right shoulder. Though she had always taken pride in being the independent sort, she had to admit to herself that it felt good to be with a man who seemed so willing and able to look out for her interests and come to her aid.

"I'm tired," she said after a few minutes.

"This is not surprising, for we have been awake since dawn," he replied absently, caught up in trying to determine what powered the watch.

"Ah, 'tis no use," he snapped after several seconds.

"What?"

"Trying to examine this thing in the darkness.

Prithee, may I take it back to our camp and look at it by lamplight?"

"Of course. For whatever good it will do us then," she answered sullenly, pushing her purse even farther behind them and lying back on the large cold slab of rock. "I could just go to sleep here. Couldn't you?"

"I daren't. Not with Booth expecting us back ere long."

"Ah, to the blazes with him! If I never see that monster again 'twill be too soon!"

Leif laughed at this declaration and tucked her watch into his belt-strap for safekeeping.

"So how much longer can we stay here?" she asked after a moment, her voice edged with sadness.

"Half an hour perhaps. But not much more, I regret to say."

"Pray, tell me about your stave-churches then. For they are among the few things the people of my century cannot seem to replicate. And, if I should somehow return to my time without you, I want to be able to add what you tell me to our history books."

He turned and looked down into her face with a knit brow and a mystified smile. "Your people do not have churches? But I thought you told me you worship Jesus Christ, as the Erse do."

"Ja. But our churches do not look like yours."

"How are they different?"

"I don't know for certain because you build yours of wood. Right?"

Again he appeared puzzled by this line of questioning. *"Ja,"* he answered with a shrug.

"Well, there, you see, is the problem. They have not

stood the test of time. Why, they don't even seem to have had stone foundations, so we've no notion how big they are or how they are laid out."

"Pray, forgive us, my dear," he replied with teasing exaggeration. "I fear we simply had no idea we were building them for *your* purposes."

Dana laughed at his feigned indignation. "You might at least consider it henceforth. For, as you can see all about you, the ancient Erse far surpass you Norsemen when it comes to fashioning worshipping places which endure."

He shook his head, continuing to smile in amazement. "And this is what I am to sail back to Norway and tell my countrymen? That some woman from a thousand years in the future would appreciate it if we'd start putting stone floors in our temples?"

She laughed again. *"Neinn.* I am sure you can think of a better explanation than that."

Heaving a put-upon sigh, he slid over to where her legs hung from the altar and flopped back next to her upon it. "Are you real, you silly maiden? Or has my mind become possessed by some sort of sorcery that merely causes me to imagine such discourse?"

She reached over and gave his right arm a sharp pinch.

"Ouch, damn it! You've the claws of a cat!"

She smirked at him. "Just letting you know I'm real."

"I could let you know how real *I* am, too, mind! Most men surely would have by now, out here without so much as a ring-fort for leagues. But I am, forsooth, too much the gentle man when it comes to you."

"Perhaps 'too much' is right," she agreed, rolling over and planting her torso upon his. "Make love to me here, upon this altar, Leif. As the man in my dream does, pray. In all my years of having that vision, I've never seen his face. So who is to say he isn't *you* and that such an act is not what is required in order to send us both into my time?"

He swallowed uneasily. "Here? Where the Erse once worshipped? But do you not think it sacrilegious?"

"Sacrilegious? Now that is a most unlikely concern for a man whose people fondle severed horse phalli in their churches," she countered, seizing the opportunity to let her right hand slip down and punctuate this observation by doing much the same thing to him.

"It sounds as though you know plenty of such places already."

She shushed him and began kissing his lips with an intensity that said she didn't intend to take no for an answer.

"Dana," he choked, reaching up and easing her face away from his. "You cannot simply order a man to service you. I mean, I am troubled, forsooth. What if the Erse gods really don't smile upon such deeds in their sacred places and they decide to strike us dead where we lie? Mayhap that would account for what I saw in my dream. A man and a woman, *you* and *me,* turned to cinders for offending such wicked powers in this way."

"Oh, don't be ridiculous. The Druids, as they were called, were pagans, as you are. Praying to their gods for fertility, that sort of thing. I'm sure, if they exist, they would be naught but appeased by such sport."

Before he could offer another word of protest, she succeeded in freeing his manhood from his trousers, and her mouth traveled down to greet it with an artfulness that made his breath catch in his throat.

"Dana, prithee, don't do this," he entreated in a helpless whisper.

She stopped her heavenly loveplay just long enough to flash a mischievous look up at him, and he knew, in that instant, that he was done for. Goddess or not, he would always be a slave to this woman.

Perhaps he'd once seen a maiden more beautiful, but he certainly couldn't remember having done so. And he was sure there was not, in all the world—in *any* century—a female more enticing.

He groaned under her continuing attentions and let himself fall back limply upon the altar. Then, as his legs began to tense several seconds later and he felt as if he might explode at the now-irresistible movements of her lips and tongue, she slid herself up onto him and replaced her wonderful, warm mouth with a sheath that was warmer and more wonderful still.

By the gods, the tightness of her! The way she could grip him! He had never experienced anything quite like it, and he realized now what a fool he'd been to resist this suggestion. Indeed, what a dolt he'd be to ever refuse such an invitation from her.

A woman such as she came along only once in a lifetime—in a millennium, forsooth—and he acknowledged that he would follow her anywhere and to any time, without question.

Dana winced slightly at taking something so stout so deeply into herself. She didn't want Leif to see her initial discomfort, however. So she let her face fall to the curve of his neck, as she began moving over him—surging, like the foamy tide upon a beach.

Lord, how he filled her! Every inch of her seemed to tingle with the electrifying sensation he generated with each long, savoring thrust.

If this had been a game to her, a temptress's victory minutes before, it certainly was not now. Indeed, as he'd begun to join in the motions of the act, she'd again acknowledged what overwhelming strength he had at his command.

He was not like the males she'd known in her own century, a voice within her warned once more. He was, by comparison, a mountain of a man—someone capable of crushing her with just one hand, if he wished. And she wondered what had made her think she could actually "take care of" him if they did succeed in slipping forward to her time.

It wouldn't be like playing "master" to a pet stallion, after all. This was a fellow with enough prowess, intelligence, and good looks to gain the advantage, no matter where or when he ended up. And, if she really had held any delusions about being in charge with him, he managed to shatter them now, as his huge palms kept pressing her down upon his tumescence and he brought her to the most shuddering climax she had ever known.

Again she buried her face beside his neck, as he peaked as well.

"Did we succeed?" she whispered weakly after several seconds.

Leif opened his eyes and tried to catch his breath.

Sadly, however—though the earth seemed to have just been shaken to its core—he could see that all was unchanged about them.

"*Neinn.* I am sorry, love, but we are still in my time. Unfortunately for us *both.*"

Chapter 18

They rode back to rejoin the others in solemn silence, their failure at the stone circle troubling them both. Not knowing what else to do to remedy Dana's plight, they had resolved to return to the site the following morning, at roughly the same hour when the time-slip had originally come over her, and see if it might be induced again.

"You know of course that Booth will likely forbid you to step back into that circle with me tomorrow," Dana noted sadly, as they rode.

"I shall try to persuade him to let me take you back to it alone. That way, he won't be there to interfere."

She leaned heavily against him, letting her chin come to rest upon his right shoulder. Then she closed her eyes in exhaustion, as the night wind continued to sweep over them with the horse's galloping. "Do you think he'll agree to that?"

"I know not. I can only ask and hope he does."

"But what if I truly am stranded in this century for good, Leif? What will we do then?"

"I've told you. I will take you back to Norway with us and ask my sire to let me wed you."

"Is he aught like Booth?" she asked gingerly, fearing the answer to this.

"Not in the least, I'm glad to tell. He is on all counts, save those concerning our captain, a just and kindly man."

"Like you then," she acknowledged, drawing in a relishing breath, as she let her arms slide up from around his waist and embrace the girth of his muscle-bound chest.

He flinched a bit at the compliment, fearful of how much he'd come to care about her and her fate—*neinn,* more rightly, *their* fate where that ridiculous ring of stones was concerned. She'd actually managed to make him want to be cast forward to her century. And now, with failure appearing to be the most likely outcome in this endeavor, he felt terribly disappointed. Terribly depressed at being forced to return to the responsibility of commanding an entire crew of Vikings while having to pretend not to be in charge. The very thought of continuing to be beset by Booth's bouts of insanity had become crushing to him.

"Leif?" Dana whispered after a time.

"Ja?"

"I know you told me you don't have a betrothed at home. But you have made love erenow, haven't you? I mean, before you met me?"

"Of course. Why? Did I seem a stranger to it?"

"Oh, *neinn,*" she answered, smiling broadly. "Not at all."

"Then why do you ask?"

"I simply wonder how many others there have been."

He gave forth a dry laugh. "A few. Some Erse chattels we have captured while raiding. A Norse maid or two, seduced on the sly when their fathers were at sea. That sort of thing. And you?" he finished pointedly.

"Ah, one 'Steven' after another, I guess."

" 'Steven,' *ja*. This is the name of the man who broke your heart, right?"

"Right. But, in very sooth, they have all done so in their own ways."

" 'All'?"

"The men I've loved. I suppose there have been six of them, at last count."

He took one of his hands from the reins and gave hers a gentle squeeze, where they still rested upon his chest. "I won't."

"Won't what?" she fished. Though she was pretty sure she knew what he meant, her great concern about her future compelled her to make him spell it out for her.

"Break your heart, love. 'Tis not in my nature. Especially with a maid who brings me so much pleasure. And pray trust me when I say that you are the only one who ever has."

"*Ja*. That is why I was asking about the other women you've known. I simply cannot believe how wonderful the lovemaking is betwixt us. I've never felt anything like it!"

"Nor have I," he whispered back.

Though they did not speak another word until they reached their Norse companions, Dana sensed that this time, being stuck between centuries might be a gift in disguise—these might be the last hours she and Leif would ever share.

Her throat began to ache at the thought of finding herself sucked back into the twentieth century and not being granted the miracle of having him come with her. And she again questioned her decision to return to her modern-day life.

Booth's tent was very dimly lit by only one oil lamp, as Leif and Dana entered it a short time later. So it was clear that the Norsemen were keeping their flaming light and heat sources to a minimum in an effort not to draw attention to their little camp.

"What ho, brother?" the commander greeted, as Leif and Dana sat down upon a fur rug that was situated near the center of the shelter, the stealthy nature of their pilgrimage having prevented their bringing any furniture with them. "No luck in finding this divine circle she speaks of, I gather."

"On the contrary," Leif replied. "We found it well enough. 'Tis only half an hour due northwest of here, in fact."

Booth sat up a bit more in his primitive sleeping bag and scowled, as he took a swig from the wineskin that was lying beside him. Then, recapping the bag, he shot a snide smirk at Dana. "Then why are we not rid of you, Your Greatness? Don't tell me *Asgardhr* doth not want thee back."

"Not tonight, in any case," Leif quickly supplied. "She thinks it best that we return to the circle at roughly half past the hour of ten tomorrow morning and try again."

Booth slanted Dana another virulent look. "Oh, is that so, Goddess?"

She stared at him before answering, her continued amazement at the fact that he was actually Leif's brother barely concealed now. His eyes, again heavy-lidded due to all the spirited drink he'd probably already consumed, looked like a sinister Arab slaver's. Dark and frighteningly unreadable, they were the antithesis of Leif's fair and usually innocent features.

God, how she'd come to loathe Booth, she realized in that instant. And how surprising she found it that, though the men were of the same parentage, she could adore one while abhorring the other.

"It is," she answered finally, her tone cold as ice.

"Well, I am in charge here, lest either of you forget, and I say we should return directly to our base, come dawn."

"Booth, *neinn,*" Leif said; and, though it was clear that he was trying to hide it, there was a certain pleading quality to his voice. "I wish to take her on my own, so there will be no danger to the rest of you at this delay."

The captain threw back his head and issued a throaty laugh. "No danger? Surely you jest. We are a day's ride from the rest of our crew and would be perilously outnumbered by any tribe of Ersemen that should decide to descend upon us, once the sun is again lighting our camp!"

Leif was silent for several seconds. Then he spoke again. "In that case, pray, do permit me to stay behind and see the goddess safely off to her realm by the morrow. I shall then try to overtake you before you reach our base."

"Leave you here alone? Are you crazed?"

"Neinn, save that I am also crazed when I go forth on my own in this land to scout for raiding sites, as you and father have permitted me to do for nigh onto six summers now."

Scowling once more, Booth gave forth a low growl. "That is different."

"In what way?"

"Well, such scouting is never done this far inland, and, forsooth, 'tis *our* bidding you do at those times, not hers."

"I am surprised at you, Captain! Have you so little regard for the ways of *Asgardhr* that you do not realize its bidding must, in the end, be ours as well?"

"Ah, fie, get out of here, both of you," he exclaimed, waving a hand at them with such violence that he nearly lost his balance, where he still sat drunkenly, up to his waist in the sleeping bag. "I grow sick unto death at your continued affronts to me! And, if 'tis your wish to perish with this . . . this *temptress* out here in the middle of nowhere, Leif, I shall not try again to prevent it. Nor, you may be sure, will I offer our sire one word of apology if we never set eyes upon you again!" With that, he emitted a loud belch and rolled away from them, onto his side.

Though Leif was astounded at this dismissal, especially in light of all the loyalty he'd shown his brother through the years, he knew better than to run the risk of lingering. Rising, he hastened Dana to her feet as well, and he seized this opportunity to leave the tent before Booth decided to flatly forbid his proposal.

"Dear Heavens, he didn't mean that, did he?" Dana asked in a whisper, as they headed for his unlit tent a moment later.

He shushed her, pointing toward the collection of freemen sleeping around an all-but-extinguished campfire just a few yards away.

Dana fell silent, realizing this wasn't a topic he wished to discuss in the presence of others. But, upon entering his quarters seconds later and finding his manservant sleeping within, she knew she still wasn't free to question him about what had just transpired.

"Garth, 'tis I," Leif greeted, crossing to the freeman and giving him a nudge with one of his feet.

"Ah, my lord, I slept within that I might be here to light a lamp for you when you returned. I'm afraid our captain forbade it erenow, with us being in such hostile territory."

"A wise command," Leif replied.

The servant, clearly still groggy, pulled himself out of his master's bedding and picked up the oil lamp he'd left at his side. Then, without another word, he rose and left the shelter, apparently in order to light the vessel's wick with a punk from the dying campfire.

"Did Booth mean what he said to you?" Dana whispered during the brief solitude that followed.

"Parts of it, I suppose," Leif answered in an undertone.

"Which parts?"

He shushed her again, this time sounding more at ease. "By troth, my dear, 'tis clear you have no servantry where you come from. You've no patience for it. But, pray, let the poor fellow do his duty, then you and I can snuggle in and whisper until the morn, if you wish."

" 'Tis just that I'm concerned—"

"Don't be," he interrupted, seeming to feign a smile, as the freeman returned with the lit lamp and handed it to him.

"The goddess will spend the night in here, Garth, given the dangers of this place," Leif explained.

The servant gave forth a light, uneasy laugh at this. Then he pushed passed them and began arranging the fur rugs and bedding into two widely spaced piles.

Leif, obviously amused at this pristine precaution, stifled his response by pressing a fist to his lips. His eyes betrayed him, however. They positively sparkled with laughter as he looked over at Dana, and she had all she could do to keep from breaking up as well.

"Should I sleep just outside, sire?" the freeman asked, as he finished his task and rose again.

"Neinn. Thank you all the same," Leif replied. "But I think it best that you join the others near the fire. 'Twill be warmer for you there."

Garth knit his brow, as though neither understanding nor fully approving of this decision. "Very well, my lord. If you are sure."

"I am."

At that, the little man was gone, and Leif wasted no time in setting down the lamp and tying the tent's door flap shut behind him.

"Do you want the right side or the left?" he asked, turning back to face Dana with a smirk.

"He's a meddlesome one, isn't he? Pray, how did we manage to escape his ministrations last night?"

"He remained at the feast with the others. I told him he could. Besides, 'tis only when we are away from our base-camp that he fusses over me."

"Leif, verily," she began again, much more soberly, "I don't like what Booth said to you. Not for the world do I wish to see thee stranded or slain out here alone in the wilderness!"

Though it was clear that he heard her, he simply walked over to the bedding, dropped to his knees and began spreading it out to form one doss again. "I won't be," he replied after a moment. "I'm going with you to your time. Remember?"

"But there are no guarantees. Did our trip to the circle not teach you that? It could, forsooth, be like one of my century's 'cars' without fuel. I may simply be stuck here until the end of my days."

"But, if we leave with the others at dawn, there will not be a second chance for you to try to make the circle take us. 'Tis very rarely that we Vikings hazard such an inland journey, as Booth pointed out. So, do keep that in mind, my dear, before protesting too much."

"Damn it! Did you not tell your brother to refrain from drinking, as I suggested? I'm sure he wouldn't have renounced you just now if he'd been sober."

"I didn't. I must confess."

"But why not?"

"Because I knew that, without all of his mead and wine, he couldn't be relied upon to fall senseless come evening and give us this time to be alone together."

"Good Lord! The risks you're willing to run for me, my dear! You're besotted!"

"I'm in love," he corrected. "And enamored men are seldom sensible. Besides, even if the circle should fail us, I will not be 'alone out here in the wilderness,' as you put it. I shall have *you* to ride back to the base with me," he declared, gesturing with a curling finger for her to come and join him on the thick, furry bedding.

She did so with some reluctance. "But what if it takes only me back to my century? What if you're left behind? I shall worry forever after about what became of you. Whether or not you returned safely to the others."

" 'What if, what if, what if . . .' " he echoed playfully, reaching out to run his fingers through her hair. "The world is filled with 'what ifs,' my sweet, yet the two of us managed to meet and fall in love across ten centuries, no less. I wager the gods will continue to smile upon us."

"I'm not so sure. I have always been unfortunate when it comes to matters of the heart."

He smiled. "So 'tis high time your luck changed, is it not? 'Tis time a true gentle man came to your father seeking your hand."

"Good God," she said under her breath in English, lying back on the furs with a dazed expression at the very thought of such a scenario.

As quaint and sweet a gesture as Leif's proposal might be, she couldn't help but believe that her parents would quickly see through him. Not even an Arrow shirt and a pair of Dockers—coupled with a blurted claim that he hailed from Iceland and simply hadn't gotten around to learning English—were likely to conceal the fact that he was a tenth-century pagan with a penchant for pillaging and eating with his fingers.

"What is it?" he queried, smiling.

"Nothing. 'Tis just that the males of my time no longer go to a maiden's father for her hand."

"But how can that be? For arranging such a betrothal is all that sets an honorable man apart from those who simply steal their brides."

"Alas, 'tis very hard to explain, love. I fear you will just have to pass some time in my century before you can understand."

He shook his head in discouragement. " 'Tis not, forsooth, a very civilized time, is it?"

"I guess, in many ways, it's not."

He donned a waggish expression. "Do you know when I first realized this?"

"I cannot imagine."

"When you were coming down the tower's ladder with the monks. That round bottom of yours looked so stuffed into those tight blue trousers," he added, fighting a laugh. "Then you turned, when you reached the ground, and I saw from the bushes that you were most assuredly not a man. And, in that instant, I knew that there was no real refinement whence you came."

She offered him a puzzled smile. "What told you that?"

"Well, do the women of your century wear breeches every day?"

She shrugged. "Some do, I suppose."

To her surprise, his cheeks suddenly reddened, as

though he was embarrassed for some reason. "But what about when they . . . they bleed? You still do that in your time, don't you?"

"Oh," she said, nodding knowingly. "Monthly, you mean. *Ja.* Of course."

He looked a trifle taken aback at her unflinching answer to this. "Then, do you not think it best to wear a frock at such times? So no one knows. I mean, 'tis unseemly for others to know when you're . . ." Again he paused, apparently having trouble finding the most delicate term. *"Unclean.* Is it not?"

" 'Unclean'?" she repeated in amazement, the resentment she felt at such a chauvinistic view reflected a bit in her tone. "Is that what you think of your women when it occurs?"

He shrugged, continuing to look chagrined. "Well, what would you call it? 'Tis some sort of scourge upon your gender, is it not?"

She took a deep breath, doing her best to remember that she could hardly expect enlightenment in this area from a man of such archaic times. Dear Lord, what a flood of backward attitudes she would have to deal with, if she wound up being stuck in this century! *"Neinn,"* she said, striving to remain undisturbed. " 'Tis, forsooth, neither a scourge nor a blessing, Leif. If you must know, 'tis merely sustenance for any unborn babes who might be conceived before that time."

He furrowed his brow. "Hmm. Are you certain?"

"Of course. Have you ever known a woman with child to bleed?"

"By troth, I have not wed or, as far as I know,

gotten a maid into such a state. So I cannot answer that."

"Well, just trust me then. Pregnant women stay 'clean,' as you put it, all of the time."

He lay back on the furs and rested his head on his upraised forearms. "How would you know this? Have you asked many of them?"

"*Neinn.* I've no need to. 'Tis a well-recorded fact."

"In your books of knowledge, you mean?"

"Right."

"But what manner of maid would tell of such things for others to read? 'Tis, verily, a matter to be spoken of only betwixt women. Or, perhaps, a husband and his bride."

She turned and glared at him, starting to lose all patience with his primitive notions on the topic. "Well, you and I are discussing it, and Heaven knows we're not wed."

Issuing a low laugh, he sat up and pulled her into his arms. " 'Tis not for lack of wanting to be," he murmured. "So, pray, tell me you'll dress as a true Norsewoman tonight, that I might show you the advantage in shedding those breeches of yours."

She raised a shoulder to her ear at his tickling yet provocative whisper. "But I've no other raiment with me."

"*I* do, however. I brought along one of my sister's flaxen frocks, so you can sleep more comfortably with me beneath these furs. Forgive me, but I've no interest in sharing my bed with those in trousers." With that, he pulled away from her. Then, reaching over to a cloth bag on his right, he turned back to her with the promised garment a couple seconds later. "Here," he continued, spreading it out before her with a soft smile. "Now this is how your good Norse forefathers meant for you to dress."

She studied the chemise for a moment, running a hand over its straight-cut skirt and long sleeves.

"Put it on, pray," he murmured from behind her, brushing her hair aside and bending to kiss her neck with melting adeptness. "I long to see you in something flowing and open once more. With no breeches and no *under* breeches to keep me from what I might wish to claim in the dark."

"You want to make love again tonight?" she asked in disbelief.

"Why not?"

"Well, 'tis just that Steven . . . I mean, none of the rest of the men I've had as lovers could do it twice in such a short span of time."

He threw back his head and gave forth a husky laugh. "Huh! Softlings. 'Tis a wonder the women of your century become pregnant at all! Now, come on," he prompted again, lowering his voice to a sultry whisper, as he reached down and began pulling up her shirt. "If I am to find myself transported to your world tomorrow, I want one last night with a Viking maid."

She let him disrobe her in the minutes that followed. Shutting her eyes and lifting her arms over her head, she allowed him to rid her of every last stitch of her "mannish" modern garb. Then, feeling aroused by the submission implicit in this, she stood unashamedly before him.

How marvelously masterful he could be, now that

he knew she was a mere mortal like him. And, acknowledging this, she let him drink in every inch of her nakedness in the warm glow of the lamplight before she slipped the flaxen offering down over her.

"Pray take no offense, love, but 'tis rather shapeless," she noted, as she dropped to her knees beside him an instant later.

He wrapped his arms about her waist and buried his face in her cushioning chest. "*Neinn.* 'Tis splendid. For don't you see? *You* are what gives it shape. And yours is, forsooth, the most glorious form this old world shall ever know!"

He brought his lips up to hers, and their mouths met with a reflexiveness that said they were already getting to know one another in the most intimate of ways. "Have you heard, in your time, of our god Frey?" he asked softly, when he finally ended their kiss.

"*Ja.*"

His voice took on an unmistakable seductiveness. "So you know which realm he rules?"

"*Ja.* That of sexual intercourse," she replied, recalling seeing several illustrations of carvings and amulets of the male god. He was almost always shown sitting cross-legged, with his erect phallus pointing straight upward.

Leif took his arms from around her, and his hands quickly moved to slide his pants downward, so he could strike much the same pose. "Then you also know how our brides worship him?"

"I can take a wild guess," she answered, half amused and half impassioned by this heathenish proposition.

"Do it then," he directed in a hot whisper, pulling her close and letting one of his palms slip up the skirt of her frock. "I'll ready you. Then do it, and, in exchange, I shall tell you all about our stave-churches and longhouses and any other bedtime tales you desire, my little maid. My sweet, *tight* little stealer of hearts . . ."

His voice trailed off, and he began drawing savoring breaths through his clenched teeth, as his loins subtly joined in the pulsing upward rhythm that his probing fingers were causing deep within her.

As usual, he closed in upon the most sensitive parts of her with such force and rapidity that she was instantly rendered almost insensible. "My Lord, where did you learn to do that?" she sighed, feeling as if she were drifting into nirvana.

Though her eyes were shut now, she could tell he was smiling at this praise as he answered.

"But 'tis a warrior's forte. Finding another's most vulnerable spot and swiftly taking full advantage of it."

She sighed blissfully again, letting her head fall back, as he continued to hold her about the waist with his free hand. She could, with no trouble at all, simply permit him to bring her to another climax, than sink back on the bedding and slip into a contented sleep. But, as he began to withdraw his pleasuring fingers from her seconds later, she realized that he fully intended to see himself satisfied again as well.

"Come along now, my dear," he urged, sliding his large hands beneath her posterior and drawing her up and over to straddle his lap.

"I . . . I'm sore," she confessed in a bashful whisper. "As with the men of my time, I'm not accustomed to this much coupling either, I'm afraid."

"Sore within or simply at the base of you?" he inquired, keeping his voice equally low, as though aware of the embarrassment she felt at having to make such an intimate admission.

"The base."

He moved her closer still and let a hint of a laugh pour into her right ear. "I'll be gentle with you then. Pray, simply relax and trust in me."

"Very well," she replied, going up on her knees, as his fingers carefully opened her once more and he slowly pressed her down upon the throbbing length of him.

In a tone that was almost hypnotically smooth, he held her tight in the minutes that followed and murmured in detail about the interiors of his family's longhouse and the stave-church nearest it. It was, no doubt, a wealth of information. Yet, transported by the gratification he was once again bringing her, Dana was only able to take in and translate about every third word of it.

With the soft rocking motion of a child upon its parent's lap, Leif gradually ignited a fire within her that caused each of them to have to muffle ecstatic outcries against the other's cheek.

Chapter 19

Dana woke with the faint glow of dawn in her face, where she lay in Leif's arms. It was early. Probably just after six, judging from the angle at which the reddish sunshine was hitting the Norseman's tent.

Today was the big one, she acknowledged with a dry swallow: her last attempt at getting back to her own time. And, as she slowly sat up and was again able to take in Leif's princely features by the light of day, she realized that she was no longer interested in returning to the twentieth century without him.

He was not only the finest lover she'd ever known, but the warmest of companions—a male whose appearance, voice, and touch were destined to become seared into the memory of any woman he embraced. She knew she would never find another like him, no matter what the century. She was, therefore, beginning to question the wisdom of returning to the stone circle and running the risk of being separated from him by another time-slip.

Indeed, she now hated to leave him for just a few

minutes, simply to go off and relieve herself in the cover of the nearby woods. But, she told herself stoically, the longer she postponed this calling, the more likely it was that the freemen would awake and start breaking camp, and she naturally disliked having to meet such a need with so many males milling around.

She considered changing back into her jeans and sweat shirt for this brief excursion; but, wanting to please Leif when he woke, she decided to remain in the frock he'd provided.

As she slipped out of the bedding and made her way to the tent's door, she smiled to herself at the joy the plain little gown had seemed to bring him the night before. She had never seen a man take such pleasure in her body. She had never known anyone else's eyes to grace her with such a cherishing sparkle. And the memory of this, coupled with his courageous offers to take her, without the protection of his retinue, to the stone circle, made her heart swell now.

She struggled with the door's flap, unable to loosen the knot Leif had put in it. But, determined to let him get as much sleep as possible, she persevered and finally managed to open the entrance.

Though she hadn't been able to take a count of them in the darkness the night before, she was pretty sure all of the freemen were still asleep in their bags as she popped her head out of the shelter and gazed at them and the brook beside which they lay. Then, being careful to look off to both sides before making her furtive exit, she stepped out of the tent and darted toward the adjacent woodland.

She'd removed her espadrilles, along with her modern apparel hours earlier, and she couldn't help wishing now that she'd remembered to put the sandals back on. Her trip across the edge of the stone-strewn campground was painful to her bare feet, and sinking into the cold black dirt of the forest floor was most unpleasant.

It wasn't a mistake she'd make again, however, she told herself hearteningly, as she found a suitably secluded spot and relieved herself before hurrying back to the tent.

It was cold for a summer morning, she acknowledged, shivering slightly in the flimsy flaxen garment. Ireland was odd that way: not seeming to get as hot as her native Minnesota even in July. She had been in fair Erin nearly a week now, give or take a thousand years, and not once had the humid heat of one day carried over to the morning of the next.

To the Vikings, though, this was probably a tropical paradise, given the year-round chilliness of their homeland. Nevertheless, they'd brought their bear furs with them for sleeping; and the very thought of returning to the warmth of them had Dana sprinting back to her beloved's shelter.

As she sneaked around to its far side, however, in an effort to further escape the freemen's notice, something caught her by the hair. And, before she could cry out and look back to see who or what had hold of her, a huge hand was clamped over her mouth.

An Erse raider! she thought in those horrific seconds. Their camp had finally been spotted by some of the locals or a band of passing thieves, and she, being the first to stir, had become the premier target.

But, when she heard her captor speak in Old Norse an instant later, she realized how wrong this deduction was.

"Witch," he hissed into her right ear; and, though the voice was barely audible, she knew it was Booth's.

She tried to gasp, tried to *breathe* beneath his hot smothering palm, but it was to no avail. His hand was covering her nose, as well as her mouth; and none of the muffled squeals she issued in the seconds that followed seemed loud enough to be overheard by Leif, who must still have been sleeping in the adjacent tent.

Although she attempted to dig in her heels and fight it, the captain began dragging her backward. With one hand pinning her arms behind her and the other still planted over the lower half of her face, he hauled her in the direction of his shelter.

A moment or two later, with her wrists and forearms already throbbing from his vicious hold upon them, Dana found herself inside his tent—where his manservant stood poised with a hushcloth.

Stay calm, a well-trained voice within her counseled. Stay calm and take stock of their weak points.

This was easier said—by her self-defense instructor—than done, however. For, as she brought up a heel to kick Booth in the groin, his freeman responded by punching her so hard in the face that she nearly lost consciousness!

She fell limp, as she was gagged and bound in the seconds that followed. Her jaw was pounding with pain and the ceiling of the tent seemed to spin with her dizziness, as she was laid out upon one of Booth's furs.

She was utterly defenseless, she realized. Trussed at

her wrists and ankles, she held no hope of striking another blow. And, with her mouth covered this way, she couldn't even try reasoning with the brutes.

Dear God, where was Leif? Was there any chance of him waking soon and coming to her rescue? Or was she destined to die at this berserker's hands?

Her frantic questions came to a halt, however, as Booth squatted near her head and began to speak once more in a growl. "I listened as you two talked in Leif's tent last night. Huh! You thought I had fallen into a drunken sleep again, but I proved far more clear-headed than either of you."

Dana's eyes traveled, in terror, down to where his hands rested on the fur flooring. Having already been dealt a mighty blow, she couldn't help but fear being hit again. Then, as he continued speaking, she looked back up into his sadistic eyes.

"Leif told you he loved you, and that alone would have been cause for me to see the pair of you rendered asunder for good and all. But, *neinn,* 'goddess,' that was not the half of it, was it? You went on to speak of that circle of stone and how it was going to return you, not to *Asgardhr* but to 'your century.' Fancy that! And fancy, too, how amazed I was to hear my brother ask if you had heard of our god Frey and how our brides worship him. Now, prithee, tell me why Leif would think you did not know of one of your own sons? And why you would consent to worshipping him by coupling with a mere mortal?"

Dana was seized by a chill of fright at this disclosure. Though the bastard knew full well she couldn't answer any of his charges with the gag on, his dark eyes remained fixed upon hers, and all she could do was give forth a piteous squeak.

Her mind began to churn with burning questions once more. If Booth had known all of this since early last evening, why hadn't he confronted them then? Why had he waited until morning to seize her?

But of course. He hadn't wanted to confront Leif. *Just* her. So he had waited until she'd emerged from the tent and grabbed her before Leif could intervene.

Now, God help her, what did the berserker have in mind?

As Booth got back to his feet with a sinister laugh, she became sorrily aware that she was about to learn the answer.

"We both know you're no goddess, wench. None of our deities would ever do what you have done. None of them would lure a Norse warrior into betraying his sire and commander. So that seems to leave only one other possibility. You are a witch! A sorceress who has cast a spell over my brother! And, by Thunder, *I* shall see you to that circle of yours now, and I shall also see it claim you in one manner or another or die in the effort!"

With that, Booth turned and left his tent. But any relief Dana felt at having him exit without manhandling her further was quickly replaced with fear as the freeman gathered her up in his arms and carried her out to a saddled horse.

Leif uncurled in his sleep, his arms and legs craving a stretch after so many hours of lying on his left side.

As he rearranged himself, however, he became aware that there was an awful lot of space next to him for expansion, and he woke with the sudden realization that Dana was no longer sharing his bed.

He sat up slowly and yawned, his eyes blinking at the brightness of the sun shining through the eastern wall of his tent.

Dana's bag was still where she'd placed it the night before, just to the left of their doss, so he had to assume she hadn't gone far. She would never have hazarded leaving such incriminating evidence unattended, not if she'd planned to do anything more than steal off to answer morning's call.

He smiled to himself and reclined again with an enamored sigh. By the gods, what a treasure she was! Strangely, she seemed even more so to him now that he knew she wasn't a goddess.

What sublime things they'd done to one another hours earlier! The very thought of her unabashed desire for him was making him grow aroused all over again. He'd been too long away from the pleasures of a woman, he realized, if this dear little maid could come along and sweep him off his feet as she had in just a matter of days.

But, bewitched as he might have become, it was the most blissful bondage imaginable. So he knew he'd be a fool to leave her alone for even an instant, once they went back into that ominous stone circle of hers.

He rolled onto his side again, as he heard her returning to the tent. If he pretended to still be asleep, perhaps he could entice her into a lingering kiss or two before they were forced to face the day.

As the tent flap was opened a second or two later, however, he realized that it was not his dear Dana but his manservant who was entering.

"Begging your pardon, sire, but I fear I have just learned that our captain has left the camp."

Leif bolted upright and turned to the freeman with a scowl. "Left to go where? Don't tell me he has already headed back to the base, the hotspur!"

"Neinn, my lord. I am told by one of his men that he rode off toward the northwest with his manservant and the goddess."

"The goddess?" Leif exclaimed, slipping out of his bedding. "But how can that be?"

Garth shook his head. "I know not, I'm afraid. I was merely told that she was taken against her will. She was trussed, as they departed with her a short time ago."

At this Leif scrambled to his feet and began searching about for the broadsword and knife he'd shed the night before. "Accursed *Hel,* man, go out and ready a mount for me at once! And see that the lady's bag is tied to my saddle!"

"Should I accompany you, sire?"

Leif paused for a second or two before answering. While he had never wanted to do anything that might cause his entourage to cross their captain, this calamitous turn of events warranted some support. *"Ja.* Arm yourself. And have Rutland join us, as well."

With her ankles still bound, Dana was forced to ride sidesaddle in front of Booth as they raced toward the stone circle. It was a harrowing trip, one made all the more terrifying by the fact that the hold of the crook of the captain's right arm was all that kept her upon his huge horse. And every time she was certain she was about to fall and be trampled by the stallion's hind hooves, the horror in her eyes was met with a ruthless smile from the commander.

When they had ridden for roughly thirty minutes, Booth was merciful enough to slow his steed and order his freeman to do the same. But, as it became apparent to him that the circle was not, in fact, "due" northwest of their camp as Leif had told him the night before, he began to lose patience with having to scout about for it.

"Your brother said 'twas only half an hour from our camp, Captain?" his manservant asked finally.

Booth nodded. Then, sniffling windedly in the morning chill, he ran a fist under his nose.

"So, should I ride off to the north a few minutes more and you ahead to the west a bit longer, that one of us might come upon it?"

The commander snarled. "The wench knows where it is. She visited it just last evening. And I fancy 'twould be easiest to simply pry its precise location from her lips."

He began untying Dana's gag, having, of course, little regard for the stray hair the freeman had inadvertently entangled in its knot earlier. Her first utterance was, therefore, a yowl at the tearing pain Booth had just caused her.

"Tell us where this ring of stones can be found, lest I strangle you here and now!"

She coughed and strove to catch her breath after so much time under the smothering hushcloth.

I know not, she wanted to answer. Or *off to the south.* The direction opposite the one she and Leif had traveled the night before. Anything to stall these two monsters so that Leif might have the time to overtake them—if, indeed, he'd even discovered her absence yet.

But the psychotic gleam in his older brother's eye kept Dana from pleading ignorance. Nor did causing them to ride off the wrong way strike her as being much wiser.

If Booth really did plan to kill her—and she had no reason to believe he didn't—she knew she'd be a damned fool not to seize this final opportunity to escape his wrath by slipping back into her own time.

" 'Tis in that direction, as I recall," she answered, motioning toward the north with her head.

After stuffing the gag into his belt-strap, the commander again wrapped an arm about her; and, without another word, he reined them off that way.

Within just a few minutes, they were across the clearing Dana remembered traversing with Leif the night before. Then came another wide stretch of woods, followed by a second open area.

It was the same field. Dana was almost certain of it. Yet, in this stark daylight, the misty moonlit scene she remembered seemed almost to have been a dream. And, far from the elation she'd known on the preceding evening, she felt only apprehension now as she again caught sight of the ring of towering gray stones.

"That is it?" Booth asked with a derisive laugh, the

circle apparently having come to his attention as well.

"Ja," Dana quavered.

He slowed the steed as they continued to approach it. "But what manner of temple has no roof and such widely spaced walls? Odin help us, these Erse are even greater fools than I imagined, building a church that cannot so much as keep out the rain!"

It's for sun worshipping, you dolt! And there is no rain, when the sun's shining, Dana thought. But, well aware of his volatile nature, she again chose to hold her tongue.

She wasn't thinking clearly enough for verbal jousting, in any case. Knowledge of impending doom could apparently, addle a person, and she was definitely in a state of high anxiety now. Her throat was parched. Her hands and feet were numb from lack of circulation. And her heart was racing like a rabbit's. A fact that couldn't have escaped Booth's notice as he finally brought the horse to a halt and dismounted, dragging her down after him.

She came to an unsteady standing position, her balance thrown off by the trussed state of her limbs. "Just what do you intend to do with me?" she dared to ask.

"Sacrifice you to the gods, of course," Booth answered with a grin, gesturing for his now-dismounted freeman to lead their horses off to the nearby woods where they could be tethered. " 'Tis not, by any means, as fine a place as a Norse temple, but 'twill do for the likes of you. And, verily, I have no care whether 'tis our deities I appease in this or Erin's. All that matters is that I shall at last be rid of you, vixen,"

he concluded. Then, issuing a demonic laugh, he un-
sheathed his knife.

Dana, thinking he was going to stab her on the spot,
couldn't help gasping.

"Silence, ye bungling witch! If you possessed an iota
of clairvoyance, you'd know I only mean to cut your
ankles loose. You've been burden enough to me these
past days, without my having to carry you to your
death as well."

She exhaled a sigh of relief. It was clear, however,
that this emotion would be terribly short-lived, for he
bent to slice through the rope that bound her, then
rose once more and nudged her forward by pressing
the flat of his blade to her thinly clad back.

"Make haste," he growled, as they both began
walking toward the circle. "I've a full day's ride back
to my base, thanks to you!"

"Leif shall never forgive you for this, you know,"
she retorted, figuring she had nothing to lose now in
light of his homicidal intentions.

His tone was as cynical as ever. "For what?"

"For murdering me."

"He will not know of it."

"He shall, I tell you. He will come here in search of
me."

"Not if I order him to return to the base with the
rest of us."

"*Ja.* Even then. He will cross you and come back to
this place."

"Keep quiet, wench, or I will start by cutting out
your tongue!"

This threat did, indeed, cause Dana to fall silent. On

the chance that there still was some hope of getting back to the twentieth century, she certainly didn't wish to leave her tongue behind! And she sensed that Booth was fully capable of committing such an atrocious act.

He deigned to speak again, as they finally reached the circle and he shoved her into it. "Besides, as I have said, 'tis not murder I'm about here but sacred sacrifice." He stepped inside the ring as well and, grabbing the back of her frock, began hauling her to the low, flat altar. "By putting yourself in my charge back at the friary, you became my property. So, now that I know beyond a doubt that you're no deity, I'm deeming you my slave. And, according to Norse law, 'tis wholly permissible for a serf to be offered to the gods. Not even my brother can dispute this with me."

Dana's mind flashed back to all she'd read about the ancient Nordic codes, and she quickly came to the conclusion that he was right. She also realized just how right Leif had been in warning her of Booth's sharp-wittedness. Indeed, there seemed absolutely no avenue for rebuttal left to her now.

Nevertheless, as the freeman finally returned to them and the two Vikings began closing in upon her, she made one last attempt to dissuade the captain. "Perhaps your law will not see you punished for this, but, by troth, mine will! For any woman who can travel through time, as Leif indicated last night, is also capable of other magical deeds. And, if you kill me, Booth Ivar'sson, I swear to thee I shall return from the dead and curse you for the rest of your days!"

Though she locked gazes with him in those seconds, and her eyes narrowed to the most spiteful slits she could produce, his cramping nearness forced her to a sitting position upon the cold hard altar. And, to her amazement, he simply responded by smiling and starting to sing.

"Did you bring the hare's blood?" he asked his freeman between the stanzas of his tune.

"Ja. 'Tis over by the stones through which I entered."

"Go and get it now then."

The manservant did so; and Booth, as if still suspicious that Dana might try to attack him, reached down and pressed the point of his knife to the hollow of her throat.

He then resumed his song. It was a chantlike melody with some of the most obscene lyrics Dana had ever heard; and she was surprised, given the generally clean vocabulary she'd learned in her Norse language classes, how many of its words she was able to decipher.

"Normally horse blood is used for such rituals," Booth said with a cruel expression, when he'd finished his sacrificial chant. "But, because you have caused us to travel so far from our base-camp, we haven't a mount to spare. Besides, the blood of a rabbit should not offend *Asgardhr* in this instance, since I offer the gods naught more now than a troublesome field mouse!"

The freeman returned to them seconds later, carrying a wineskin, a little wooden bowl, and a small tree branch with a three-pronged end on it. With Booth's knife at her neck, Dana wasn't able to look down to where the servant squatted with this menacing paraphernalia an instant later. But she did manage to see, from out of the corner of her right eye, that he was pouring blood from the skin into the bowl. Then he placed the stick in the vessel, and, to her dismay, he lifted it out and began whipping it toward her as he got to his feet once more.

She reflexively shut her eyes, as the first round of it splashed upon her face and neck. It had an odd, almost nauseating smell; and, were she not afraid that Booth would cut her throat, she was sure she would have pulled away and started to retch.

"Ugh, God! Jesus," she exclaimed under her breath in English, wishing with all her heart that she could raise her bound hands and cover her face.

She could feel the dreadful stuff on her *lips* now; and, though she hated to admit it to herself, she thought she could even taste its saltiness!

How on earth could she have sat reading so passively about such gruesome ceremonies in her college textbooks? How could she ever have been so detached as to find these accounts merely interesting?

She would certainly never think so again! If she somehow managed to survive this ordeal . . .

"An incantation," the freeman accused at hearing her foreign expletives. "Pray, sire, kill her now, lest she bewitch us as she did your brother."

"Neinn. Neinn. Dying quickly is far too good for her," Booth countered, throwing down his knife. "I think I shall try choking her for a while instead." With that, he wrapped his fingers about her throat and began cutting off her air.

She stared up at him in those fateful seconds. With

her eyes wide and beseeching, she saw what sick satis-
faction he was taking in attempting to strangle her
with his bare hands. It was naked flesh upon naked
flesh—warm blood dripping from her chin onto his
clenched digits. . . . And, all at once, she saw a strange
haze form around his head and shoulders, and the
sudden detachment she felt from his ever-tightening
grasp told her that she was slipping away from him.
Indeed, slipping away from his very century!

"Fie," Booth barked, nearly falling forward, as his
hands slid off of her fading neck.

His freeman caught him by his right elbow and
helped him recover his balance. "What is it?"

"She *is* some sort of sorceress, for my fingers just
moved through her as if she were nothing but vapor!"

"But how is that possible?"

"I know not," the captain replied, clenching his
teeth and again taking hold of her throat.

He had a grip on her once more, Dana acknowledged. She was experiencing the pain and panic anew,
as she again felt his fingers close in upon her.

The time-slip still seemed in effect, nonetheless, for
his words, and those of his freeman, were becoming
drawn out and slurred—just as with the utterances of
the white-robed strangers she'd seen in this very circle
nearly a week before.

Then again the strangling grip upon her loosened,
and she saw the manservant, now functioning in a
kind of otherworldly slow motion, turn and point toward the southeast.

"Leee . . if, si . . re," she heard him drawl.

Booth removed his hands from her entirely as he turned and looked in that direction as well.

Everything was echoing in Dana's mind at this point, as though she'd been given a light dose of ether. Nevertheless, she rallied her concentration and forced her eyes to travel to where her captors were looking. There she saw, to her delight, that it was indeed Leif who was riding toward them and that he was flanked by two of his mounted freemen.

If she could only hang on for a moment or two more, he would reach her, she told herself bravely. If she could just keep from slipping out of this time or dying at Booth's hands in the next several seconds, Leif might be reunited with her and she could catch hold of him and lead him to wherever this encompassing "slip" was taking her.

She squinted, struggling to get as clear a view of him as possible. But the blood the freeman had splattered upon her eyelashes, coupled with the strange glow that now seemed to outline her beloved, made him little more than a blur for her. Only his long blond hair and the blue-gray of his tunic across his broad chest told her it was Leif growing larger with each quick stride of his steed.

God, don't let it end this way between us! she silently prayed. Just as with her first trip to this circle, the terror of having someone trying to kill her seemed to have accompanied the time-slip. And, if she could only calm herself, if she could just become convinced that she was safe now that Leif had finally come to her rescue, she believed she might stay anchored in his century until he reached her.

Her focus upon him was brought to a sudden halt, however, as Booth—desperate to do away with her before his brother could prevent it—again blocked her view and resumed his stranglehold upon her.

It was the most peculiar mix of sensations she had ever experienced. In one instant, she was gasping for the air that her body couldn't get past the captain's crushing fingers. Then, in the next, she felt nothing at all. It was as if she were floating outside of her own form, as though she were a ghost who could slip from any grasp, like air escaping the mouth of an untied balloon.

All of a sudden, Booth again stopped his efforts to kill her. And, in that same instant, as his huge form was jerked backward, she saw that Leif had finally, blessedly, reached the circle and was turning her would-be murderer about as though to attack him.

Leif, so near now. Just a few feet away. *Leif,* her avenging warrior, with his sword drawn, was . . . was running Booth through with its broad blade!

"Oh, *neinn,*" she heard herself exclaim, knowing he'd surely stand trial for murder for such an act. And this was hardly the fate she wanted for either of them, if they wound up being stuck in his century. *"Nei . . . inn,"* she pleaded, her voice starting to sound as protracted to her as the Norseman's had in the past few minutes.

With his weapon now bloodied to its hilt and his villainous brother quivering at the impalement, Leif turned and locked eyes with her.

Why? she tried to ask. Why did you stab him, when you could have just knocked him out?

She desperately wanted to speak, but, all at once, it felt as if she were swimming through gelatin. The slightest movement, even just forming words, became an impossibility.

Then, to her great relief, she saw that the glow about Leif had gone. He, unlike the others in the circle, was apparently in sync with her somehow. He was slipping *with* her, she acknowledged, the corners of her mouth curving up into a jubilant smile.

He smiled as well, his large blue eyes filled with both joy and a trace of sadness.

"I am coming with you," she heard him declare. His voice as clear and undistorted as ever. Then he winked at her. Their agreed-upon way of saying they loved one another.

She winked back, now feeling better able to move in their eerie straddling of centuries.

Then, to her utter horror, he simply disappeared! He and the rest of the Vikings suddenly vanished, and Dana looked down and saw that the stone circle was once again filled with crushed white rocks!

Chapter 20

Dana froze in the seconds that followed, hearing only the sound of her own voice as she cried out Leif's name.

Her eyes traveled back up to where she had just seen him, directly before her, and some part of her—some frantic portion—seemed to believe he was still visible there.

Transparent, specterlike, stuck in the act of withdrawing his heavy broadsword from his brother's torso, he wavered in time and space, like a phantom shimmering upon a dipping stretch of highway. His eyes and all of his emotions seemed pinned upon her in that petrified instant.

But it was only an illusion, she realized, springing off the altar and stepping over to the very spot where she had just seen him. Only she had been transported by the time-slip. And now she was as alone as she'd ever been—back in modern-day Ireland.

Yet, knowing all of this, she again raised her voice and called out for her lover in the echoing early morn-

ing haze. Though she suspected there was no one for
miles to hear her, the sudden rage she felt at this cosmic
injustice made her screech until her throat burned.

She was definitely back in her own time. Back to the
well-kept tourist site, which apparently wouldn't begin
welcoming its daily stream of visitors for at least a few
hours. And, still trembling from the trauma of both
Booth's attack and her sudden flight through one
thousand years, she backed up to the altar, sank down
upon it once more, and began to sob like a child.

She'd returned all right. Her stony perch and the
rock-covered ground all about it showed absolutely no
trace of the blood sprinkled over the front of her. But,
Heaven help her, Leif had been left behind! And now,
with her hands tied, she had to face the future on her
own. She'd somehow have to make her way, without
so much as a credit card or a single Irish penny to
sustain her in this still-foreign land.

Oh, God, what was she going to do? How would she
explain her bizarre plight to whomever it was that
found her in this state?

The locals were sure to think her story the product
of a deranged mind. Even her parents were likely to
feel that a psychiatric evaluation was in order, if she
dared to tell the truth.

She sniffled and began to cry once more, her tears
mixing with the blood of that poor tenth-century hare.
She felt totally helpless, unable even to wipe her own
eyes, with her hands bound.

She thought about getting back up and going in
search of someone, *anyone* who might be able to call
the authorities and see her returned to the guidance of

Worldtrek Tours. But then, still desperate to get back to Leif somehow—or to stay put in the hope that he had also gotten caught in the circle's time-slip and might soon appear—she lay back upon the altar and let her hot tears stream over her temples and into her sleep-tousled hair.

She woke an hour or two later to the horrified gasp of a pudgy, redheaded man in a fisherman's sweater. He was leaning over the right side of the altar, staring down into her face; and he looked pale enough to swoon, as she opened her eyes.

"Ah, sweet Jesus, woman," he exclaimed, jumping back from her, "you were lying so still, I thought you'd been murdered!"

Dana scowled, feeling a bit taken aback at hearing someone speak English to her, after so many days of having to converse in Old Norse. Then, with some trouble in her bound state, she managed to sit up on the stone slab. "I . . . I very nearly was," she croaked, her voice hoarse from her previous outcries.

The middle-aged stranger took one step forward and peered around to the back of her. "What's the matter with ya then? Who tied you that way?" he asked charily, glancing all about him, as though fearing her attacker might still be in the vicinity.

"They . . . they did," she stammered, unable to think of a thing to tell him in lieu of being honest.

"And who would 'they' be?"

"The same ones who spattered this blood all over me," she answered impatiently. "Listen, do you think you could unbind my hands? I've been this way for quite some time, and it's very uncomfortable."

"They're not still about, are they?" he inquired guardedly. "Because I can tell from your accent that you're a foreigner, and if it's some kind of occult thing you were doin', some coven activity, you should know that we've had that sort of trouble in these parts before and we'll tolerate no more of it! The gardaí aren't mucking about when it comes to that!"

Dana shook her head. "No. I swear to you that's not what happened. I was just hauled here and attacked by some strangers. And, the next thing I knew, you were staring down at me."

He drew a little closer. "That's not *your* blood on ya, is it?"

"No."

He folded his arms over his chest with a sternly defensive air. "Whose is it, then?"

"A rabbit's."

His bushy, reddish eyebrows drew together. "A rabbit's?"

"Yes. That was what I was told, anyway. Please, could you just untie me? I promise I won't hurt you. I'm in no shape to harm anyone," she concluded, her voice cracking as she again found herself on the verge of tears.

He appeared moved by this show of emotion. "You've been weeping, haven't ya?" he acknowledged in a suddenly sympathetic tone. "I can tell from the two white streaks down your cheeks."

Dana sniffled again. "Of course I have. You would

have too—if you'd been punched in the jaw and nearly strangled to death!"

"Dear God, miss," he replied, hurrying around to the other side of the altar and finally beginning to unbind her. "How long ago did this happen?"

One thousand years, she wanted to blurt out. But, knowing that no one—except her tour guide, Ian Preston—could ever hear the truth, she told him an hour or two.

She sighed with relief, as her hands were at last freed seconds later. Then she brought them around to the front of her and began rubbing her chafed wrists.

"I think I'll keep this rope, if it's all the same to you," he declared, stuffing it into one of his pants' pockets as he circled back around to face her. "The gardaí will want all the evidence they can get in this crime, I'm sure."

"Who are these 'gardaí' you keep referring to?"

"The police, of course."

"Oh, I don't want to talk to them."

"Well, maybe not. But I'm thinkin' you'll have to, just the same. I mean, how are we to find these attackers of yours otherwise, miss? Miss . . ." He faltered, clearly waiting for her to supply a name.

"Dana Swansen," she offered without hesitation. "And you are?"

"Matt O'Brien." He extended a hand and gently shook one of hers. "I work here. At reception, I mean. Not as a guide . . . Dana Swansen. Swansen," he repeated, as though searching his memory. Then he donned an ecstatic grin for some reason. "The Saints be praised! You're that American woman who went missing about a week ago, aren't ya? Your photograph has been all over the telly, and I think I would have recognized ya right off, if not for all the blood on your face."

"The telly?" she questioned blankly. Though media attention was hardly what she needed now, this was the first indication she'd gotten that she had indeed slipped back to the right month and year; and she couldn't help feeling greatly relieved.

"Aye, well, that's big news here in the Republic, one of our top tour companies losing all track of a client. Ian's sure to be beside himself with joy when he learns I've found ya."

"Ian Preston, you mean?"

"Yeah. The very same. We see him here at the circle at least twice a week the summer through with his groups. He *was* your guide, wasn't he?"

"Yes," Dana replied, taking great comfort in the prospect of being able to see her time-slip confidant again. "Could you call him for me? Do you know how to get hold of him?"

"Sure. It should be easy enough. I'll just call the Darby Hotel in Dublin, and they'll get a message to his home. He's off today, I think. Most of Worldtrek's tours end on Mondays and their guides take Tuesdays to deal with personal business before the next batch of tourists arrives. Anyway, it's so early, I'm sure we can catch him before he leaves to run errands or whatever he's got planned for the day."

"Oh, that would be great! I'm really indebted to you, Mr. O'Brien."

"Matt," he amended, wrapping a kindly arm about

her and trying to help her off the altar and onto her feet. "We'll go back to reception and place the call now."

She balked. "No, please, Matt. I want to stay here. Could you just go phone him for me?"

He looked confounded by this request. "But why on earth would you want to stay behind? It's cold out here, as you can plainly tell in that flimsy thing you're wearin'. I mean, just look at yourself! No jacket, no shoes. You're sure to catch your death. That is, if ya haven't already."

She swallowed uneasily, scouring her rattled mind for some acceptable excuse for wanting to stay in the circle. She could hardly tell him, after all, that she needed to await the possible arrival of a tenth-century Norseman caught in some sort of time-slip delay! "Well, you may go and get me a blanket or something then. But I think it's best you don't move me, because . . . because they somehow hurt my back. I mean, I don't think we should risk injuring it further. Do you?"

"Well, no. I suppose not. But, if I leave ya here, you must swear to me you'll stay put," he added with great concern. "There've been a good many people searching for you, and I can't have ya disappearin' again!"

"I won't move even an inch. I promise." Though Dana felt certain her eyes shone with sincerity now, he still appeared hesitant as he began backing away.

"All right, then. See that ya don't. We've got this whole place fenced off and the entrance gate locked through the nights. So I have to confess to being a bit on edge regardin' how these 'attackers' of yours got ya in here in the first place."

"Ah, God. It's really hard to explain. I mean, they knocked me unconscious for part of the time," she lied again, growing increasingly uneasy with this web of untruths she was being forced to spin. "Oh, please, just get Mr. Preston for me, and I promise to tell him everything I can remember."

"Well, the gardai will likely be the first to arrive, with Ian having to come all the way from Dublin."

"Oh, no," Dana exclaimed, suddenly realizing how disastrous matters could become, if she were dragged away from the circle to go off and help file a lengthy report at a police station. "I must speak to Ian first, *please*. I mean, he's the only one I've come to know at all in Ireland, and I couldn't possibly face being questioned by your police without him at my side!"

O'Brien shook his head slightly, as if still rather perplexed by her requests. "Very well, then. But," he continued, pointing a finger at her emphatically, "if I get Preston for you first, I want it understood by all concerned that *I* was the one who found ya!"

It was Dana who looked puzzled now. "Yeah. All right," she replied with a shrug. "Of course you were. Why would I claim otherwise?"

His finger remained leveled at her. "Just see that I receive full credit for it."

She tried to don an allaying smile. "A call to Preston and a blanket, my good man, and you have my solemn vow that I'm putty in your hands."

* * *

"Abducted by extraterrestrials?" Ian echoed skeptically a short time later, as he and Dana met alone in the stone circle. "No. You'll never get anyone to believe that."

"So what am I supposed to tell them? Do you think it's any more plausible that I accidentally slipped back ten centuries in time because of this ring of stones?"

Preston heaved a discouraged sigh and let his chin come to rest in his upraised palms as he sat next to her on the altar. "Ah, Jesus, Mary, and Joseph, the whole thing is so dizzyin', I'm not sure what's believable anymore."

"Well, I can tell you which story is less likely to land me in a mental institution. We've had lots of people in the States claim to have been abducted by aliens, and they're at least taken somewhat seriously."

He shrugged. "You know your parents better than I do, that's for certain. I've only spoken to them the once by phone the day you disappeared at the monastery. So, if ya think that's the best thing to tell 'em, go ahead with it. But I can't promise ya the gardaí will believe it."

"Ah, damn! Oh, Ian," she went on, her voice cracking with both desperation and her continued hoarseness. It wasn't even eight in the morning yet, but already she felt so exhausted she simply let her head fall onto the tour guide's shoulder. "What am I going to do? You tell me what's credible. You saw me run to a locked round tower and then just disappear from view. Now what? What's the end of that story?"

He wrapped an arm around her—a comforting reminder of the hearty embrace he'd offered when

O'Brien had first led him to her a short time earlier. "I don't know, ya daft little Yank. I've been in the tourism business for over two decades now, and I thought I'd heard and seen everything. But this episode definitely tops them all! I mean, even I, with all my reading about quantum physics and time travel and such, am having trouble graspin' the fact that, only a few hours ago, you were sleepin' with an honest-to-God Viking!"

She raised her head and fixed him with an indignant glare. "Well, it's the truth!" She reached under the wool blanket O'Brien had supplied and pulled at the fabric of the frock Leif gave her. "Have these fibers examined in a lab if you don't believe me! Carbon-date them, why don't you!"

He patted her back and gently returned her head to his shoulder. "Lord, woman, I believe ya, all right. It's the rest of the world we're talking about here."

"I don't see why I have to discuss it with the police in any case. I mean, really, even if I simply told them I was kidnapped by terrorists or some such thing, *who* would I press charges against? What could I say their motive was? And how do I explain the fact that there was no ransom note?"

"Again I've no answers, except to remind ya that there are tall bushes all about the base of that friary tower, so we didn't actually see you disappear. We just walked up there a couple minutes later and there was no sign of ya. No sign of any unidentified flying objects either, mind. So I'm thinkin' a claim that you were simply abducted by an everyday earthling or two will hold more water in the long run. And I'd just as soon see ya leave out the part about them being terrorists, if it's all the same to you."

"Yeah. O.K. But how could said kidnappers have gotten me out of there with so many tourists around?"

Ian pondered this for several seconds. "Ah, it's probably more doable than you realize, given the rather overgrown acreage at the back of the place and the fact that the stone wall about it is fairly scalable and not too high. And, since you were screaming like a banshee when last any of us saw you, it shouldn't be too hard for the authorities to believe you were being pursued by someone."

Dana considered all of this for a moment or two. "All right," she said finally, drawing in a deep breath. "That's the story I'll go with then. That is, if you really think I have to discuss it with your gardaí at all."

"Oh, yeah. I see no way round it, I'm afraid. Not with Mr. O'Brien planning this very moment how to spend the reward money your parents put up for your recovery."

She pulled away from him once more, suddenly enlightened. "So that's why he was so hesitant to call you before he phoned the police. He was afraid he wouldn't get his pot of gold out of it, huh?"

"Precisely."

"And just how much did my parents offer?" she asked gingerly, never having had to face the monetary worth her family might assign to her.

"One hundred thousand."

There was a hopeful rise to her voice. "Pounds?"

"No. Sorry. Dollars, my dear. But it's a very respectable figure as such rewards go, you must admit."

"Yeah. I guess so."

"You know, it's really a pity you can't simply tell everyone the truth. Just think of what you'd earn on the lecture circuit at colleges the world over. History departments would be houndin' ya night and day. To say nothing of the chat shows!"

" 'Chat' shows?"

"Yeah, you know. What are they called in the States again? . . . Oh, yeah, 'talk' shows. That's right. I met your Sally Jessy Raphael one time, by the way."

"You did?"

"Oh, sure. She was over here, staying at an old castle-turned-hotel with her husband. Lovely couple! Very gracious and unassumin'. So, I'd go on her show first, if I were you."

"Ian, please! When I need a press agent, I'll let you know. But I don't want to be made a celebrity over this. I couldn't stand to have people staring and pointing at me. If that was what I wanted, I wouldn't have spent my entire adult life buried in history texts, right?"

"Still, we must find a way to disseminate what you've learned to the other scholars in your field. I mean, it would be a pity if we didn't. . . . Just think of it! Makin' it with a Viking! It's darn right astonishing to realize that the two of ya could have been lying here, havin' your ways with each other on this very altar only last night!"

"Yes," Dana replied wanly, the whole encounter truly seeming a thousand years in the past now. "What are we going to do, if Leif appears in this circle?"

"I'm not sure I fully grasped that part of your story,

I'm afraid. Please tell me again why you think he might."

"Because he was solid for several seconds when the time-slip came over me again. Everyone else—the three freemen and his brother—were surrounded by that blur I told you about. But not Leif. He was in sync with me. I thought we were 'slipping' into the twentieth century together. He even acknowledged it. I could have sworn I heard him say, 'I'm coming with you.' Then poof, he just vanished. And I found myself back here alone."

"Well, if he'd been coming, don't you think he would have arrived by now?"

"Not necessarily. Remember how long it took me to leave this century? The slip started here at the circle and it wasn't until we got to the monastery that it really claimed me. I mean, you said you saw me all the way up to the time I reached the round tower, right? And Mrs. Goldfarb had been run through before that."

"For the third time," Ian put in testily, "Barbara Goldfarb was *not* slain by Vikings! And, in view of the fact that I lost you to unknown forces, I do wish you'd stop saying as much. It's hard enough trying to keep a job in this country without that sort of ruinous rumor getting started! For the record, Mrs. Goldfarb is alive and well and on her way back to New York by now, I assure you. I overheard her having a dustup with her husband just yesterday mornin' in the lobby of the Darby. My guess, based on what I've read about time-travel experiences, is that you saw another woman killed. Someone who happened to be occupying the same space as Mrs. Goldfarb, only it was exactly one thousand and seventy-eight years earlier."

"O.K. Fine then. Barbara's alive. And there's no one more relieved to hear it, believe me! It's just that this proves my point that I must have, at least for an hour or so, been caught between the two centuries somehow. And I can't help but think that same thing may be happening to Leif now."

"So, if he appears, you think he'll just pop into this circle?"

"Yes. After all I told him about what happened to me, I think he'll stay right here until he appears to us or has reason to give up all hope of doing so. And that's a risky business, Preston, let me tell you. Because, back in his time, these stones were planted in the middle of a very hostile foreign wilderness. After a century or so of being attacked by Vikings, the ancient Irish became pretty formidable foes!"

"Sweet Jesus, woman, I've been listening to tourist lectures at our historical sites since you were in nappies. Do you honestly think there's need to explain all of that to me?"

"Sorry. I just wanted to make sure you understood his perspective."

"Well then, here's mine. We're safe for today, with this site closed for repairs to the reception building. But, as of tomorrow mornin', no fewer than three hundred unwitting sightseers are going to pour into this circle. And we can't have this Viking friend of yours suddenly turning up and startin' to lop off their heads with his broadsword! If you think your disap-

pearance was bad for our tourism business, that would
be the bleedin' end of it!"

"Oh, no. Leif won't kill anybody. You don't need to
worry about that."

"Don't I now? You just got done telling me he
stabbed his own brother. And what about what you
claim his crewmen did to Mrs. Goldfarb? Why, you
told me yourself they only spared you because they
thought ya some sort of goddess."

"But those situations were entirely different from
this one."

He was clearly unconvinced. "In what way?"

"Well, they were raiding when they came to the
friary, and you know how fierce the Norsemen were on
raids. As for Leif's brother, well, the man was trying
to strangle me, for heaven's sake! What was Leif supposed to do? Yell 'stop it' to a berserker?"

"All right. So you're fairly sure he won't hurt anyone?"

"Positive. He's really such a sweetheart. Such a
lamb. Honestly, I've never known a kinder, more gentle soul. I think you'd like him very much."

"Ah, fine, then. I'll take him out for a couple of
pints the moment he shows up."

"You're making fun of me."

"No. It's just that it's far-fetched enough, having
you back here, covered with the blood of a thousand-
year-old hare. So, naturally, I'm having a bit of trouble imaginin' another visitor on his way from that
same dimension."

"Well, he's real enough. I can assure you of that,"
Dana declared, suddenly feeling tearful once more.

"Dear God, Ian, I'm scared to death I'll never see him again! I mean, I know you and I didn't get the chance to discuss my pathetic love life before I disappeared. But, just trust me, it was awful! One two-timer on the heels of the next. For an entire decade! And now I *finally* find a man I know will cherish me until the end of my days and he's a *Viking* from the year 916 A.D.!"

With that, she leaned into him, burying her face in his flannel-clad chest, and began to weep bitterly again.

"Faith, girl, it's all right," he whispered, reaching up to pat the back of her head. "We'll take turns keepin' an eye on this place, you and I. And, if he should show himself, we'll see that the pair of ya get back together. . . . Now, you go off and talk to the gardaí when they arrive. Then phone your parents and assure them you're well and that I'll look after ya while you finish up your research over here. And," he continued, withdrawing a tiny tablet and pen from his shirt pocket and handing them to her, "if you'll kindly write a note in Old Norse, which I can use to communicate with your friend, I'll take the first shift in our little 'Viking watch.' "

Chapter 21

The gardaí report indicated that Dana had bruises on her face, throat, wrists, and forearms. Attempted strangulation was apparent, and tests revealed that, in accordance with her claims, it was, indeed, the blood of a hare that was splattered all over the front of her. In addition to this, the investigating physician found semen within her and evidence of recent and repeated intercourse.

The police did, however, mercifully release her after a couple of hours. Bathed, shampooed, and dressed in modern-day apparel, she was returned to her former tour guide.

"Any sign of Leif?" she whispered to Ian, once O'Brien had seen her back to the stone circle and again left them alone.

"No. But I can tell you that Matt is beginning to wonder why the two of us prefer hangin' about out here to sitting in the comfort of the reception building."

Dana sank down next to him on the altar with a

worried sigh. "Yeah. We're going to have to cook up a story for him, aren't we?"

"I'm afraid so. How did your visit with the gardaí go then?"

"As well as could be expected, I guess."

"They think ya a bit unhinged, don't they?"

She rolled her eyes. "Just a trifle. I mean, they seemed to believe my claim that I never got a good look at my kidnappers. That is, until their damned doctor examined me and informed them there was evidence I'd had 'recent and repeated intercourse.' "

Preston's cheeks flushed at this, and Dana couldn't tell if he was embarrassed or angry.

"Those Vikings raped ya, didn't they? Bleedin' savages! Dear God, Worldtrek still isn't in the clear, is it?"

She offered him a consoling smile and gave his shoulder a pat. "Don't worry about it. I was a consenting adult from beginning to end on this one. It's just that Leif was rather. . . . Oh, I don't know how to phrase it. Rather insatiable with me, to put it delicately."

"The beast," he snarled, continuing to look galled.

"No, no. I could have refused him at any time. It was just as much my fault as his. It takes two to tango, as they say."

"I see," Ian replied coolly.

"I've embarrassed you, haven't I?" she said.

The tour guide squared his shoulders. "Not in the least. I'm sure you were quite deserving of the . . ." He broke off, obviously searching for a tasteful term. "Of the amorous experiences you knew with him, after what you've told me of your love life prior to that.

Well," he continued, clearly wishing to change the subject, "I see the gardaí were good enough to clean you up and get you some jeans and such."

"Yeah. My parents promised to wire money over right away, and, fortunately, the officers believed they'd follow through. Which of course they will. My family is nothing if not responsible."

"And how did that part go? The talk with your mum and dad, I mean?"

"They're worried about me, of course. They wanted me to fly home right away, but I somehow managed to talk them into letting me stay for a few more days."

"Well, that's a relief! I don't want this Viking fellow turnin' ferocious on me when he shows up and discovers you've moved on to another continent!"

She sighed again. "I'm tired."

Ian pulled cigarettes and matches out of his shirt pocket and lit up. "Little wonder, after all you've been through."

"I'm going to want that frock back from those pests, too," she went on resentfully. "It's the only thing I have that Leif gave me, and don't think for a moment that I intend to let them keep it!"

"Well, no. Of course you shouldn't. Especially in view of the fact that it dates back over a thousand years and is, therefore, probably worth an incomprehensible sum. Do you suppose the gardaí will figure that out?"

"I doubt it. Short of some mail and leather garments, very little clothing has survived from Viking times. And probably nothing as lightweight as that dress. So I can't imagine why they'd question its age."

"Probably just wanted it in order to run more tests on the bloodstains."

"Yeah."

"Are ya hungry?"

"Come to think of it, I guess I am. I haven't eaten since last night. And, because we were 'on the trail,' as it were, all the Norsemen brought along was dried fish and some bread."

"How revolting."

She gave forth a soft laugh. "Yeah. It was, come to think of it. I wasn't impressed with their food, on the whole."

"That's not surprising." He reached into one of his pants' pockets. "Here's some change for the vending machines in reception. Go and get yourself somethin', and I'll continue to stand watch."

She rose. "No. Thanks anyway, but I've got money now. The gardaí gave me some to tide me over until my parents' mailing arrives."

"Well, off with ya, then. See you in a few minutes."

"Do you want anything?"

He threw his head back with a dry laugh and exhaled a puff of smoke. "Yeah. I could really do with a bottle of whiskey. But Matt doesn't stock that, I'm afraid."

"Nothing then?"

"A Coke, I guess."

"All right."

Dana returned a short time later with two cans of the requested beverage, two packets of cheese-filled crackers, and a chocolate bar.

"Luncheon *and* dessert?" Ian noted teasingly, as she

sat down on the altar once more, handed him his Coke, and spread the snacks out between them.

"Yes, well, it will have to do until Leif gets here and we can go off to a restaurant."

Preston opened his soft drink and took a sip of it, his green eyes focussing upon her soulfully all the while. "You really think he's on his way, don't you?" he asked with a trace of sadness in his voice.

"Oh, yes. I *must* or I'll lose my mind. Hope is my only solace now."

Exhaling uneasily, he tossed his cigarette to the ground, and put it out with one of his feet. Then he picked the butt up, conveyed it to a nearby clump of bushes and tossed it into them. "We can't leave even a scrap of litter in view, mind, or the staff will have my hide," he explained, as he made his way back to her and sat down again.

She nodded. "O.K. I'll be careful not to."

"You know, I was rememberin', while you were gone just now, how you told me last week that you'd had a recurrent dream about this circle. Perhaps Leif was one of the characters in it. I mean, you have to admit it's odd to have nearly found yourself 'sacrificed' here. It's as though that nightmare, or whatever you want to call it, really was prophetic, isn't it?"

Dana hurriedly finished chewing her mouthful of crackers. Then she washed them down with a swallow of Coke. "Yes. And what's even more odd is that Leif claims to have seen this circle in one of his dreams, too. But, in his version of it, two people die here. A male and a female. Well, I'm not dead. So far, anyway," she added with a nervous laugh. "So maybe what he witnessed was Booth's demise."

"Do you think Leif succeeded in killing him?"

"Oh, yeah. I mean, how long could a man live in the tenth century with a wound the width of a broadsword blade running all the way through him? And it looked to me as though Leif knew what he was doing. He stabbed the brute right up under his rib cage, so he must have hit his heart or one of his lungs or something important. . . . Ugh! Just look at me! *Eating* while I'm talking about this. I guess they've made a barbarian of me as well," she concluded with a wry smile.

"Oh, I hardly think that's possible. But one thing is certain, my dear. You've learned more about the Vikings than any Irish museum curator could ever hope to teach you!"

"Yeah. I suppose it's kind of ridiculous for me to try to study under my Dublin contacts now. But I had to give my parents some excuse for wanting to remain in Ireland for a little while longer. . . . Hey, thank you for believing me about all of this and offering to look after me while I stay," she declared, locking her emotion-filled eyes upon his once more. "I mean, if it weren't for you, I don't know what I'd do. Everything I owned, including my airline ticket back to the States, was in the purse I was forced to leave behind in Leif's tent."

"No, now. Not 'everything' you owned," he put in hearteningly. "Your luggage is still at the Darby. Remember?"

Feeling another surge of weepiness come over her,

Dana suddenly reached out and gave him a deeply grateful hug. "Well, thank God for that! And thank God even more for you, Ian Preston," she gushed.

Though he seemed caught off-guard by this outpouring, he reciprocated her embrace, his face coming to rest against the side of her freshly washed mane in those seconds. "My pleasure, Dana," he said in a hushed voice, patting her back.

She shut her eyes. How good it felt to be held again! It had only been a matter of hours since she'd been in Leif's arms, yet his warmth and protection seemed a lifetime away from her now. And, after the lengthy and blatantly suspicious questioning and examination the gardaí had put her through, she'd begun to feel as if she didn't have a friend in the world.

But this simply wasn't true, thank Heavens. She was discovering what an ally she'd really found in Ian. And she knew that, no matter what the outcome of the watch she was keeping for Leif, she'd have to find some way to repay the tour guide's kindness.

This hug seemed a good enough way to start, she supposed. But, as she suddenly felt him tense up on her and begin to draw away, she wondered if she'd been too forward in initiating it.

She opened her eyes once more; and, all at once aware of a heavy, racing footfall coming up behind her, she realized that Ian was pulling away for a very different reason than she'd thought.

She turned in that instant, thinking that O'Brien was approaching with some news from the police or her parents and that Preston felt it too incriminating to be spotted in such a pose. To her astonishment, however, she saw that it was *Leif* who was charging toward them and that he had his sword drawn!

"Dear Lord," Ian exclaimed, pulling himself down off of the altar and dragging Dana along with him.

"Leif, *neinn,*" she screeched, holding up her hands defensively. But, before she could put herself squarely between the tour guide and the blade, the Norseman stepped around and pressed the point of his sword into the hollow of Ian's throat!

"Stefan! You dare to touch her again after wronging her so?" Leif growled in Old Norse.

The Irishman, looking as though he might simply die of fright on the spot, managed to get to his feet and begin backing away from his threatener.

"Oh, *neinn,* Leif," Dana cried out again in his native tongue, springing up to put herself between the two men once more. "This isn't Steven! *Neinn! Neinn!*"

Obviously aware that such a weapon could prove every bit as deadly as a cobra poised to strike, Preston froze where he stood and addressed Dana out of the corner of his mouth. "Is *this* the 'lamb' and 'sweetheart' you spoke of earlier?"

"Yes. Well, he thinks you're someone else. He must have seen us hugging and concluded that you're my old boyfriend."

Ian continued to speak under his breath, this time trying to don a placating smile for the Viking. "So tell him I'm not, for the love of Jesus!"

"I'm trying to! *Leif,* listen to me," she went on, switching back to his language. "This is *not* Steven!"

To her relief, the Norseman looked her in the eye for

the first time. "Then why was he holding you thus?" he demanded.

" 'Twas I who embraced him. He's my 'guide.' Don't you remember?" she asked anxiously. "I told you about having a guide here."

"But you said it was a woman."

"Ja. My guide at this site was. But my guide to the rest of Erin was this man. And you mustn't hurt him, for he has been most kind to me since I came back to my time!"

"Too kind, me thinks," Leif said from behind clenched teeth, as though still having half a mind to dispatch Preston.

Fortunately, however, he did withdraw his blade an inch or two from Ian's neck; and Dana seized the opportunity to take hold of his sword hand and pull it toward her, her body curving about his long arm as she hugged it to her torso.

In spite of this show of affection, Leif continued to appear rankled. "I slay my own brother for you, only to see you next in the arms of another man?"

"Leif, *neinn.* I pray thee, stop this now! He is no more than a friend, a helper, I tell you, and you simply must believe me!"

He went on glowering at her for several seconds more. "See that he does not touch you again!"

Dana clutched his huge arm even tighter and pressed her lips to his shoulder, elated at finally being able to express how wonderful it felt to see him again. *"Ja.* Of . . . of course he won't," she faltered, feeling choked with joyous tears.

Leif seemed to give in to his warmer feelings as well

in that instant. At last lowering his sword tip to the ground, he turned and wrapped his free arm around her.

"Am I safe now?" Ian whispered, continuing to back away stealthily.

"Yes," Dana replied, smiling through her tears.

"I think I'll go wait for you in reception, then," he declared, his voice still hushed with wariness. "I'm sure you two lovebirds have much to discuss."

"No. It's all right. You can stay. He's not angry anymore," she assured, shifting her gaze back up to Leif's now-adoring eyes.

Preston reached up to wipe the trepid sweat from his forehead. "Sweet Jesus. Are you positive?"

"Yes."

"Lord, he's the jealous sort, isn't he?"

Dana went on smiling, her gaze still intertwined with Leif's. "It appears so."

She heard the Irishman crunch his way across the rock chippings, back over to the altar. Then he plopped himself down upon the stone slab with a pained sigh. "I think he ruddy well cut ten years off my life just now."

"Mine, too," she confessed with a light laugh.

"Will he mind then, if I simply sit here and study him for a moment or two? I mean, I've never seen a real Viking before, and I have to admit to findin' him rather awe inspiring."

"Yeah. That'll be all right, I think. We're going to be kissing for a while, near as I can tell."

She was right, as it turned out. Within an instant, Leif let go of his broadsword altogether. Then he

wrapped both of his arms about her and pressed his
lips to hers with heart-stopping ardor.

"By Thunder, I feared I would never again see you,"
he whispered feverishly against her cheek, when he
finally stopped to let them both catch their breath.

Dana felt almost too touched to reply. "Oh, I know.
I *know*," she finally gasped, hugging him with all her
might. "Thank the Heavens the 'time-slip' claimed us
both!"

"Prithee, don't ever leave me again," Leif murmured into her ear, the penetration of his breath bringing the memory of her more intimate mergings with
him racing back to the depths of her in hot waves.

"Oh, no. Of course I won't. Of course not! 'Twas
not by design, in any case, you know."

"No wonder you liked swivin' with him. He's as big
as a house, for Christ's sake," Ian interjected.

Dana took one of her hands from Leif's broad back
long enough to wave the tour guide off. "Just look,
please, Preston, and save your comments for later. All
right?"

"Fine. Lord knows I'd be better off trying to come
between a bull moose and his doe," she heard him
mutter, before Leif swept her up into another earthshaking kiss.

The next thing she knew, Ian was again addressing
her, this time from much closer by. She turned, as her
lover finally took his lips from hers once more, and
saw the Irishman standing only two or three feet from
her.

"I am goin' to leave you now, my dear. It's clear
that he wants ya all to himself for a while, and it's

probably best that I keep watch on the path so that O'Brien doesn't come out here and see him." He shook his head. "That Viking garb is far too authentic to be anything but genuine, I'm afraid. So steal a few minutes more to yourselves, and then we're going to have to move on to the serious business of sneakin' him out of here and getting him dressed for the times."

"Wait," Dana blurted, stepping away from Leif just long enough to catch hold of Preston's right hand, as he was turning to leave. "I'm sure Leif is sorry about that rather unholy entrance of his and wishes to see you both properly introduced."

"I wouldn't be too sure of that, if I were you, lass."

"Oh, come on, Ian," she insisted, tugging at him until he was facing them both fully again. "Offer him your hand, now that he's dropped his sword."

To his credit, the Irishman did so, albeit cautiously. Unfortunately, however, Leif failed to respond. He simply arched a brow at Dana peevishly.

"Clasp his palm," she said in Old Norse. " 'Tis our way of offering a greeting. By joining right hands men show one another that neither is armed."

"*Ja.* I am aware of the significance of such an act," Leif countered coldly, "but I do not wish to engage in it. I neither want him touching you nor *me*. What is more, I'd have no care if he were armed, for 'tis clear that, whatever blade he carried, I could gain the advantage and snap him in half as I would a fowl bone."

For a second or two, Dana was at a loss as to how to react. She knew that extending this courtesy to Ian was the only decent thing to do, yet she feared angering Leif anew. Then, realizing that he would simply

have to conform to some of society's rules if he was
going to survive in this century, she narrowed her eyes
at him sternly and tried again.

"Greet him thus, lest . . ." She fell silent as she
searched her mind for ample retribution.

"Lest?" Leif echoed tentatively.

"Lest I withhold myself from you."

His expression said he knew exactly what she meant
by this. "For how long?"

She crossed her arms over her chest. "Mayhap a
very long time, indeed."

This was, apparently, the ultimate threat to him.
One that would, admittedly, make Dana feel quite
deprived as well, should she be pushed to enforce it.

"Accursed *Hel*! All right, woman," he snapped after
a moment, finally reaching out and giving the Irishman's hand a very hurried shake.

"His name is 'Ian,' Leif. Can you say that?"

The Viking rolled his eyes at being asked such a
patronizing question. "Why on earth would I want
to?"

She donned a broad smile, for the tour guide's benefit, and continued to speak to her lover in a warning
tone. "Because, in my day, as I explained to you, we
thrive by trading, not raiding, and this is part of proving yourself a gentle man."

Leif drew in a deep breath and locked the back of
his jaw. Then, with a burst of thinly cloaked mockery,
he drawled, "Eee . . . an."

"Your name, Preston," she heralded brightly.
"There, you see what a civilized guy he can be? He's
just said your name."

"Bravo," Ian gibed. "Now all you have to do is teach him the other five billion names for things in the English tongue, and he's primed."

" 'English'?" Leif repeated with a foreboding rise to his voice.

Dana instantly stepped forward and took hold of his arm again. *"Neinn,* Ian is not English, love. He simply meant that that is the language we speak."

"What's the matter with him now?" Preston put in.

She gave forth an uneasy laugh. "Well, I'm afraid I managed to paint the English in rather a bad light when I was telling him about our century."

"Ah, Mother Mary, that wouldn't take much effort, now would it?"

"Anyway, he's decided he doesn't care for them."

At this, Preston dared to reach out and give Leif's hand another sporting shake. "That's the spirit, man! It looks as though we're going to be gettin' on better than I thought!"

Chapter 22

As upbeat as Ian's parting exchange with Leif had been, he was right in assuming that the Norseman wanted to be alone with Dana. The mood between them was, indeed, easier once the Irishman left the circle and was out of earshot.

"Need I keep this drawn any longer?" Leif asked Dana, as he bent to pick up his sword.

"Oh, *neinn*. Forsooth, there was no call for it at all. This is a fairly peaceful land now, as I've told you."

He sheathed the weapon and stood taking in their surroundings for what seemed the first time. "This place is very different in your day, isn't it? So . . . so primped."

"*Ja.* There are many people who come to see it, so it is tended with great care."

"By whom?"

"By . . ." She was tempted to tell him that she found this hard to explain. But, remembering how irritated he'd become at that sort of answer from her before, she struggled to finish her sentence. "By those who rule southern Erin now."

"Her high king?"

"Neinn. The South has no king anymore. But a sort of ruler, *ja,* whom the people all take part in choosing."

"Hmm." He nodded and pivoted slowly once more, studying everything around him. "Oh, I've something for you," he began again, suddenly looking rather self-conscious, like a schoolboy bringing a flower to a girl with whom he was smitten.

Dana knit her brow, unable to imagine what this might be. *"Ja?"*

He opened his cape and slid her purse straps off of his left shoulder. Then he handed the bag to her.

"Oh, *thank you."* She clutched it for several seconds, then tucked it under her right arm with a relieved sigh. "I'm so glad you remembered it!"

He smiled softly. "But of course. When my freeman awoke me to say Booth had ridden off with you, I knew I could not hazard leaving it behind. . . . Come. Sit," he directed, wrapping an arm about her waist and moving her toward the altar. "And tell me what happened. I remained in my time long enough to hear what our captain's manservant had to say of it, but I know that only you can tell me all which came to pass."

Dana moved the snacks and beverages she'd purchased far to the rear, as they reached the stone slab. Then she set her purse between them and they both sat down.

"Food?" Leif inquired, reaching back and picking

up one of the cellophane packets with an intrigued expression.

"*Ja.* They are called 'crackers.' "

" 'Crack . . . ers,' " he repeated, lifting the opened package to his nose and giving it a sniff.

"*Ja.* They are like . . . like flatbread. *Hardr taka,*" she said triumphantly, having stumbled upon what she considered to be an Old Norse equivalent. "But they have a soft cheese spread betwixt them. Try one," she invited, reaching over and tearing the wrapper open more widely for him.

He pulled one of the crisp sandwiches forth and bit into it tentatively. Then, a second or two later, his lips curved up into a subtle smile. "Good," he praised.

"*Ja.* They are, aren't they? You can eat the rest, if you wish."

"Thank you. How did you make them?"

She issued a light laugh. "Oh, I didn't. I bought them."

"From whom?"

"From . . . from what you would call a 'contrivance.' I promise to show you one of them, once we have left here."

"Where are we going?"

"To a—an inn. You know what those are, don't you?"

He nodded. "Where is it?"

"In Dublin."

He looked as though this name was unfamiliar to him.

" 'Tis a very large village far to the north of the monastery where you found me."

"But that is many, many leagues from here," he noted.

"You forget, though, love. We have 'cars' in this time."

His smile widened to an all-out grin. "Oh, *ja,* that go thirteen times farther in an hour than a horse?"

"Right."

"And you will allow me to ride on one?"

"In one, *ja.* Most assuredly. Along with Ian and me."

His grin faded. "Must he travel with us?"

"Indeed. For, you see, 'tis *his* car."

"Oh," he half groaned. "Can we not ride in your car instead?"

"I haven't one in this land. Mine is back in America. So, you see, we really must be kind to Ian, as I told you. . . . He's wed, Leif. Long married to a woman in Dublin," she continued in a placative tone. "So, prithee, do stop worrying that he fancies me."

He popped a couple more crackers into his mouth and nodded as though he did, indeed, find some comfort in this claim. "To drink?" he asked, reaching back to one of the Coke cans a few seconds later.

"Ja."

He grasped the container, but, once he got it within a few inches of his mouth, he thrust it away from himself and averted his gaze.

She took it from his outstretched hand. "What is it? What troubles thee?"

He looked back at her, his eyes wide with consternation. "Can you not hear it hissing? 'Tis the same sound that fiery rain of yours made!"

She laughed. "Oh, *neinn.* It won't hurt you. You are simply hearing the bubbles in it."

"Bubbles," he echoed in bewilderment.

"Ja. See?" She lifted the can to her mouth and took a long swallow. "It cannot harm you." She handed it back to him.

Still appearing somewhat unconvinced, he accepted it from her. "What precisely is it?"

" 'Tis called 'cola.' It's a sweet brown drink with many tiny bubbles."

"It is spirited?"

"Neinn."

"Foamy, then, like beer?"

"Ja. That's right. 'Tis a bit like beer. But you cannot become drunk from it."

"Odd," he replied, continuing to furrow his brow. Evidently trusting her, however, he tipped the can to his mouth and took a sip.

"What do you think?"

He pressed his lips together tightly, as though considering it. Then he tried a little more. " 'Tis sweet, as you said."

"Do you like it?"

He gave his head a shake and crinkled his nose at the titillating carbonation. "I don't know yet. 'Twill take me some time to decide."

"All right." She offered him a tender smile. "It appears we've all the time in the world together now."

"I hope so," he said uneasily.

"Oh, *ja.* Why wouldn't we? And you'll love this century, Leif, I promise. Believe me, you will soon

learn that there is far more to like about it, than to
hate."

"Very well. Now, tell me, pray, why Booth stole you
off to this circle."

"Because he eavesdropped on us last night. He listened outside your tent, and he heard you speaking of
my 'century' and how you wanted me to worship Frey
by . . ." She broke off, unable to think of a tasteful way
to finish the sentence.

He pressed a finger to her lips. *"Ja.* I remember.
You needn't say more. So, he realized you weren't a
goddess?"

"Ja."

"And for this he sought to kill you?"

"Ja. And because he said he thought me a witch."

Leif nodded slightly and fell quiet, obviously trying
to make sense of the nightmarish chain of events that
had led up to his being catapulted into this modern-
day world.

"So the freemen saw you slip into this time?" Dana
inquired softly.

"Neinn. They left me before then."

"Left you?"

"Ja. Having made myself their chief with my own
hapless blade, I ordered them to return to the camp.
Then I told them to head back to our ships, with the
claim that I would rejoin them when I could."

"So Booth did die?"

He dropped his gaze, clearly remorseful. *"Ja.* But
with merciful swiftness, I hasten to tell."

She reached out and hugged him to her once more.

"Ah, by all that is sacred, my love, I am so sorry it came to that!"

He wrapped his arms about her as well. "I know," he whispered against her cheek. "But 'twas not your fault. 'Twas not truly by cause of either of us. For it was he who chose to begin the battle."

Keeping her voice low, she eased away from him enough to look into his eyes as they continued to talk. "And do you think your crewmen understood this?"

"They seemed to. Forsooth, they seemed not at all disposed to see me tried for the act. But then," he added gingerly, "they were, none of them, very fond of our captain, as I am sure you guessed."

"Oh, *ja.*"

A mournful silence came over them, as they both contemplated what a wretched soul the berserker had been.

"What reason did you give them for wishing to stay behind?" she pursued.

"I told them that it would not be Booth's wish to further endanger them by slowing their return to our base with the hauling of his dead body. So, I was, in keeping with that, remaining at this site in order to bury him."

"And did you?"

"*Ja.* Fully four hours passed, by my count, before the 'slip' befell me. So I was afforded plenty of time in which to give him a shallow grave."

She looked down at his hands and noticed, for the first time, how dirty and battered they were. "Without aid of a shovel?"

"With a small spade one of the freemen had in his horse's pack."

Feeling sad at his having to inter his sibling alone, Dana raised one of his soil-dusted hands to her lips and graced it with the whisper of a kiss.

"Ah, 'twas not as loathsome a task as you might imagine, my sweet, for it helped me pass the empty hours without you," he explained.

She looked into his eyes once more, seeing the eternity of a cloudless sky in their light shade of blue; and she wondered how she could ever have doubted that the universe meant for them to be together.

But then, as always, she sensed that they would simply melt into each other's arms and begin making love again if she kept staring. Since this was hardly the time and place for such an act, she let her gaze fall and she issued a light, sobering sort of cough. "So, um . . . you were not in the circle when the slip claimed you?"

"Neinn. I felt it coming. Surely you must know how it feels. How all about you becomes unclear to your eyes and any sounds around you echo."

"Ja."

"Well, I experienced all of this. And, chancing to remember that I had brought your bag from the camp, I hurried to my horse to fetch it. And 'twas then, when I was walking back to the circle, that I saw you hugging that man," he concluded, his voice still edged with resentment.

"Ian," she prompted.

"Eee . . . an," he pronounced again, rolling his eyes.

"Pray, what manner of race could have given rise to such a doltish name?"

She bit her lip, fighting a laugh at his continuing jealousy. "The Scots, I think."

He scowled in confusion.

"From the mountainous land just to the northeast of Erin."

"Ah." He nodded his understanding. "Scraggy, though, isn't he, for one from such warring stock?"

"Oh, Leif, verily, you mustn't speak ill of him, for he has shown me every kindness since my return."

" 'Every,' *ja,* " he retorted. "That is precisely what troubles me."

She shook her head, as she repressed another laugh. Thank heaven he was going to have a few days to cool off before she returned to the States with him. Given the rage he'd twice displayed already that morning, she knew she shouldn't be too quick to convey him to the same continent where the real "Stefan" could be found!

"Ian did naught more than return my embrace," she began again firmly, making a point of looking him squarely in the eye.

The adamant way in which she said this made him recoil slightly. "I caused your 'watch' to begin counting again," he declared, as though suddenly wishing to change the subject as much as she did.

She gaped in surprise. *"Ja?"*

"Ja." He pulled her purse forward, began rummaging through its side compartment, and his fingers emerged with it seconds later. "See?"

She accepted it from him and sat studying it. The

pulsing colon in its digital display had, indeed, begun flashing again with the passing of each second. "By Thunder, 'tis amazing! How on earth did you manage it?"

"I know not, I must confess. If the truth be told, I was tinkering with it, after I buried Booth, and I chanced to drop it to the ground. And, when I picked it up, it was beating in that way, and the last column of numbers or whate'er they are, changed with what seemed each moment that passed."

Dana gave forth an astonished laugh. "You *dropped* it and that was all that was needed?"

He laughed as well. "So it seems."

She fastened it about her left wrist, then leaned over and gave him a kiss on the cheek. "Well, thank you, good sire. I shall ask Ian the present time and reset it when he returns. . . . Mayhap you have a future in repairing such things, after all," she added, wrapping her arms about his waist once more and giving him a squeeze.

As she did so, however, her hands seemed to slip through his very flesh somehow; and she pulled away to see that he appeared to be fading!

"Ian," she cried out frantically. "Ian, please come back here at once!"

Digging her fingernails into Leif's cape, she clutched him to her desperately in the seconds it took for the tour guide to return to them. And, by the time he had entered the circle, the Norseman had slipped back into solid form.

"Did you feel that?" Leif whispered apprehensively.

"Ja. Shhh. 'Tis nothing," she assured, continuing to

cling to him. "You mustn't fret, love, for I'm afraid 'twill only make it worse."

"What is it? We'll be lucky if they didn't hear ya clear to Kilkenny, for God's sake," Ian exclaimed, his tone reflecting great concern.

Afraid to let go of Leif for even an instant, Dana waited to respond until the Irishman got close enough to circle behind the Viking and look her in the eye. "He started to disappear," she answered, her voice breaking with the fearfulness she was trying so hard to suppress.

"Oh, no! Sweet Jesus, lass. There must be some sort of paradox then."

"Paradox?"

"Yeah. You know, some change in events caused by his leaving his time. But maybe it was simply that purse of yours remaining behind."

Dana's eyes traveled downward to where the bag rested between her lap and Leif's. "No. That can't be it. He brought it with him. See?"

"Aye. But are all of its contents still in it? Because even the smallest item, just a camera or a paperback book, could conceivably have changed the face of history."

"Nothing was removed from my bag, was it?" she asked Leif.

"Neinn. Forsooth, it was with me all morning."

Dana translated this answer for the tour guide.

He responded with a worried sigh. "Then it must be something else."

"Like what?"

"Like some deed your Norseman was meant to stay

behind and carry out. Or a child of some importance, whom he was destined to father in his own time."

"Oh, God," Dana gasped.

"Yeah, well. Don't panic, my dear. Just keep hanging on to him, and maybe we can figure a way to anchor him here or to help you return to his century with him."

"I don't know if this is significant, Ian, but both times I slipped, I was about to be murdered, or so it seemed, and I was frightened out of my wits."

"In that case, it's all the more important to stay calm now and tell Leif to do the same."

"I did," she confirmed.

"Can you get off that altar, the pair of you? Maybe that's what's causing it."

"We'll try," she replied in English, then returned to speaking in Leif's tongue. "Ian says we should attempt to stand. Slowly, mind, and *together*. He thinks the altar is what caused you to slip a bit just now."

"All right," Leif agreed, willing to do whatever was necessary in order to remain with her.

"On the count of three, then?" Dana suggested.

"Ja."

She proceeded to say the Norse numbers aloud; but, as they both began to lift themselves from the stone slab, Leif again dissolved slightly in her hold.

Horrified by this, they sank back down upon the altar in shuddering unison. Fortunately, however, the Norseman was back in his entirety an instant or two later.

"Did you see that?" Dana hissed to Ian.

"Aye. Indeed I did, my dear. And I'm afraid all I

can recommend is that you keep holding him that way until I can think of some other course."

"Such as?"

"Well, I don't know exactly. You have to remember that I'm hardly an expert on time travel. I've simply made a hobby of reading about it. Actually, I think it's more likely that you hold the answer to this riddle."

"Riddle?"

"Yes. *You* tell me. You're the one who has studied the Vikings. What is Leif's surname and what outstanding part could he have played in history?"

"His father's name is Ivar. So we would know him as Leif Ivar'sson. But that's all," she concluded in a despairing tone. "I'm wracking my brain, but, for the life of me, I don't recall that name from any of my reading!"

"All right, girl. Calm yourself. It will do no good at all to get wrought up. Just tell me who might be able to help."

"Some of my curator contacts, maybe. Since it was Leif's habit to raid Ireland, perhaps it's a piece of history that only your people have."

"How do I reach them then?"

"Their names and phone numbers are in the little notebook in the center section of my purse. Just slip it out from between us and you'll find it."

"What is he doing?" Leif growled, as the guide stepped forward and began withdrawing the purse.

"He's getting something from my bag. Something that might help us come to know why you seem to be slipping again . . . Ian, I just don't understand this," she went on anxiously. "If he was never meant to leave his century, why did it happen?"

The Irishman set the now-freed purse on the ground and dropped to one knee to start searching through it. "It was due to his sheer bloody will, I imagine. He's clearly the headstrong sort, and he appears to be very much in love with you. A great many physicists would contend that love is among the strongest forces on this old earth."

"So, if I just love him enough, I'll be able to slip back with him if he goes?" she asked hopefully.

"Maybe. And then again, it may happen that we'll simply be forced to realize that he belongs in his time and you in yours," he replied sadly.

"Oh, Lord, no. I think I'll off myself if I lose him again!"

"Now, now," Ian replied, finally rising with the specified notebook in hand. "Let's not draw any conclusions, my dear, until we have more of the facts. I'll go and make a few calls. You'd be surprised how many friends 'in high places' a fellow acquires after twenty years in the tourism business," he added with a smile. "And you two just go on clinging to each other for dear life. I promise not to be long."

"Where is he going?" Leif inquired, as Ian left the circle.

"To talk to some of the people who study your times, as I do."

"They are *here?*"

"Neinn." Dana felt almost too distressed now to explain. Yet, knowing she had to do all she could to relax them both, she strove to keep her voice even and

her tone unruffled as she spoke again. "They are in Dublin, love, and Ian will talk to them through a device we call a 'telephone.' "

"This allows you to speak to those so far away?"

"Indeed it does. So, you see, it is, forsooth, a wonder-filled time to which you have come." She donned a brave smile, but it must have been apparent to him that she was already fighting back tears. "Leif?" she began again, after several seconds.

"Ja?"

"Ian knows far more about these slips through time than I do, and he thinks you may have some important deed yet to accomplish in your century. Pray, do you know what that might be?"

He was silent for a moment. *"Neinn.* I cannot imagine, for it has always been my place to simply do my sire's and brother's bidding."

"But you became the commander of your crew before you left your time. So what would you next have ordered your men to do?"

He shrugged. "Return to our land."

"And your sire. Did he have any designs for your future or Booth's?"

"Neinn. We were to go on raiding each summer, of course. And we always chose Erin, because we knew much of Erse ways and where the most booty could be found. But . . ." He paused, as though suddenly lost in thought.

"But?"

"But my father had, of late, begun speaking of a permanent base which some of my cousins had established in what you call 'England.' He urged Booth to consider taking our crew and settling with them there, that we might attack Erin with greater ease and with the intent of procuring one of her provinces."

"And Booth opposed this?"

"Oh, not gaining such power in Erin, of course. But he was against settling with our cousins. He hated them and they him."

"Perhaps that is it then."

"What?"

"The 'paradox' Ian thinks took place."

"The what?"

"The 'paradox.' Do you remember how I explained to you that the centuries betwixt my time and yours are like a loosely woven cloak?"

"Ja. And that we must not drop or cut a stitch of it by changing events, lest it begin to come apart."

"Right. Well, as I have said, Ian thinks it possible that you faded a few minutes ago because you were meant to stay in your time and achieve something of great significance."

"Hmm," he replied, the uneasiness he felt at this apparent in that one simple syllable.

"Or perhaps 'twas a child you were meant to beget, one who somehow altered matters."

"Oh, *neinn.* This, I can vow, is simply not possible. For you returned to your time, and I would have no other woman after thee."

Dana's tearfulness came to the fore once again at this touching declaration. "Well, umm," she choked after a moment. "Then we must assume, save that I slip back there with you, the deed in question is to be yours."

"Ja."

"So, tell me. Having become the captain of your crew, would you have heeded your sire's counsel and gone to settle with your cousins for the purpose of winning part of Erin?"

Leif pondered this, having never before been put in the position of being able to make such long-range plans. *"Ja.* I suppose I would have. Since I was third-born in my family, there was no hope of my staying to claim my father's farmstead."

"Well, maybe that *is* it then," she replied with a dry swallow, scared stiff at the prospect of his century reclaiming him.

"Ja. Perhaps. But know this," he continued in a tone that bespoke an iron resolve. "I shall not go back without you!" With that he hugged her all the more tightly, and she did the same. And neither of them dared to turn and look, as Ian came back to them a short time later.

"I've some good news and some bad, my dear," he announced soberly, once he'd circled around Leif and was again able to look Dana in the eye.

"The good first," she said tensely.

"I think I've found your paradox. Your contacts were of little use, I'm afraid. Either not in their offices at present or as much at a loss to place one Leif Ivar'-sson as you seem to be. So I had an old mate of mine in the history department at Trinity log on to their computer, looking for both names—'Leif' and 'Ivar.' And, faith and begorra, he found the Ivar dynasty of Dublin. Now, surely that must ring a bell for ya, girl."

"Yes, of course. After the battle at Climashogue in

919, the Norwegians ruled great parts of Ireland for the next fifty years," she replied. "But don't they still assume it was a Norseman named Ivar who began this reign?"

"No. According to what my friend found, they've recently discovered that Ivar was, in fact, the surname of the fellow in question. And, since they've now also learned that he brought with him a wife named *Dana* to rule at his side—a woman who was said to possess magical powers, I might add—I think we may be safe in assumin' that we've found your paradox."

"Oh, my God, Ian! You mean to tell me Leif will become the first Nordic king of Dublin?"

The Irishman smiled. "Aye. And you the queen, if we can believe a word such eggheads tell us. But you have to admit it's as good a guess as any. I mean, the dates are right enough for it. And that's more than can be said for the other Ivars and Leifs my friend turned up. They seemed to be in the wrong centuries altogether. Anyway, it stands to reason you're meant to go back with him. That is, knowing all you do about what battles the Norse won and lost in those chaotic times, I think it very likely you'll prove to be the reason why this great galoot succeeds in claiming the throne."

"Heaven help me, I'm speechless," she replied, continuing to gape at him.

"Well, at least you can rest easier now. Knowing the pair of ya probably won't have to part for good. Which brings me to my bad news."

Dana grimaced, imagining the worst. That he was about to inform her Leif was destined to die in some horrible fashion soon after taking power. "What is it?" she asked warily.

"O'Brien came by, while I was on the phone, and informed me that he's alerted the press about having found you and they'll be here within the hour to cover the story."

"Damn it," she blared.

"Yeah, well, the long and the short of it is, we'll have to get Leif out of here and the sooner the better."

"But what if he starts to disappear again when he stands up?"

"I'm sorry, lass. But there'll be no reasonable way of explaining that getup of his, and there isn't enough time to buy him some modern clothes. So, even if we just hide him for a while in the bushes, he is going to have to leave this circle."

"I don't want to talk to any reporters, Ian," Dana began again pleadingly. "So, if he hides, I'm hiding with him. I'm not letting him out of my sight!"

"I wouldn't either in your place, but I had an idea as I was walking back here."

"What is it? *Anything!* Just don't let me fall into the hands of more questioners!"

"Well, didn't you say that Leif and his men had to travel from a base-camp in the southeast in order to bring you here?"

"Yes."

"Well, we'll sneak him out to my car and I'll drive you both in that direction. Save ya havin' to make your way back through hostile territory on a horse, if the slip should claim you again."

"Yes! That's brilliant, Preston. You're a genius!"

He blushed slightly at the compliment. "Hardly. I just want to prove helpful to the pair of ya. I mean, on the chance you do end up becoming some of my town's first royalty," he added with a chary laugh. "Now, you'd better let the man in on our conversation and see if he's willing to leave here. And I'll go stand guard again and make sure no one's comin'."

"Ian," Dana called after him, as he started walking away.

"Yes?"

"You . . . you didn't just make up the part about a queen named Dana in order to keep me from balking now, did you?"

He frowned. "I'm surprised at ya. Accusin' me of such a thing! Good Heavens, no! The truth is, though I know this news probably means the two of you will stay together, I pity ya having to go back to such a beastly time. Your parents will worry themselves into early graves, if they ever get wind of it."

Dana's eyes welled up anew at the thought of her family and the probability of never seeing them again. "But you'll think of something to tell them, won't you? Some story that won't make them worry?"

"Ah, sure. I'll probably just claim that you ran off on me. It'll make you seem like a loon in the long run, but it may prevent my being accused of doing away with ya."

"Oh, Lord! People *are* apt to suspect foul play, aren't they. I never even considered that."

"It's a chance we'll have to take though. I'm in on it now, aren't I?"

"No. There is something I can do about it. I want

you to come back here and take a few things from my purse."

"Why?"

"Because they could be worth quite a bit to you. Enough to pay a good attorney, should you need one."

"What? More Viking paraphernalia?"

"No. But my camera is filled with pictures of it. I took several shots the morning we left Leif's base. And, in my cassette player, is a tape of him conversing with his brother in Old Norse. A language never spoken today. If you can get these into the right hands—Heaven knows, my notebook is filled with suggestions—you'll probably be paid quite well."

"All right then. If you insist, my dear. I'll collect them when I come back for you in a few minutes."

"Oh, and Ian?"

He clucked, as though seeing little call for the urgent tone that remained in her voice. "Yes?"

"Just for the record, the tenth century wasn't really as 'beastly' as you might think. I mean, in some ways, it was nicer than now."

"In what ways would those be?" he asked skeptically.

"Well, Ireland had lots of trees then, for one thing. Beautiful, vine-covered forests, spreading across the land. And the Irish Sea was crystal clear and safe to fish from. I saw it myself. I sailed on it with Leif and his crew."

There was a half-dreamy smile in the tour guide's voice as he replied. "Aye. That does sound nice. . . . Well, let's get on with this," he began again briskly.

"Tell your future husband, or whatever he's to be, what I found out and ask him if he'd like a twentieth-century lift back to his base."

"I will. And thanks, Ian. Thank you for everything!"

He clucked again at the finality in her tone, obviously convinced that their time-slip, if there was to be one, would be as slow in coming as Dana's first.

She knew better, however, for she had begun to hear his words slide into the echoing drawl she'd perceived twice before in this mystical land. She had started to see that dizzying blur form about everything which surrounded her.

She waited until Ian was well away, hidden from view by the border of tall bushes that separated the circle from the path which led to it. Then she somehow found the courage to pull away from Leif and confirm that only he remained in focus for her.

Her hands dropped down and took hold of his. Her chieftain, her earl. A man who might one day become a king. God knew, she thought, studying his high cheekbones and jewel-like eyes, there would never be a more noble countenance for one.

She began to translate all that the Irishman had shared with her. It wasn't really such a complicated explanation but lengthy enough, as it turned out. Amply long to comfort them both as their rightful century claimed them and they gradually vanished into the sunny haze of that warm Erse day.

Epilogue

Ian returned to the stone circle a few minutes later and saw that Leif and Dana had gone, leaving only her purse behind. Though he sensed that the Viking's time-slip had probably taken them both, he called out their names once or twice and scouted about the surrounding trees and bushes for them.

When there was no sign of either of them, he returned to the reception building and informed Matt O'Brien that Dana was again missing and that he believed the gardaí should be called to come and search the grounds for her at once.

This was done, and the local press was informed of Miss Swansen's second disappearance. Though every effort was made to find her, she was not heard from again; and, after several months had passed, the police closed their file on the case.

Ian was, of course, questioned several times as to the exact circumstances of the American's "abscondence." But the gardaí never found enough evidence to charge him with any wrongdoing.

In keeping with Dana's suggestion, he did manage to smuggle her camera and the cassette tape in her recorder to his car, before the authorities arrived and seized her purse.

Though he was fortunate enough to receive a good price for the tenth-century treasures Dana left to him, he went on to be vexed by questions and concerns about what fate had really befallen her and her Viking lover. It was not until some six years later, in fact, that his theory about Leif becoming the first Norse king of Dublin was verified for him.

Several silver goblets, dating back to the mid 900's, were found at an archaeological dig not far from Dublin. Engraved on the base of each of them was a crown-shaped design with the initials *L* and *D* intertwined within it. Beneath this, each goblet bore the following message: You were right, Ian.

Because such modern English words were not used in the British Isles until after the 1400's, the participants in this dig were at a loss to explain these curious tenth-century inscriptions.

Ian Preston, on the other hand, was not.

Author's Note

"Time-slips" really have been reported at sites such as the stone circles of the British Isles. If you would like to read some nonfiction works about them and other time-travel phenomena, here are a couple of titles that Ian Preston would, no doubt, recommend:

The Eagle's Quest (A Physicist's Search for Truth in the Heart of the Shamanic World)
by Fred Alan Wolf
(Ian Preston's dialogue in Chapter 2 of this novel contains a sentence or two from the above-named book.)

Time Journeys—A Search for Cosmic Destiny and Meaning
by Paul Halpern

The origins of the Old Norse berserker will probably always remain a mystery. Leif's disclosure to Dana on the subject was, therefore, simply conjecture on my part, based on research I've done on Vikings.

I also took literary license in this novel to make Leif the first Norwegian king of Dublin. Though the half century in question really is referred to as the "Ivar dynasty," the known names of its Nordic rulers were Sigtrygg, Olaf Cuaran, and Gudrod.

Because I traveled to Dublin myself some years ago, I made it a point in the opening chapters to mention some of the places and establishments I visited there. It should be noted, however, that the names of the hotel and tour company given in this book are fictitious.

Now, having addressed the "nuts and bolts," as it were, I would like to take this opportunity to thank all of you readers who have shown so much support for my work over the course of this Viking trilogy. In 1993, I received over 150 exuberant letters from you on *VIKING ROSE* and *VIKING FLAME;* and I did my best to see that you all received a personal response from me. Please know, in any case, that I will keep and cherish your words of praise always!

Many years ago, when my husband and I were wed, we had the presiding pastor read this well-known passage from Kahlil Gibran's *The Prophet:*

And think not you can direct the course of love,
for love, if it finds you worthy, directs your
course.

I *still* can't read those words without tearing up! Yet, I couldn't have known back then, as a bride of twenty-two, just how true they would prove for me. Not only do they apply to my love relationship with my spouse, but to all of the pairs of lovers I'd one day begin writing about in books such as this.

Six years were to pass between my wedding day and the sale of my first novel to a publisher. And you have only to ask one of them how closely we authors stick to our original plot synopses when actually writing our novel, to discover just how right Gibran was! The pomposity of assuming we can direct love's course, either in life or in fiction, is quickly dashed in this business.

If we're lucky, however, our romance characters allow us to peek into their lives and just follow along, feeling our way through the story—as one might "feel" one's way home through a very thick fog.

Alanna and Storr, Meara and Brander, and Dana and Leif were all good enough to share their most intimate moments with me during the creation of this Viking trilogy. And you readers, in turn, have been terrific about encouraging me to continue writing about love. In a world filled with far too much cruelty and sorrow, it's an honor to be able to take part in a genre as positive and uplifting as romance!

I thank all of you for helping to make this possible and for sharing so much of yourselves and your lives with me in your letters. Please feel free to write to the address listed and let me know what you thought of *VIKING TEMPEST* and whether you'd like to see more time-travel romances from me. I always have bookmarks or other promotional pieces on hand to mail back to you, if you'll enclose a self-addressed stamped envelope.

Ashland Price
c/o Zebra Books
850 3rd Ave.
New York, N.Y. 10022
P.S. My next historical romance, which will feature a
ghost, is due out from Zebra in August of '95.

About the Author

An award-winning author, ASHLAND PRICE holds a B.S. degree in theater arts/English secondary education and teaches novel writing in the Minneapolis/St. Paul area. She began writing fiction in her spare time while working as an advertising copywriter. She has written and sold ten books and one novella to date, including a saga, two suspense novels, and seven historical romances. Her Zebra titles include: *CAPTIVE CONQUEST, AUTUMN ANGEL, CAJUN CARESS, WILD IRISH HEATHER, VIKING ROSE, VIKING FLAME,* and "Spirit of the Manor," a novella in Zebra's first Halloween historical romance anthology, *SPELLBOUND KISSES.*

Taylor—made Romance From Zebra Books

WHISPERED KISSES (3830, $4.99/5.99)
Beautiful Texas heiress Laura Leigh Webster never imagined that her biggest worry on her African safari would be the handsome Jace Elliot, her tour guide. Laura's guardian, Lord Chadwick Hamilton, warns her of Jace's dangerous past; she simply cannot resist the lure of his strong arms and the passion of his *Whispered Kisses*.

KISS OF THE NIGHT WIND (3831, $4.99/$5.99)
Carrie Sue Strover thought she was leaving trouble behind her when she deserted her brother's outlaw gang to live her life as schoolmarm Carolyn Starns. On her journey, her stagecoach was attacked and she was rescued by handsome T.J. Rogue. T.J. plots to have Carrie lead him to her brother's cohorts who murdered his family. T.J., however, soon succumbs to the beautiful runaway's charms and loving caresses.

FORTUNE'S FLAMES (3825, $4.99/$5.99)
Impatient to begin her journey back home to New Orleans, beautiful Maren James was furious when Captain Hawk delayed the voyage by searching for stowaways. Impatience gave way to uncontrollable desire once the handsome captain searched *her* cabin. He was looking for illegal passengers; what he found was wild passion with a woman he knew was unlike all those he had known before!

PASSIONS WILD AND FREE (3828, $4.99/$5.99)
After seeing her family and home destroyed by the cruel and hateful Epson gang, Randee Hollis swore revenge. She knew she found the perfect man to help her—gunslinger Marsh Logan. Not only strong and brave, Marsh had the ebony hair and light blue eyes to make Randee forget her hate and seek the love and passion that only he could give her.

Available wherever paperbacks are sold, or order direct from the Publisher. Send cover price plus 50¢ per copy for mailing and handling to Penguin USA, P.O. Box 999, c/o Dept. 17109, Bergenfield, NJ 07621. Residents of New York and Tennessee must include sales tax. DO NOT SEND CASH.

DISCOVER DEANA JAMES!

CAPTIVE ANGEL   (2524, $4.50/$5.50)
Abandoned, penniless, and suddenly responsible for the biggest tobacco plantation in Colleton County, distraught Caroline Gillard had no time to dissolve into tears. By day the willowy redhead labored to exhaustion beside her slaves . . . but each night left her restless with longing for her wayward husband. She'd make the sea captain regret his betrayal until he begged her to take him back!

MASQUE OF SAPPHIRE   (2885, $4.50/$5.50)
Judith Talbot-Harrow left England with a heavy heart. She was going to America to join a father she despised and a sister she distrusted. She was certainly in no mood to put up with the insulting actions of the arrogant Yankee privateer who boarded her ship, ransacked her things, then "apologized" with an indecent, brazen kiss! She vowed that someday he'd pay dearly for the liberties he had taken and the desires he had awakened.

SPEAK ONLY LOVE   (3439, $4.95/$5.95)
Long ago, the shock of her mother's death had robbed Vivian Marleigh of the power of speech. Now she was being forced to marry a bitter man with brandy on his breath. But she could not say what was in her heart. It was up to the viscount to spark the fires that would melt her icy reserve.

WILD TEXAS HEART   (3205, $4.95/$5.95)
Fan Breckenridge was terrified when the stranger found her near-naked and shivering beneath the Texas stars. Unable to remember who she was or what had happened, all she had in the world was the deed to a patch of land that might yield oil . . . and the fierce loving of this wildcatter who called himself Irons.

Available wherever paperbacks are sold, or order direct from the Publisher. Send cover price plus 50¢ per copy for mailing and handling to Penguin USA, P.O. Box 999, c/o Dept. 17109, Bergenfield, NJ 07621. Residents of New York and Tennessee must include sales tax. DO NOT SEND CASH.